VERY STRANGE SHORT STORIES YOU *HAVE* TO READ

Short Stories From A Long Life

EDGAR J. GOLDENTHAL

iUniverse, Inc.
New York   Bloomington

VERY STRANGE STORIES YOU HAVE TO READ
SHORT STORIES FROM A LONG LIFE

iUniverse books may be ordered through booksellers or by contacting:

iUniverse
1663 Liberty Drive
Bloomington, IN 47403
www.iuniverse.com
1-800-Authors (1-800-288-4677)

Because of the dynamic nature of the Internet, any Web addresses or links contained in this book may have changed since publication and may no longer be valid. The views expressed in this work are solely those of the author and do not necessarily reflect the views of the publisher, and the publisher hereby disclaims any responsibility for them.

ISBN: 978-1-4401-1647-6 (sc)
ISBN: 978-1-4401-1649-0 (dj)
ISBN: 978-1-4401-1648-3 (ebook)

Printed in the United States of America

iUniverse rev. date: 3/19/2009

Contents

EPIGRAPH

"At every crossway on the road that leads to the future, each progressive spirit is opposed by a thousand men appointed to guard the past. Let us have no fear lest the fair towers of yesteryear be sufficiently defended. The least that the most timid among us can do is not to add to the immense dead weight which nature drags along. Let us not say that the best truth always lies in moderation, in the decent average.

Let us think of the great invisible ship that carries our human destinies upon eternity. Like the vessels of our confined oceans she has her sails and her ballast. The fear that she may pitch and roll on leaving the roadstead is no reason for increasing the weight of the ballast by stowing the fair white sails in the depths of the hold. They were not woven to molder side by side. Let us ride with the cobblestones in the dark. Ballast exists everywhere; all the pebbles of the harbor, all the sand on the beach will serve for that. But sails are rare and precious things; their place is not in the murk of the well, but amid the light of the tall masts, where they will collect the winds of space."

Maeterlinck
"Our Social Duty"

DEDICATION

This book is dedicated to my three sons
Dr. Michael J. Goldenthal
Dr. Mark H. Goldenthal
Dr. Jonathan L. Goldenthal
Because they were "brought up" by Dr. Janice Goldenthal
Their Mother and my Love

READING MY HARD DRIVE

This neurologist, for reasons all her own, decided that she could not make a proper diagnosis of "my condition" without an MRI of my brain. An MRI is a Magnetic Resonance Image—an exact replication of the anatomy of one's brain. Great! So they got me to lie down in this tube (which reminded me of the torpedo tube of a submarine) and strapped me down so that only my eyelids were able to move. They had given me rubber ear-plugs to dull the grinding sounds of the magnetic resonance machine.

It is not exactly possible to imitate with written word the kinds of sounds that these machines can create. The MRI makes such rough sounds as grrrrkkkchgchgchg and twunggggggrrrrkkkzzzz. These are all noises and they reminded me of someone using a lathe or a drill to scrape or gouge metal. They are not the sounds one likes to hear during a medical procedure. It is more like having your Mercedes repaired.

It took about forty minutes of inhuman, vicious chirping and screeching as the device traveled backward and forward up and down my skull. Of course the tones grew more as the electronic rays had to pierce the heaviest bony area of my skull in order to be able to produce an image of the delicate organ that lay within. So mechanical was the whole "operation" that when it finally ended I was told *by the machine* where I was to go in case I required another visit and then, in a different voice, when my neurologist and internist would receive their copies of the analysis of my scanning by the radiologist at the Marlton Imaging Center.

Strangely enough the voice on the "disc" sounded quite familiar to me. It seemed to have come from the Middle East. While putting my eyeglasses, watch, wallet, pen, keys, small change, belt and shoes back in their accustomed places I mentioned to the attendant that the voice on the tape sounded quite familiar. She replied that the MRI machine was actually manufactured in Israel. It was the newest item on the market and the manufacturer had provided, gratis, (the total cost was a little over one million dollars) that disc with whatever message the new purchaser would require. Since I had many friends and patients from Israel it was no wonder that the accent and the voice sounded as though I had heard it before.

When I subsequently visited the neurologist she seemed unsure whether this particular MRI reading told her what she really needed to know about "my condition." She prescribed that I return to the Radiology Group to have an "MRA", (a Magnetic Resonance *Arterial*), the very next week! So back to the tube I went.

It seemed to me that it would be the same old thing to be undergone but I was mistaken. First of all, they forgot to give me the rubber earplugs. Then they injected a radio-active substance into my bloodstream. This enabled the mechanism to read the anatomy in a different way. Most of all, I had a chance to listen very carefully to *all* the sounds which had previously been partially blocked by the earplugs. As it turned out this was more than merely "interesting".

While the noisy "examination" went on this particular procedure had periods of silence because the idea was to trace the major and minor arteries of the neck and the brain. When the scanning of a major arterial complex reached its termination there was a momentary pause while the machine was set up by the attendant to trace another large arterial complex. This was all very interesting to me. Some of those pauses only lasted a few seconds, others were lengthier. The examination of the neck area was not as noisy or as interesting as the examination of the head and its contents but when the attendant directed the machine to penetrating my bony skull the real heavy grinding noises began in earnest.

It was during those "pauses" that *I began to hear "replies"* to the violent-sounding grindings of the MRA machine. I was not at all sure that I was hearing those feeble tones but each time there was a pause in the action I took the opportunity to listen particularly closely for them. After all, what kind of sounds were they if the MRA was not in action at that moment? Was it possible that my brain had been stimulated to "reply" in some way to the impositions of that electronic machine? I could not differentiate whether those sounds were all within my head or whether they could be heard by someone else in the room. It was strictly forbidden for the patient to speak while being examined. It certainly was not sensible to do that while the MRA was actively probing. However, I took one of the "pauses" to ask the attendant, *"Are you sure you aren't reading my hard drive?"*

"What do you mean by that?" was her reply.

"I mean that whenever your machine pauses after tracing one of my arterial complexes there is a reply, possibly from my brain tissue possibly from other sources, but definitely audible to me. Can you and your associate try to listen for those sounds while you continue?"

Of course they agreed thinking that I was at least slightly mad and that they had nothing to lose by catering to my madness. As a matter of fact, I was not entirely sure that I had heard those sounds or whether they were indeed imaginary.

When the MRA machine was imaging the neck area there had been no "reply" from my brain. It was only when the imaging had moved to the skull to trace the vascular system of the brain that the grinding sounds became most intense since the rays had to penetrate the dense casing of bone that is my skull. *Then* the sounds became really wild as the probing MRA tried to image the furthest reaches of the brain with its radio-activated blood-flow. After about twenty minutes of such probing of the deeper areas, there was a brief pause, and it was then that I was almost sure that I had heard vigorous "replies." The pause that followed the grrrrbrrrrkzzzzzz rasping sounds of that procedure was followed by an almost excited reply from my brain. What had been done to stimulate such activity? Did I really hear those replies in my ears or was there another sound communicator in my head? Was there also an external auditory sound? Was that really my innocent brain speaking up for itself? What section of my brain could respond this way to an electronic imposition? Was it possible (or probable) that I was so mentally or emotionally involved in this procedure that I could not deal with it in a sane manner? All these ideas— *this whole page of ideas* —passed through my mind in the few brief seconds that the machine had paused in its raspings.

When the test was over, in about another half hour or so, the attendant walked into the room and said to me, "I don't know if you are nuts or I am nuts as well but I distinctly heard some kinds of sounds in a cadence, like someone was speaking in a foreign language. I think that should be looked into."

"I heard it too!" said the associate with the severe acne. "That's enough to scare me! Are you sure you're not some kind of ventriloquist? It really sounded like you were talking out of the side of your mouth!

"I feel better now that I know there really was such a collection of sounds and that none of us is really crazy," I said. It had occurred to me that there might be side-effects with all that grinding and probing imposed upon my most sensitive organ. After all, the brain is an electronic organ that is much like a natural computer. In anybody's office there is always the possibility that accessory electrical or electronic components might well impinge upon one's own computer and disturb its workings. Apparently the MRI and MRAs had impinged upon my natural computer causing an unusual reaction....and gotten a reply!.

When the neurologist received the report of the analysis of the MRA from the Marlton Imaging Laboratories I also received a copy of that report. I was pleasantly surprised that most of that report was very positive. Where is it written that the brain (or any other vital tissue) of a man in his late eighties should be pristine in its state of wear and not compromised? One has to accept what nature provides. Yet there are certain aspects of an arterial scan that bear close watching and anyone with half a brain in his head (a likely case!) has to recognize that certain hazards do exist when an older person finds that a few arteries are either clogged (stenosed) or bent at an unusual angle. From the first MRI that I had taken I learned that my diet, containing too many fats and carbohydrates, (or age itself) was indeed clogging some of my "minor" arteries, producing an atrophy (deterioration) of some of the brain tissue. This is definitely something for younger people to know about and to plan their diets as though their lives depended upon it,: which indeed is the case. Among the possibilities with stenosed arteries are "strokes", black-outs or even loss of some cognitive or physical functions. The clogging might come from deposits of cholesterol or calcium, or just an unfortunately sharp bend in an artery. I suspect that just such a possibility was what the neurologist was searching for. My brain scan did reveal a few "bent" arteries which might have dangerous possibilities.

So it was back to the tube once again for me. The plan was to undergo another MRA, this time at different angles to try to study those probably angled arteries. They really got to recognize me at the Marlton Laboratories! But *this time* I had a long discussion with the director of the laboratories a few days in advance. I asked permission to have someone bring in an intense, highly sensitive sound-recording system that could make audio discs of the sounds that transpired in that laboratory. He was excited about the situation and delighted with the opportunity to serve. He offered to bring in some of the most sophisticated sound equipment available.

And so it was back to the tube for me. Once again they strapped me in and once again I was allowed to dispense with the rubber earplugs, just in case I might be able to hear my brain speaking to us.

This time we had a terrific high-tech audio system in the operatory, with discs that could not be affected by the radio-activity in my blood-stream or by any waves that might be emitted by the MRA machine. That was an achievement in itself. And again, as the MRA ground its way through the depths of my brain-case recording the arterial system from various angles the better to study the anatomy of several unusually-disposed smaller arteries there were again a considerable number of "pauses" in the activity of the machine. And this time, as my brain tissue "replied" in its own way to the excitatory rays of the MRA, we had that first-rate audio system to pick up the sounds that the two laboratory attendants and I distinctly heard.

We have known for many years that the brain can emit electronic "waves" but what is their significance? What areas of the brain can originate those rays? What areas can actually reply to the inspiration provided by MRIs and MRAs? What sort of specialized training would a scientist have to undergo in order to decipher what the brain had to say? Is there only *one* center in the brain that can communicate its ideas or its reactions without the usual voice of an individual? For many years scientists and writers have suggested that there is something called "extra-sensory-perception" (ESP) in which one brain can communicate by an invisible, non-auditory manner with another brain (or brains).

No scientist of note has ever said, flat out, that there is no such means of communication. However, those who allow that possibility have been seeking the location of the brain tissue most likely to be involved in ESP. Perhaps the pineal gland could be associated with ESP. We all know that Nature has a way of protecting most intensely those organs that are extremely important. The heart and lungs and most of the liver are encased in a bony cage (the chest) and the brain, the eyes and the other sensory organs are thoroughly encased in a hard, bony skull. Why is the pineal gland, of all organs, kept in the deepest, most protected and most inaccessible area in the head? Is, perhaps, that most protected of areas the central location for extra-sensory-perception? Are we, perhaps, constantly radiating electronic messages that only sometimes get answered? As my Internist, Dr. Jeffrey Oppenheim, once said, "We should be everlastingly in wonder at the size, the power and the expansive capacity of the human brain."

These were the thoughts that went through my mind while the MRI and MRAs were performed. And what was ultimately recorded on the high-tech audio system that was at work in the Marlton operatory for Magnetic Resonance Imaging?

Aha! Surprise of surprises! That audio-sensor *did pick up a form of electronic chatter that could only have come from my brain tissue itself!! That highly sensitive organ had had an MRI and two MRA's within three weeks and apparently resented it!*

Of course, no one had the temerity to hazard even a guess as to what the messages were that my brain was transmitting. Perhaps it was a variation on *"Oy vay iz mir"*, or as the olde Englishe used to say it, "Oh! Woe is me!" But then again, perhaps my brain, in response to the impulses it had received, was unconsciously divesting itself of data that I had been storing up there for lo these eighty-seven years! More work has to be done, for perhaps even another century, to learn accurately to interpret those brain chatterings that are stimulated by electronic proddings. It would indeed be wonderful to learn what my brain was trying to say during those tests at Marlton.

It is amazing that I never heard my brain speak to me at all except for those occasions when I was undergoing those tests. Maybe—and this is a wild supposition—maybe that brain has a personality all its own! Now I wondered what would be the significance of all that brain-chattering? Could there be ramifications beyond the field of medicine that would be interesting, say, to politicians, to the CIA, to foreign governments, to the IRS? *That is the main part of this story. All that you have read thus far is introductory!*

When I played the disc for my three sons on my DVD they were stunned. All three of them, who are all doctors of one sort or another, noticed a special, familiar cadence of the almost staccato sounds my brain had emitted. They all sounded like Dad! There is no one else's personality it could represent. It was **me,** even in dits, dahs and dashes! It was in the same cadence and in the same "Type A" pace that I use, unconsciously, when I speak. Whatever the area of my brain was affected it replicated my personality. "This is important." my sons said. "Let's find out what it is saying."

If my younger brother, Allan, were still alive he might have shortened the search for clues. He was a cryptographer, having translated, from codes in Chinese and Japanese, secret messages during World War II and during the Korean and Vietnam wars. But let's not take any respect away from newer, younger scientists who have tremendous new techniques for deciphering strange codes, even those assumedly from "outer space." Wouldn't it be wild if what they were trying to decipher *was not from outer space but from the brain of the scientist at the next table?*

It was in the long run, six years later, when I was 92 years old and had been subjected to many more MRAs that the breakthrough came. I had written many, many more short stories over those years, most of them autobiographical or with a personal bias that distinguished my writings from anyone else's. A psychoanalyst, a friend of my son Mark, (who is a 'shrink') was told about my "story" and had heard a couple of the discs of my brain-chatterings. He phoned me early one evening and asked if he might visit with me real soon.

"How about this evening," he urged. "At about eight o'clock?" At my age I appreciated the value of immediacy rather than postponement. I agreed at once and at eight o'clock sharp the psychiatrist entered my modest little home,

"Would you like some Scotch?" was my opening gambit. "That would be fine, thanks," was his immediate reply. That important relaxant established, we sat on comfortable leather recliners opposite each other. Over several glasses of Chivas Regal we tried to solve one of the most exciting puzzles in my lifetime.

This psychiatrist was about the same age as my eldest son, probably close to sixty-five years of age. He thought that it would be important for me to learn that he was not only a psychoanalyst but also a cryptographer. He intimated (it was obvious to me the longer, he spoke) that he had been used for years by the CIA in analyzing complex problems that had defied the experts. As he spoke I noticed that, whenever he was searching for a particular phrase to describe his thoughts on some subject, he stroked his full (pepper and salt) beard as though he were an orthodox Rabbi in a *shtetl* (a small town). He was bright, all right, and bold. His mind was incisive. I use that word knowingly because to incise is to cut and he trimmed away the fat and inconsequentia from whatever I was discussing, leaving only the lean meat of the topic to be considered. I admired him, thinking that I never had that kind of a mind. I always had the habit of "decorating" whatever I was saying with personal attributes, leaving some people downright annoyed.

In a very few minutes (one ounce of Scotch) he asked me a key question. As he spoke he seemed intense and he slid forward in his chair a little. "In all your life has anything ever happened that was so traumatic to you that you simply have never gotten over it? It is always somewhere in back of your mind ready to come to the surface."

"Yes!" was my prompt reply. He was not surprised. But what I was about to open up was a Pandora's box of trauma and guilt. He had been primed for this visit by Mark who told him that I was a "Type A" individual, quick to speak, quick on the trigger, quick to hurt and quick to apologize and with an imponderable sense of recall.

"Speak up, old man!" he said. Apparently he felt that he could get away with such a personal approach. And why not? I certainly couldn't be called "young" anymore. I chose to overlook his poor taste at the moment. Actually I planned to get even with him at a subsequent date but this was not the occasion!

"During World War Two I was in an Infantry division on a number of South Pacific islands. At one time, on the island of Bougainville headquarters company my section of the Americal Division had sustained a serious setback. A small combat patrol of ours was overwhelmed by a much larger Japanese force and in just a few minutes we had lost about sixteen men with about eight or nine more wounded. By radio one of the medics advised us about this tragedy which was not over by far. Immediately a much larger force from the First Battalion was dispatched to encircle the entire combat area, not only to relieve our small patrol but to wipe out the Japanese contingent altogether. About two hours later we received a call for four trucks (six-by-sixes) to go to the battle area, one to carry back the dead and the others to bring back the wounded.

Since several of our MD's were unavailable at this critical moment (they were victims of wounds, malaria, nervous breakdowns), it seemed only appropriate for the Dentist to help with the care of the wounded. I had participated quite a few times before, giving plasma, bandaging and splinting. There were only one physician and me to treat all those wounded. These soldiers were from my own company and I knew all of them by name. In fact, the morning before I had treated several of them for routine dental problems at about six o'clock.

When I got my chance, it was to give plasma to a youngster a big burly young man of twenty-one. His color was already gray, his skin was cold and clammy to the touch and I was not sure that he was breathing. He was definitely in shock. My problem was that I couldn't find a vein to insert the needle and he desperately needed plasma to survive at all. If I had seen his wound, which was on his back and was already bandaged partially I would have reacted differently.

I struggled to open the package of plasma, which contained a long plastic tube and its own needle. I secured the bag of plasma to a rack in the medical tent. Then I searched both his arms and his hands and then his feet looking for a vein. Nothing materialized, even though I placed a tourniquet on both arms and then on his legs hoping a vein would show. I used a scalpel blade to cut open his trouser legs in hopes of finding the greater saphenous or some other vein, even a little one, to insert my needle. Nothing showed up. I called out to Tom Cogswell, our chief medic and explained my problem. I was really upset. He raced over to the soldier, turned him over partially and showed me the ghastly wound (some shrapnel had ripped open his back, exposing his lungs and damaging his spinal column).

"This man is about dead. There's nothing you can do for him, Ed. Better find another customer." And Tom raced back to his own patient who was not quite as bad off as my patient. We were so short-handed that we didn't have enough men to select patients knowledgeably on the basis of the severity of their wounds. Tom was in charge of triage, but in this case he was more hopeful than the situation deserved. This poor kid had been handed to me and I felt guiltier than I have ever felt before in my life. For the first time I had failed in something vital and as a result somebody's "little boy" was dead. I have never forgotten that incident and apparently it is of sufficient importance for my subconscious that it must arise every once in a while to plague me. I have never felt so guilty in all my years."

The psychiatrist, who had sat through this long recitation without interrupting even once, took at least four minutes before he replied. I have to remind you that he is quite a brilliant man, with a string of degrees after his name and a Talmudic approach to the problems of life that people bring him.

Finally he stood up, stroked his beard and looked at me with what might be considered "gentle approbation." I thought I detected elements of admiration and respect in his attitude even though, when he spoke, he acted as though he had "seen through my charade."

"I don't believe a word of that story. *You know and you know that you know the true story that's so active in your subconscious.* No one with your intellect and experience would waste a lifetime of guilt on a case like that—where a man came in who was virtually dead and in deepest shock. Most of all, I doubt that your buddy Dr.Tom Cogswell would have let you waste your valuable efforts on a man already almost dead. I'm sure that Dr. Cogswell had done a quick triage on all the wounded before you even started working. It's a major part of his training.

"Your story is all wrong. What really happened? You must have done something really awful to remember it deep down for sixty-three years. "He had me, and for the first time ever I was forced to admit to a desperate failure that was entirely my fault.

"Of course," I promptly replied. But it took me a few moments to bring myself to admit my "guilt".

"The first story I told you was absolutely true but it is not the reason that I have remembered it all these years. He was given to me just to give him some plasma. I think I might have forgotten about it almost entirely if it were not for this other case that came just a few minutes after they carried the first youngster away. He died before I could even begin on the second case. And I did feel helpless in the presence of problems I could not solve, but nothing compared to the way I felt after my next patient who was lying in the next litter waiting for me.

"Of course most of these wounded were completely unconscious and in varying degrees of shock which means that their blood-vessels had receded deeper into their musculature making it almost impossible to find a vein to use for the plasma.

"As to my next patient, I was prepared to save that kid's life. But I struggled with the package of plasma (with its attached tube and needle) that I was given. The manufacturers of these packets had been experimenting with new substances called "plastic". This was in 1943. Somehow this particular packet of plasma had been dried out or over-heated inadvertently. It was virtually impossible to get that damned needle out of its plastic cover until I finally tried cutting it free with a scalpel. Of course, and you must have guessed it by now, in the heat of the fray I managed to break that needle!

All this took valuable time away from my patient which is the one item he could not afford. Of course I then reached for another packet which was a cinch to open and to set up. But by this time, although my patient had veins that I could find and enter, he did not respond to the plasma and went deeper into shock. Again I called for Tom and he came running to my aid. "This is another case that you can never save. Better let the corporal tend to him and get to the guy on the next littler. You've had some tough luck." And Tom raced back to whatever life-saving attempts he was succeeding at. Tom was not at all as cold and cool as he was that morning.. He had risen to the occasion the way I wish I had. He was all efficiency and heart, but heart is useless when you don't have efficiency.

"All I can say is that two kids died, leaving two families bereft and eternally to mourn. They were deprived of their youngsters because I couldn't find a vein and I broke a goddamned needle that was stuck in some hardened plastic. This was in 1943 and it is now 2009. That's sixty-six years that I've had to live with these horrors. It's a wonder I could ever smile again—or sing–or have fun. Two deaths in less than half an hour was too much for my psyche to take. Two youngsters dying in my arms: literally. Even though I kept on working and did succeed in helping to save three more men my batting average was too low for comfort As long as I have a brain those two kids and my part in their deaths will everlastingly be a black time in my life, a story that I have never told before to anyone."

"That's quite a story. No wonder you've felt guilty all these years. But you have been too tough on yourself. If you had seen a psychologist years ago you might have concluded that there wasn't a chance in the world for you to have saved either man. And someone else is basically to blame for that second death. Whoever manufactured those plasma packs had to give you a fighting chance to get the stuff out easily and in a hurry, without having to cut the package with a scalpel blade. You had every right to anticipate the same sense of cooperation from the manufacturers that you were employing to save those kids' lives. This was combat. This was the unexpected that stymied you despite your training and eagerness.

"I can understand your feelings of frustration and guilt but you did what any other sensible and well-meaning person would have done. Has this feeling of guilt ever disabled you in any way, besides being stored as a failure?"

"Not in any way that I know. Normally I have very good manual dexterity and no one, even jokingly, has ever called me a clumsy klutz. But that's how I felt. Actually I've done surgery all my professional life without a hitch or a pang of guilt. I've tried to continue as a professional taking things as they came. But there is something that you have not mentioned and there is where my sense of guilt is most acerbic. I think of the mothers and fathers of those two boys. And I think of their kid brothers and sisters. They rightfully consider their brother as a hero and a victim. But they have no idea that part of the death scene for each man was a klutz who couldn't find a vein and a klutz who broke a needle. I cry for these people in my sleep as they cried. I share a good part of the guilt for their endless memories of their loss. Whatever you say to mitigate my guilt, I was there and their blood is on my hands. No wonder my brain is talking back to these machines. They have pried open a Pandora's Box and the worms of guilt and shame are set loose."

The Doctor had no answer. He simply had no reply. My conscience was *my* conscience and I was not prepared to share my sense of responsibility with anyone else. But what he *did* do was to open another Pandora's Box that was part of the reason for writing this story.

"Have you thought about the consequences of your making those audio-discs of your experiences under the MRI and the MRA?" he asked.

"Of course. Now that I know that you are a cryptographer as well as a psychoanalyst no man's mind will be safe to retain its personal secrets once you've learned to decipher the codes that the brain uses to express itself. Besides, you will soon be working on refined ways of stimulating brain tissue more easily, thereby giving you a double-edged sword!"

"You're amazing! Why did you say "codes" instead of "code"?"

"Because the white matter of the brain, having a different composition from the gray matter, as well as different functions and different types of memories, is most likely to have a slightly different electronic co-efficient and probably has one or more different codes. A great deal would depend upon the nature of the stimuli that you will be using. This is the beginning of a very dangerous technology. As time goes by you guys will employ non-therapeutic doses of electronic rays, not only to draw out more and more data from the brain but to eliminate some of it—delete it—as you would from any other computer. And, worst of all, you might be able to force-feed data *into* the brain without the individual being aware of what you are doing! Talk about dangerous technologies!"

"As I said before—you're amazing! And I thought you were just a Dentist with a penchant for romantic stories: but....but....you're just damned unbelievable!"

"As soon as I learned that you are a cryptographer as well as a psychoanalyst, I knew what you were really trying to accomplish!"

"It's really a secret, Dr. Ed."

"I know."

"But," said the psychiatrist, "there is also the possibility that by using certain as yet unknown doses of electronic stimulation we may be able to enhance the brain's normal capabilities. We may be able to sharpen up the accessibility to numerous memory banks. We may be able to enhance the creativity of a brain, to compensate for areas of atrophy that may have developed from strokes and dietary excesses. We may enable Man to create more and better devices and techniques for the world to live by."

"Of course you will. *And* you might be able, surreptitiously, to detect the knowledge, the plans, the ideas and the techniques of some of the world's leaders. Suppose you got the Secretary of State—or the President himself—and while they were in the hospital for a regular check- up you gave them sleeping pills to allow eight or nine hours of continuous exposure to an MRA or an MRI or whatever technique you have developed to extract information from someone's brain.

"A cabal, using members of the medical profession, could pump all the pertinent knowledge out of someone's mind and disc-record it. Then other members of your cabal could decipher what you have extracted. The leaders of your cabal who would remain in possession of very important documents of State would have tremendous power. Those members of the cabal who are least important or least to be trusted could simply be made to disappear. It's a great scenario. Happens all the time."

"It is more than a scenario!" exclaimed the Doctor. "We are working furiously to decode what your brain has revealed. You may be really surprised how close we are to a break-through. This particular session with me has, I think, confirmed most of what we have suspected. The confidences that you have exposed to us today confirm what we have been most reluctant to admit. The white matter of your brain, much of which has seemed to be atrophied because of your age and the stenosis of much of your arterial supply, is really not atrophied. For some reason, that area is still a premier focus of your subconscious power. Now that we know the story that has been deepest in your mind, that will aid us immeasurably in deciphering your mind's language. Just wait and see!"

"I'm waiting! I'm waiting! Meanwhile I am sure you will want me to be subjected to more tests, right?"

"Of course. Starting next Tuesday we'll invite you in for another series of brain stimulations and recordings. Using the information we were given by you today we can now zero in on refinements of our understanding of your brain's language. Stay alive, Doctor Ed. We need you! Humanity needs you!"

"And the cabal needs me!" I retorted.

"Okay, if you say so. As you said earlier on, we opened up a Pandora's Box of scientific possibilities. *It all depends on what values we use in our lives.*" The psychiatrist was excited and very intense as he spoke.

It was now my opportunity, once again, to reveal my innermost thoughts about the experiments that "the cabal" were working on. "Actually, I would *love* to be alive when all sorts of challenges face humanity! I would be less than honest if I did not admit to a certain excitement over the work that you are doing. *May I make a few suggestions for the further use of the techniques you will be developing?*"*

"Later. Not now. We have plenty to think about as it is!" And in this way the *"vunder-kind"* of the cabal brushed me off. No matter that he was putting me in my place! No matter that my excessive imagination was already three steps ahead of them all and it will take another wild short story to reveal a way to remove the tendency towards violence and hatred that is so typical of modern Mankind! Just wait and see.

*By the way, almost two years after the author wrote this (untrue) story he had a severe heart attack and two "strokes." He's still alive and kicking!

A COLD CASE

There is a program on TV called "Cold Cases" which describes in routine television manner various legal cases, usually of murder or worse, which have been solved after a number of years have gone by. Usually, these cases are solved by using DNA samples which had been unavailable or withheld at the time of the crime. Then there are the cases which are solved because of a late admission of guilt or because a previously unknown spouse had been discovered. Sometimes a policeman would have a red face of embarrassment or the red hands of guilt. It is all routine. You can solve any one of these cases in no time at all, especially if you have a tendency to secrecy or what is known as a "criminal mind."

This story is a little different, although it fits in the category of "Cold Cases". If you have the sensation that the people in this story seem familiar that would make sense. Some incidents recounted here are indeed very ordinary: the usual behavioral patterns. The strangest things happen to the most ordinary people—sometimes.

Jeffrey Lynn was an ordinary man. He was an accountant trying by all means legal and shady to make a decent living. He had several bad breaks and unfortunate mishaps that deeply affected his mind; perhaps too deeply. He was sued by a couple of clients who thought that Jeffrey had used some skullduggery in filling out their income tax returns. The IRS also didn't like what appeared to be fraud.

It *wasn't* fraud. It was tricky and clever, which most of his clients liked about Jeffrey. But the IRS examiner was in a bad mood, or something akin to that, and fined both Jeffrey and the clients a lot of money. He might have presented charges against Jeffrey but he didn't. Jeffrey was allowed to keep his license, but he received a "warning." These cases were blatantly "exposed" by the media, one of the writers being the younger brother of the IRS examiner. Would you say that the examiner (or his brother) was guilty of something illegal?

Jeffrey also had bad luck with women. His first wife Elaine, fooled around, shamelessly and shamefully with every Tom, Dick and Harry. Jeffrey found her nude with Harry, which led to a messy divorce. It is amazing how many handsome young men testified in favor of Elaine. The female Judge who heard the case was very impressed with Elaine. She didn't care for Jeffrey, who was an ordinary man. Jeffrey got his divorce but Elaine won the case: she walked off with a bundle. Jeffrey had to pay her like forever—more than he really could afford.

Jeffrey married again, but this time it was to a darling little woman who wouldn't hurt a fly. She bore him three children and brought them up nicely. You couldn't ask for anyone nicer. Nancy was a good house-keeper, good cook and good company. Everything about her was good. But what Jeffrey neglected to check up on was Nancy's family history. Her maternal great-grandmother, her grandmother, her mother and Nancy died when they were in their middle-forties of a strange disease called sarcoidosis of the lungs. This condition caused a smothering effect because it clamped down on the amount of air coming into their bodies, as well as depriving their brains of the essential oxygen necessary for normal living.

So Jeffrey found himself alone again, a widower with three young kids. Knowledgeable about women at last, Jeffrey was leery about getting married again. He didn't even have a girl-friend, so fearful was he about the other sex. Jeffrey was also up against some dreadful expenses, with the college years for the kids coming up and the endless payments to his ex-wife, Elaine.

The former examiner from the IRS managed to get an executive position at the IRS, from where he pitilessly saw to it that Jeffrey's simplest cases got examined in the unfriendliest manner and Jeffrey's own returns were given the same "treatment". It did not take long before Jeffrey's practice took a permanent dip.

However, just after his eldest son graduated from law school, Jeffrey made a contact with the man who would save his life. This man, who dealt in the international sale of armaments, was looking for a person with just the accounting skills that Jeffrey had. This arms dealer sold in the neighborhood of a billion dollars worth of armaments to all the most irritating and immoral of the nations that come under the category of rogue nations. Some people think that a few powerful atomic bombs could wipe all of them off the face of the earth and no one would cry. That might be a scenario for the near future if diplomacy fails. As the rogue nations develop the few nations who have atomic weapons are afraid to use them because of the obvious consequences for the future. And the "insurgents" are not fearful of bombs and rockets. They'll take their chances with those.

Anyhow, the arms dealer paid Jeffrey many millions of dollars for the cleverness and trickiness that the situation required. If you noticed, I didn't say a word about the ethical aspects of Jeffrey's recommendations. And it was these many millions of dollars that impelled Jeffrey do what he felt he had to do. First of all, when the "money-man" had contacted him, Jeffrey Lynn changed his name and altered the dates on his license and diplomas. He had to do this because of the snake that was after him in the IRS. Then he opened secret accounts in Swiss-type banks in the Islands off-shore in the Atlantic. I'm not sure but I think he had two accounts, in Barbados and in Saba, an Island near St. Johns. He also had about a million, six hundred thousand dollars in cash in a safe in his basement.

All these moves were temporary. Jeffrey suffered from lack of security and lack of 'permanence' in his life. The facts were that the judge's decision in the Elaine divorce case hamstrung him permanently and the attitude of the mean man at the IRS destroyed any sense of security that he might have had.

Do not worry yourself.....this is not going to be a murder case where he kills either Elaine or the man at the IRS or both. I had both in mind and so did he. But he is not a killer and neither am I. What he had to do dominated almost every aspect of his waking hours and also kept him sleepless most of every night. He really became very nervous and uptight until he made his ultimate decision.

Finally, after making sure that his sons would be left with more than adequate resources and had their futures mapped out plainly, Jeffrey simply disappeared. He did not intimate that he had any plans for the future He just went to a lawyer and filled out, signed and had notarized , with two witnesses, a simple Power of Attorney, which gave his eldest son control all his assets in case anything happened to Jeffrey. He owned his own home, had some securities and a few bank accounts: the usual. He told his son, Jeffrey junior, that he was simply being sensible, knowing what the world was like in "these perilous times." Jeffrey junior thought he understood. He had no suspicions that his Dad had "secret plans."

Sixteen years then went by without a word from Jeffrey. Talk about "cold cases"! Jeffrey Junior had hired all kinds of detectives, some of whom were former classmates of his. They searched the airline records, checked on bank accounts all over the world, checked marriage records in every country that was civilized, investigated the DNA and finger-prints of every "unknown" murder and suicide victim that was a white male in his sixties for the present and the next five years. Jeffrey Senior had just plain disappeared. Of course that IRS executive sought Jeffrey in all the known refuges: Miami, Las Vegas, San Diego, Puerto Rico, Paris, London, Rio de Janeiro, Tokyo, Israel, Australia, New Zealand, Hawaii and Mexico. Elaine had her lawyer look in the same places, without success. There was nowhere else in the world that was worth living in for a man of modest means. Even the "money-man" tried to find Jeffrey, for obvious reasons. But Jeffrey had just "fallen off the Earth", as the ancients used to say.

Jeffrey had gotten the idea of disappearing when he studied the Power of Attorney that his lawyer had given him. It read: *"Definition of Disability, a principal shall be under a disability if the principal is unable to manage his or her proper affairs for reasons such as mental illness, mental deficiency, physical illness or disability, advanced and chronic use of drug chronic intoxication, confinement detention by a foreign power or disappearance."*

Aha! As soon as he read that definition Jeffrey knew what he had to do! He had been searching (using his computer) for a place to move to: somewhere nice, climate-wise, somewhere stable politically and socially, somewhere that American tourists would not flock to on the odd chance that someone might recognize him from "back home." After several months he made his decision. Using his computer, he immediately located four banks in the area he wanted to live in and placed five hundred thousand dollars in each bank, using his "new name" (We are going to have to start calling him J. Rand soon) and identity. He used his lap-top computer to locate real estate brokers in the area and sent a money order for sixty-thousand dollars to pay for a small house in a nice part of town.

He bought, at Barnes and Noble, a quick way to learn the conversational language for that island. He bought airline tickets for the first section of his flight under an entirely fictitious name. He knew that he would have to get each section under a different name and had a different credit card for each new name. He had a different address and a different location for each credit card. He set up the whole scam in advance. By the time he reached his destination no no one would be able to trace his disappearance.

On Thanksgiving, when he knew that the airlines were at their busiest and when he knew that all of his boys would be out of town, Jeffrey took his flight towards anonymity. For sixteen years he lived a full life. He had a modest home where he took one or more native women to satisfy his needs. One thing he didn't need was to get married. He paid them amply for their services. He also had a cook and a housekeeper. He stayed away from the tourist areas, although his house was near the ocean. He kept a low profile. Mr. J. Rand bought himself a small Korean car and made sure that he knew the rules of the road for that area so that he wouldn't get into any trouble. He dressed like the natives. He ate like the natives. He faded into the background and although he was liked by the natives they forgot that he was a foreigner.

After a few months he spoke their language like a native. He went to the beach nearby frequently and swam for hours in the Indian Ocean, until he for no reason at all became an accomplished, strong swimmer. For sixteen years he lived like this. He was relatively happy. His bank accounts were no more than any other successful retired businessman. He always paid cash for whatever he bought. He was an ordinary man and was happy to be that way.

He had "disappeared "on Thanksgiving week-end in the year 1988. That's a long time ago. On Christmas day (actually on the 26 of December) in 2004, J. Rand noticed something different about his island. All the animals seemed disturbed. The horses in a horse-farm near his house were nervous and excited. The dogs and cats were running around as though they were being chased by an invisible spirit. Some of the old-timey natives in the hills began to chant and beat their drums for the gods to be moderate in their punishment, which they felt was due imminently. J. Rand was busy fixing his neighbor's washing-machine. He was always good at mechanics and his neighbors often brought their problems to J. Rand. They called him J.

Suddenly the Earth revolted. A 9.6 earthquake shattered the calm of this lovely Eden. Houses fell in a heap, the "business-district" of three-storey brick buildings collapsed, trapping many hundreds of people in the rubble. Land-slides in the mountains covered over a multitude of towns, creating fresh, unmarked graves for thousands of residents. The water and sewage pipes which had been engineeringly sound in their placement under the ground were fractured in many places, leading to a combined flood of fresh water and raw sewage in the city's streets .Trees and power poles were shaking and waving in the unsteady earth until they too, went crashing to the ground, with the consequent exposure of the public to high tension wires. J. Rand was wise enough to rush out of the house when he felt the first rumblings of the earth below his feet. He ran to the field behind his home (he was careful to avoid the orchard) and lay down on the lush grass to await the end of the earthquake.

Loud shouts in the most agonized manner emanated from both of his neighbors' homes. How could he lie there quietly in the safety of his field while his friends were trapped by an unheeding Fate in the rubble of their homes? He couldn't. J. Rand raced to the neighbor to his north and found that the man and his wife and two youngsters were trapped beneath the rubble. J. freed the man first, so that he would be able to help in freeing the others. That was relatively easy. But when they went to free his neighbor's wife they discovered that she had multiple fractures of her limbs. Gingerly they created a litter from the siding of the house and placed her aside in the field to await medical treatment, whenever that might be. When they searched for the kids they found them barely conscious, stunned but otherwise unharmed. They got the kids out and they helped their father to minister to their mother. J. Rand then raced to the other neighbor, to the south of his house.

There was suddenly an unnatural quiet all over the area. Someone raced by in a car and yelled, "The Ocean is disappearing!! The water is moving backward towards the sun!" No one knew what to do about this screamingly unnatural news and J. Rand went to free his neighbors on the south. He managed to free both the husband and wife in a few minutes and they were about to reach in to salvage the three kids when the most impossible event took them all by surprise.

A thirty or forty-foot wall of water, carrying houses and autos and trees from the shoreline bore down upon them. There was no warning that anyone could have heeded—no action they could have taken to avoid that violent tsunami. Estimates exist that, on the periphery of the Indian Ocean at least 210,000 people lost their lives. On Banda Aceh, this island in Indonesia, more than 100,000 people perished. Mountains of debris *flowed* up *the rivers instead of* down *the rivers*. People, from areas near the shoreline, were seen running around *on top of the floating debris*! Many people were seen floating on trees, boxes, mattresses and other remnants of houses, stores, trains, autos, hotels and other structures.

Many towns on Banda Aceh were annihilated by this tsunami. Those villages that were not destroyed by the water had been virtually wrecked by the preceding earth-quake.* Almost everyone

*If you have a computer and look up under "Google" about Tsunamis in Indonesia you will find the research of what this story says about that tsunami and the 9.6 earthquake that hit Banda Aceh on December 26, 2004.

This is not a true story, with the exception of the earthquake and tsunami that struck Banda Aceh in the direct path of the 30-foot wall of water that swept through the shoreline was killed, by either drowning injuries or disease.

When the international and Indonesian authorities got around to estimate just who was killed and who was left alive they used certain lists. They knew, approximately, who the residents were that lived on Banda Aceh. They procured the lists of persons who were staying at the various hotels and rooming-houses. They knew who was active at the various businesses, the police and fire and other domestic services on the island. They had separate lists of foreigners and domestic personnel. When they located a body, and those people who were not carried out to sea were left, rotting in what must have been the most putrid manner, on the beaches, in the rivers, on the shores of the rivers, among the multitude of buildings that were not washed away, in basements and in vehicles that were usually overturned and wrecked.

When they did not know how to identify a body they did the obvious procedure. If the body, for instance, belonged to a Caucasian, they checked the lists first. Then they took his finger-prints and a sample of his DNA. In the case of an elderly Caucasian man, for instance, whose body they found high up in a tree in an orchard near the beach, they also searched his pockets, where they discovered that he was, for the past sixteen years, a resident of Banda Aceh. He looked like a European or an American. The authorities sent a copy of his DNA and fingerprints to the various governments in Europe and the Americas. Surprise of surprises! The Indonesian Government received information that this individual was an American, from New York City, who had served in the Vietnam War as a volunteer and he had three surviving sons. Oh, yes, and his name was originally Jeffrey Lynn, not J. Rand.

Only four of J. Rand's neighbors were still alive: both men, from homes north and south. Two of the sons from the northern house were still alive and were trying, manfully to reconstitute their homes. When the local newspaper, The Aceh Star, sent a newsman to check on the progress of the rebuilding, all of a sudden there came an outpouring of sadness for the loss of their late neighbor, a Mr. J. Rand. "He was the most decent and helpful neighbor any man could want." both men said. "He risked his life while we had that earthquake still going on. He freed our whole family from the wreckage of our house," said the eldest son from the north house. "And then he raced to free my own late family from the ruins of our house," said the sole remaining survivor of the south house. "And that's not all!" said the second son of the north neighbor. "When that gigantic wave hit us he suddenly materialized in the water and screamed, 'Grab onto my neck. I'll save you!' and he did, he saved my life by grabbing onto one of the trees in his orchard. I hung onto his neck for dear life. He was a terrific swimmer and very strong!"

The media people were delighted that their editor had published that story about "Mr. J. Rand, hero!" But J. Rand was, in reality, just an ordinary man and so was Mr. Jeffrey Lynn.

I REMEMBER, I REMEMBER

Who cares what an old man remembers? Right? Well, wait a minute. Memories have a genuine purpose. Suppose you couldn't remember anything at all: you could never learn and would have to keep taking the same old trial-and-error tour instead of going right ahead and doing your job. No one would recognize your face if they didn't have memories. And how could you love someone if you kept forgetting who she is? Societies would forget what got them in the last economic depression or the last war. You wouldn't know your friends from your enemies without a memory.

Maybe that's what's wrong with human beings in the first place: they have defective memories. They seem unable to remember history and those who study that subject know *history keeps repeating itself because people forget the lessons it teaches!* But there's nothing wrong with *my* memory and sometimes it gives me so much comfort. And sometimes, I gotta say it: remembering is awfully painful. It can make you wanna cry.

For instance:

I remember the thrill of the first snow each year and how the windows used to get all frosted-up so that you could scratch your name in the ice on the glass.

I remember before they had pneumatic tires on automobiles. The cars had solid rubber tires, sometimes with holes bored through them and they sounded so different! And they gave a real bumpy ride, too.

I remember how the wind used to whistle as it raced through the alleyway between our house and the Farley's, next door: Oooooooooooooooh!! That was scary to a six-year-old kid.

I remember when I was almost three years old and my baby brother, Allan, wearing one of those "sweet-pea" nightshirts, had crawled too close to the gas heater and his nightclothes went up in flames. "Baby fire!" I screamed. "Baby fire!" and my mother broke the twenty-yard speed record and plopped the flaming kid into the sink with all the dishes and all that water. Nobody got hurt, but how could I forget that incident?

I remember the clop-clop of horses hooves as wagons of all sorts used to pass our house: especially the milkman's. He would leave a few bottles of milk in a crate on the back porch early in the morning. By the time we got to breakfast the milk in the bottles had frozen stiff and pushed up the cap on the bottles. In the wintertime it was as though each bottle had an erection of ice. Never thought about it that way, I must admit!

I remember the ice-man, who used to drive up to the house in his horse-drawn wagon and deliver a chunk of ice to put in our refrigerator. Usually a ten-cent piece of ice would fit snugly in there. We didn't have an electric refrigerator in those days. It was called an "ice-box", which was literally the case.

It was not that we were poor because we didn't have many conveniences in our lives. It is simply that the industrial revolution had concentrated on improvements for business and manufacturing. The home and the women who tended your home had to wait an interminably long time for those conveniences. We, who are used to everything in the home being electric or even electronic, might sneer at a home that didn't have an electric or gas stove or a micro-wave oven. My Mom had a large, black cast-iron stove which she heated by starting a fire with newspapers and twigs and then throwing chunks of wood (later, coal) into a veritable furnace. It cooked just fine, but my Mom had to clean out the ashes every day (after a few years she hired an Irish immigrant maid, Mary Doyle, for $30 a month and all she could eat). I remember she came from

County Cork, in Ireland. There was no such thing as a day off or two weeks off for vacation. And I remember the rags she used to hang on a line near the furnace in the basement when she had her menstrual period. I never had a clue about things like that.

We didn't have a dishwasher, a clothes-washer or dryer. We didn't have electric can-openers, orange-juicers or mixers or garbage disposal units. We didn't have vacuum-cleaners, electric coffee-pots or even electric drills for my Dad to use around the house. (And, being a dentist, he didn't have an electric drill in the "early days of dentistry." *He used a foot-pedal that he had to pump, the way I did in the Army until I got a motor I hooked-up to my Jeep.)* We had a lawn-mower that you had to push yourself and when it came to removing the snow from a couple of hundred feet of sidewalk my Dad, and later his eldest son (I was that son) had to shovel a path to rid the place of that arctic appearance that makes Christmas cards such a pleasure to receive.

Dad used to shovel the ashes from the coal-burning furnace *and then drag a fifty-gallon can of ashes up the cellar stairs and spread those ashes* on the poorly-shoveled sidewalks for safety's sake. My Dad must have been very strong. I remember that Mom or Mary had to carry the wash upstairs and hang it out a rear window on a line that my Dad had attached to a nearby telephone pole. Come to think of it, how did Dad ever get that high up on the pole to place that line up there? But I remember that wash: how sweet is smelled; stiff as a board from drying in the wind.

I remember the snow that used to get under my collar when I went sleigh-riding in the park across the street. It used to occur to me that the snows were much deeper in my childhood than they are today. But then again, I have to remember that I was, at best, a very little boy and that snow would naturally seem very deep to a little, little boy. (I think I'm going to cry!)

However, I also remember the silly clothes we had to wear: knickers that had to be tucked into long, long stockings and then secured in place with a garter of some kind. I remember that many, many times those long stockings would fall down to my ankles. And those stiff, white, starched collars that had to be attached to your shirt with collar-buttons! Listen, you out there—I'm not making this up, nor am I reciting the costumes from Rebecca of Sunny-Brook Farm. We actually wore those high shoes with those metal "buttons" on them that had to be tied by a couple of two-foot-long shoe-laces!

I remember going to my uncle's funeral and not being allowed to go into the graveyard. Instead I was ordered to keep the limousine and hearse drivers company, "And see to it that they don't get into any trouble!" my mother commanded. I had never seen the inside of a hearse before and got a thorough explanation of how the casket slid over metal spikes in the floor and didn't require too much lifting on the part of the funeral people. I don't think I was quite three years old at the time but it seemed that everybody was very sad there and no one cared to talk to me very much when they came back from the cemetery. I wondered if I had done anything wrong. This uncle whose funeral it was (Dr. Carol Goldenthal), had caught the flu from his patients in the flu epidemic of 1919. So I must have been a little past two years old!

I remember those delicious gingerbread houses that we used to buy at Christmas-time and then you had to soften the walls and roof of the house in milk because they had all dried out by New Years day and you couldn't eat it otherwise. And I remember that we used to hang our longest stockings up on the mantel so Santa Claus would fill them to the bursting-point. Of course we always knew that it was my Dad who filled them up because Santa would never be so cheap as to put an apple, an orange and a banana with some cracker-jack toys in a Christmas stocking. But we enjoyed the holidays anyhow, even though, as Jewish kids, we had other holidays of our own to enjoy. Even so, I was pretty old before I stopped fantasizing about some fat old man coming down a chimney in the dead of winter when the fireplace was still smoldering and hot.

I remember the trolley-cars on Kingsbridge Road, especially in the winter. You see, Kingsbridge Road is a very, very steep hill and when the trolley cars which have to travel on steel tracks in the roadway try to negotiate either an uphill or a downhill trip when the weather is icy it can be a very exciting experience. The trolley conductor when driving that electric vehicle downhill would have his brakes on fully tightened. The last thing he would need is to get some speed when he can't stop the trolley from sliding all the way down that long hill completely out of control. As it was, I personally used to take that trolley in the wintertime just to experience that thrill! We used to take that trolley to Van Courtlandt Park for the free ice-skating it offered on its small lake. That was a delicious experience provided the lake was sufficiently frozen to be a safe place to skate. Sometimes it wasn't and some kids actually fell through the ice! By the way, it/ just cost a nickel to ride on the trolley-cars (and the subway to the end of the line!).

I remember the trouble the Bronx and Van trolley had in negotiating the *uphill* trip on Kingsbridge Road when the chill of the late afternoon iced over the rails that we were supposed to ride on. Aha! Many a time we all had to get out of the trolley and helped push it up that long hill before it would slide all the way down again, which it did sometimes! What a great climax to an afternoon of ice-skating!

I also remember that it was pretty rugged living in those days...... but I'm still here, aren't I? And I haven't lost any of my marbles yet, either. Which reminds me *I remember my marbles,* those little glass balls that in my neighborhood we used to call "immies." Of course there were variations on them, like the "steelies"...little balls of polished steel which were indestructible.

I remember going with some kids to Poe Park, a block away, and crawling *under* the bandstand while the bands would play dance-music for people to dance to on the cement dance floor in the park. In this park was the home of Edgar Allan Poe. You may not want to believe this but I and my brother Allan were named after that Mister Poe. My mother could remember every word and every line of every one of Edgar Allan Poe's poetry. And so could I, after a while. My youngest brother was not named after *that* poet but after my maternal grandfather, who was also a poet. But Maurice, my youngest brother, was always called Poe by his friends! Poe Goldenthal?

And I remember, in the late nineteen-twenties, sitting on the living room floor *under* the old Colonial Radio listening to "The Shadow Knows!!" That radio had a speaker *on the bottom*!

Well, "The Shadow" is gone, the trolleys are gone, the milkmen and the ice-men have gone the way of all flesh and all that's left, besides the present, are those memories. I may not have to rake up any of those memories ever again, but they are still on my mind's hard drive in case I ever have to. Right now, I'm too busy thinking about tomorrow.

(This is absolutely true.)

DEMOLITION

My name is George Earnshaw. All my life I had been a resident of Palm Beach County, Florida. By the time I married Helen Finch I had been living in the city of Palm Beach for about eleven years.

Our marriage was a total fiasco. We didn't get along at all and never had any kids because Helen kept on losing those fetuses. It was mostly because she kept doing some violent exercises and taking some kind of pills. I was not sure whether those were actually *my* children she was carrying and she wasn't sure either. There is no doubt in my mind that she was involved in several "illicit romances", especially with a guy named Timothy O'Hearn.

Timothy was a butcher. His father and grandfather were butchers. Although they had made a fortune at that trade, especially during World Wars I and II, they were not happy as butchers. They all wanted to be builders and in 1947 the whole family formed a corporation, "O'Hearns of Florida, Builders". Helen was very impressed with their monetary success. At that time almost anybody could be a builder. Even *nobodies* could be builders in Florida!

One afternoon, although I didn't feel badly at all, the doctor I went to for my annual medical exam prescribed something to keep my cholesterol down. When he said, "You seem a little tense. What's your problem?" I had to tell him about me and Helen.

When I said, "I am basically a non-violent man but if I was a different kind of guy I would have bashed both Helen and her many boyfriends to the ground. I could do it, physically, but that's not my way of doing things." he seemed genuinely disappointed and prescribed a mild sedative for me. "I would rather have you tell me that you bashed the lot of them!" he commiserated. However, my laid-back attitude led to a wild and woolly story that finally made headlines in the newspapers. It was even on TV, under the caption, "Strange Stories!"

On one particular evening in 1974 Helen brought in some Chinese food for dinner. "This is from a real gourmet Oriental restaurant and it might seem a little strange to you at first. But everybody raves about their food so you'll love it!" She chose certain dishes for herself, mostly seafood, which I don't like. What she chose for me was very highly spiced but also unusually sweet and rather purple in color. Helen said that the purple color was a trademark of this gourmet restaurant.

I immediately knew what Helen was up to. When I had come home from the doctor's office I had told her that I had something wrong with my heart and that he prescribed some very strong medication. "I dare not take more than *one* of these pills every other day or it will knock me off!" I lied. "These pills are purple in color so that we won't be able to confuse them with any other pills we might have in the house. I have to be very careful." Of course it was all a fake-out, because the pills were actually white and very mild, but I had stopped at one of those "Party Shoppes" after I left the pharmacy and bought a whole box of purple-colored sugar pills that kids just love. I exchanged them in the pharmacy's bottle and took my white pills early in the morning before Helen woke up. So when I saw that this Chinese food was really purple I knew just what Helen was up to.

When I ate the Chinese food it was wild; very spicy but terribly sweet. I made believe I was enjoying it but it actually made me want to barff! "It's purple, all right, but very spicy. I really like it!" I lied again. She must have put about twenty of those candy pills in the Chinese food. Obviously, the intention was murder: *my* murder! So I went along with her scenario. Right after the meal, despite the excess of Chinese tea, I became---for Helen's sake—terribly sleepy. Before she could stop me I fell to the floor in an apparent deep sleep. She didn't know if it was a coma or death or whatever. The next act in her scenario was for her to call Timothy O'Hearn to come over and take me away in his Econoline Van, which is exactly what happened. Timothy and Helen had a heck of a time carrying me to his van, mostly because I made myself as heavy as possible and kept slipping through their grasps to the ground. I had great difficulty in not laughing out loud. But it really was not a funny situation, since the object was murder and Timothy was an accessory to the "crime."

I wondered where Timothy was going to dump me. I hoped it wasn't one of the many canals in the Palm Beach area where there are often alligators prowling around. Timothy revealed his plan, fortunately, just before he drove away with me in the Van. He said, "I'm gonna hang him in that great big new freezer I put in my backyard. He'll hang there and in a few hours he'll be as stiff as a board. When we're ready to start re-building that old courthouse that we're partially demolishing now I can easily bury this guy in cement in the basement floor or build him into one of those big foundations for the new elevators we're gonna install. He'll be out of our way from now on!"

So I knew my fate, if I wasn't alert.

When we reached Timothy's house it was already dark outside. He drove around to the back of his house and wrapped me in what looked and smelled like a horse-blanket. He went into his house and called a handy-man to help carry me into the freezer. "This is an expensive-quality piece of cow-meat." he explained to the handy-man. "I'll hang it all up on one of hooks myself, after I cut away what I don't want to keep. You can go on home after we get it into the freezer." The handy-man, who wasn't too swift on the intelligence scale, didn't think too much about what he was asked to do and agreed in a docile fashion. After helping Timothy load me into the freezer he took the twenty-dollar bill that he was offered and went on home, as directed. Actually, I think he must have gone to a bar in his neighborhood and drunk up as much as he could tolerate.

Timothy then proceeded to tie my arms together at the wrist and, being quite strong, was able to lift me up, the way he would lift a side of beef, and hang me, by the wrists, face to the wall, to a very cold steel hook in the side of his freezer. I knew at once that if he didn't leave relatively quickly that I would be in real trouble. The temperature must have been about thirty-three degrees and that's not recommended for anyone's health. Timothy must have felt the same way because he worked faster and faster and, almost precipitously, ran out of the freezer into the very warm yard of his house. He had never, even once, looked at my face. He had never tested my pulse, which had been racing. The fact that I was still soft and flaccid was, he must have figured, the norm for someone who hasn't had enough time to develop rigor mortis. But an hour hanging in that freezer would have been the end for me.

I felt sure that he had locked the freezer from the outside and wondered why there was still a little bulb lit in there. It didn't take me five minutes to wriggle free of that hook and, standing on the floor, which was not icy, untied my wrists. Timothy was not one to tie knots the way the hoodlums do in the movies. It was a cinch to wriggle free and then try the door. It opened easily from inside so I guessed that the manufacturers, knowing that many a poor soul had been locked in freezers made it easy to get out but difficult to get in. It's not the "insiders" you have to worry about but the "outsiders."

I had just enough time to look around at the contents of the freezer before I was ready to leave. The first things I saw were a number of "sides of beef"; about half the torsos of a number of cattle hanging from hooks such as I had been hanging from for a few minutes. Then there were a number of expensive fowl hanging on racks.

But most interesting was an old man, fully clothed, wearing an Irish cap, sitting on a wooden crate---frozen stiff. I later learned that this was Timothy's old uncle Shamus O'Hearn, who, in his dotage and partially anesthetized by an excess of Irish whiskey, had found his way into Timothy's freezer. The old man must have been very tired. So he sat down, on what was a very warm summer's day outside, on this crate in the freezer, which was to be his final seat.

Later that day Timothy and his brothers had discovered the old uncle frozen like a popsicle and they left him there on that crate. They had all cared dearly for Uncle Shamus and, sad to relate, he would never again bend their ears with those phony stories of his childhood in good old Ireland that they knew by heart. They would surely miss the songs he used to sing in his fine Irish tenor and his brogue, which got more unintelligible the more he had to drink.

I quickly departed from the freezer before I became frozen stiff like Uncle Shamus, putting a small stick in the path of the door so that, if necessary, the police might be able to gain access. But I didn't want to bother with the police at this time. I had to get something to warm me up after that icy experience, so I walked a few blocks to the nearest bar. Of course, I knew where Timothy and Helen would be at this time. Four double brandies finally warmed me up.

I was not alone at that bar, naturally. One man, as tall and as husky as I was, had been watching me as I shivered and drank and shivered and drank and shivered and drank. He walked over to me, friendly fashion and said, "You must have been in a freezer, to be so cold."

Amazing! How the devil could he know a thing like that? "How the devil do you know that, buddy? I *was* in a freezer!"

"Easy," he replied. "First of all, I am a private detective. Secondly you have sawdust on your shoes and thirdly the rope that was used to tie your wrists which are still rubbed raw, is still hanging from your jacket pocket."

"Wow! How easy that was to figure out!" I had just enough to drink to have loosened my tongue so, as though on a shrink's couch, I couldn't help telling him about Helen and Timothy.

"That's a terrible story!" he opined. "But I'm sorry I can't drink and celebrate with you. My doctors tell me that I am four drinks away from a collapse of my nervous system. Just as I knew you'd been in a freezer these guys have my life expectancy pegged to the actual number of drinks it would take to knock me off."

"How many drinks have you had tonight?" I asked.

"One cup of coffee and one glass of club soda with lemon juice, that's all."

"Well," I guessed, "I guess if you have only one drink to help me celebrate my freedom it can't knock you off. Okay? It's on me!"

"Why not?!" agreed Ralph Boyd, which was his name. "One straight shot of Chivas Regal!" he called to the bartender. He drank that Scotch down the way only a true lush can drink. "One more Chivas Regal!" he called. To me he confided, "I'm not going to put my doctors to the test. This will be my last!" And it was!

Two drinks and Ralph was on the floor. His doctors had given him too much leeway. Two drinks and Ralph was gone.

"I'll take him to the hospital if someone will help me get him there."

"I have a panel truck," said a non-descript wino. "I'll take you to the end of the earth, if you choose!" he exuded in his alcoholic generosity.

So Frank (that was the wino's name) and I got Ralph into the bed of the truck and I gave instructions how to get to Timothy O'Hearn's house. We drove around to the back of the house where I announced to Frank, "This man's doesn't need a hospital. He's dead! Help me carry him into the freezer and I'll take him to the morgue in my car, later on."

"As you wish. You have but to ask." It was the alcohol as well as Frank's good nature that was talking. Frank and I hung Ralph up by the wrists on the same hook I had been hung on and Frank drove off, twenty dollars richer. But he had seen Shamus sitting frozen on that crate and I had to explain that it was a wax dummy and that sufficed for a drunken mind.

I made sure that there was no trail that could lead to me (except for the wino, and who would believe that drunk?) Then, after I left the same twig leaving the freezer door unlocked, I walked back to the same bar that I had been at after my first experience with Timothy's freezer. I ordered a simple whiskey with a water chaser. Fortunately that wino did not come back to this same bar. He *did* go to another bar in West Palm Beach and couldn't stop talking about the old man in the freezer. Someone finally got annoyed hearing the same inebriated story and called the police, who took one look at the wino and called the hospital EMS service, who took the drunken man away to sleep off his hallucination. Only it was *not* a hallucination!

About forty-five minutes later a bedraggled Ralph Boyd re-entered the same bar we had met in before. He came right over to me and I said," I have a shot of Chivas Regal Scotch waiting for you. Here it is. I knew that if you weren't dead you'd wriggle loose and come right back here again. If you were dead you would wind up in one of the walls of the old courthouse the O'Hearns are rebuilding

So Ralph and I became good friends. He only drank that one Scotch and it didn't hurt him a bit. Eventually, we walked to the railroad station together on my recommendation and got two tickets to Tulsa, Oklahoma, where we lived separately but as very good friends.

Every once in a while I'd buy a copy of the Sun-Sentinel, Palm Beach edition, just to catch up on old times. In 1974 it was written that the O'Hearn company was rebuilding the old courthouse. They had put in some elevators, added a floor and built the building out in all directions. It was said that they had cut one of the courtrooms in half just to put in a hallway! They had all the taste and sensitivity to human sensibilities that you would have expected from a bunch of butchers. The original had been built in 1916 and it been renovated in 1947, when Palm Beach began to grow more populated. From the moment that the old courthouse was rebuilt by the O'Hearns it was constructed in such a way that nobody, but nobody, had a kind word to say about the taste, the design, the conveniences or the quality of the workmanship. The O'Hearns decided to go back into the wholesale meat business. But they did manage to conceal several items of considerable value. Just recently, on January 23, 2004, the Sun-Sentinel had an article describing what a struggle it was for some far-seeing politicians to undo the work of the O'Hearns and once again rebuild that old courthouse the way a sensitive public would like to see it done.

A family of builders named Hedrick, the scions of a long line of prominent builders, was chosen for the job. I can tell you at least one thing that the Hedricks will find once they get to dis-mantling the old elevators. They will find a skeleton of a man wearing the clothing typical of the mid 1970's. That was supposed to be *my* skeleton and it nearly became Ralph Boyd's skeleton. Let's see how good a detective you are. Can you guess whose skeleton it really was?

Sure enough! They *did* discover a male skeleton in the rebuilt section of the old courthouse a few weeks after the original articles were written in the Sun-Sentinel in January, 2004! How did they go about finding who that man was and who had put him there? After all, if the O'Hearns had rebuilt that courthouse in 1974 at least one of them or their workmen had to have been involved. Right? Right.

Remember, the crime or crimes were committed in 1974. That is about thirty years ago. Who can be expected to remember what happened thirty years ago? Well, at least one fellow did remember enough for the police to have a viable lead to follow. A man who now works as a dispatcher for the Lincoln Hospital in West Palm Beach does have a vivid memory of what occurred because of the peculiar nature of the individual involved. Here is his story: "I remember that in 1974, when I was a young EMS worker at Lincoln hospital, we were sent to a bar on Military Trail where a husky wino couldn't stop talking about a freezer in a back yard in Lantana where he had seen an old man, frozen stiff as a board, who was sitting on a crate.

The old man was wearing an Irish cap and was covered with a light frost. This wino was so excited by his hallucination and had been drinking so heavily that one of the "customers" in the bar became annoyed and called the police. Of course, knowing the source of the information, the police never checked out his story. They called *us* and we took him to the hospital to "sleep it off." He also added, in our "wagon", that he had helped someone hang up in the freezer a guy who had passed away on the floor of the bar. We were so sure that he was hallucinating that we never passed that information to the police." This was the tale of a middle-aged man who still worked at Lincoln hospital. He had read, in the Sun-Sentinel, about the skeleton the Hedricks had found while dismantling the renovations to the old courthouse.

But this time the police *did* take an interest in the case after the Lincoln Hospital employee called the police and informed them of the "wino" of thirty years ago. They put a top-notch detective on the job of investigating the role of the O'Hearns, who had rebuilt that part of the courthouse where the skeleton was found. Timothy O'Hearn had just retired at the age of seventy-four. He admitted that his uncle, old Shamus O'Hearn, was still in the freezer.

"Sure now," he added with an Irish accent, "What better way is there to honor the dearly beloved after they've passed on than to freeze them and still be able to see them pretty much as they were! I wish we had done that intentionally!" He proudly took the cops to his freezer and showed them his old uncle and they were inclined to agree with him that a deep-freeze is the way to go as he dusted off the fine powdery ice that had settled on old Shamus. But Timothy denied having anything to do with the body in the foundation for the elevator in the rebuilt courthouse. That story was actually on television!

Then the detective, whose father had been a "private eye" before and had strangely disappeared thirty years ago, had an epiphany. The hospital dispatcher had told him about the wino who had claimed he had seen a man in a freezer in a backyard in Lantana and then added that the wino had claimed he helped a man hang someone who had passed away at another bar in Palm Beach County in the same freezer where Shamus was sitting. Where was that bar? Was it still in existence? And it suddenly occurred to the detective that his father, Ralph Boyd, might have been the man who had passed out in that bar. Ralph Boyd had been forbidden to drink alcoholic beverages by his doctors, but Ralph simply liked the ambiance of those bars and had a lot of friends there. He might, indeed, have been the man who passed out.

So Lionel Boyd, the detective, went from bar to bar in the Palm Beach area looking for some information about a man who fell to the floor in a bar from having too many drinks. *Every bar* had at least four such stories. But the owner of a bar on Lantana Boulevard remembered one special case. Salvatore Brusiglio remembered a man—a regular—who had fallen to the floor many, many years before and that another man said he'd take the man to a hospital but that he didn't have his car. A wino, also a "regular", offered to drive them to a hospital in his panel truck.

Lionel felt that he was on the right track, alright. The case was melding! But the barkeep nearly spoiled the story, "However," he said, "forty-five minutes later the guy who had collapsed on the floor and been carried away came back to the bar—alone—and resumed his drinking. He was ice-cold, which was unusual for a summer's evening. He had only one more drink: a Chivas Regal!"

Lionel almost exploded. "Did you say Chivas Regal?!" (He knew that his Dad always drank Chivas Regal.)

Salvatore was certain, "I am absolutely certain! The nice guy who had driven off with the victim and returned to the bar to resume his drinking had bought a glass of Chivas Regal and set it aside next to him. He distinctly said, 'If that guy is still alive he'll be back for that drink!' and sure enough, the guy came back!"

Lionel had one more ploy to try to locate his long-lost father. He took out his wallet, which contained a few photographs and picked out two representative photos of Ralph Boyd. "Do you think you could remember if this was the man who drank and fell to the floor in your bar?" He showed Salvatore the two pictures. Sal pondered a while. He took the pictures to a better light, next to the big mirror behind the bar, and then he spoke---"I know it's been thirty years, but I am absolutely certain that this is the man. He's actually wearing the brown topcoat and fedora he always wore!"

Lionel sank into his arms on the edge of the bar as he said, "That's my father! That's Ralph Boyd. He was a private eye. He *always* wore that topcoat and fedora no matter what the weather was outside."

"That's amazing!" observed the barkeep, "Originally, when the other guy had come into the bar and taken four drinks in a row your Dad mentioned to the other guy that he was a private detective and to prove it he told him, "You look like you been in a freezer!" And the other guy was amazed! 'I *was!*' he said."

"Wow! This case is really moving!" Then he started to cogitate some more, spending at least five minutes thinking. "What happened to the two men, the "Good Samaritan" and my Dad?"

"The other guy kept looking at his watch, which he wore on his right wrist, which means that he's a lefty (left-handed) and finally he said, 'We can make it to the train-station and catch the ten fifty-five if we leave right now!' And I never saw either of them again!"

For a good detective to prove his mettle Lionel had to use all his intellect, which means he had to use his imagination as well as his cleverness. He decided that Timothy O'Hearn and his freezer needed more investigation. Why had "the good Samaritan" and Ralph Boyd both shown evidence of having been freezing cold in the hot summertime? Why had the so-called 'good Samaritan" taken Lionel's father Ralph to the freezer and, with the help of the wino, hung Ralph up on a meat-hook? Was it "to take his own place", thinking that Ralph was dead, so that Timothy would have someone he thought was the "Samaritan" to bury in the new courthouse? It certainly seemed to be a likely scenario. This guy seemed to like Ralph very much and, if Ralph was not actually dead he must have figured that Ralph should be able to wriggle himself free and find his way back to the bar—which is exactly what happened. The question that had to be answered was "if the Good Samaritan" had been in the freezer first who had put him there and why?

Lionel had to figure out why Timothy would want to put *any* man in a freezer—dead or alive. No one else had access to that freezer, which was supposedly locked from the outside after Shamus had wandered in and died. Did Timothy want to kill someone intentionally or did he think that the man was already dead? We *know* that Timothy *could* have planned to secrete that frozen body in the cement-works of the new courthouse, once they started rebuilding it. Did Timothy have any enemies? A business competitor? A lover for his wife? A girl-friend's husband? Someone else that Timothy could have hated? Somehow, Timothy did not seem to be someone who was capable of a "great hatred".

Every detective who has a great reputation is often dependent upon some unlikely collaborators to help him solve his cases. Very often apparently innocent people make critical mistakes, like writing a note to or telephoning a suspected person. Often such a note may be sent to the press or even the police to embellish the ego of someone who really could not bear the scrutiny of a thorough investigation.

After the doldrums of several succeeding months, during which nothing of substance had appeared to break this case, a nasty person, for whatever reason, sent a note to Timothy O'Hearn. Helen Earnshaw was just such a nasty person and although she was now almost eighty years old, she was still nasty to Timothy, whom she had not seen for almost 28 years.

One of the men working for Lionel in the police department had only one job: to screen all the mail, E-Mail and phone calls that were directed to Timothy O'Hearn. Many a letter was steamed open to no avail but this letter, from Helen, was a bonanza! It simply said, "The furniture man can't sell if he can't work." Why would Helen have done this? There are no answers for that question except perhaps sheer nastiness. Unquestionably she had read the newspapers that told about the imminent renovation of the old courthouse and she must have thought this a good occasion to irritate Timothy who might be having some explaining to do with the police. After all, she was not an utter idiot, having planned and almost executed the perfect crime. But Timothy had ditched her after a couple of years and returned to his homely, sexless wife from whom he had wandered quite often. At least she was harmless.

Who was Helen Earnshaw and who was 'the furniture man,' Lionel wanted to know. And why did Helen think he couldn't move? Lionel had to investigate. He soon discovered that Helen Earnshaw's husband, who had mysteriously disappeared thirty years before, was a model citizen named George. George had been in the furniture business, owning a store called, "For The Home". Ever since George disappeared in 1974 Helen had been living on his insurance money and on the proceeds of that store. Her younger brother, who was very out-going and practical, managed the business quite successfully. George's physician, who knew about George's problems, always had the impression, although he never said anything about it to anyone, that George had either committed suicide or just plain run away. But Dr. Abbott knew when to keep his mouth shut until Lionel got to him.

Now Lionel had some solid intimations that Helen and Timothy had been "an item" thirty years ago and that it was her husband, George "the furniture man" who could not move. Obviously she thought he was dead. She must have *known* that George could not move! Why was she so sure of it? Only if George was dead or paralyzed could he not move. She had waited the appropriate length of time then filed for his insurance and his Social Security checks. Helen came out smelling like a rose! But what did Timothy smell like? Why did he have to be reminded that George couldn't move? Only if you can imagine the nastiness of that Helen would you know that she wanted to get back at Timothy and destroy him to the degree of emptiness that now described her own life. Things were beginning to connect to each other for detective Lionel Boyd.

Lionel was certain that George Earnshaw was the "Good Samaritan" who had spent some time in Timothy's freezer. He had obviously escaped from that freezer in Timothy's backyard. Ralph had also escaped from that same freezer and met George again in Salvatore's bar. So since both men had escaped from Timothy and taken a train for someplace far away neither of them could be the skeleton that was recently found in the old courthouse. Whose skeleton was it, then?

It is easy for an author to intellectualize about whose body it was. But just put yourself in the place of the detective and you can see how many choices he had. He had actually almost run out of choices. There would have been no excuse for Timothy to have buried anyone else but George Earnshaw. Anyone else who made his appearance on that meat-hook would have resulted in a call to the police and Timothy, too, would have come out smelling like a rose. But Timothy never had any idea that George had escaped. There was almost always somebody hanging there, except for a few hours late one night after Ralph had escaped. Timothy, who was really not a bad sort, went into that freezer many, many times, but he could not bring himself to look closely at the body he thought was George's. He figured that dead people change too, and the fact existed that the man's body hanging there soon became covered with a coating of ice-dust that concealed his identity totally.

Lionel figured out that the body belonged to the wino, Frank, who had spent a few hours in the local hospital recovering from those hallucinations that were actual reality! Lionel conjectured that Frank the Wino was truly so enthralled by what he had seen in that freezer that he sneaked back in there at about six o'clock the next morning. He had gone to a bar for his early-morning four shots of whiskey and, already slightly high, had gone back into the freezer. How did he get in? The twig that George had left in the doorway had prevented the door from closing entirely.

So Frank, the wino (we didn't learn his last name until much later on) soon found himself in that freezer. He turned the lights on fully, so that he could see old Shamus more clearly. It would not take long for an inebriated man to freeze to death. Frank disregarded any precautions. He might have had a suicidal motive as well as old uncle Shamus had. Why else would they become alcoholics in the first place? It would not be long before Frank would find his ability to move and maneuver quite limited and he would then fall to the floor, helpless, and soon freeze as stiff as any of those sides of beef—as stiff as old Shamus.

"I can just see the whole picture in my mind's eye." said Lionel to one of his lieutenants. "Frank was talking to old Shamus and getting increasingly perturbed as the old Irishman remained silent. I can just hear Frank singing Mother Macree and The Little Drummer Boy and other Irish melodies in a tenor that needed some repair–just to get a rise out of old Shamus. I can just see him kneel before the frozen Shamus, begging him to answer. I can see him gradually freezing to death!" And Timothy, when he saw the wino's body on the floor figured that it was George who had freed himself only to freeze to death looking at Shamus. So Timothy, never looking at the body, hung the wino on the same hook that he knew that George had hung on. He shivered at the thought that George had wriggled free, only to die of the cold.

In less than a month Lionel located George Earnshaw in Tulsa, Oklahoma. He simply had his squad check out every State in the Union for the middle 1970's to detect a new furniture store being established. They found one in Tulsa owned by a man named

George Antell. Mr. Antell had a manager named Ralph Zuloft, who passed away from natural causes in 1984.

It does not take all that long for an airplane to fly from West Palm Beach airport to Tulsa, Oklahoma. When Lionel walked into the "Homestyles" furniture store George saw him at once and nearly had a seizure. He walked right over to Lionel, after peeking at his watch on his right wrist, and said, "You look so much like your father that for a moment I thought I was seeing a ghost! Hi! I'm George Earnshaw and I imagine you've been looking for me."

"Hi!" said Lionel. "You mentioned seeing ghosts. Am I to assume that my Dad has passed away?"

"Yes. He died of a heart attack about twenty years ago. His doctors never thought he would live that long but I saw to it that he stayed away from alcohol and all aggravation. He was my best friend. We just never found anything that we disagreed about. He told me all about you and your late mother. He had completely lost any interest in women and sex after she passed away. He also said he left you on your own to stimulate you to succeed without being in his shadow."

"He was a very dear man and really didn't have to leave me. I think he was quite troubled."

"He resented the fact that his heart condition limited him so much. Any moment might be his last on earth. He was frightened. There were occasions when he had considered suicide but I think that when he met me and learned about *my* troubles he decided to stick around. Misery loves company."

Lionel wiped away a tear or two. He was very much like his Dad. We went to a local restaurant for a real good dinner (Austrian cooking). I no longer frequented bars and had dropped alcohol as an interest. Lionel asked me a load of questions and there were no surprises in any of my answers. (George was very sincere and had not changed despite the years.)

"What charges can you bring against Timothy O'Hearn and Helen?" I asked.

"Well, Timothy never knew the man he finally placed in the foundation of the old courthouse. The man was already dead. He wasn't surprised that the person he thought was you had worked loose from the hook he'd hung you on. He never looked at the face of his victim—he really wasn't a bad person. He figured that dead people change also, so he thought that all these years he had secreted George Earnshaw. The real villain was your wife, Helen. She actually tried to murder you and could be held on attempted murder, but she's eighty years old now and what could we do to her?"

"Lionel!" I barked, "She's a witch. She should have all her money taken away from her and be forced to live in an old folks' home for the indigent. That would be only fair!"

"Well, it would take a mean lawyer to propose that to a judge. She's not only old but a little out of her mind, so she wouldn't feel punished for the right things. And she's ill. She has whatever-it-is that produces creepy-crawly sensations in her skin. It may be nerves, the consequences of a lifetime of meanness. I don't think she experiences a pleasant moment in a year's time."

"Then forget her! I forgot her but I never forgave her. The law may also be forgiving but Mother Nature is not. She's being punished the way no man could punish her."

"I'll have to fly back to Florida on the eleven o' five plane. Could you bring me to the airport?"

"Sure. By the way, what was the real name of Frank the wino?"

"Francis X. O'Toole was his name. And dig this: he was once a prominent Irish-born psychiatrist! Oh, by the way, I must thank you for being such a good friend to my Dad, even though you did hang him up in O'Hearn's freezer!"

"I really thought he was dead and by hanging him there Timothy would not have suspected that I escaped. But I gave your Dad an out. If he was still alive and wanted to live he could wiggle loose, the way I did. I didn't tie his hands very tight. And he just knew he could meet me at the bar! And if he was really dead, then he would make the newspapers in 2004. *And,* if he actually wanted to die he had Shamus O'Hearn for company.

A copy of part of the newspaper article in the Sun-Sentinel of 1/23/2004 follows. Wouldn't you have written a story like this if you had read that article? It is not the truth, naturally.

The Sun-Sentinel   *1/23/2004*

Officials begin chiseling away at court-house wall
by Anthony Man, Staff writer

WEST PALM BEACH- With a few dozen gentle taps—and some energetic whacks from County Commissioner Warren Newell—Palm Beach County got a bit closer to its history on Thursday.

It will take months of work before people get to see the ultimate treasure: the 1916 county courthouse, hidden for the past three decades by a now scorned expansion.

And even then, architect Rick Gonzalez warned, it will look pretty bad at first.

Gonzalez said it could take a little more than three years for the original courthouse, now entombed by an ugly beige shell typical of 1970's architecture, to open as a historical museum and county office space.

Demolition of the wrapabout six months, Gonzalez said. First, five to ten feet of the addition to next to the 1916 building will be carefully removed to create a buffer to protect the historic structure. He said others involved in the project are passionate about the cause. "People who know the history, they develop a sense of community, they develop a respect" said Michael Bornstein Lantana Town Manager. "Nothing gives me more pleasure than taking an ugly structure and converting it into a beautiful thing" Gonzalez said.

He's especially interested in restoring the original 2-story courtroom to its early, but brief grandeur. When the first of three additions was put on, in 1927, the courtroom was sliced in half to add a hallway.

It's also more than a job for Dale Hedrick, whose Hedrick brothers Construction is managing the project. Generation of Hedricks—his great-grandfather, grandfather and father----have been builders.

County Commission chairwoman, Karen Marcus, said "There wouldn't have been anything to work on if it were not for Mike Bornstein. He pushed restoration when few were interested. County and city plans called for demolition of the new courthouse after the newer one opened in 1996. (Continued on page 2B)

AT THE CROSSROADS

Everybody in South Florida knows about The Crossroads. It is one of the noisiest eateries in Boca or Delray, but the food is quite good and the service is excellent. Its floor is littered with peanut shells the result of the free peanuts you get before, during and after the meal is served.

Long ago, on the S.S. France, during its heyday as a luxury liner, you would get a selection of fine French wines and mounds of caviar with all the chopped eggs and onions you could eat *free* at every meal as well as at all hours of the day or night on the Promenade deck even at breakfast time or at three in the morning. That tells you something, doesn't it? The French gave caviar and fine wine and the Americans give peanuts. The floors on The France were spotless, too. The French Line went broke, ultimately.

You would expect that an establishment such as The Crossroads would attract only the young and the Beat, but, on the contrary, lots of senior citizens patronize this restaurant. They must enjoy being among young people who are more relaxed and do not have, as yet, the history of problems and disappointments that identify the usual 'seniors'.

The waiters and waitresses are all in their late teens and their twenties. The young woman who was our waitress the first time we ever ate at The Crossroads seemed to be about nineteen years of age and offered the observant patron the sight of a very tight blouse with a bosom to match. Her jeans must have been applied with one of those power-suction devices. So molded to her lithe figure were they that one had to wonder if those jeans had to be incised and peeled off at bed-time like the skin of an orange: a Florida orange, of course.

She was not at all of Spanish descent but her name was Maria, according to the card that was pinned to her blouse. Even if you were dreadfully near-sighted you would not need eye-glasses to read the name "MARIA". That yellow card was stuck right in your face.

I usually try to engage our waiters and waitresses in a limited form of conversation. It is a form of speakus-interruptus because these people are usually too busy and hurried to dilly-dally in long, fruitless conversations. But this was not the case with Maria and it was her fault for leading me on. All I had to do was ask her why she was named "Maria" instead of the usual "Mary" and I got a touching story that grabbed you by the heart.

"Oh! My mother must have been so romantic!" she gushed. "She originally wanted to name me "Marybelle", which was her mother's name, but she had seen West Side Story so many times in the movies and on TV that, when I came along, she just *had* to name me "Maria" and then, when I was only seven years old she died and left me alone with my mean old father!"

Maria's eyes were focused on something in the very high ceiling of the restaurant and it was as though she was transfixed by some power beyond her control. "My Daddy used to beat her regularly even after he was arrested several times for his brutality, but she loved him anyhow and would never press charges against him. I would never stay with a man like that even though I have a three-year-old at home."

Jan was surprised. "Do you actually have a three-year-old in real life?" she asked, incredulously.

"I would also have had a one-year-old son if my husband and I hadn't been in that terrible crash on I-95 last year. He was killed and I lost my little boy! What will you folks be eating?" and that was all of her story that Maria could get out to us that evening.

Needless to say, we were filled with sympathy for Maria and left her a very large tip.

Jan and I were determined to visit The Crossroads again real soon just to get the rest of Maria's story. It was less than a month later before we could get to The Crossroads again. Jan had sort-of stopped cooking dinners any more. She had been preparing three meals a day for fifty-six years and didn't need any excuses for wanting to "eat out" at dinner time.

We entered The Crossroads and asked the girl at the "desk" for a table in Maria's section. ("The Desk" was actually two large, sixty-gallon barrels of roasted peanuts in the middle of the entranceway.) We could see Maria's blonde head bobbing around and sat at the table right next to the one she was attending at the moment. We tried to get her attention but her eyes were fixed on something in the far reaches of the high ceiling of the restaurant. She was telling her "life story" to two other couples who were simply fascinated. We could hear every word she said.

"Oh, my mother and father would never allow me to get married at this early age! My father never likes any of my boyfriends anyhow and my mother thinks I should wait until I am thirty. That's what she did and my father, gentle as he is, is much older. I guess that's the Irish way. My boyfriend says I shouldn't listen to them. He'd love to marry me right now and have a lot of kids. I think he just wants a lot of sex and I am too young to have any kids right now. Will there be anything else you'll be wanting?"

Her eyes moved down from the clouds. Once again she had revealed what was thought of as her biography. Her eyes had tears at the corners, ready to gush out at the slightest provocation. As in the "biography" she had created for us, we were sure that she believed the whole story and was pained by it. Would you say she had multiple personalities? Was she just an excellent actress and was putting all of us "on"? She had to share all of her "tips" with the other employees so she received very little benefit from her histrionics except, perhaps, the discharge of a sick mind.

Another waitress came to our table to take our order but The Crossroads has never been the same for us. We have been there four more times and always ask for Maria's section. We never got her again as our waitress and although she saw us a few more times she never seemed to remember us. She actually; looked right through us—as though we were transparent. Three times she saw us but we never again got her as our waitress.

On our last visit to The Crossroads Maria was nowhere to be seen. I asked our waiter, "Where's Maria today?

"She died two weeks ago in a terrible car crash on I-95." he replied. Were those tears in his eyes as he scrunched up his face in a sad grimace.

This story is true including the names..

THE BARBER

Okay, I'll admit it. Most of my stories, even those that I say are 100% true, must strike you as contrived and you now feel that you can't believe even one word that I say. I don't blame you at all, even though, on occasion, I honestly state that whatever I have said was true is actually the unvarnished truth.

So what category should this next story be in? Fiction? Part fiction? Actual bull-shit? How about if I swear to you that this mad, mad story is what my forebears would have called "*the emess*"—the honest truth: would you believe me? I swear to you that this story about "The Barber" is the undecorated truth. Will you please read it, already?

Many of my most unusual patients were recommended by fully certified weirdoes. (Fully certified?) I was not actually a specialist in either, the strange, the sexy, the gay, the obscene, the orgiastic or the deeply religious, yet many of my patients were in one or more of those categories *at the same time!* And I had to do straight dentistry on some of the most disturbed people: like The Barber.

I did not make them what they were but I suspect that the tensions of our society, with its concentrations on religion, on money, on mortality, on morality and on achievement are responsible for the large number of twisted, knotted personalities that you and I meet all the time. You *must* have come to realize that all these pressures on the psyches of individualists to conform to a pre-set formula for behavior has to deny a whole world of natural tendencies with a consequent distortion of a whole world of individuals.

Imagine the effects on a child to be told, constantly, that his savage little ways are not socially acceptable and that he'd better shape up or some ogre in the sky will force him to live in perdition even after he is dead! Imagine someone who is truly original and creative to be forced to conform to someone else's standards of creativity and of behavior or else he will be denied acceptance into the society of "normal" people. Imagine someone who has been "gay" all his life, who was forced to change his name and the other facets of his identity several times in order to gain some iota of credence and identity in our world of "normalcy." This is the situation of "The Barber" we shall be discussing in the next few pages.

Let it not be assumed that just because someone has become unacceptable to his family and their friends, because he has had to move his residence several times and change his name more than once and struggle to find a way to make a living because of his strangeness—let us not assume that this person continues to act honestly or by anybody else's rules of behavior and is a delight to know. Usually such a tortured soul becomes particularly "creepy" and this is the story of just such a person whom I befriended, treated with gentleness and kindness, handled with respect and consideration and was victimized by the object of my generosity.

It is very rare for me actually to forget the real name of such a person. I have tried for years to recall his name so that I could write this story. Sigmund Freud would have said that I forgot his name because I really don't want to remember it! He is right! I am a master at making up names but, somehow, I have the feeling that one of the names I give this man might be one of his real names! However his story is going to be told regardless, now. Time is not on my side anymore.

Let us call this man Gary Kanton, because I am sure that was *not* his real name. Gary was recommended to me by my former chair-side assistant, Dolores, whose story is as wild as anyone's could be and some day I'll have to write about her too. For that reason even Dolores is a name of expediency.

Gary came to me because of considerable discomfort in almost all his teeth, which meant that, if he was able to pay the price, he would have to mortgage his soul for thousands of dollars. Of course, he was not able to handle such a responsibility but I started on the work anyway and figured that if I continued on his treatments for five or ten years, slowly but comfortably, he might be able to meet the tab. So Gary was always behind in his payments and that never really bothered me.

I guess I should have told you at the beginning of this story that Gary was almost a caricature of gayness. He was so effeminate that sometimes I wondered whether he had more female hormones than male hormones. He dressed in regular masculine clothing but wore earrings and jewelry that only a woman would wear. He had a purse and would affect a "nasty temper" at the slightest provocation. He was also jealous of the fact that I had a wife and that so many of the women in my office were beautiful and sexy. When he got annoyed or when I brought up any serious matters he would purse his lips as he thought through the problems, very much as I thought a woman might do.

Gary's name at the time of his birth was Marvin Josselson (that is a phony name) but he felt that he had to change his name and move out of his parents' home in Brooklyn, New York, when he was seventeen years of age. According to his view, his parents were ashamed of the fact that he was obviously effeminate and they simply didn't know how to handle the situation. Sending him to the family doctor was a fiasco because the doctor thought that they should send him to a specialist to inject him with male sex hormones. "But that is an unusual form of therapy for this unusual young man, and, to tell you the truth, I don't know any social way to cure his problem. Injecting him with hormones might turn out to be very dangerous." said Doctor Kramer. Gary left high school, moved to Manhattan and changed his name to George Josst. He also met an older man, an experienced homosexual, who paid Gary quite liberally for the sexual services that Gary would perform for him. It was the first time that Gary had ever done any overt sex with another male, although he had been fantasizing about something interpersonal almost all the time since his early puberty.

Gary got a job that was not too demanding in the garment district in Manhattan. He was wiry and quite strong, as he grew older, and was able to do almost any physical work. In the garment district he met many men who were gay and expanded his homosexual activities to a broad range of men. He also learned to broaden the talents that he had for all sorts of demands. He became an accomplished homosexual partner, developing, at the same time, into a jealous, almost vicious personality. In terms of education, he learned much, but none of it was formal education in a school.

How do I know all this "biography"? Gary gradually told me about his life, in a form of braggadocio that was not at all becoming but it was his manner. He never made 'a pass' at me for the simple reason that I never emitted the vibes of a latent homosexual. For that reason I always felt "safe" with him. I never had any influence at all on Gary because I never tried to "change" him, so he felt safe with me, too.

By the time Gary came to me as a patient he was already thirty-seven years old. He was very ingrown in his style of living and was an obvious "fag": unsocial, unchangeable, hard, untrustworthy and mean, but, for whatever reasons, I liked him and trusted him. That says something about my common sense, but I'm also a victim of unknown forces, as are you.

It soon became apparent to Gary and me (and the girls in my office) that Gary would never be able to deal properly with large dental bills, so one afternoon, after he had noticed that I sorely needed a haircut, that Gary, who had by then worked for years as a hairdresser in a posh women's salon, could reduce his indebtedness a bit by attending to my own hair. So we arranged for him to come home with me sometime after five-thirty once a month and cut my hair. The first time that he walked home with me the doorman, elevator-man and lobby attendant all raised their eyebrows as I walked and Gary swished into the lobby. As we arrived on the sixteenth floor I decided that, to put everyone's mind at ease: that Gary could cut my hair in the foyer, on a plastic tablecloth that I placed over the costly Persian rug we had there and I left the front door open so that everyone and anyone could see that Gary and

I were involved in nothing more than the usual barber-barberee relationship and nothing else. Jan, as usual, was away at NYU where she was working towards her Doctorate in English and the kids were all away at college.

For well over a year Gary gave me my monthly haircut, for which I reduced his monthly indebtedness to me by thirty dollars. That was pretty good for the 1960's. The haircuts stopped when Gary started taking long cruises on the largest ocean-going liners, all at the expense of the man (or men?) for whom Gary was "working". He took six or eight such cruises each year and must have received considerable sums of money for his activities. It's not that he began paying me more for his dental treatments. That cash went into designer clothes and expensive jewelry for Gary to wear. Who knows, maybe he actually saved some money? After about six years of treating Gary and two years of not seeing him at all, the girls in the office asked me to make some effort to collect the nearly six thousand dollars that Gary still owed me for work actually finished. So we sent him a bill on the bottom of which I wrote greetings to him with the suggestion that he could pay the whole thing off at two-hundred dollars a month, more or less.

The letter came back with the advice from the post-office department that Gary Karton had moved and they didn't know to where he had relocated. As I had expected, it looked like I had been completely bilked of all that money. However, unexpectedly one day about two months later, my former nurse Dolores walked into the office just to pass the time of day. We were all overjoyed at the sight of that kid, who had been employed for about two years as the head of the design department of a major fabric supplier to the garment industry. Would you believe that Dolores was being paid $80,000 a year in the 1980's? It was the innocent-seeming hygienist, who had know Dolores for about twelve years, who asked, "By the way, do you know Gary Karton's new address? He's due for a prophy." Dolores, unaware of our struggles to collect from Gary, was only too pleased to give us his new address: on the lower East Side of town.

We sent Gary our "final" statement, without my usual friendly note at the bottom of the page. He *had* to know that we really meant business and wanted to collect. Gary by now had been given great sums of money for the services he rendered to some wealthy homosexuals.

Finally I went down to the small claims court where one could now sue for up to five thousand dollars without the use of an attorney. We received a date and a number for our case. I felt very confident that we had an open-and-shut case against Gary and, if I have to say so myself, I had been a very efficient and successful plaintiff in the dozen or so cases I had brought before the judges at the small claims court. You have to know that being a good professional practitioner of dentistry was not sufficient for making a living. You either had to be a better business-man than I was or a darned good lawyer for your own cases

When I arrived at the court on Centre Street in Manhattan I found close to five hundred people who had already beaten me to the seating facilities. I knew I would have to stand somewhere until my case was called, which could have been three to five hours. The Clerk took a look at the slip I presented to him, checked his records and told me to stand along the wall close to the judge's desk. I figured that I would be out in no-time. Wrong again! There ultimately were almost one hundred and fifty people who were standing, uncomfortably, along the walls on both sides of the Judge. The court opened at six-thirty. I was there at six. Would you believe it if I told you that it was at ten-forty-five, when most of the cases had been adjudicated and a mass of people had come and gone, that the Clerk droned out my name. He took one look at my slip of paper that they had sent me, checked his records and said to me, emotionlessly, "Gary Karton is deceased. Next case Irving Goldberg."

Gary Karton is deceased! I was filled with mixed emotions and had to stand there for some time to absorb all the ramifications of what the Clerk had said. First of all I was filled with a spontaneous sadness. I didn't want Gary Karton to die! *I liked him.* I just wanted to collect some money. This was in the days before the Aids epidemic became known, but I thought that maybe some beastly pervert had killed Gary. Maybe my bill was just too much on top of a whole heap of serious problems and Gary had killed himself.

All these ideas must have taken as much as ten seconds to rumble through my over-tired mind. I was suddenly aware that the police guard was grabbing me by the arm and leading me away from the courtroom. I apologized for delaying the Court and tried to explain to the policeman that I really didn't want to sue Mr. Karton, but the cop had already vanished. To say that I was "disconcerted" would be a gross understatement. For the first time in my life I felt confused. The idea ran through my mind that I really should go back to the Clerk and ask to see the evidence that Gary was dead. In a regular court of law they would never get away with that sort of take-it-or-leave-it-announcement. But the policeman was too intimidating and I just felt exhausted and confused.

When I got home it was many hours before I could fall asleep. So many gruesome possibilities crowded my mind! You know as well as I do that the newspapers are overly filled with the wildest examples of violence and the loss of appreciation of the value of life. How did Gary die, anyhow?

I managed to arise the next morning and had to tell the girls the story of my lawsuit against Gary. They were awfully sad—shocked. No-one would have wanted to have even a misfit like Gary die.

Several weeks passed and we sort-of forgot about Gary. I shouldn't say "forgot". The whole story simply edged to the rear portion of our memories so that we could go on with our lives comfortably. On a Thursday I told the girls that after taking my lunch I was going down to the Chase Bank on 79th street and Broadway to take something out of our vault. The vault is in Janice's name and they always give me a hard time to get access to our security-box. Finally I accomplished what I had to do and was walking across Broadway, through mighty heavy traffic, when I heard some violently loud horns blowing at some lunatic who wanted to cross 79th street against the flow of traffic. He scooted safely to the north side of the street and turned around to snicker self-consciously at the drivers who had nearly killed him. It was Gary! And he saw me! I don't know what made me do it but I mouthed the name he was given at birth, "Marvin!" He nodded to me and raced off as though the Devil was at his back.

So Gary, which was just a name and an identity he had improvised, was dead. But the original soul was still alive! I rejoiced!

This story is true, except for the names.

THE PIPE

Every once in a while you read something in the newspaper that makes no sense at all and you rub your eyes in disbelief and then read the same little article again—and again. And it still doesn't make any sense. Why did they print it in the first place?

This short story is the result of my having read, and re-read, just such an article last Spring in the Sun-Sentinel, in Boca Raton, Florida. (That article follows this story but don't read it, please, until you finish this story.)

What happened, anyhow, in room 511 on the fifth floor of the Mango Hotel in Fort Myers? John Barlow was all ready to go down to the swimming pool with his wife of twelve years, Helen. He was waiting for her to put some make-up on her face and a sun-screen on her forehead and shoulders. John and Helen had just returned from an archeological expedition to the jungles of Ecuador. They had a fine reputation as proper scientists, despite their youth and physical attractiveness and had published many scientific articles to prove their abilities.

Among the notes and tapes and discs they had recorded while making their "digs" were many artifacts which they had legally taken with them from South America. John and Helen had every intention to study these artifacts and write them up before giving them to the Museum of Natural History in New York City. They were so excited by their "finds" that they took every opportunity to study what they had found and discuss the details and the implications of the small statues, jewelry made of precious stones and gold. There were religious items that needed a lot of understanding and investigation and numerous small objects that were probably used by the natives in their homes. Many of these small, detailed items could be very revealing about the life-habits of the ordinary residents of tiny towns that really could not be described as "primitive". They showed that the average native, although he may have dressed in the comfortable, home-made clothing that he and his wife had created, was interested in a very social way as everything that pertained to his tribe.

For instance, there were small tablets that contained some form of writing scratched on the slates by a sharp stylus. There were tapa-cloth hangings in their homes that had a religious significance as well as some that were simply there for the adornment of their simple, stark residences. There were cups and dishes made of baked clay (but no "silverware") and actual candles made of some kind of organic oil placed in shallow flasks with wicks made of some strands of a plant that must have been growing nearby. There were flattened, round, preserved objects that looked as though they had been the bladders of some fairly large animals and when blown up they could have been used as balls to play games with. Those artifacts would have to be analyzed in a laboratory in New York to find out which organs of which animals the Ecuadoreans had been using for their games. And how did they embalm that organic material so that it would have lasted for the thousand or so years until John and Helen had discovered it?

While looking through the mass of their collection, each item of which had been carefully wrapped in straw, John's hands roamed about the sides of a very small item that felt to him as though it were a pipe of some kind; a pipe for smoking something akin to tobacco. He didn't remember putting that pipe in there (and neither did Helen), but he was not concerned about it. Probably one of their native helpers had found the pipe and wrapped it up for them when it came time to leave Ecuador.

John carefully removed the object from the mass of straw and it was indeed a pipe, made of baked clay, with a stem and a mouthpiece that was obviously a thousand-year-old reed from one of the swamps in the valley. The pipe bowl was about two inches in depth and the stem, which had broken off at its far end, was about four inches long. It must have been much longer, once upon a time. John called to Helen, telling her about the details of his find and asking her how much longer she would take to feel that she was finally presentable enough for the half-dozen or so strangers who were sunning themselves beside the pool.

"I'll be ready in two or three minutes. Why don't you look into that pipe and see if there's any tobacco in it so that we can smoke it when we get back from the pool?" Helen was known for her ability to create problems by just such a jaunty suggestion as she had just made. She was scientific, alright, but also had an impish side to her nature that had previously led them to other narrow escapes in their wanderings all over the globe.

"Whaddaya know! There is quite a bit of something like tobacco in there! I think I'll take a puff or two and then we'll save the rest of it for a study." said John, as he took a cigarette-lighter out of one of the valises in the room.

"I'll take a puff or two also." said Helen, who didn't want to be left out of any excitement at all.

John took three puffs of the ancient "tobacco" and Helen took three puffs. They both gasped from the sharpness of the acrid smoke they had breathed in and did not dare smoke any more of whatever substance was in that pipe. Helen sat down on the easy-chair next to the bed and her eyes glazed over as she seemed to stare unseeing directly before her. John had difficulty breathing normally and they both could be seen twitching nervously. Neither Helen nor John looked at one another. They were both going through a severe shock to their nervous systems. Suddenly John stripped his swim-clothes off his body and stood on the bed stark naked making weird sounds that sounded very much like the apes in a zoo. He began to wave his arms primitively and to all appearances was acting like any agitated anthropoid in the jungle. He stomped around the room wildly and onto the patio and did not look at any time towards his mate. He was psychedelically transformed into a primitive creature.

If John had looked toward his wife he would have seen that she was likewise transformed into a different persona. She was sitting on that easy-chair going, "Cheep! Cheep! Cheep!" like a bird. Like her husband, she had stripped off her bathing suit. She had been psychedelically transformed into a bird just as he had been transformed into an ape. Her lips and her entire facial mechanism were involved in acting and "speaking" in bird-like fashion while her husband, to all intents and purposes was acting like an ape. How long could this situation go on? After all they had only taken three puffs of that substance and they had not inhaled much of it at all. It was only a matter of time—a few minutes—before they would return to normal.

But they were not to be granted a normal recovery. Helen stood up and made wing-like movements with her arms. She seemed to fly around the hotel room but that was not satisfactory enough for her. She actually wanted to leave the ground and fly! Of course she did not have actual wings and could never fly like a bird. *But she did not realize that!* She dashed out onto the patio and tried to climb over the railing to jump off and fly.

Meanwhile John had sat down on the edge of the bed and held his head in his hands. He had a terrific headache which was a precursor to returning to normalcy. At that moment he thought about Helen. Where was she and how had the smoke affected her? He looked toward the easy-chair and didn't see her. She was no longer anywhere in the room. She was on the patio trying to climb over the railing! And she was gesticulating and making the same sounds as a large bird, waving her arms as though she wanted to fly off the patio!

John "woke up" just in time to grab at Helen's legs as she stood on the railing of the patio and had actually jumped off, waving her arms and eager to fly. Helen did not weigh any more than a hundred and thirty pounds but that is quite a weight to hold onto, especially since she had actually jumped into the air, which adds many more pounds to her actual weight. Helen was completely under the spell of the drug that she had smoked.

She "thought" she was a bird and resented anyone who kept her from flying. John's grip on her legs kept slipping down to her ankles as Helen kept maneuvering to free her legs from John's grasp. What made John's task so impossible was the sun-tan cream that Helen had rubbed onto her legs. It was only a few minutes of desperately trying to pull Helen back up despite her efforts to fly before she slipped eternally out of his grasp. She reveled in her newfound freedom and "thought" she was flying until the earth came up with a rush and crushed her beyond recognition.

John went to court in Fort Myers to fight for his own life. He was charged with first degree murder and the prosecutor had a great imagination as to why John wanted to kill Helen. It was all about money and pride and selfishness and inhumanity. John refused to have a lawyer, although he did consult with several attorneys and paid them well to advise him. When the prosecutor had completed his case and was smugly waiting for John to defend himself, John simply told the story of Helen's death exactly as it had occurred. The prosecutor and several of the members of the jury had to laugh as he acted out the scenes in the bedroom and on the patio.

Then he brought out the clay pipe and a cigarette lighter and asked if any of the jury or the prosecution would care to puff on that pipe to see how it would affect them. The prosecuting attorney himself and the female chairman of the jury volunteered to puff on that clay pipe. Previously, one of the attorneys whom John had consulted called the police and asked them to dash into the courtroom to prevent anyone from harming himself under the influence of the drug they had smoked.

After three puffs from that pipe the prosecutor and head of the jury performed almost exactly as John and Helen had. The prosecutor stripped off his clothes and ran around naked---like an ape. The jury chairman stripped off her clothing and tried to fly like a bird, both of them with glazed eyes and making sounds that one usually hears in a zoo. The woman wanted to fly out of the window and had to be restrained. The prosecutor ran around like an ape until someone came into the courtroom with a blanket and covered him up.

You may wonder what the jury's verdict was under those circumstances, and reckon whether John wouldn't be held in contempt of court for the antics that had occurred but the Judge was an honorable man and the newspapers published the very article that we include here.

Take a look at the article in the Sun-Sentinel that inspired this story. It is on the following page. If you had read that article what would have gone through your mind? This is an untrue story...but it takes a great imagination to write it.

Taken from the *Sun-Sentinel*
2006

Fort Myers
**Jury acquits man
in wife's fatal drop**

A jury Friday acquitted a man
accused of dangling his wife by
the ankles from a hotel balcony
and then dropping her nearly 60
feet to her death on Fort Myers
beach.

Christopher Dame had been
charged with manslaughter in
the death of his wife, Colleen
Dame, 46, died in the drop from
the fifth floor of the Lani Kai
Island Resort into the sand on
July 2002.

The six-member jury
deliberated just over two hours
before returning its verdict, the
News-Press of Fort Myers
reported in today's editions.

THE KILLER

Once in a great while one of my sons, who is supposed to clue me in to what the modern world is really like, gives me the cold shoulder. It seems that one of the crimes that have taken up much of the print media and many hours of "authoritative analysis" on television has inspired me to write a short story about this crime. "How can you, in all good conscience", said this son, "write an alternative to this case that has already been thoroughly treated by the media and, in fact, has been decided by the courts. How would *you* feel after you had suffered the way all these people have if someone with your ignorance and your imagination came up with a most unlikely killer. Someone might be excused if he took a shot at *you* for your insensitivity and callousness?"

"The media and all the people it tells about are fair game for an author." I replied. "Didn't Arthur Miller write a play about his ex-wife, Marilyn Monroe, even after she died a very strange death? Do you think that all those war stories and those events that took place on 9-11 that made great movies are an imposition on the sensitivities of those parents (and veterans) whose lives are portrayed on the screen? Do you think that all those district attorneys, defense attorneys, witnesses and victims who had to do with "The Son of Sam" and all the other serial killers are better left unwritten about?"

After that we left the discussion unresolved. I did *not* say, "What do I care about the family of so-and-so?" because *I do care.* And I do say that if I come up with a different killer and can write a respectable murder mystery I should be regarded as an imaginative writer. If I were to write a different ending for the O.J. Simpson case, for instance, what would you say to that? The very fact is that no one else in the world of writers has come up with a different definitive ending to that case, even though there is a substantial feeling abroad that there was a great miscarriage of justice performed right in the face of the public."

Okay then, this is a story based on the Tracy Pressman case (the names in this story have all been changed) that had the world's attention from the moment she was discovered to be missing to the moment when the jury not only found her young husband guilty but decided upon the death penalty for his crimes. "Only a person who never read or saw the basic facts in this case or witnessed the coldness of Dred's expressions, his lack of sympathy for his wife's family, including the "fact" that he had a girl-friend to whom he told a pack of lies, would write a story such as this." you might say.

But that is a key part of this story: his attitude. Didn't it strike you strange that here is a person, Dred Pressman, whose life depended upon his making a decent defense and showing remorse. He never, once, expressed a love for that woman who carried his child and who had such a miserable death? For some unusual reasons this man acted as though he *wanted to be found guilty. He seemed to want the world to hate him.* Certainly he was not a fool.

Certainly his attorneys knew tricks of appearance and attitude to ameliorate the severe charges that were leveled against him. Did anyone ever say, "I can't believe that a criminal, even a subnormal specimen from the lowest reaches of "Da Mob", who does not know and does not have the instincts to act innocent?" What were the reasons that went through his mind? Didn't his attorneys impress upon his consciousness that *his life* was at stake? Even an innocent nerd like this writer knew that *that* jury was out for blood if there was any way for the prosecutor to prove his case. But that young man maintained his impassiveness even though, if there was ever a time for a passion for life, *this was it!*

Let us take a look at some of the highlights of this case. All during the days, weeks and months that this anomaly dragged on not once did the "killer" publicly proclaim his innocence. Not once did he weep, nor did he get angry at the accusations and occasionally snide references to his sensibilities. Not once did he refer to his lost wife in terms of endearment. *He actually seemed to want everyone...even his own family...to consider him capable of that heinous crime.* When his attorney placed a boat similar to Dred's boat on the grounds near the courthouse (.why, I do not know) Pressman did not say a word about it. When the jury ultimately found him guilty and, a few days later, sentenced him to death he *acted* unconcerned. If he *was* in any way concerned *it took a tremendous amount of dedication and will-power to repress his normal reactions!*

What would be his reasoning, assuming for the moment that he is not so psychopathic as to be beyond the pale of normalcy? Can *you* think of any sensible reasons for his behavior? Was there, perhaps, a reason for Tracy to have been killed? Did *she* commit some sort of crime that was also "beyond the pale" of reasonable behavior? If Dred was *not* guilty, he *seemed to be* guilty. And if he did not kill his wife who did? All the evidence seemed to show that it was he who attempted to dispose of her body. Is it even conceivable that someone else committed the murder and prevailed upon him to dispose of the evidence? Is there anyone whom he cared for enough to take the punishment of a murderer? Who would it be that he would have forgiven the killing of his wife and unborn son and assume a role that he did not really deserve—before the whole world?

And what about the girl-friend that he had while his wife was missing and then was found? What would his excuse be for that piece of skull-duggery? Wouldn't that make him seem guilty of insensate murder of an innocent young wife and child? *Was even that not part of a calculated plan to cast all suspicions, and the possibilities of all suspicions, in his direction and away from the true murderer?* Please promise that you have it in your heart to even consider such a possibility, as impossible as it may seem.

Among the many discrepancies in the trial was the locus of the actual murder. Where was Tracy killed? What was the weapon that was used to kill her and was there much blood on the premises? This leads to the question of what was used to get rid of the blood and where did the killer dispose of that material? If paper or cloth were used where did all that stuff go? If a carpet or furniture or wood flooring were involved how in the world did the culprit clean it up? The police haven't found clue one on that subject. The body that was found in the bay off the California coast revealed that no gunshot was used but that would only be true if bone damage had been found. A strictly soft-tissue gun-shot wound, with considerable bleeding, could have led to her death and then we would have to find a gun. Has anyone suggested that such a weapon be looked-for? Perhaps the killer used a sharp knife. That would be a good start for something to find.

Some damage to the scalp was found but no bones of the head or neck were broken and a scalp damage could be incurred while carrying a dead body to dispose of it. There were no evidences in the autopsy of a poisoning or a strangling. Poisons might be found in the residuum but strangling would only be patent if there were damage to the trachea or neighboring tissues. No such damage was found. So how did Pressman kill his wife: if he killed her? Did she die of pneumonia, of a heart-attack, some rare disease? There was no evidence of anything of the sort, but then the body was not in the best condition, having been in salt water for several months. The question I asked was, *"How* did someone kill Tracy?" Can you answer that for me, please? The trial was especially vague on this score.

And vague, too, was the location of the crime. *Where* was she killed? This is a very rare trial, where someone is convicted and given the death sentence for carrying a dead body to the bay and throwing it in the water (and for having a mistress and lying to her and everybody else about her!) No one says how or where she was killed. Can the authorities execute Pressman on those grounds?

Under those circumstances there is room for further intellectualization on this case---to solve it. Let us start with Tracy herself. What was she like? Well, she was a mighty attractive brunette and she was very pregnant, enough for her gynecologist to be able to differentiate the maleness of her fetus. What was her family like and was she happy about it? Well, she lived in a nice house with her husband who earned a lot of money and all we know about him was that he apparently became bored with Tracy and got himself a mistress, which is the usual for at least 60% of American households. There is no need to go crazy and kill this man for infidelity.

Was Tracy happy or bored with her husband and did she have a 'role model' for an unhappy marriage? Well, her mother had given Tracy a prime example on how to handle an unsuccessful marriage. Helen had gotten rid of husband "number one" (by divorce) and remarried a strikingly hand-some man in his fifties. I don't know why she got rid of "number one" but when "number two" is in a room he is very charming and very attractive. You can see at a glance why Tracy's mother would prefer "number two."

Nobody asked Tracy how she liked father "number two." However, I have noticed that many young women are attracted to some men in their fifties (even in their sixties and their seventies). I am trying to figure out why young Dred had seemed out of love with his wife. I cannot get the feeling out of my mind that Tracy was so bound up with her step-father that, if he were macho enough, it had to become an "affaire." Of course, Pressman suspected what was going on right away. Nobody said that Tracy was a talented actress. Not a word in that regard was mentioned at the trial. *But the police did a DNA test on the fetus!* Why? Was it possible that someone other than Dred was interested in Tracy? Is it at least possible that Tracy was emotionally and physically involved with someone other than her husband?

So let us visit with Tracy in the kitchen of her mother's home.(Why the kitchen, because the kitchen and the bathrooms are the only rooms with ceramic tile flooring!) Tracy's mother had brought her daughter into the kitchen to read a couple of notes *from Tracy to her mother's second husband* that had been found in the husband's sock drawer. Ordinarily only the Spanish-speaking housemaid and Frank would have had access to that drawer. However this maid had brought the notes from the bedroom because it didn't seem correct for mail to be in the sock-drawer. That's what you get for having a compulsive maid----it can lead to God-knows-where.

Helen took one look at the notes which were signed with "I love you.....Tracy" Helen, at first, only thought in terms of a young girl having a crush on a middle-aged man and was prepared to treat it as such. But Tracy is in her twenties and is married and pregnant. Instead of passing off those letters as a piece of girlish silliness Helen took them seriously.

Tracy mishandled this revelation foolishly by expressing pride in the relationship that had developed. She "pushed her weight" around to the point that Helen suddenly realized that her daughter was actually a threat to her marriage (and her last chance for happiness?).Tracy even told her mother that, "We began wondering *what place there was for you* in this triangle. We both spoke about 'What are we gonna have to do with Helen?'" While she spoke, Tracy had forgotten the lesson she and her family had learned from husband "number one," when he had mentioned, every so often, that "You have to be very careful when your mother gets that peculiar smile fixed on her face. She's not enjoying your company at all at that time and is at her most dangerous!"

Tracy had taken her eyes off her Mother and was looking away--expounding on what plans she and 'number two' had for 'that lady' 'That lady' had a fixed smile on her face and a fixed stare in her eyes. Ordinarily one would never have thought of violence from a dignified, loving woman such as this but she reached over and grabbed the neck of a bottle of a good French wine (Macon Villages Blanc) and slammed that bottle at the base of the neck of her daughter Tracy. It was just when Tracy had said that she "hoped the child she was carrying was Frank's" that Helen struck.

Of course murder was not at all in Helen's mind. She just wanted to emphasize her distraught condition which Tracy couldn't care less about. But Tracy never moved again. The force of Helen's blow was insufficient to break any of the bones of Tracy's skull but the shock of the whole experience was enough to end her life and the life of her unborn child. (Did the autopsy doctor investigate the integrity of the occipital bone?)

Talk about shock! Helen was in a state of excitement, shock and confusion. She had just learned of the affair between her daughter and her second husband, Frank. She had just learned of Tracy's callous description of the plans that Tracy and her lover had for Helen. And it was when Tracy hoped that the fetus she was carrying was her lover's instead of her husband's that Helen's emotions ran out of control!

There was practically no blood involved. There was only a maze of loose ends to mull over. "What am I going to do about Stacy? What should I do about Frank? What about that unborn child? Shall I phone 9-11 to try to get that baby out of Tracy's womb and see if he would live? Why? Whose kid is it, anyhow? Dred's? Frank's? Someone else's? What's going to happen to dear Dred, who is the best thing that ever happened to Tracy? Shall I call Dred?"

Helen dialed Dred's number and he knew by the tone of her voice that it was an urgent call. He was there in less than five minutes. He bounded into the house and hurried to the kitchen (where all the lights were on) when he suddenly saw Tracy sprawled out in the classless sprawl of the dead. He impulsively knelt by her side and showered her face and neck with kisses. Tears, those unwanted icons of tragedy, poured from his eyes. He was a man in the throes of despair. As he reached for Tracy's hands, in a gesture wracked with grief, he caught a glimpse of Helen. Dred suddenly reached out to her to provide whatever comfort he could. He rose to her side and held her in his arms. She was always one of his favorite people and he knew that she was not having an easy time of it in navigating the stressful seas of life.

"What happened?" he asked after a few moments had gone by.

"You won't believe what I'm going to reveal to you." Then she told him all that had transpired. Helen thought that her story would shock Dred to the core, but she was mistaken. Apparently Dred had been aware of Tracy's affaire for about five months until she told him that she hoped it was Frank's baby she was carrying. From then on until this very moment he had not spoken with her and had not kissed her or shared any of the charms of conjugal life with her. He had also avoided speaking with Frank and wondered what he was going to do in that regard.

He said to Helen, "I love you very dearly and do not want to do anything that would cause you pain but Frank is not one of my favorite people."

At that moment, as though Frank had been called to account for his actions, he appeared at the kitchen door. When he suddenly spied the body of Tracy lying lifeless on the kitchen floor he was at a loss for words. He had no idea what had transpired during his absence and he was in such a state of shock that he could just do what any lover would do—he simply burst into tears and kissed her unresponsive face madly. There was no doubt that he was crazy about her. Tracy's eyes were still open in surprise at the immediacy of death. As far as he was concerned was no reason to carry on a vendetta among the three survivors who were, each in his own way, wild about this victim of her own passions. Each one bore his own responsibility in her demise and each one would bear the scars of her killing to his grave.

When Frank was able to, he commiserated with Helen because he felt she had lost her dearest friend. And he even hugged Dred as though to say, "Let's let bygones be bygones. We have both lost our loves. We have the rest of our lives to make accusations and cast blame." It seems that both Dred and Helen were taken-in by Frank's show of deep emotion.

Helen then did not wait for Frank to ask, "What happened?" She repeated in full the true facts she had recounted to Dred. Frank entirely understood at that moment the complications of unrestrained passion. He and Tracy had broken up a marriage and turned a mother into a killer. He had let his wild feelings for an impulsive young woman destroy what was left of a normal family. His mind raced over the alternative actions he might now take and he promptly decided that he would share the blame for Tracy's death and try to ameliorate as much as he could the attitude of the authorities, whom he felt would have to be informed of the whole tarnished mess.

"We'll have to call 9-11 and tell them exactly what happened," was Frank's contribution.

"That's exactly what I figured you'd say," accused Dred. "This way, you can get rid of Helen while she spends a lifetime in jail and then you can inherit half of her money, which is a very tidy sum. *And then you could pretend to commiserate with the relatives about the tough break* you *got!*"

"I haven't had as much time that to think about this as you have." said Frank. "But I figure that if we follow the law strictly we have the least chance of getting in trouble. We're already in a mess. If you or I tried to dispose of Tracy's body illegally we might wind up being accused of her murder and perhaps even have to serve time in prison for our part in the crime....and it *was* a crime!"

"How would you dispose of Tracy if you wanted to," Helen asked Dred. "I'm looking to save the trauma and the expense of a series of trials. I need some help here."

Dred mused aloud at Helen's question. He had never considered such a possibility before. "Well, *I would do anything* to prevent you from having a trial as an ordinary murderer. You know how big a deal the TV and print media would make of this. Let's see—if I could take Tracy's body and put some plastic around it and put some heavy weights on it then I could—mayb with some help (he looked at Frank, who looked aside) —I could take her out to my boat on the Sound and throw her overboard. It might not be for ten years before they would find any trace of her at all----if we're lucky."

"That sounds reasonable to me," said a muddled-thinking Helen. She was, at this point in the discussion, already overly tired and unreliable in her decision-making.

"I'll do anything that the majority wants me to do because of my guilt in this situation, but I really feel that if we report the incident to the police right now Helen might get off with a slap on the wrist and we will not risk a very messy trial and the consequences. I know some excellent lawyers and I'd pay all the legal costs in this case. How about that?" This was Frank speaking in his most persuasive and sensible manner.

"It all depends on Dred," said Helen. "I just don't know what to do. I really got you men in a real mess. Maybe what Frank suggests is best. What do you say, Dred?"

"I am not sure either," said the inexperienced young man. "I wouldn't expect the police, who are not always reliable, to locate Tracy at the bottom of the Sound. Frank and I could handle it alright. How about it, Frank?"

"Well, I made my case for your approval. I'll help you if you want me to."

And the rest is history: Dred Pressman had to declare his wife missing. He and Helen and Frank had to *act* as though Tracy (and her unborn child) were missing for weeks. The police left no stone unturned in attempting to locate that "beautiful young mother-to-be". The media "went bananas" over this case, especially when Dred went into his mode of being non-committal about every-thing. The authorities were careful not to accuse Dred in advance of having some real evidence. The most difficult cases to try are those without a *"corpus delictus"* to present so there was a tremendous search for Tracy's remains: if she were dead. When they heard about Dred's boat everyone heaved a huge sigh of relief. All they had to do was to search the waters where Dred always went fishing.

What the police had to do was drop some explosive charges into the water and the ropes or wires that are usually employed in tying weights to a body would loosen up and the body would float to the surface of the water. There are specialists in that field and that is exactly what they did. And the results were as expected. Tracy and her unborn child rose in the water and were driven by the tides to the shore. The prosecutors and media had a field-day. Dred behaved as though he had killed Tracy. The DNA of the fetus showed that the unborn child was Dred's. Helen and Frank *acted their roles* as the bereaved parents. All the do-good-nicks were full of "I-told-you-so's".

Dred now lies in prison where most people think he belongs. We are waiting for another trial as if it were an after-thought. Frank and Helen are off scot-free. And my son, who is very moral and proper, still thinks that I not only should not have written this story because the families involved have suffered enough, but, additionally, because like Frank would have said, the law is very tough on writers who use real names in their stories. *You noticed I am sure that nobody with the names of Dred and Tracy Pressman and Helen and Frank Cartwright have been involved in a murder mystery lately.*

By the way: who paid for the attorney who defended Dred? It was a lot of money.

This is an extrapolation of a series of newspaper articles and TV 'shows' with all the imagination and alternative thinking I could employ.

TERMINATION

According to a program on the Discovery Channel at noon on Sunday, 6/26/05, this important fact was revealed:

In five billion years our aging Sun will implode and its vast, inconceivable heat will overcome the Earth and Mars and other planets relatively close to this Sun. The seas will boil away and become clouds of immense density. All life will become extinct— all animal and plant life that is, including insects and bacteria. The Earth will be sterile, characterized by a seemingly endless violence of the topography as well as of the internal mechanisms of its existence as a planet.

Earthquakes and the flow of lava in unpredictable areas will continue for aeons as our Earth goes through its terminal convulsions with the destruction of all that had seemed permanent and changeless to the human mind. All the coastlines and the mountains will shift. Many islands will disappear under the seas and new islands will rise in the seas before they boil away. Ice and snow on the Earth will entirely vanish until it cools again as a corpse. Even the polar areas will shift in their locations as the Earth's weight changes with the vaporization of the seas and the ice and the burning off of all the vegetation and the consequent changes in positions of the tectonic plates. Ultimately the shrinkage and contractions will signify the end of this beautiful little planet of ours.

Do you estimate that your love will last forever? Forever has to be only five billion years, *so make your plans.* What will happen to all the art and literature that Mankind has created in the past few thousand years? DaVinci and Rodin, Rembrandt and Dali, Tschaikowsky and Beethoven, Mozart and Richard Rogers will disappear together with Jazz and Rap and Rock. Even *rocks* will be melted and vaporized!

Shakespeare's plays and sonnets and Tennyson's poetry will disappear in smoke together with the Iliad and the Odyssey, the Bible and the Koran. Even *my* paltry few poems and my time-honored short stories will be lost—for eternity! Oh, dear, what a catastrophe!

Of course Mankind will likewise vanish unless—*unless*---spacemen, sometime in the next few billion years find a way to travel to another little planet, far, far away from our explosive, aging Sun. And when they find this beautiful little planet it will have to be basically very much like our own planet Earth. It will have to have those soothing, cool breezes in the summer-time and the summers should be warm but not too hot, as the winters should be cold but not unbearable. And the salty seas (salty with sodium chloride, of course) can be as rough as they want to be, but they must be navigable to Mankind and they must have those white, sandy beaches that we love so well. We have been spoiled by the beauty and considerateness of our little planet.

This new planet, which we could name Earth Two, must have all our varieties of verdure: those trees, bushes and gorgeous flowers and the greenest grass—and all the animals that characterize our Earth! Also, what would Earth II be without the insects which we always complained about and which turn out to be so useful? Certainly this new home for Man must have sunrises and sunsets, fresh water and fresh clean air and be fertile for all the foods we must plant there. Most of all, our new planet's climate has to be hospitable to little kids. It has to allow our little kids to play outside the house all year 'round.

Of course, this new planet has to have a future. What is life without a future? We need a future to dream about and to create for. Those whose belief is not in the future of life on the Earth, and there are over one and one third billion of them today, are condemned by their beliefs to live in poverty, in hatred and in violence. These people would *not* be invited by me to make the journey to our new home. I happen to believe in life—in *this* life! As a matter of fact, the topic of my Bar Mitzvah speech, over seventy-five years ago, was "The Importance of Life (Chai) To Humanity." I did not realize at that time the importance to the world of that topic. The lessons of childhood are often lost in a lack of understanding.

We must wish the Space program Godspeed in its efforts to find Earth II before it is too late! However, as a writer of poetry and short-stories, with a mighty imagination, I am willing to leave to you, the discriminating reader, the description of the last three, or so, billion years of the existence of human life on this small planet. For instance, who can say, with scientific assurance, what will be the course of human history over that projected period of time? Will mankind "progress" in a relatively orderly fashion towards the goal of a moderate, humanistic society, with all the "liberal" ideas of civil rights, humane behavior, equality among men—and women—and religious freedoms or will we continue on the present trend of economic global interests which put the economies of every area under the selfish stewardship of an increasingly few megalopolies that do not have the interest of the great masses of the Earth's population at heart?

What trend will win out in the struggle between the Muslims and the rest of the world to live a varied life without being castigated and *hated* as "infidels"? Will religion indeed win the struggle for men's hearts and minds with the totally imagined existence of deities who become ever more primitive in their powers? Will the exigencies of famine and the expanded need for water remove whatever "humanity" still exists in this world? Will the information that our world is really going to come to an end in the foreseeable future have a hysteria-producing effect on human behavior? After all, that implosion of our sun will not be a sudden event. Most assuredly there will be billions of years of erratic behavior among the elements of our solar system, with weather inconsistencies and the shifting of the Earth's innards with volcanoes and earthquakes, with tsunamis and hurricanes, violence of the winds and the seas and the earth that no one can predict with accuracy.

Our considered hope is that human society will have drastically changed from what it is today. Hatred and violence, intolerance and discrimination should become a rarity instead of the norm. After all, Mankind is only 40,000 years old (since the end of the Neanderthal era and the arrival of "modern man"). Another five billion years should witness some real positive changes in Man's nature; hopefully. Why do you suppose the "powers-that-be" allowed us, just recently, to invent the atomic sciences, cloning and the rest of the technological revolution? Wouldn't it be a shame if, just when Mankind had finally reached the ultimate phases of being "Homo Sapiens" and "Homogenesis Societas" our Sun decided to blow up? If that is the scenario they have planned for us we had better find that little planet, Earth II, long before the Sun reaches its fiery termination.

I will leave to the more expressive of my fellow writers to imagine, with concern, the details of our future human society, together with the possibly erratic behavior of our fellow animals on this planet, whose sensitivity to the Earth's behavior is more naturally geared to the physical rather than the ethical and historical aspects.

Write about this, you guys. Tell me what our human society will be like and what will become of this beautiful little planet. I'll be long gone, I expect, but we will not suffer a lack of imaginative writers; especially those with an esoteric turn to their minds. I would like to hear what the more thoughtful, scientifically and historically-trained estimators of our physical and social future history have to say. Very possibly it might be a religiously-inclined maven who comes up with the real answers.

You might even describe the wild, violent, inconsiderate behavior of those who have learned about the daily trips to our new Earth II that we will be having and are trying to hitch a ride on one of those space vehicles. Do you remember the incident when the Americans were evacuating the South of Vietnam by helicopters and other planes? Did you ever imagine that there would be a similar event in our future when *billions* of people were trying to get onto the spaceships before the earth literally went up in flames? And who would be the select few who were permitted on the spaceships? And who would make the decisions? Tell me about it. I'll be here, either above or below my favorite earth. One item I have to offer is that I will not accept the demands for any Muslim to move, with me and mine, to Earth II. Anyone who has no regard for *this* life, on this lovely little planet, has no place on Earth II. No one who believes in Death should be invited to our next home.

"OH YOU WHO SLEEP........."

Leonardo Da Vinci was quoted as saying, "Oh you who sleep, what is sleep? Sleep resembles death......." This quote was mentioned in a book that I read about the Da Vinci Code* and it came to my attention *after* I had been mulling some special ideas in my mind for several weeks: days and nights. It is about the story that succeeds these first introductory paragraphs. As you must know (or suspect), once the basic concept for a story creeps into your consciousness it lingers there and begins to dominate a good percentage of your waking hours, with nagging suggestions from your muse about the best techniques for telling that exciting tale.

I was overjoyed to find that Leonardo shared so many of my ideas. He had lived in the 'dark ages' when no intellectual in his right mind would have dared to express what he really thought lest some cleric report him and the hierarchy that controlled the world might remove his entire head for daring to think.

Anyhow, this is a story about someone very much like I am. He has the same concerns and interests, the same habits and peculiarities, the same libido and characteristics that made me very popular in some quarters and very unpopular in others. I cannot say, for sure, whether this story is really true. All I can say is that it scared me and excited me for about three weeks, until I

*Secrets of the DaVinci Code" by Dan Burstein, CDC Publ., NYC, NY, 2004

was finally able to get it out of my system and tell somebody about it. And *you* are the first person I am confiding in! I think that you, too, might now become afraid to go to sleep.

It seems to me that everyone has dreams. I'll have to ask my son, Mark, who is a shrink, whether everyone has dreams. I have such an active mind that there is not enough time during my waking hours (about eighteen hours a day) to consider all the improbabilities and actual events that my mind is exposed to. The wild events that take place in the news programs and newspapers, the gratuitous violence on almost all the "shows" on television as the product of all that excitement—and then some!

The excitement and suppressed involvement of the history and historical novels I read created a backdrop for more than the usual number of dreams that I might ordinarily have. All I can say to you, my intellectual friend, is that the following story is almost true.

About a month ago I had a peculiar experience after I had gone to sleep. It is not certain that this experience can be called a dream. Whatever it was, I was in touch with some of the dearest friends I ever had. Somehow they knew all about the good and the unfortunate events of my most recent years and I had not seen any of those people for many years! I just assumed that they had been, in some manner, corresponding with our more active friends in one way or another.

For instance, there was a friend from West Orange, New Jersey, who was, for years, the chairman of the Board of the condominium complex (The Woodlands) we used to live in. Jerry Fien was an accomplished politician as well as a highly-considered accountant in Newark. He had been the chairman of a major firm of CPA's.

"How's Jan" he asked in his usual manner. Frankly, he *usually* didn't wait to listen to my replies because he was almost always too interested in what *he* had to say. But this time he really listened and I felt that he was indeed interested. At the same time two of my best friends at the Woodlands came in to share the bottle of wine I had opened and they were very glad to see me, as though we had not been apart for many years. *Actually,* they had all been taken by the "grim reaper" at least six or eight years ago and I was really surprised at how youthful and hearty each one of them was.

Then, all of a sudden, they all just plain disappeared from my presence, like in a dream. But it didn't feel like a dream. It was too real, too close up, too sensible for a dream. I don't know what that experience was, but it was really good to see my old friends again, especially since we hadn't seen each other for a long time. I had a few more "regular" dreams that same night but they were obviously "just dreams" and left me unfulfilled.

There were then many such "events", at least two per night, which brought friends and relatives back, sometimes even from the dim past, to enhance my sleeping hours. It didn't occur to me, for several nights that all these people were actually dead! I suppose that everyone must dream, once in a while, about people who are long gone from this world, but I just wonder if everyone dreams in this particular manner.

Just a few nights ago I "dreamt" about my Dad and my brothers, Allan and Maurice, all of whom have been deceased a long, long time. The contents of that "dream" are not germane, but one subject came through very clearly. We have always been an affectionate family and my Dad always kissed us "Hello" when we come into the house and "Good-bye" when we were about to leave. The startling thing about this "dream" was that my Dad's face was just as soft as I always remembered it, and do you know what?—his skin always had a characteristic fragrance to it, kind-of a personal aroma—and I was particularly aware of that fragrance and as a result, the dream came to an end and I woke up. The very idea that in a dream I could even remember the fragrance of a person's skin was just so unusual that it woke me up!

The next day we happened to be celebrating one of my grandchildren's birthdays and the whole family was gathered at my eldest son's home. I selected the "right" moment to mention to all three of my sons, together, about those unusual "dreams" I had experienced. It was when I mentioned that I could even remember the scent of my father's skin that it brought the whole conversation to a temporary halt; everybody was suddenly trying to remember whether the sense of smell was usually part of a dream. Since all my sons are doctors, of one sort or another, you can be sure that my "case" got their closest attention.

Our middle son, Mark, a psychologist who is particularly aware of the nature of dreams, looked at me very intensely and then suggested that I see a neurologist right away. Michael, who is a molecular biologist, suggested that whatever condition I have, I'd better have it cleared up soon because, knowing DNA as well as he does, he was concerned lest one or the other of our progeny might inherit the same wild "condition" and that would not be so pleasant.

I explained to our three men that my dreams were not unpleasant nor scary. It was just when I thought about them after I awoke that I could remember every detail with a sharpness and clarity that you wouldn't get if you were to remember that everyone in those "dreams" was actually dead.

My son, Jonathan, who has inherited my Dental practice and a whole slew of my talents and interests, looked at me in a strange way. He had taken several minutes to think about me and then he made a truly zany suggestion, which was exactly what the neurologist whom I visited later that week had recommended. "I think, Dad, that you should be hospitalized for a few days and that they should connect you to an electro-cardiogram machine that works continuously 24 hours a day and also have your pulse and blood-pressure and your brain-waves monitored during that same period. In this way they can cover your system whether you're asleep or awake."

My sons are so close to me that we can almost read each others' thoughts. As I looked at them and they looked back at me, we had to start laughing. "Crazy, isn't it?" I asked, "Do you think it's really possible?"

Mark said, "It's wild; but it's possible—I think!"

Mike said, "It's too wild to be true; *but suppose it was possible?*"

Jonny said, "It's possible! But what can they do about it?"

And so, without saying out loud what each one of us was thinking, including the neurologist, I found myself, two days later, in a private room at the New York Hospital hooked-up to all kinds of sophisticated machinery. I expect Medicare and United Healthcare will pay for all this hokey-pokey, but it must cost a fortune to have

24-hour-per-day care with a *trained nurse and an intern* on watch full time to check on my vital statistics!

I spent three nights at that hospital and each night I had two or three of my "specialized dreams" and the hospital had a record of my body's reactions to them. On the fourth day, Dr. Freudenheim, the neurologist, and all three of my sons were in attendance in my private room at the hospital. It was a beautiful, sunny day and Dr. Freudenheim had an avid audience as he spoke. The only others allowed in the room were the three nurses and three interns who had attended me since I had been in the hospital. "I have been in consultation with two other world-renowned neurologists for four hours," said Dr. Freudenheim.

"Yours is indeed a most unusual case, and nobody has come up with a fully-agreed-upon mode of treatment yet. But we all concur that we have never before witnessed a patient who has managed to die for a few seconds, or even a half-minute several times almost every night and then recover his full strength for the rest of the day! It is unbelievable!"

As he paused to give himself an opportunity to organize his next thoughts I looked at my loving sons and we all smiled that familiar smile that signified that we had all guessed correctly: but *"now what"*? Dr. Freudenheim then continued, "Each time you had one of those strange "dreams", Dr. Goldenthal, it was not a dream at all! Apparently, from your EKG and the other machines you were on, your vital signs all signified that you had actually died for those few seconds or half a minute while "those so-called dreams" went on! Your pulse, your brain-waves, your blood-pressure, the electricity that supplies all of the muscles of your body, including your heart were all shut off for those minute periods of time. You were not dreaming, Dr. Goldenthal, *you were dead!* And for several incidents per night! What defies all our rational thinking, is how in the world was your mind able to make those connections to dead people, so clearly, so recognizably, when your brain was actually dead at the time?!"

THE FORTUNE-COOKIE
COLLECTOR

Once in a while you think of a story that seems too ridiculous to tell. If you put it down on paper and take it seriously you might be surprised at what happens. I created a few characters and gave them an opportunity to live on their own. This story is just such an event.

Who knows about Orientals that "escape" the rigors of a dictatorship and live for a while in America? What do I know about such a character? I invented him. Maybe he's real enough to be believed.

The police were called to 172 East Canal Street, in the heart of New York's Chinatown. In apartment 7B a Chinese gentleman was lying on the floor, dead. He was obviously very wealthy and the reason for his death was probably poison. There were no signs of a gunshot, a knife wound, a heart-attack or a stroke. The clue that gave away the cause of death was a pervasive odor of almonds which was inescapable.

A beautiful young Chinese woman, his wife, was mourning discreetly in a corner of the living-room. It was she who had called the police and let them in the front door. The nature and perpetrator of this crime, murder, were never solved by the police. Let's see how good we are at the problem.

The police veritably ransacked the extravagantly-furnished apartment. All they were able to come up with was a hobby of the deceased man, the collection of fortune cookie "fortunes" and that was all. Oh, and they discovered a "bug"—a listening device–discreetly located in the chandelier in the dining room over the main table. But there was no clue as to the location of the receiving area for the "bug."

If they had had the man's biography they would have known more about the Of course, the media had to call him "The Fortune Cookie Nerd", as though he were addicted to Fortune Cookies and they left out the other, more redeemable qualities that he had.

There is something about crime in Chinatown that frightens even the most experienced metropolitan policemen. Even the Chinese cops are prone to shy away from crime in Chinatown as though every case has an aura of mystery about it instead of it being the usual human-type of crime.

The dead man's name was Hu Shung. Originally he came from Beijing. He was lucky enough to get, somehow, an opportunity to live in New York City where there are many, many Chinese of all sorts who live in "their own world." Certainly it is not *my* world. I could not eat their kind of cooking (the hot grease would get to me in time), the MSG would lead to all types of problems and the salt they use in such profligance could be fatal. I could not do laundry for a living if you paid me a bundle. And I could not live in apartheid with all the prejudices active against Orientals. I could not live without the Jewishness that I am used to. I am a different kind of cat, that's all.

But Hu Shung was relatively happy in those circumstances. This description says "relatively"; *not perfectly.*

Hu Shung was superstitious, that was his problem. He believed in all sorts of things that you don't cater to. He believed in Fortune Cookies, for instance. He never considered that some business people hire writers to express those banal "sayings" and put all kinds of numbers on the reverse side of the "Fortune" to be played in whatever grubby, chancy game you choose. He firmly believed that a "Higher Power" was behind all these writers. They simply wrote what "this power" put into their minds. Socrates expressed this view of poets. It was Fate, not business. Your "luck" was really not good fortune: in a way you had to earn "the luck" that you had.

How did Hu Shung earn his "luck"? He lived a clean life. He was not dishonest in any way at all. He donated to all the Oriental charities. He supported whatever Chinese ethnic groups were interested in China as a god-given-residence although he was temporarily living in America. Most of all, he "believed" in the verity of the Fortunes that came in Fortune cookies.

He saved all those 'Fortunes' in a great loose-leaf notebook. He didn't paste them in the blank pages, because he felt that the 'numbers' were also somewhat holy. He kept them between transparent pages to which they clung by a form of magnetism. You see, he took his "fortune" very seriously.

Only one among the two thousand six-hundred seventy-three "fortunes" that Hu Shung collected was chosen by him to be valid. It was a simple sentence like ever so many: "Your fortune awaits you" but the numbers on the back of the "Fortune" were "3333"— a good number to play. What is so overwhelming about "Your fortune awaits you"? It is simple: unadorned by excessive wordage. It tells you that the fortune is there, go get it: Just figure out where it is and how to get it. And the numbers at the rear of the slip of paper were significant as well. Simply find an address with all those threes. That's all.

Obviously to Hu Shung, he would have to go to China to retrieve his fortune. Do you believe that a choice existed as to the location of that fortune? Not at all! Only in China would such a treasure be found. *He* believed it so why should I doubt him? It's *his* story, not mine!!

If you think that for a decadent (anybody who chooses to live in America must be decadent) to return to China in this day and age is no trial, think again. Everybody (in the government) thinks he is at least a spy. Maybe even a serial killer. You never know what you can catch in New York City. The average Chinese did not have such suspicions. They sympathized, surreptitiously, with anyone who wanted to go to New York. The only thing that bothered the average guy was, "Why did he come back?" They all figured that his mother must be dying. In fact, that's what the government figured, too, so they did not bother Hu Shung at all. His mother cooperated by taking sick and dying as soon as Hu came home. She figured that he came home because she was dying, so she died. I forget what illness the Medical examiner wrote as the cause for her death. Oh yes, he wrote, "Surprise!" because she didn't know she was dying before her son came home.

What is the significance of the number, "3333"? Well, China has a set number of districts. Because of the gigantic size of the country there are 1,876 such districts. Hu Shung found that district 333 is in Nanking. He went to Nanking right after his mother's funeral. He actually carried her ashes around with him and got so excited when he found his fortune that he broke the urn holding her ashes and spilled them all over the place. He had to leave her where she was; it was a nicer place than she was used to, by far. But I'm getting ahead in my story.

He had to find building number 3 in district number 333. What building was number three in District 333? It was the Treasury building of the District. He was particularly careful about what he took from the Treasury building. He didn't want to get in trouble. When he asked someone about fortunes the answer he got was, "Anything you find in this building is a fortune to the average guy!". So he kept looking.

In the Social Services waiting-room, which was beautiful beyond belief because they spent more money than they could afford to so they couldn't deliver any social services. He saw a duffle-bag with his name on it, saying "This is yours!" He knew right away that this was his fortune and got so excited that he broke his mother's urn of ashes in trying to lift the duffle-bag. The ashes didn't look too much like Mrs. Shung but the duffle-bag was so heavy that he had to pay someone to help him carry it outside the building and put it in a cab. The first place that Hu Shung visited was a safety deposit vault at one of the Banks that had large boxes for storing large amounts of gold, securities, diamonds and cash. Then Hu took the cab home to his hotel, the Excelsior of Nanking.

In China they have a problem with excess women. The Chinese Government looks askans at people with a fortune who are not married. To the average bureaucrat in modern China a wealthy man should offer to take care of the expenses of a single woman. That generally means marriage, but not necessarily. So before Hu left the Treasury building someone handed him a piece of paper with some official statements on it. It said approximately, in officialese, "In this life you get nothing for nothing. You get a fortune—you have to share it."

Actually, Hu sort-of expected something like this. It's a lot better than paying taxes. You don't have to have intercourse with a tax-collector. The Law had found a way for you to do the numerical equivalent without paying official taxes. It made sense.

This is a round-about way of letting you know that Hu had to find someone to support and he had three weeks to find her. So the rest of this story is not about Fortune Cookies but the results of getting that fortune.

Does anyone know what the SSAOGC is? Most likely, unless you were a Chinese female who was considered excess baggage, you never heard of the Substitute Sex Association Of Greater China. This is an organization of talented women of Greater China who use substitute sex instead of taking a chance of doing the real thing and getting pregnant or a sexual disease. The Government of China was concerned about the large number of children who were being produced, especially to women who had no visible means of support. This was a social effort to provide the women with some degree of sexual satisfaction without a male partner.

They had classes where the instructors claimed that they get as much satisfaction from substitute sex as from real sex. Genuinely talented women (girls, really) put on demonstrations where they show how much satisfaction they get from the techniques they use. The grunting and howling are like the real thing.

What has this harangue got to do with this story? Well, when Hu Shung asked around about getting a wife or a paramour who would meet the requirements of the National Government he was routinely directed to attend a meeting of the SSAOGC. He was told that these girls were all virgins, unaffected by any disease and could perform a substitute intercourse that has no equal in the history of humankind. So Hu Shung went to a meeting of the

SSAOGC and was greatly surprised at the large number of men who were in attendance.

There were three women who would give demonstrations that evening. The first two were pedestrian in their demonstrations. Granted that they used various substitute sexual devices but they were personally unattractive enough to turn the average man off. What everybody knew was that the third woman really turned everybody on, men and women alike. She had a sweet personality and seemed to endow the devices with a personal charm. At each climax she would be aware that the audience was having a communal climax as well. Everybody fell in love, physically and emotionally, with Mi Sin Li. When I say everybody I must include Hu Shung.

Hu made up his mind that he had to pursue Mi Sin Li if it took forever. He found his name near the bottom of a list of four hundred men and women. How would he defeat the other hundreds? He added a note after his name that said, "I have just won the National Fortune Cookie Title." If ever there was a successful inspiration that was it. At ten o'clock that night the hotel-room phone jangled. It was Mi Sin Li. She wished to visit with him.

To make a long story short, they agreed to live together for two months and then to figure out whether marriage was practical. Of course, a substantial monetary settlement was to be paid to Mi Sin Li in case of no marriage. It didn't matter to Hu that Mi Sin Li was experienced at substitute sex. He had talents all his own which made substitute sex seem an unwanted thing of the past. Maybe you don't realize it but there is no substitute for the "real thing". The Government plan is okay for substitutes.

Two months later Hu Shung and Mi Sin Li were married. Six months after that they booked passage by ocean liner to New York. They actually took fifty days to reach New York! What they did was take a world cruise to the Orient, the Islands of the Pacific, Africa, the Mediterranean, South America and the Islands of the Caribbean and thence to New York. It was a dream trip, from start to finish. They collected all sorts of expensive goodies to decorate their apartment in New York, which was being renovated while they took this trip. If you have great wealth why ask what anything costs? It does not matter. On the ship, the Volendam, one of the people they had as friends was a man (Hing Shen) whose nature and employment were kept as a secret that must never be discussed. He seemed to be with his wife, but he really cared for another, prettier, female. They were all Chinese and a group of more secretive, tighter dudes you'd never want to meet. But they seemed to enjoy the trip, all of them, and took pictures of all the scenery. But they never even suggested that a picture of one or all of them on a bridge or some place of interest would be apropos. There were no pictures taken of any of them at all. That was strange.

When they met in New York it was always at a formal place, like at the United Nations, instead of at one another's apartments. There was nothing personal about their relationship.

One evening, after they had met Hing Shen and his two afficionados at the U.N. and had a few too-many drinks, Hu Shung and Mi Sin Li were having a late dinner at their own home. The conversation revolved around Hing Shen, as usual. Hu Shung questioned, "I wonder which one of those two women he really cares for."

Mi Sin replied, "I don't think he really cares for *either* of them. They are both utilitarian and the question should have been, 'Why would either of them let herself get into a situation like that. It's so demeaning!"

"We haven't decided yet what he does for a living. What do *you* think?"

"It really does not make a difference. He's happy with it and that's what's important."

"Does it look like he is happy? He seems like he's under extreme pressure to "produce" something, and he is not pleased with the result."

"What would he have to produce for someone else?"

"I don't know. Let us suppose that he works for the Secret Service. Just suppose!(This over her objections.) He would be under pressure to come up with a spy and he doesn't have one so he's unhappy. His job and maybe his life have to depend on that. Maybe he's been told that some cabal or other require him to come up with something dramatic. Are there any cabals that need resolution right now?"

"I really don't know. Why don't we discuss something else? We wouldn't know about these things, would we?"

"Well, I'm not sure. Certainly there is the attitude of the Chinese government in regard to the Middle-East and their attitude towards the production of oil recently in Kazakhstan. Those are items to make espionage a field day for the right person. You have to be aware in this day and age. You can't simply live your life as though it didn't count!"

"I didn't know you were so interested in worldly affairs. Most people are just satisfied thinking about where their next meal is going to come from."

"I firmly believe what someone in America once said, 'If you don't remember History you are doomed to repeat it!'"

"That is very clever."

They finished their repast and went to bed. Knowing what kind of a job Mi Sin had before they got engaged. I have to state that, "they went to bed but not to sleep!"

Three days later Hu Shung and Mi sin Li were enjoying the privacy of a lunch in their dressing gowns. They had, of course, a cook and a maid, a valet for him and valet for her. For Hu the cook had made the most marvelous western omelet with four eggs and all the ham, onions, cheese, celery, mushrooms and olives one could want. Mi Sin was satisfied to have simply two eggs, over easy, some strawberry jelly and one piece of toast with margarine. Hu said, "She must have put some almonds in there by mistake. I can try it. I've never had almonds in a western omelet before." So saying, he took a large mouthful of the omelet and promptly fell down to the floor, dead.

Mi Sin dialed 9-11 immediately and said, "My husband is lying dead on the floor. I think he had a heart attack!" The EMS and an ambulance with a physician came almost at once and they agreed that, with the odor of almonds rampant, he was probably poisoned with cyanide.

The police came and spoke to the cook and she said that, once in a while, she used some oil of almonds in her western omelets and she gave the mostly-filled jar of oil of almonds to the detective, who discovered, at the police lab, that that jar was primed with a ninety percent solution of cyanide. The question, which nobody was able to answer, was, "Who would have put the cyanide in that jar?" So far this case is getting colder and colder as time goes by. Nobody was taken away by the police....everyone seems innocent.

Strangely enough, another poisoning took place in Chinatown the same day. A man named Hing Shen was having roast duck at a well-known restaurant, and as you know, the Chinese of Eastern China use almond oil for their roast duck. This jar of almond oil, also, was laced with a ninety percent solution of cyanide. It was a coincidence that only writers of short stories would know about.

Don't worry. We will not kill off Mi Sin Li, yet. She has not been connected with either of these murders, although a Secret Service operative told me, just yesterday, that Mi Sin Li has been in the Chinese Secret Service since she started working in the SSAOGC. You never know about things like that, do you?

AN INTERESTING NEIGHBOR

Every once in a while we change our residence. We move to another community and have to get acclimated to a whole new set of rules and regulations, customs and neighbors. As one grows older it becomes increasingly tedious to accommodate to the varying egos that constitute the "way of life" of new condos and to abide by their artificial community. To put it mildly, not all the neighbors are our "cup of tea."

We had just moved into our new residence and the task of unpacking and putting all the manifold items in their proper places was left entirely to me, since my wife is ill and it really is not the job of her live-in caretaker to drag heavy boxes of books and kitchen gear as well as the clothing and multitudinous cartons for my "office" (where I write these stories and the mass of checks to pay our bills). Of course my sons helped with the shelving and hanging up of the museum-like number of paintings and photographs we still possess.

I wondered, one time in a fit of despair, whether I would not have enjoyed one of my neighbors offering to help me out. But they are almost as old as I am, some of them, and it would not seem proper for me to invite one of the many comely (and uncomely) widows to give me a hand. So, in a bold attempt worthy of a man one-third my age, I 'bit the bullet' and we now are fully "moved in."(There is no question that frequent moves at old age are a prelude to disaster. A heart-attack and two "strokes" later ask me about that!

Subliminally, I guess, I *had* noticed something unpleasantly strange about the house next door to us (on the north side). In a patent attempt to appear wealthy and artful in their decor, the people there proved that "nouveau riche" is newly rich. There is no escaping the premise that "nouveau riche" means that we will be exposed to all the bad taste that goes with throwing money in the direction of gardeners and in the direction of those who sell all those tawdry little statues and trees and bushes that are carved to look like animals of all sorts.

At the time we moved in I could not help noticing that the man next door, in clothes that seemed too expensive for such work, was busy washing his Volvo convertible. A Mercedes was in his garage. The entire outside of the house and the grounds looked grotesquely "patched-up". If I hadn't had a premonition of other interesting, bizarre goings-on (such as you will learn about in this story) I would have told the moving-men to re-take all our belongings, put it all into storage and we would have flown back to live in Florida forever.

We succeeded in having as little to do with our neighbors as possible. I *did* go to that fancy house on the evening that we had finished moving in and asked the madam of the house if she knew which days of the week garbage and trash are picked up and which days are reserved for aluminum, tin cans, glass and newspapers. The answers I received were replete with sighs of confusion, as though she was trying to say that, "Oh dear! We *do* need those dirty men and, really, my dear, they're so declassee!"

I also learned that the family name next door was Ginzburgh, with an "H" at the end and that her husband's name is Morris but everybody calls him "Mahr." I've not yet had occasion to meet that guy although I really haven't tried. It's only been two years and we have lots of time left. At least I thought so at the beginning of this story.

And so we started to re-lead our ordinary lives in the manner that Jan's illness dictated. Jan is a victim of Alzheimers disease and if you have ever loved anybody as unreservedly as I love that lady then your life is endangered merely by the unending efforts you would take to see to it that she is always comfortable, fed, clothed, medicated, entertained, has her exercises and is always neat and clean and sweet-smelling. We go through a very tough regimen and the caretaker who administers most of the care works a straight two weeks before I take notice that she, too, is beginning to look as though she was on the brink of "whatever" and then we have to bring in a substitute while Sylvia gets a few days off, preferably in a place at least a thousand miles from where we live. She has friends and family in Canada, Jamaica (the island), Long Island, Florida, Massachusetts and upper New York State. How can she afford such an expensive series of air-flights? Do you think her pay is sufficient to maintain such a life-style? I can tell you that it most certainly is!

Sylvia (Jan's caretaker) never once recommended that we try to "make friends" with the neighbors to the *North.* The neighbor to the *South* had already been invited by Sylvia to share in a dinner of spaghetti with meat sauce. That character never said thanks and his upper lip curled as though he had been asked to participate in a meal laced with arsenic. I overheard that conversation and I'm glad I held my tongue and didn't tell him that Sylvia's spaghetti with meat sauce is one of her premier dishes and, although we are careful about eating animal fats (and refined sugars), he was really missing a great meal. I shop for the leanest meats and we grind them ourselves with an electric grinder. That meat has to have less than 4% of the daily requirement of fat even if you eat two heaping dishes of spaghetti! And that's what I do.

It must be the "socialist" in me that resents people who go to such pains to show off their supposed wealth as do our neighbors to the *North.* I have to admit that neither of those people look particularly educated or seem to emphasize any genuine talents or even have the appearance of those of our friends who are truly cultured and also wealthy. There's something in me that can detect a phony a mile away. So it wasn't until last week that I asked the owner of the house we rent from him if he knew in what profession or business the man next door had earned so much available money. If I tell you what that business was will you promise not to spread the news? Okay. The man next door, age 67, was formerly an ordinary patrolman in the police department of New York City! What's the first thought that comes to *your* mind when you hear that this "rich" man was a cop on a "beat" in lower Manhattan? As a matter of fact, *that was the same thought that immediately came to my mind!*

Actually, as a short story writer, I quickly thought of at least twelve scenarios where a former city cop moves to the sticks of New Jersey and has a very inquisitive neighbor who is determined to "get to the bottom" of whatever dirty story is really mixed up with these people. But I didn't have to do a single thing—the story unfolded before my very eyes and I didn't have to use too much imagination to tie one thing to another and get the answer I was after all along!

It was well into the third year we had lived in that house in New Jersey, about a month after we had come up from Florida to trade the heat, humidity and hurricanes of the South for the heat and humidity and traffic of the North. I was working at my computer when I happened to look up for a moment. We keep the windows wide open up here and there's just a simple screen between us and the neighbors of the North. The neighbor was washing his Mercedes and it looked like new. A man had been driving up and down our street but I only caught a glimpse of him subliminally. Ultimately he stopped right in front of the Ginzburgh residence and it didn't take a practiced ear to hear the man shout in his best Brooklynese accent, "Hey Mario! *Que se dich?*" (Whaddaya say?)

Of course Mahr Ginzburgh heard him. So did everyone in the neighboring quarter of a mile. But the sight of "Mahr" shifting gears from a staid, Jewish, respectable New Jersey condo owner to an Italian Brooklyn mobster was priceless. He didn't take his foot off the clutch as he slowly–ever so slowly–turned to shift gears in reply to his former buddy on the streets of the Italian ghetto near 18th Street. "It's a-good to see yez." He said trying to resume the accent and inflections he had lost forty years earlier. He failed miserably because his old-time friend had also progressed in his Americanization and had only reverted to Brooklynese to impress Mario about how long they had known each other. He was involved in private motivations that Mahr immediately recognized. "H'ya, Fish?" continued Mahr. Of course he had to stop washing his Mercedes.

Needless to say, Fish got out of his car, walked over to hug his old buddy and they went into the house to give Mahr's wife, Betty, the surprise of a lifetime. The story of their life did not all reveal itself to my snooping gaze. It was revealed later on by Frank, the former owner of our house who was a wealth of information. In fact, he later testified in court on the "Fish and Related Cases".

Apparently, according to Frank, Mario Berlongaza met Betty Friedman when they were still in high school. Mario was about four years older than Betty. He was from a nondescript Italian immigrant family and she was from a nondescript Jewish immigrant family. There wasn't an accumulation of two years of high school in either family before these two kids had made it through high school. There had been much more important things to do than getting an education, like putting bread on the table of a large, hungry family.

Whereas Betty and Mahr had always been in love with each other there were no overt problems when they decided to get married. Neither family was particularly religious. Neither one could afford to belong to the houses of God which seemed to bestow benefits excessively on the wealthier patrons than on the poor strugglers of the Friedman-Berlongaza type. The problems had just arisen when the time came for Betty and Mario to move to a condo in New Jersey. Apparently something that Frank didn't know about had arisen and Mario had to leave New York and the Police Force and assume a new life with a new name and new identities.

Mario left the matter of relocation almost entirely in the sure hands of his wife. He had been just an ordinary cop for many years and did not seem to be particularly bright. He left things to Betty because "them Jews are too smart for their own good" which was telling you something about himself. She decided that since they had been married for over forty years he could get away with trying to assume a Jewish identity. From Mario Berlongaza he became Morris Ginzburgh. Mario, in his native Italian neighborhood was pronounced "Mahrio"—so he was always nicknamed "Mahr". But this time it was for Morris instead of Mario. The Italians and the Jews really got along well with each other in the ghetto (and they got along well together in this condominium); nobody could afford to be uppity about anything. He had known many Jewish expressions all his life and loved to say them at the right occasions. In order to fit into the condominium group in New Jersey, which was about sixty percent Jewish and thirty percent Italian, he contributed to all the charities, using the name Ginzburgh on his checks. Frankly, whenever I saw him I was sure he was Jewish. That's telling you something about me, too.

Mahr and Betty never had any children, which was too bad, because they had so much love to spare. Any child they brought up would have had the benefit of all that love and an interesting background as well. Instead of a child they had a bulldog for the past fourteen years. This bulldog was named MUSSO because he looked so much like Mussolini. He was a very devoted watchdog and sounded much more dangerous than he really was.

Having a sixth sense would be marvelous for people. But this dog really had an sensibility. If he as much as suspected a person of harboring impulses that were inimical to his "mother and father" he would act very macho in badgering that individual so that the suspect would feel much more comfortable in leaving the house rather than be pestered by a personalized dog. Betty and Mahr would never interfere with that dog. He knew what he knew and he was always right.

When Betty saw Mahr's old friend Fish she knew right away why Fish was there. So did Mahr, although he didn't "let on" that he was aware of the problems that were now about to occur for them all. Fish insisted on looking at the entire premises, inside and out, and he automatically sat at the head of the table when Betty brought out some home-baked chocolate cake and coffee. Fish took the lead in whatever conversation took place and dominated the conversation. Soon he was asking himself, out loud, how it was that an ordinary patrolman, even a sergeant, could afford such a munificent spread as Mahr and Betty seemed to have. "You must have hit it real big when O'Flaherty got stuck with all that dope that time."

Mahr knew this was coming and he had an ordinary reply. "Well, you know us, Fish, and you know we always lived pretty tight when we lived in Brooklyn. Now we have a chance to expand a little bit and let loose some of the cash we saved all those years."

But Fish didn't buy Mahr's story; not by a long shot. "I dunno, Mahr. I really think you oughta share some of the wealth with your best friend. Whaddaya say, Mahr, how about five hundred a month to start?"

"I thought you had your share of the ripe pickins all those years from Shea Stadium and all the businesses in that area. You mean to say you played it straight when your natural inclinations were to play it dirty?" Mahr knew just what kind of a guy Fish was and he laid it out to him straight. "Are you really so hard up for money after all these years? To tell you the truth I'm kinda disappointed in you!"

"It's not that way at all." said Fish, who was getting hot under the collar. Meanwhile Musso was pestering Fish because he sensed a threat to Mahr and Betty. That dog just kept on barking and pulling on the left pants leg of the unwelcome guest. Neither Mahr nor Betty made a move to stop their pet from badgering their guest. They knew what their dog had sensed and he was right!

"Say, can you keep that mutt offa me? He's a real pain in the ass!"

Mahr made believe he didn't hear Fish. "I'll tell you what, Fish. Since you're now on my list of the neediest people I know, I'll donate five hundred this month and we'll talk about it more next time. This way we can let you get you back to "The City" in time for your next begging job and I think we can assume that you'll be back one month from today, which would be May fifth. Okay?"

"That'll be just fine with me. But Betty doesn't have to serve me no cakes and coffee next time. It'll be just business." But Fish was not satisfied with his acquisition of the day.

While Mahr reached into his left front pants pocket and withdrew a large wad of fifty-dollar and one-hundred dollar bills Fish had one helluva time shoving Musso off his pants leg. When

Mahr stood up and extended his left hand with exactly five-hundred dollars Fish stood up as well and prepared to leave. Musso sensed that his target was about to leave and relented, but he maintained a deep-throated growl and looked Fish right in the eyes. In much less time than it takes to tell this part of the story Fish reached into the holster that was not very well concealed under his left inside jacket pocket. He withdrew a .38 caliber pistol with a silencer on it, aimed it precisely between the instead of using the word "God.". instead of using the word "God.". eyes of Musso and squeezed the trigger. In less than two minutes Fish had taken his five-hundred dollars (without saying "thanks"), made his good-byes, shot the dearest friend that Mahr and Betty ever had, scooted out the door and drove away.

Betty and Mahr were forlorn about the loss of their beloved pet but they were not lost otherwise. They had simply been reminded that what they had just experienced was the unconscionable brutality that had marked their former life before they had removed themselves from the big city. They simply had to plan around any such recurrences and defend themselves as best as they knew how. But there was one item that could not be kept waiting. They had to clean up the mess that was left when Musso was shot. This was done with dispatch as Mahr brought a sizeable tarp from the garage and put his old friend's carcass on it while Betty mopped up whatever she could find. They both regretted the bullet-hole that was left in the entrance foyer wall but Mahr knew just how to repair that damage. He had done so many times before in his earlier days.

Both of them had the same idea when it came to the problem of burying Musso. They would get, from the nearby Home Depot, a relatively large flowering bush that would bloom almost all spring and summer. Then, in place of the Ficus tree that was a useless ornament, they would plant Musso about two-and-a-half feet deep under the large blooming bush they had just bought. In this way Musso would nourish and aid in the blooming of that new bush and add more beauty to their lives. Also, they promised each other that, as soon as things became settled again, they would get a duplicate bulldog to replace their beloved Musso.

Later that night (I actually saw them doing this when my unconscionable bladder got me up at about three A.M. and I saw them planting Musso and then planting the new bush.)Then they held a brief service for their beloved pet. I didn't know whether to cry or micturate again. I could understand their not spreading the news of Musso being shot necessitating those late-night funeral rites.

The experience they had with Fish engaged them in other ways. Apparently they started re-evaluating the design of their flower beds. They got a gardener to remove and rearrange a whole mess of plants, leaving an area about twenty feet long that was now entirely denuded of shrubbery. Then, exactly a month later, on the fifth of May, they received a delivery of six large flowering bushes of varying foliage and several different colors. Early on that Wednesday morning those bushes were delivered. At just about three o'clock in the afternoon Fish himself made his appearance. He didn't bother to ring the entrance chimes or even to knock on the door. "I'm here!" he announced imperiously, as though Mahr and Betty would not have known he was there.

"This won't take long," he informed them. Betty acted very disappointedly. "Oh! I spent two hours making some cookies for you and putting up a pot of coffee.

"I asst you not to make a fuss over me. I ain't got any time to waste. Maybe next time," he commanded.

"Well if that's the way you want it I guess we have to go along with you. But I wanted you to come out here on the patio and see the new bushes we just bought. You gave us an inspiration in something you mentioned last time." Mahr's imploring tone had the desired affect on Fish who then walked out, following Mahr to the patio. Now this patio was entirely screened-in so that the mosquitoes and other insects that were in the tall bushes that enclosed the sides of the patio would not gain access to the charming sitting area. The whole effect was of coolness and privacy yet it was bright and cheerful. Fish was duly impressed with the carefully planned privacy of the scene. "So where are them bushes you were talkin' about?" he asked.

"Well, Fish," drawled Mahr, "if you'll just turn your head very slowly to your left you'll see exactly how we feel about you, old friend!"

Fish turned his head very slowly to his left. He saw Betty holding a .38 with a silencer about four inches from his neck. Mahr continued with a very pronounced slowness in his speech, "We have gotten you onto this patio where nobody can see us. We carefully planned this so that the bullet will just cut your spinal cord and kill you right away without hitting the arteries in your throat. This will make it a very clean job without all that blood and brains like the way you shot our dog. If you hold very still Betty will do a surgical (as he used the word surgical Betty carefully, slowly squeezed the trigger) treatment." Fish collapsed, dead, to the floor of the patio. There was no blood on the tile and no brain tissue at all. In addition, the bullet went out the open door of the patio and lodged somewhere in the grass, which meant that this was a very inexpensive execution. And there were remarkably few clues left behind.

Mahr then wrapped Fish in the tarp he was lying on. (Didn't I tell you that Mahr was a very efficient policeman? I had said he was not too bright, but that was when I had just started this story and I didn't know my neighbor very well at that time. I've learned a lot about him since then and about Betty too!)

Of course you know now why Mahr had taken so many bushes out of the ground and bought six new ones. And you know, if you have a little mayhem in your system, how Mahr and Betty spent four hours between two and six o'clock early that next morning. I never knew a thing about all these goings on until I had another nature's call at about five A.M. and spent an hour watching them put the finishing touches on the installation of those six bushes. I am certain that Fish (Gianni Abalone) was more than ample nutrition for those six bushes. We'll see, as this story goes on.

But nothing had been told to me about how Mahr and Betty got so wealthy on a mere policeman's pay. You have noticed, I am sure, how Betty and Mahr are an efficient team. Nothing is ever done in that family except through well-thought-out teamwork. So we must assume that Betty was as much a part as Mahr was in the earning of that money. What happened is what always happens when there is a big drug bust. I mean tremendous! The police had private information that a relatively small freighter was going to dock at that old pier number fifty-eight, on the Hudson River and 43 St.

If my memory serves me correctly, the Araguaya, of the old Royal Mail Shipping line had a dock at that very spot in 1929 and Dr. Leon Goldenthal and his eldest son, Ed, left from there on a two week cruise to the Bahamas, Florida and Cuba. That was so long ago! But I do remember that dock and I knew how old and decrepit it was. And the fact that this small freighter had come from Central and South America, as I was told, made me suspicious that it probably had lots of drugs on board.

The police also had their suspicions about that vessel, tipped off by a disgruntled waiter at a restaurant, the Munson, on Twelfth Avenue and fifty-second streets. Captain O'Flaherty had participated in many such raids as he now planned, but he had never hit it very big. This time there was all of a ton and a half of marijuana and at least a ton of cocaine on board that ship, as innocent as she looked with all that rust on her ironwork and as dirty as she was in every other regard. At least a ton of cocaine was what Captain Guinness O'Flaherty figured it was that they carried in all sorts of containers to his office on West fifty-fifth street between ninth and tenth avenues. And that dope stayed in his office until he could find a real connection to unload it and make himself several million dollars.

You read every once in a while of a great big drug bust. Whatever becomes of that dope? Did you ever, just once, read about how those drugs were disposed of? I read the newspapers every single day and watch the news programs on television all the time. Not once have I ever heard how they were going to dispose of those drugs so that they should not get into the hands (and lungs and blood-streams) of the public. What happens to it? If I tell you that Captain O'Flaherty waited for *six years* with approximately three tons of dope (including the marijuana) in his office you can believe it. He employed six policemen twenty four hours a day to guard that dope. One of those policemen, whom Captain O'Flaherty trusted to watch the drugs for him, was Mario Berlongaza.

For three years Mario had nothing to do but watch everybody who went in and out of that office to see that nobody walked out with a package of goodies. Suddenly one day, when he and the other two night-working patrolmen were making a count of the drug containers, they discovered that approximately one thousand pounds of cocaine was missing! How could that happen? Three cops on duty at all times and someone walked off with all that "snow"! No wonder Guinness O'Flaherty was furious! Here he had been negotiating, surreptitiously of course, with all kinds of drug dealers for a real good price and someone beats him to the punch! The Captain couldn't flat-out accuse any of his especially-chosen paragons of virtue of stealing his stuff. But he had to remove them all from duty and get new guards.

He felt bad about relieving Mario, mostly because Mario, of all people, was such a goody-good that he was above suspicion. But all six cops who had been on duty for the Captain were given jobs where he could keep an eye on them and see, if only for a moment, any one of them went on a spree and spent money he never could have had before. If one of those cops had to buy a new car it had to be a cheap car, and none of their kids could go to expensive colleges. Also, and this is important in this case, if any of the cops went to Atlantic City or Las Vegas to gamble, a detective was appointed to check on the nature of that gambling, to be sure it wasn't for "big bucks".

Mario was given a very demeaning job. He was required to wash the two cars that belonged to Captain O'Flaherty every day; his own Volvo sedan and the Chevrolet Impala that the department let him use. Mario washed and simonized those two cars so that they gleamed beyond belief. For three years he washed those cars and neither he nor his wife spent one penny that anyone could say came from the proceeds of the sale of five hundred pounds of cocaine.

But then it was time for Mario to retire. There are written rules for the retirement of policemen. He went to the Captain, with tears in his eyes and asked permission to retire. Guinness O'Flaherty had tears in his eyes as well, because he had felt all along that he had been punishing Mario for a crime he simply could not have committed. So Mario retired from the police force at a fairly good pension and went home to his modest little house on 18th Street in Brooklyn. For five years after that Mario suspected that the Captain had a detective check out all his expenses. If he and Betty had been the recipients of a couple of million dollars from the sale of all those drugs they certainly did not act like it. They spent exactly what they had spent for the previous twenty years. You can't beat that for will-power!

Betty and Mahr spent the several years preceding his retirement planning just what they should do. You know and I know that Mario had somehow stolen that one thousand pounds of cocaine from the Captain's giant stash of drugs. Actually speaking, the cocaine was never the property of the Captain. It all belonged to the State of New York or the City of New York. The fact that Captain O'Flaherty illegally kept that stuff around his office and illegally employed six policemen to guard it was the *Captain's* crime! He had plans for selling it all off to the highest bidders but those clever men knew that once the Captain had received his many millions from the deal he would know just whom to go after to make the most important "catch" of the Century. That is the time for Captain O'Flaherty to be assassinated. We're all smart but these guys are smarter. They put Captain O'Flaherty in an impossible spot. It was under these circumstances that Mario was able to get a very satisfactory price for the drugs that he stole from the Captain. He wasn't greedy; just dishonest in a greedy sort of way.

After those five years of living in penury in Brooklyn Betty and Mahr decided to move to a condominium unit (real estate prices had gone down sufficiently for them to have gotten a good buy) in nearby New Jersey so that he could always keep in touch with people who were important to them: their attorney, their accountant and some relatives who seemed stuck in Brooklyn forever. There were also a few (very few) of their old-time friends who would never do the kind of debauchery that Fish was guilty of.

Betty and Mahr did not expect that they could disappear eternally from the long reach of the New York Police. All they planned on doing was to up-scale their life-style and have a few luxuries. The one thing they could not resist was temptation. For instance, Mahr and Betty would go to Atlantic City and gamble the way they never used to gamble---and very often. They actually won considerable cash! It was there that Fish saw them for the first time in many years and, as you might have supposed, he followed them home! Mahr had noticed him following their car but, mistakenly, he thought that Captain O'Flaherty had finally located him and put a tail on him. But the Captain, himself, finally did see Mahr in person at the Trump Palace, and they made a date for the Captain to visit them in Marlboro at his first convenience. After all, the Captain and Mahr were actually friends for over forty years and with a little bit of luck there would be no repeat of the "Fish story".

It was about three months later when Captain O'Flaherty called to set up an appointment to visit with Betty and Mahr. Because they had no genuine idea what the ultimate attitude of the Captain would be in regard to the "missing" drugs the younger couple took certain steps to protect themselves. They certainly knew that they couldn't plan on simply killing off anyone and everyone who presented a threat. Somewhere their luck would wear out and they felt that maybe–just maybe–they should rely on being "just folks." By being nice and decent perhaps the ogres in society would forget their atavistic impulses. That's a nice idea, isn't it? Do you think it would ultimately pay off? Did it ever pay off?

The Captain arrived promptly at three o'clock and was a delight to his hosts. He was as nice as he could be and was delightfully surprised--- and pleased--- with the large, roomy, though tastelessly decorated ranch house that Betty and Mahr had bought. When he was shown the grounds he noticed that some of the bushes were more colorful than the others and he inquired what the reason for this was. It may seem strange to you, but Mahr and Betty had decided, if asked that question, to tell the truth. It seemed to them that the Captain would only respect boldness and bravery to any challenges that life might bring and, in a way, would accept it as an implicit threat to anyone who threatened the placid life that Mahr and Betty had set out of themselves.

"That one bush, over there, is more colorful and healthier because we buried our dog, Musso, underneath it and it seems to have nourished that bush more than some of the others." was Mahr's simple explanation.

"Oh, I remember that dog!" said the Captain. "He looked so much like Mussolini that you used to call him Musso, didn't you? How did he die?"

"I had an old acquaintance from the early days in Brooklyn and when he came to visit us he took a particular dislike for that dog. When he tried to blackmail us because he thought we wouldn't normally have enough money to live like this, the dog growled and sensed that this guy represented a threat to us. The dog was right so the guy just lost his cool and put a bullet right between the dog's eyes. It was the worst experience of our lives!"

"That is the vilest, most inhumane offense I ever heard of!" exclaimed the Captain. "What was the name of that guy?"

"Fish. We all called him Fish but his real name was Gianni Abalone."

"Oh, I knew Fish. We used to use him as a snitch whenever we needed some information about the Mob. I hope you beat him up good and proper."

"I'm too old for the physical side of retribution. After all, I'm almost seventy years old. But we took care of Fish, in the only way he would understand."

Guiness O'Flaherty timed his reply perfectly. He looked at Betty and Mahr with his steely blue eyes and burst out laughing. "I see it all now! And you buried him under those other bushes that are thriving so beautifully! You're very bold and extremely clever. *I really appreciate that!* I had no idea you were such a creative thinker and so brave. If I'd had any such conception of you I'd have promoted you to the highest grade detective. "He thought a little more about the stories he had been told by Mahr and almost to himself, continued his musing. "Imagine that! The son-of-a-bitch comes into your home and brutally kills your beloved pet dog and how do you react? You get rid of him just the way you should have! I'm proud of you, Mario! Really proud of you!"

Mahr and Betty didn't expect such effusive praise from their guest. Betty was very proud of her husband and said so to the Captain. "Oh, I'm so pleased that you didn't feel offended by the way we have behaved. After all, we always realized that a policeman has a different take on the outrageous anti-social actions of the general public."

"That's the basis of the attitude I've worked with for my forty-five years in the service of my city!" exclaimed Captain O'Flaherty. "The law is one thing but the way you work within the law is another!"

Betty then brought out a whole array of home-made delicacies and a pot of Brazilian coffee, which, by its very aroma, titilated one's very taste buds. She just knew that the way to a man's heart was through his stomach. Captain O'Flaherty didn't even wait to be asked. He simply sat down at the dinette table and, after his hostess had sat down and made herself comfortable, they all dug in with a vengeance.

Obviously the Captain liked his hosts and would never do anything to harm them. In fact, he told them that, as soon as he had received his second cup of coffee. "I've always liked you, Mario, even though, for appearance sake I had to humiliate you for a few years. Most of all, I respect the way you handled that drug business. You took a course of action that there was no real opportunity for me to take. The drug king-pins just knew that after they would pay me off for the sale of the drugs to them I would have to nail them in the biggest smash against the drug trade in history. They would all go to jail for long terms and I would be killed for double-crossing them.

"What happened was, in the long run, that I had to give all that dope to the State and who the hell knows what they did with the stuff? You protected me for several years and then you did what you had to do. There were no hard feelings. There were *never* any hard feelings about what took place.

"My poor, late wife always told me to do the right thing and turn the stuff in to the State. That's one more thing we have in common, Mario. We both married Jewish women and there's something very proper and practical about those women." Guiness O'Flaherty had to wipe his eyes and his nose as he recalled his wife of over fifty years.

Either the Captain had eaten too much or had too much coffee, or he was in some way overcome by his memories of his late wife, but he suddenly became very short of breath and got exceedingly flushed in the face. Betty saw that he was distressed and immediately called 9-11. She told them to hurry, that an elderly gentleman was either having a heart attack or a stroke. Within less than six minutes the emergency squad was there and the Captain reached out to pat the hands of both Mahr and Betty but despite the excellence of the care he was dead before they could even get him to a hospital.

I saw the ambulance come to their house and noticed that both Betty and Mahr were beside themselves with grief. There was no question that whoever had been to their home was a welcome guest and whatever had happened to him was an act of The Almighty. It was then that Betty and Mahr noticed the driver of Captain O'Flaherty's car. A uniformed chauffeur had been sitting outside in the limousine all the while that the Captain had been visiting Betty and Mahr. If only they had known, they could have invited him in and made him comfortable in the house. His name was Kevin Muldoon and he had been an experienced driver for O'Flaherty for six years. He was a very handsome man in his late forties. Betty was immediately smitten by the youthful manly appearance of this chauffeur, and since she knew that she was about four years the junior of Mahr (actually she was almost sixteen years older than Kevin Muldoon but her libido lied to her) and it appeared that Kevin liked youthful-looking older women as well.

However, this was no time for an illicit romance. It was a time for grief. But grief does not have a future and sometimes romance does, if it can wait. So Betty invited the handsome Kevin into their home and wondered how she could hide Mahr from their sight. It was really easy, because Mahr had no time for chauffeurs and excused himself because he wanted some quiet and some privacy. So he went to their bedroom and closed the door. Is it at all possible that he could have done such a self-destructive act while he *had* to see that Betty was making an ass of herself in front of that young man?

Maybe, like so many other people, you only see what you want to see and your mind does not allow you to soak up the significance of what your eyes definitely have seen. Anyhow, despite the death of *his* boss and *her* guest, romance got a good start at that moment.

A couple of weeks later Mahr and Betty made one of their bi-monthly trips to Atlantic City, to invest a few dollars in the nebulous advantages of "gambling". It is only "gambling" to the player. To the "house" it is a sure thing. They have a few strict rules which guarantee the "house" the edge in all the odds. This is called "the vigorish". And one may actually hit it "big" in one hand or two, or in one throw of the dice, but all-in-all the customer doesn't stand a chance to beat the "house."

However, the romance between Betty and Kevin had its best chance at Atlantic City because Betty had reserved a room for Kevin in the same building that the gambling was going on. The room for Betty and Mahr was in a different building entirely. So Betty and Kevin had many hours together while Mahr was so delighted that he had come out ahead in the first three throws of the dice and, like all addicts, he couldn't resist trying to duplicate those successes. Of course, he lost all that he had figured he'd lose except that it took four hours instead of one.

When he returned to their room to freshen up before dinner he found that Betty was already in the shower, softly singing a song that was out of date twenty years ago. Every two weeks, like clockwork, Betty, Mahr and Kevin enjoyed a week-end at the Trump Palace but Mahr didn't know about Kevin being there.

Time passes quickly when you're having fun and six months elapsed before you can realize that you are now six months older and looking it. One day, in the middle of the week, Kevin showed up at the Ginzburgh "palatzio." His excuse? He felt that he wanted to see his old friends, that's all. Actually he had the hots for Betty and that set up a whole situation in which Mahr, for the first time, was exposed to the sexual interplay that he had avoided noticing before. Of course, he didn't say anything about this. He quietly figured it would go away if he didn't exacerbate the affair.

After all, he was now a man of nearly seventy, not the man he used to be and Betty had a right, if she wanted it, to live her own life. He didn't like the situation but he figured he'd wait a while before acting. The couple, Kevin and Betty, decided to take a ride in Kevin's new car without inviting Mahr. Of course they would go to a nearby motel and spend a few hours. This happened every week from then on. Mahr waited for the affair to cool off to indifference.

One Wednesday Kevin showed up as usual. Mahr thought it unusual when Betty asked Mahr to please sit out on the patio, which for some reason had a tarp on it. Mahr figured that Betty had finally gotten so tired of him and so excited by Kevin that she was about to do to him what they had done to Fish. Since Mahr *had* had *to do something* to satisfy himself that he was protecting his own interests, one day, while Kevin and Betty were at a motel, Mahr went to see his lawyer and accountant in Manhattan. He stripped Betty from his will, leaving her just the house but leaving a note for the district attorney telling him about the bodies under the bushes. That's all he did to protect himself. Of course Kevin thought that whenever Betty became a widow she would be a widow with millions of dollars.

So Mahr dutifully sat on the patio with the tarp beneath his chair and knew that if Betty was as good a shot as usual he would feel no pain and just go to heaven with all his money. He knew that Kevin was sitting somewhere on the patio watching how Betty dispatched her husband and then Kevin and Betty would transplant some of the bushes late at night, as usual. Because there was a silencer on that pistol and he was also dreadfully hard of hearing, Mahr knew that he would hear practically nothing.

When he figured Betty was pretty close behind him, and because he knew the timing of this procedure pretty well, he spoke gently to her. "If you look slowly to your left you will see that Betty has a .38 caliber pistol with a silencer which she will use to sever your spinal cord without injuring the large arteries in your neck. As you know, this is done with surgical precision." He waited for Betty to pull the trigger on the word "surgical". He slowly turned towards Betty and saw that Kevin was lying dead, on the floor behind him.

And Betty was lying, dead, right behind Kevin. Apparently, she had committed a murder and suicide. Mahr called 911 and burst into tears. *He had never expected that!*

(There is not a word of truth in this story.)

HANS

This is a story that I haven't told before for several very good reasons. But, now that Hans has passed on, I think I should tell it. First of all there are four, or more, bodies that have to be accounted-for and I am not entirely sure who did these killings. I always believed in "first-suspicions," but I am not certain that Hans did them. Let's see whether you are as sure about your suspicions.

I knew Hans and spent many a day and evening in his home before his wife passed away. He gave up his home and lived with one of his daughters. That is where I found Hans to be a source of information about the holocaust. Some of the data he gave me was confidential. I will allude to that data here but let you make up your own mind in how much he was involved.

When Hans was ten years old his father and mother had just had enough of Hitler and the Nazi approach to government and decided to leave Koln (Cologne), Germany, as soon as possible. You just don't walk away from a place without planning the whole bit in advance. Hans' father was a very successful "junk" dealer. He had considerable property with several trucks and automobiles—a large establishment that he had to sell. And he owned his own home, which he had to sell. He had to make arrangements to go to America and be sure that the whole family was acceptable to the US government. He had to arrange tickets for a steamship (in Spain) on a certain date.

Hans' Dad had to know what to do with his fortune, which was considerable, and not let the Nazis in on the deal. He and his wife had to take some cash with them to France and then to Spain and then to the United States. Heinrich knew that his family would have more security, after ages living in Germany, if he established a bank account waiting for them at their future home. This was done so that they would not be paupers and have to depend on someone else's "charity".

All these things were planned and executed in advance by Heinrich Rozen. So on a Thursday morning, in May 1939, the Rozen family left their home in Koln and took their places in a truck which Heinrich and Betty had fixed up for the occasion. There were seats for the children, Hans, Rosalie(eight) and Kurt(six). There was, of course, enough food for breakfasts, lunches and dinners, if necessary, for three or four days, an emergency "potty", and three mattresses. Heinrich had figured it would take a day and a half or two to reach the Spanish border, having their dinners at various restaurants on the way, and then they could make it to the port in Spain within a day or two. A German orderliness was in Heinrich who had two spare tires and all the tools that he would need to repair anything on the truck, which was practically new.

They made it in the planned day and a half to within five miles of the Spanish border. Heinrich and Betty and the three kids were going to stay at a small hotel on the way to Spain.

They all entered the hotel and the man at the desk asked, "Do you have your license with you?"

Heinrich produced his license, which told the owner of the hotel that the name of the family was Rozen, a Jewish name. "I cannot let you stay at this hotel and you cannot eat at our restaurant. You know why!"

The wife of the owner held her nose as though there was a very bad odor coming from the Rozens.

Heinrich then said, "Of course we don't want to stay at any place that is so unfriendly, but I resent having your wife hold her nose as though we had some bad smell. We bathe every day and are probably cleaner than you are!" And he took his family to the truck and parked it across the street.

It was while the Rozens were eating dinner that a couple of French policemen came by, heavily armed. They roughly dragged Heinrich and Betty out of the truck and then came after the children. Hans, who was tall and well-built for his age was very athletic (in fact he had extremely powerful hands all his life) and didn't give the men a chance to lay hands on him. The entire family stood outside the truck and were very respectful.

The first policeman (he was a Captain in that area) stated, in a very harsh tone, "We understand you were nasty to the hotel owner and his wife. That's not the way we behave in France!"

Heinrich replied, being careful not to irritate the Captain, "We were refused service because we are Jewish. The woman held her nose as though we smelled bad. I told her we bathe every day."

"I have a good mind to give you a taste of this gun for being so fresh to a Frenchwoman!"

Heinrich was aghast and his tone of voice reflected that shock, "We have reservations on a ship to go to America. Please, if we have offended someone we are sorry and apologize. Can we please finish our meal and if you please, tell us where we can park for the night."

"I don't like your attitude"...and with his automatic rifle he shot Heinrich, Betty, Kurt and Rosalie to death. Hans ran to the woods behind the hotel and disappeared. Nobody knew that he had been within earshot of the house. After an hour or two the policemen and the owner and his wife gave up the search. "He'll come out when he's hungry!" said the owner of the hotel.

"I'll be nearby in case you need me." said the Captain.

"It is very comforting to have a captain of the police in the very next house." said the owner's wife. "We appreciate what you have done to rid the neighborhood of these criminals."

It was around ten o'clock at night when the Captain decided to go to bed. He had heard a scratching sound outside his front door, so, taking his automatic weapon he opened the door to investigate. That was his big mistake. Someone slipped a length of clothesline around his neck and quietly strangled him to death.

The same thing happened to the owner of the hotel, who was strangled the same way. The wife of the owner was strangled while she was at the stove making a cup of tea. She didn't even know that there was someone in the house.

Hans lived in the woods in France for several years, until the end of the war in Europe. He grew taller and stronger on whatever food he was able to scrounge from various kitchens. He was almost twelve years old but was a hefty five foot nine inches tall; all solid muscle.

Hans ultimately found a camp in the north of France that was primarily a place for homeless children...orphans, really...that was run by a charity in the United States. The great war was over and the Europeans had to make a power arrangement that would get rid of the possibility of war again for good. It took about fifty years for the Russians to agree to do this, but one has to have reservations about the British. They were as guilty in starting that war as anybody. They simply would not join with France and Germany in establishing a fast union!

Of all the people available, Hans was the least likely to assume a position of leadership. But that is exactly what happened! Hans took naturally to the job of leader of the young people in that camp. His great strength led to an aura of gentle power. Hans was a natural-born leader! He protected the weak and innocent among the youngsters against the natural 'operators' who thrive in our society. He was exceedingly popular and no one would believe he was only twelve years old. He had grown to almost six feet tall and was exceedingly strong.

His firm "grip" was the method Hans used to establish his power. All he had to do was "shake hands" with the men who were employed around the camp to inform them that there was a powerful phenomenon on the premises. It would take a dim-wit to attempt to compete with Hans.

One evening one of the men decided to take the services of one of the prettiest minors amongst the members of this group of children. The only thing he did wrong was to fail to have her permission. He used the total darkness of the camp to grab this beauty and attempt to rape her. She was prevented from calling for help by his scarf, which was stuffed in her mouth.

Suddenly, while she was struggling against what seemed like a losing cause, someone grabbed the rapist by the throat and pulled him off the girl. Within seconds the man was strangled--dead--and whoever it was who strangled him pulled the scarf out of her mouth. No one knew who did this killing. Most people would suspect Hans because only he was that strong. Whoever it was, it established the fact that unwanted sex was forbidden at that camp. The camp was now safer than it had been before. The man was allowed to lie where he was for two days as an example to the other men.

Hans ultimately came to New York, where some distant relatives took him in hand. He had since discovered that the banks that his father had sent all that money to didn't know anything about that money! Would you believe that? (If I mention their names, and I know them since Hans told me his story, I could be sued!)

So Hans was now a pauper, which he never been in his normal life. He was totally reliant upon his relatives. He attended the public schools, through high school. Of course he took on a job and earned enough for his "keep". He also got work, for his working lifetime, when he was eighteen years old.

Hans found a job that made use of his large hands and powerful grip. He found employment in the garment industry where he became a "cutter". This job requires a steady hand and considerable strength because you had to hold, in a firm grip, as many as fifteen or twenty pieces of fabric and use the razor-sharp blades of the cutting-machine to cut all those pieces precisely.. Of course there was an advantage for the manufacturer to cutting fifteen or twenty items at the same time instead of five or ten. Hans earned a sufficient sum to retire at the age of sixty or so.

Now it is proper to mention the lady he married at the age of twenty-two. This is an important story for me because I assume it is the truth: mostly because Hans told me these stories himself. It is also interesting in its own right because, true or not, it is exciting. And it confirms one of my particularly prejudicial opinions, which is that the major cause of Alzheimer's disease is a traumatic mental experience early in one's life. I'm not talking about love-affairs or disappointments about getting into the school of your choice.

I refer to the type of experience that Hans went through or that my wife, Janice, went through when she lost her mother on our honeymoon. Essie (Jan's mother) was the alter-ego of Janice; Jan never made a move without her Mom's okay. She was not as mature as we had thought. She was too dependent on Essie. When Essie died, Jan was left all alone to deal with marriage and the acquisition of a new family and all the responsibilities of a new life. She handled it okay but it cost her a piece of life. She really needed her mother. A lifetime later she told a neurologist, as soon as he walked into the room, "I lost my mother on my honeymoon!" *Fifty years after the fact!* Jan and Hans ultimately died of Alzheimer's disease.

Anyhow, Hans met Florence in a relative's house. Florence was a particularly attractive woman (she was a native of France) who had gone through the holocaust as a kind of heroine. The trauma of those experiences took its toll on Florence's life as well as Hans. She died relatively early of a heart attack. She must have been in her early sixties!

Her parents had died in a concentration camp. I don't know which one. Florence escaped being in such a camp because she and one of her sisters were at school when the Nazis came to the house and took their parents away. She went from home to home with all their friends and relatives but the Jews were in a state of flux and there was a great deal of nervous tension in those homes. Her sister (older by about six years) had married a German man and she wouldn't take Florence into her house even for one night --or a meal--because she was afraid that the Nazis would find a Jewess there! Ultimately her married sister *was* taken to a concentration camp with her husband and murdered. But it was not because of anything that Florence had done. It was a Nazi law that forbade marriage to a Jew!

Ultimately, Florence got to stay with a Catholic family who risked life and limb to take care of this pretty, young Jewish girl. They hid her, gave her food and treated her like a member of their family. To this day every time one of Florence's granddaughters visits France (every year!) they visit this Catholic family.

Florence, when she came to America, she stayed with relatives and went to school. She ultimately taught "English as a Second Language" at a high school in Brooklyn. She and Hans had three children who all went to college and have interesting careers. But this story is basically about Hans and I have to pick it up when he reached his "seventies."

When Hans reached about seventy-two he had two fatal conditions: Alzheimer's and Parkinson's diseases. His eldest daughter and her husband, with the acquiescence of Hans' other children, put Hans into the best nursing-home in Cherry Hill, New Jersey, because they both worked at very demanding jobs. Hans considered the place to be like a Nazi prison. He always thought the employees were vicious and anti-social, but that may all have been in his head. They had no idea how heroic his past was. He did not seem to have a single pleasant day in that nursing-home. We do not know what images go through the mind of a person with Alzheimer's Disease, especially one who had gone through the horrors of the holocaust.

Hans and Florence had one son and two daughters. His son was named Henry, after his Hans' father, Heinrich. Henry was a dead-ringer for Heinrich. He looked just like Heinrich and had the same build and posture: and the same gigantic power in his arms and hands. But Henry had an ego that was not entirely reasonable. When he would visit Hans in the nursing-home Hans did not seem to remember him. He would call Henry "Papa!" or "Heinrich". Hans thought that Henry was his father! Henry would not go to see Hans any more. He never put two and two together. Hans was trying, sub-consciously to renew his father's life which the Nazis had taken away from him but Henry's ego took over.

When I first heard that story I asked Hans who had been brought to his daughter's house for the Holidays, if he remembered me. He was quick to reply, "Of course! You are my friend Ed." So his failure to remember Henry was entirely psychological.

One day one of the male nurses seemed to be having particular difficulties with another of the patients at that nursing-home. He became violent towards that patient and was in the act of crippling him. That's when someone intervened and started to strangle the nurse. No one knows who it was. Hans was now wheel-chair-bound, but someone with super-strength in his hands tore into the throat of that male nurse and would have killed him but, whoever it was, relented and didn't take the life of the nurse and also saved the life of the patient. The nurses at that institution were very careful not to carry their "techniques" too far from that time on.

Hans died this spring. I knew that he suffered from more than Alzheimer's and Parkinson's diseases. He suffered from the Nazi attitude towards the Jews, which is still the rule in many countries. He suffered from being driven out of his home-land. He suffered from the cruelty of the world, particularly the German and French and Russian and Polish and Muslim people. He suffered from the historical inability of the world to live in peace.

Hans was a gentle man with tremendous physical strength. He was a social man who loved his family and was deeply loved by all who knew him.

But he had unusual courage and bravado.

What do *you* think? Did Hans do all those strangulations?

THIS IS A NORMAL LIFE

I

What is a normal life, anyhow? I'm beginning to have second thoughts about it now. Of course everything that happens in my presence is not my fault but why am I so frequently in the presence of tragedy or near-tragedy? My parents brought us all up to abhor violence. Just listen to the next few examples in this story and you will see what I mean by "tragedy".

When Jan and I had been married about thirty-seven years we lived in an apartment on the West Side of Manhattan overlooking Central Park. It wasn't all that expensive since the owners had in mind selling those apartments to us or some other suckers at a really exorbitant price. It was probably because I was quite verbal in my refusal to sign any documents that the landlord put forth that the other tenants elected me to become Chairman of the Tenants' Committee, just as, when we finally bought our apartments, that they elected me Chairman of The Owners' Committee. For the least wealthy of all the owners I became the biggest "big-shot" of them all. Maybe I had the largest mouthpiece of them all!

Our next-door neighbor a single young man who had a pretty girl-friend and spent very little time in his apartment was a very bright young man. He was already, by the age of about thirty-two, a PhD in economics and he was also a Bachelor of Law. He received all his degrees from Harvard and had an enviable job as the advisor and alter-ego of the senior Senator from New York State, Jacob Javits. As such, he toured the world gathering as much information as Senator Javits thought he needed to represent the business interests and the common citizens on the world stage.

On speaking with David several times I learned how important knowledge of law economics and history is to "big business." This young man, I figured, had a great future. Although he was Jewish, as was Senator Javits, the position of Justice of the Supreme Court of the United States was not too high a goal for him; ultimately.

And so, one day about twenty-five years ago, David went to Europe and the Middle East on behalf of his boss. He must have been a huge success in Europe because he unexpectedly flew back to Washington to consult with the Senator and some business people to tell them what he had accomplished for them. Then he flew, on El Al, directly to Israel and Turkey, where he duplicated his successful mission to Europe. On the way back, it was while he was waiting in line at the El Al office at the airport in Istanbul, of all places, that some terrorists exploded a suicide-bomb killing six or eight individuals, including, of course, our wonderful young man. ,

All the tenants in our building were in varying degrees of shock at the news. About two weeks later an older lady, David's mother, who obviously had the keys to his ten-room apartment, was busy throwing out all his possessions. Now there is something about some people that bugs me! She was very religious, so why didn't she want anything at all to remind her of that wonderful young man? She even threw out all his letters and many pictures of David. It was when I went to the "service elevator" to dispose of some of our own trash that I saw her again.

"Are you really throwing out those brand new golf-clubs?" I asked her incredulously.

"What else should I do with them?" she retorted. "If you want them, take them!" she continued. " I don't think my son ever used them!"

So, later on, I took that brand new set of Calloway golf clubs, without that brand new golf-bag. They didn't help my game one bit. It's not the equipment, you know, that is most important for playing a good game of golf. *It's what goes on in your head that ruins your game!* But what I *did* take, in addition in those clubs, was a very long, interestingly carved ivory shoe-horn, which I have used to put my shoes on for the past twenty-five years! It all may seem kinda grubby to you, but it's the only time I ever took something from someone else's trash.

II

During World War II there were many occasions when violence, inhumanity and inconceivable destruction occurred and I was a witness to much of it. Of course, in a war you expect such things. That is what we were taught. We could not mourn and become useless due to our grief just because even close friends had died in combat. Strangely enough, this is by way of an introduction to my next little story.

After we had defeated the Japanese forces on Guadalcanal we were taken by ship to the Fiji Islands where we were ordered to get some much-needed rest and rehabilitation. We changed our top leadership and added a large influx of fresh troops. We also went through a modernization of our uniforms and our military equipment. After all, we were the first troops who had seen action since World War One and we were still using the old Springfield '03's (rifles dating to 1914-17)! By the time I reached the 'Canal they had actually swapped our WW I helmets for the typical WW II helmets, which you already know about. We had fought on Guadalcanal using khaki's and were glad to get camouflage clothes for the next combat. We didn't get our Garand rifles until we had been on Guadalcanal for about six months! We used the old Spingfield rifles dating to 1915. (Talk about being unprepared for a war!) The Marines stole our Garands from Headquarters Company and left their old Springfields! War *is* hell!

Finally, after about eight months on Fiji, we were deemed well-enough trained to be able to make a landing without needing the Marines to help us. Our next target was another of the Solomon Islands, the large Island of Bougainville. So they piled our whole

Division on a cluster of LSI's ("Landing Ships Infantry"), which were not the epitome of comfort. These ships were all brand new and suffered from frequent breakdowns and the problems of all new vehicles, land, sea or air.

We then tried to outsmart the Japanese submarines by weaving around in semi-circles and took forever to reach our *preliminary* destination, the island of New Guinea. Let me tell you, very briefly, about the island of New Guinea. That is definitely one of the scariest islands in the world! There are always black clouds over the Eastern half of that piece of real-estate! To me, a perpetually black sky is an omen of danger. If you want to know about the natives: they were out-and-out savages—but I mean almost like Neanderthals!

We anchored outside the port of Finchhaven, which is a moderately-sized city on the East coast of the island. We had stopped for about eight or ten hours, to load up on fresh water and food, which were in short supply on Fiji and, of course, on Bougainville, which is where we were to make our next landing.

A few of us wanted to go ashore, just for the heck of it. I had just been promoted to Captain and wanted to flash those silver bars to any native girls who wanted to look at them. A few of us were permitted to go ashore but with the proviso that we make some semi-official mission of it. We were told that it was doubtful if there were any Japanese in the area, but to wear our helmets at all times, to take our weapons and, "For God's sake, don't do anything to stir up trouble!"

We went ashore on several launches, about forty of us, and were in groups of ten. We were supposed to walk through about a mile of Kunai grass (grass that grows to a height of seven to eight feet, or more) until we came to a native village which, they said, was entirely friendly. Then we were supposed to have lunch there and return to our ships. The whole excursion was not to take more than four hours. A cinch! A pleasure! And we were not to expect any trouble, except of our own making!

There were about fifteen or sixteen soldiers who preceded us in the file of men taking this almost invisible through the Kunai grass. We were in single file because the trail was so narrow. Those who know me best are aware that I have difficulty being quiet for an hour continuously, so you have to know that I kept up an almost constant barrage of jokes and stories with the soldier who preceded me in the file.

He was, believe it or not, the only Jewish second lieutenant in Headquarters company. His name, for some psychological reason (although I swear I remembered it until I started to write this article) eludes me at this moment. He was one of the replacements for the National Guard men who had to be replaced because of wounds, death or psychoneurosis. He was about twenty-one years old and already had a bachelor's degree from Rutgers University. As a matter of fact, this young man was a perfect foil for my jokes and stories, since he usually demonstrated an interest in my stories and flashed a sweet smile, revealing perfect teeth and lots of pink gums. By the way, in those days we were able to walk quite quickly without becoming out of breath and without getting tired. I wish I could walk that way now!

We had just about exhausted the subject of Rutgers being a premier school in New Jersey for pre-law or pre-politics when Marty (*That* was his name!) suddenly tumbled to the ground. I was on the verge of making some kind of joke about people who cannot even walk straight, when it occurred to me that there was something peculiar in the way he fell to the ground. He seemed to have jerked backwards before he crumbled in a heap. When I reached his side (in a second or two) and tried to lift his head a little I noticed the blood pouring out of his body. He was dead before he hit the ground! Someone had shot Marty to death by hitting him in one of the few areas that no surgeon in the world could have repaired for him: the throat. Marty was gone!

When the others, a few steps behind us, came to our side they all remarked, "We didn't hear any shots!!" and "Who could have done this? No one could even see us on this trail! The grass is so high!" I couldn't believe that a silent shot had killed my friend right in front of me!

This was death so sudden that it made us consider our own mortality. If someone could nail Marty so noiselessly what chance did we have that we could survive? Years later I read a book by a previously unknown author, Norman Mailer, in which the writer described just such an event, where a soldier loses a buddy to a similar "stray shot" that seemed to be directed towards that one man. That story, "The Naked and the Dead", told of sudden death that was a replica of the shock and disturbance that engulfed our entire group on New Guinea. There is no doubt in my mind that Mailer had to have had a similar experience somewhere in combat. Once was enough for me.

We never did find out where that shot came from, although our top officers were more annoyed than disturbed by the event. We were just going to be on that island for another few hours and the last thing they wanted was to launch an "investigation". I always thought that some hot-shot soldier ahead of us had simply let out a burst from his automatic weapon into the Kunai grass, not even thinking about the people behind him on the trail. He's lucky that he didn't get *me!!*

III

This next brief story is likewise true, the same as the two tales that precede it. As a matter of fact, I have come to the conclusion that, regardless of how ordinary my life has been, you too, and everybody else lives through the same kind of excitement and frustration, but you just never think about things enough to write these experiences down; that's all.

For instance, who cares about the fact that I am a "Reformed" Jew and haven't been to a strictly orthodox synagogue more than twenty times in my entire life? Who cares that I am a "liberal" Democrat ever since I was old enough to distinguish between political parties? Anyhow, these two aspects of my life have everything to do with my awareness of the utter violence and hatefulness of an event that took place just a few years ago.

It was in West Orange, New Jersey, a pleasant enough town, that I continued with my liberal leanings as I attended one community meeting after another of various committees that had to do with education, voting, social responsibility and other aspects of community life that interested me. One of the people sitting near me at this particular meeting honoring the new Superintendent of Schools was a tall, dignified man who seemed to share my views: at least he clapped his hands at the same time that I did and groaned in dismay whenever I did too. When the meeting was over I leaned over towards him and said, "You look familiar to me. Aren't you a member of the Conservative Synagogue of Livingston, on Livingston Avenue?"

"No," he replied, "I admire their Rabbi, who is very intellectually inclined, but we belong to the deeply Orthodox synagogue just down the street here on Pleasant Valley Way. We must know each other from one of the other groups that meet in town here. We are quite active in politics because we have a couple of children and we want this to be the best township for them to grow up in." And that was that. We saw each other again and again at other meetings but never seemed to find another occasion to converse. However, there was something to be admired about that man and I decided that, just once, if I could find the time, I would visit his synagogue on a Sabbath and see what he found in orthodoxy that was so great.

A few weeks later I found time on a Saturday morning to visit at his temple. Actually, I did not like their old-world ambiance and what I thought was a regressive stance that was true orthodoxy. I've been wrong in my life, on occasion. This might have been one of those occasions, but I did get to see that man and his family. They did not sit together, as we do in all other sects of Judaism. The women and the girls sat in another section of the temple: they sat "upstairs"and the males sat "downstairs".

When the Service ended the females came "downstairs" and met the male members of their family. The gentleman whom I had met at several meetings had a charming family: a very attractive wife and two daughters, one a gorgeous teenager. I was about to introduce myself to his family but could not, in good conscience, find a satisfactory reason for such a move. That is the second mistake I made that morning, because I would have learned then that the teenager was leaving in about two weeks on a tour of Israel, with a group of other teenagers. This became important only when I learned (weeks later) that this girl was killed in a terrorist attack in Israel!

There is now a street named for that girl; the next street after the corner on which her synagogue stands. She was very pretty, very charming and socially very popular.

You see, there is something terrible going on in our world today. Anybody who differs from certain Muslim sects is an *infidel* and must be destroyed! That's how it is these days and no one dares to implement an effective counter-measure to such madness. In truth, there are more than one billion, six hundred million Muslims!

How would you fight with an eight-hundred-pound gorilla? *Very carefully!*

IV

This last little vignette is the most painful tale I have ever told—and what is so sad is that it is an honest story; it really happened to me. This is another "war story" It happened on the island of Cebu, in the Philippines. I had been, as told you in another story, promoted to be the Division Dental Surgeon of the Americal Division before we left Bougainville and I had settled in with all the unpolished brass that the Army could offer. We managed by dint of some heroics by our GI's to move further inland to what I thought, in my ignorance, was a safe area. After all, there had not been any shooting in the area we were occupying.

We were to spend the next two or three nights, possibly a week, in this area so Headquarters Company GI's began putting barbed-wire all around the compound. Actually there was a little stream running along the northwest segment of our encampment and I was assigned to sleep in a foxhole (which I had to dig) right near the edge of that stream, which I thought was "just lovely".

My anticipation of a terrific night of rest was totally spoiled when the Major in charge of the layout of our defenses told me that I was a part of the *perimeter* of our defenses and another GI was ordered to put his foxhole close to mine so that we could "spell" each other for the hours of sleep we were supposed to get. He would be awake and observant for two hours and then I would be "on guard" for the next two hours, all through the night and day. Apparently we were short of men to take over such duties. It seems that the resistance of the Japanese in that area had over-taxed our resources.

You may wonder why that night-time duty was so onerous to me. Well, first of all, I am not the most heroic person in the world. And then there were the very large frogs (I didn't know about them when I got that assignment) which kept jumping in and out of that water, all night long, which made me think (all terrible night long!) that those sounds were the Japanese infantry sneaking up on us. May I utter a frightened "Oy, vay!" at this juncture?

Dawn took a long time in arriving. It seemed, actually, like a thirty-six hour night. But as dreadful as that seemed to me it was really routine to the average GI. However, the next night has bothered me for over sixty years. *Nothing* has ever been as dreadful as what occurred the second night we were in that area.

As I have already mentioned, the first thing the GI's did when the campsite perimeter was established was to put up the barbed-wire everywhere except where there was water. I cannot imagine why that shallow stream with the frogs was considered a sufficient deterrent for a determined infantryman of the Shintoist persuasion. But starting about twenty-five or thirty yards from where I had my foxhole the barbed-wire began. There were soldiers every five yards in foxholes and everyone was cautioned "not to get out of your foxhole for any reason whatsoever during the night-time hours. Keep your head down, don't expose any part of your body unless there is a fire-fight." Certainly, *this soldier,* this misplaced dental nerd, had no intention of sticking his head, arms or fanny anywhere near the surface of that foxhole. The earth was very soft and it didn't take too much digging to prepare a tidy little grave for one. By the way, the moon was covered by some treacherous clouds, which made our situation chancier..

At about twelve o'clock midnight, when I was just starting my second shift on the watch, there were some shots from somewhere 'out yonder' that began to come into our compound. Were they really from the Nips or were they mistakenly directed by an American force in the same general direction? That has happened too often, as everyone knows. Suddenly there was a pronounced rustling about seventy-five yards from me. GI's rose from their foxholes and turned on such a vicious counter fire that one had to wonder if anyone could live through that. The Japanese firing ceased altogether. A few minutes later, one of our GI's walked from his foxhole. He apparently wanted to check on the security of the barbed-wire. Was that wire continuous or was there a space sufficient for one or more Nips to slip through? At that moment, one of those treacherous clouds moved from the moon exposing him to full view.

Suddenly there came a burst of small arms fire from the Japanese, enough to wound that poor soldier severely. He was simply unlucky to have fallen forward, onto the barbed wire—and just hung there. The Japanese didn't fire at him anymore. They just let him hang there. Apparently he was wounded seriously enough to be unable to detach himself from the wire. There was not a soldier alive anywhere nearby who did not peek over the edge of his foxhole to gauge whether or not *he* would be able to rescue that poor kid on the wire. You'd think that the Japanese would yell–in English–"we'll hold our fire–get that kid off the wire!" But they never did that. Several of our men, including my immediate commanding officer, yelled to the Japanese, in English, "Let us get that soldier off the wire! Cease firing for a few minutes. We'll use a white flag!" But there was no answer.

For the next three hours that youngster hung on the wire, moaning and crying. After some time he got much weaker and less assured that he would survive. Every once in a while the Japanese would use their automatic weapons as "grass-cutters" to make sure that we were going to stay in our foxholes. Then the wounded soldier began calling for his Mother and Dad for help. From then on we knew he was out of his mind from pain and fear. If we could have seen where the enemy was I know that any number of men would have put a crushing burst of fire on them so that the medics could go out with some wire-cutters and free that kid. But that didn't happen early enough. Everyone who was near enough to hear his cries was consumed with feelings of guilt, as though anyone could have helped him.

At about five-thirty A.M. his cries ended. Daylight was just approaching and our commander gave orders to pour a terrific barrage in the direction the Japanese were supposed to lie. While that barrage was going on the medics did indeed bring that youngster to safety, but too late. His body, I understand, was still warm and supple, but his life had vanished. And so had the Japanese. When a contingent was sent out to evaluate the situation they found evidence that only a few Nips had been involved and that, in fact, if we had taken a riskier course, we could have saved that young man. But once more, intelligence was lacking as to the number and disposition of the enemy and tragedy was the result.

When I had written this last story it was just before lunch and I thought that Janice and her caretaker, Sylvia, would like to hear it. When I finished reading the manuscript I suddenly burst into tears. Apparently I did not realize that the accumulative effect of all four of these little tales which I had actually lived through could affect me that way. Also the fact that my wife who has Alzheimer's and did not react at all to the stories was one more reason to cry. All-in-all, although my life did not seem so sad to me while I was living through all these zany experiences, the totality of all this madness just got to me.

THE GREAT FLOOD
Written by Chung Sho

This is the year 9,556. A great many people have written to us to get a better idea of the great floods of the past and we have responded by providing this listing of the articles concerning that world-wide flood.

There was, thousands of years ago, (actually 7,003 years ago) considerable concern that the vast ice-packs that covered the North and South poles would melt and lead to tremendous floods on all the islands of all the oceans and on all the lowlands that lay on the shores of all the oceans of the world.

There are *two floods* that we must consider. *The first one (the Great Flood of Mankind's history)* an intense melting of as many as seven miles of thickness of ice that had formed on a large portion of the Earth that occurred after the great ice age that ended approximately twenty thousand years ago. This melting was accompanied by what many folks would consider excessive volcanic activity and earthquakes in response to the shifting of the weighty pressures on the tectonic plates of this planet.

The second flood occurred as a melting of the *residual ice and snow* of the polar areas, with all the consequent rains (which lasted approximately six hundred and seventy-six years). Earthquakes, volcanoes, intense winds and tsunamis resulted from the changes of the interior of the earth because of the alterations in pressure over the tectonic plates that lie beneath the ground and was the finale of the previous ice age. This melting and these geologic and meteorologic incidents **occurred late in the *second millennium,* Anno Domini (approximately seven thousand five hundred years ago**).

How do we know that such floods actually took place? First of all, there is a well-substantiated history of ice ages on this Planet and the consequent melting of all that ice, which has to lead to thousands of years of flooding of the lowlands of the Earth. Secondly, we have evidence, if it can be called that, of the reactions of people (mostly primitive people) who experienced those inundations, with the intense rains and the severe weather conditions. *Most of these primitive folks had ridiculous conceptions of what caused these changes in the geology and the meteorology of this planet.* But, regardless of the causes they gave, the fact that they all wrote about these floods at relatively the same time has to be given serious attention.

We know that there are several oceans on this planet: the Atlantic ocean, the Arctic Ocean, the Pacific ocean, the Indian Ocean, the American Sea, separating the three sections of the North American continent, and the Mediterranean Sea, covering that area between North Africa and Asia.

There have been studies concerning the "previous "locations of the North and South poles. Those studies have our present South pole over the once tropical islands of the Pacific (The Fiji Islands) and carried over to the Southern end of Africa. The North pole is now located over northwestern China and northern Canada, with portions of the Arctic ocean also involved, according to the most recent studies. The previous North Polar area was over the Arctic Ocean and the South Pole was somewhere on the present Cold Land, which I understand was called the continent of Antarctica.

The following is an example of a few of the articles that have survived the flooding of the previous lowlands all over the world and the steps the natives of those lands took to deal with the geological and meteorological problems they faced. Not one of the continents has been eliminated: Asia, Europe, North and South

America, Africa, the Cold Land and the newest continent of all, Australia.

Of course when you read these articles you will understand what we think is very primitive. The beliefs of the world's population and the steps they took to deal with these acts of Nature are to be believed only if you suspend your intellect for a few moments. Moreover, this listing of articles is not complete. There are actually articles for the whole world. We (the Editors) decided that we would write about those articles that are most convincing that floods actually took place. We could not find any articles that could prove that those floods did **not** actually occur. *The flood that **these** articles refer to was at the tail-end of the last ice age,* involving the final melting of the vast amount of snow and ice at the former North and South poles, due to a combination of forces. It took place late in the second millenium, Anno Domini.

We would appreciate your responding to us by advanced ESP (Extra Sensory Perception) or by any other means of personal contact.

GENESIS
Written by Chu En Salaam

Many religious people *and most of the evolved persons* believe that a flood actually happened as recorded in Genesis and a multitude of documents from every country in the world. *This major flood ended approximately twenty thousand years ago.* The first cause of these floods is the natural, recurring history of this planet, It seems there is an ice age every 1,000,000 years When these ice ages melt there is a gigantic flood of epic proportions, just as when there is a maximum period within each ice age there is a withdrawing of so much water (to make all that ice) that the ocean bottoms are revealed along the coastlines of all the shores on this planet. *This withdrawal of water would reveal all the cities that were built-up to modernity,* places that were occupied for many centuries and then were re-inundated. To be built up and then to be inundated by an uncaring Mother Nature is a story in itself. The history of the Earth is much more complex than we would imagine.

Think of the billions of human beings that have been sacrificed to such a schedule of eternal change! Think of the animals and plant varieties that have been drowned....or frozen to death! *If there is a Deity Who cares* (and is responsible for these tragedies) He, She or It has a different plan than we would have.

It is only natural for there to be as many myths and tales as there are natives who were given such a rough treatment. The Gilgamesh flood myth which inspired a multitude of flood myths in every religion that we know about has obviously had its origins in the last ice age, which finally ended in about the year 2070 with a bang and with inundation of much of this planet.

We currently are in the status of being in the preliminaries of another ice age, with a partially-iced North and South Pole and ice-sheets over a portion of China and northern Canada as well as the Southern-most areas of Africa and some "tropical" islands in the South Pacific area.

FLOOD MYTHS IN VARIOUS CULTURES
Written by Chu En Salaam, Director of Antiquities

This is a listing by countries of the causes of the floods and the "suspected" causes of the extreme rains that were supposed to have occurred many millenia ago. They were actually written in reaction to the Great Flood but the subsequent floods, knowing how primitive people still are, are similar in content to those letters written in reaction to the **Great Flood.**

Actually, geologists and meteorologists have claimed that since the Arctic and Antarctic waters were deprived of their icy components there was a drastic change in the worldwide weather. The warmer streams in the oceans such as the Gulf Stream and the Humbolt Currents would have been much cooler due to the melting of the polar ice but they were still much warmer due to submarine volcanic action. That led to an indescribable intensity of rain. Such rains for many hundreds of years had to lead to vast floods

Many of the remaining residents of these countries claim that a deity, or a combination of deities, destroyed civilization as an act of retribution for some sinful behavior on the part of the residents of these countries. (Guilt is a ploy among most of the world's religions but to create guilt for nature's actions is sticking it in a bit!) Among certain people there still remains a 'personal aspect' of the creative process that formed the universe. Religions have always prided themselves on their ability to create feelings of guilt, without which you can have no religion. Some people take literally forever to be educated.

The means of "escape" from the severe inundation that apparently occurred very often was a vehicle of some sort. For instance they named a canoe, an ark, an airplane, a rowboat, a motor-boat, a horse and a mule (sic!), reeds, hollow trees, an automobile or a van, helicopters and various other devices that were too primitive to be useful.

Some mythologists claimed that rivers existed and other bodies of water that we never heard of. For instance did you ever hear of the Great Lakes and the Mississippi River? Did you ever hear of the Hudson River (or a city named New York?) or a State named New Jersey? or a State named Louisiana, or Texas? A map that we located from 2007 revealed all these places to us. The saddest was the State of Florida, (these are all in the *sophisticated* United States of America) that experienced entire inundation and had some vicious toothy monsters that were endemic to that "Paradise". Most of the world had these floods and seemingly endless rains and all kinds of earthquakes and severe geological shocks that destroyed as many as four billion "civilized" people and overwhelmed many islands and countries.

The letters quoted here are copies of those written in the **Great Flood,** the greatest that Mankind has ever seen. Knowing how primitive people still are these letters show how those people still react to natural disasters

The Earth Press, Asian Branch,
By Loo Kassim, the Middle East

Allah, in his impeccable wisdom, decided that he would rather have all his children come to Heaven at the same time so he created a great flood that destroyed the Infidel nation of Israel and also took the countries of Iraq, Iran, Abu Dabi, Libya, Lebanon, Nigeria, parts of Egypt, all of Syria, Kuwait, Jordan and Saudi Arabia. He also caused an inundation of much of Indonesia but those islands were united by volcanic eruption and earth movements to create an extension of the continent of Australia. Allah was displeased with the sinfulness of the Jews and the Christians and he couldn't find a way to drown all the Jews and Christians without drowning the Muslims at the same time. *But the Muslims wanted to die* so they welcomed Allah's procedures! (Did anyone mutter "Madness!" behind my back?)

The Earth Press

By Loo Kassim *Akkadian, the Atrahasis Epic*

This was the Babylonian (Iraqi) Epic. *Atrahasis* means, 'exceedingly wise,' Atrahasis gives overpopulation as the reason for the great flood. After 1200 years of human fertility, the god Enlil could not get a night's sleep due to the noise of the populace. He tried to get rid of the people by a series that included a plague, a drought, then a famine, then a saline soil. (That sounds like one of the episodes of Passover!) He could not get rid of mankind by these means until the gods decided that a flood would just about do it. Enki, the flood god, objected so they devised a survival vessel, very much like Noah's Ark. Enki then created new forces of society to keep the number of the populace under control. He created non-marrying women, barrenness, miscarriages, and infant mortality. It all sounds like Satan at work. Was Atrahasis exceedingly wise? (These inane procedures actually happened!)

The Earth Press

By Loo Kassim The Hebrews

The book of Genesis tells that God "Grieved in His heart" that "Man's sole intent was only evil continually" and decided to destroy the Earth and all the people on it. He chose Noah, who was very righteous, and told him how to build an Ark. After Noah had built the Ark and populated it with all the known animals and all the known human beings God created an immense flood. One year and ten days (one has to wonder about the time that such primitives had) from the beginning of the flood the ground was dry enough for the survivors to leave the Ark. This account was derived from the Sumerians who ruled Babylon once upon a time. They were a very creative and inventive people. Due to the influence of the

Hebrews, who were an important race at one time, this story of the great flood exerted a large influence.)

The Earth Press

By Ante Capri, Afghanistan,

Whereas this nation is not known for its changes, we understand that a World-wide deluge is referred to in times past normal recall. We have written records that in the year 2,070 (or there-about) a vast body of water from intense rainfall seems to have inundated all the low-lying lands even those that had no coastline and *also* the coasts of the entire earth. This flood was apparently the end of the ice age melt-down that officially ended 12,000 years previously.

The source of this water (year approximately 2070) seems be attributable to volcanic activity in the area of the South Pole, with the consequent melting of vast quantities of ice and snow. The warm ocean currents then melted the ice at the North Pole, which was an ocean of ice and snow. For the preceding hundred years a "warming effect" had been taking place leading to vast tectonic rearrangements. Large areas of this planet were inundated with an intense quantity of water with a consequent loss of life.

We were subject to a series of immense rainfalls which lasted, according to our records, 646 years! (One has difficulty believing this but there been so many letters describing the rainfall as 640 years why not believe it?). If that is to be believed, there would have been considerable flooding all over this planet. The consequent shortage of food water and other essentials, was responsible for an enormous loss of life.

The Earth Press

By Cho Nissan, Turkistan,

The Emperor, Shao Ji Nibrim, was washing his hands in a small stream near his castle, when a little goldfish told him that a tremendous flood would occur in this very stream and that he had best take his family and his staff to high grounds as soon as possible. The Emperor always believed what this little fish told him and took her advice. The only people in this particular area who survived the subsequent deluge were the royal family and their aides. For many years there was heavy rainfall and much flooding.

Only on the mountain-tops did people survive. The survivors traveled by helicopters!

The Earth Press,
European Branch,
By Alpha Numero, Greece,

The Ogyges, Platinum age, expired about fifteen thousand years ago: perhaps even longer ago than that. The Ogygian flood is named after a mythical king of Attica. His name is synonymous to "Mythical" or "Primeval." In many traditions the flood is said to have inundated the entire earth. These floods are recurring. It has been more than 20,000 years since there has been such a flood, according to Plato, in his Laws book III.

People who survived were left without rulers and without a regular source of food and water. The last preceding such flood occurred during the time preceding Solon, during the 10th millenium, BCE. This time would occur at the end of the last ice-age. We can expect another such flood in roughly one million years, if geologists and meteorologists are to be trusted.

The map for the preceding time to the accepted second flood would show that the coastal waters would be approximately 130 meters shallower (approximately 400 feet). It was very interesting investigating the areas 400 feet beneath the surface of the water all along the coasts of the Earth and in the "inland seas" in the North American and Mediterranean Seas. Those may have been the residences for a multitude of people. These geological findings may convince doubters to support the hypothesis that the Ogygian deluge may well be based on a real event.

The Earth Press
By Mani Dhongro, India

A President of India, named Manu, had a little fish which warned him that a great deluge would occur soon which would destroy all who could not hurry to the mountain tops. *This fish suddenly became very large and very strong and towed the boat which the President had in his home* (Italics because of the state of surprise of the author!) Not only the President was thus saved but also his entire family and some *"seeds of life"* to start a new life for everybody of consequence.

The Earth Press, Orient Branch
By Siki Chingso, China

Many folk myths have references to repair the broken heavens after a deluge that did not cease for 640 years which led to devastating floods all over the world. A goddess named Nuwa led the group in the repairs to the heavens. The Yellow River became a veritable sea due to this flooding and it is estimated that over a billion-and-a-half Chinese people lost their lives from the flood waters and the effects on agriculture and the food supply. Also, dysentery took many more lives because of the contamination of the drinking water. The people who survived traveled by horse(?)

Australia
The Earth Press
By Reginald Cho

Australian "primitives" tell the story of a huge frog who drank all the water in the world. The only way to correct this situation was to make the frog laugh. The eel was funnier than even *he* expected and the frog squinched his face in a spasm of laughter that was preceded by vast peals of thunder and lightning. The frog emitted vast quantities of water from his mouth and the water filled the deepest rivers and inundated the land; enough to drown millions of people and animals. The mountain-tops were the only places of refuge from this deluge which lasted 646 years.

The natives who survived did their escaping by automobile (?)

The Earth Press
By Heinz Chu, Germany

Frost Giants Biergson and his wife Brunhilda were murdered by the rulers of Saxony. The blood from the butchering of these Frost Giants created a deluge of blood that lasted well over 650 years (!) His descendants crawled into a hollow tree where they ultimately found other Frost Giants.

The Germans were known to have a penchant for blood-letting. There is a story that 6-8 million souls were murdered in a series of "camps" a long time ago. In a World War that ensued almost 20,000,000 more people lost their lives. (I ***believe*** this!)

The Earth Press
By Frank Nissan, Americas
Aztec

When the Sun Age finally arrived it was 676 years that we had of the deluge. The oceans and the skies drew near to one another. All was lost except in the highest mountain-peaks. Even Emilio and his wife, Flornaza, had a difficult time in surviving. Tituan had warned Emilio to hollow out a log of mahogany wood and keep a vast supply of ears of corn to last all those years but Emilio and Flornaza succumbed due to the length of the deluge.

The Earth Press
By Frank Nissan, Americas
Menominee

The evil and wickedness of Man causes them to kill each other. According to mythology a trickster shot two underground gods when they were at play. In revenge they created a huge flood which rose to the mountain-tops. The populace ran and they ran but the waters of Lake Michigan (we never heard of this Lake Michigan) chased them faster and caught up with most of them and they drowned. The bravest animal of all, the Muskrat, recreated the world as we know it today. The natives who survived traveled by automobile and van!

The Earth Press
By Frank Nissan Americas
Mayan Mythology

From the Popol Vuh, Vol 1, Chapter 3, it is said Huracan (one-legged) was the god of wind and storms. He created the Great Flood after the first humans angered the gods. He was a resident in the

THE ICE AGES

Written by Cho En Salaam

Talk about cold weather! Do you know much ice was on our polar regions? Did you know (and I am certain that I did not realize it) that three-to-five kilometers of ice formed sheets that were in our polar areas! A kilometer is a little more than a mile. *Three to five miles of ice... that is a lot of water that was locked up*

there. That is more than enough! *(Some scientists estimated the depth of polar ice at **seven miles!**)* It was enough water to make our oceans many feet deeper, world-wide,. No wonder those primitives worried about inundation! *(I would worry about it myself!)* So now let us get to work and analyze what happened, because in the five billion years that the Earth has been around there have been four ice ages.

The first ice age was the most complete frosting that this planet ever had. Every bit of land was covered by a mile or more of ice. I am glad I wasn't there! But what is the difference? Nobody lived on the Earth at that time. Oh, possibly, deep in the ocean, near some volcanic openings, some bacteria lurked. So there were two hundred thousand years of melting ice to conclude that first ice age. Two hundred thousand years sounds just right to me to make all those oceans. *But those were the first oceans Mother Nature had made on this planet.* She is not done yet! Did you ever look at the present-day map of the world? A map of the world in the year 9,556 is enclosed with this article.

Nature insists on making ice and then melting it which wreaks havoc on our maps. Only a deity knows what lies under those waters. Do you know (or care) which deity? I am a writer, so I do not know or care. A scientist or a preacher would care. But nobody *knows!*

CAUSES OF ICE AGES AND THE CONSEQUENT MELT-DOWNS
Written by Cho En Salaam

There is a rule that all scientists should abide by. This rule has to do with Mother Nature. Do not ask, "Why?" or, "Why not?" Nature has her secrets and whoever is responsible for the rules of Nature they are the rules and that is that. *Let me give a few instances:* how about the electric poles of negative and positive? Can you change either one? How about sodium chloride being the main salt in sea-water? Can you change that? How about the laws of gravity? Can you circumvent them? (The aliens from other planets seem to have circumvented those laws!) How about the sunlight being bright and warm during the day? Can you change that? How about Ice Ages and the meltdowns? Can you change them?

How about the rotation of the Earth? Can you change it? Or you might tilt of the axis of the Earth or change the long-term increase in the Sun's output. The Earth moves in and out of dust-bands in the solar system. Do you want to change that? There are a lot of things that Man cannot do to help himself and who knows to what degree something has to be changed and if it will help....or hurt?

Do you want to change something important? There was a time when people were concerned about "global warming" with concentration on the burning of fossil fuels as a cause for the holes in the ozone curtain that protects the planet from rays that would melt the polar ice quicker than usual. And freon, a gas that was used in air-conditioners to chill residences, was supposed to be a culprit in the destruction of the ozone curtain. Maybe. But the main culprit is a law that you cannot change, the Milankovitch Cycles, which determine the orbit of the Earth around its Sun. Did I answer your question?

QUESTIONS I REALLY CAN ANSWER
Written by Cho En Salaam

If you have a little goldfish and the question is whether that little fish knows when a flood is coming, *I would say she does and the question is, "Who can discuss this with a goldfish?"* Do you want to drive yourself crazy?

If you think your Deity has to do with the floods and you'd better go to church or synagogue, I would say *she (he) does and you'd better go there right now and apologize.*

If you think all the other guys are infidels and god is angry at them for doing what they do naturally and wants to drown everybody, I'd say you should go right now to a shrink. *There is something wrong with **you!***

If you think there is something you can do to alter the global warming that everybody thinks is going on I have no answer, but do it!

If you think that high ground is safer than low ground even if it makes your nose bleed (and is more expensive) I would say you are probably right. But do not go by horse or mule. Hay! Hay! But be careful about landslides in the higher areas!

If a muskrat, eel, pigeon, dove, or any other animal talks to you and gives you advice, see that shrink right away! And if that shrink takes advice from animals, change doctors right away!

If you think there is something you can do to alter the cycle of ice ages because of something I wrote, I apologize and will go to that shrink immediately.

If you think horses and other animals sense whether you are about to have a tsunami or an earthquake and they act like it is imminent, I would agree. Animals seem to have a sense that something geologically important is about to happen that is unusual. Too bad people do not have that "sense.' But what can you do to protect yourself from an earthquake or a tsunami?

HOW PRIMITIVE ARE WE?
Written in the year 9,556 by Chang Sho

What is "Primitive"? Once again I have to look in Webster's dictionary (Webster's is ageless) to find the various terms for the word "primitive." There are several meanings to that word:

1)-of and existing in the beginning or earliest time or ages; ancient; original

2)-characteristic or imitative of the earliest ages; crude; simple; rough; uncivilized

3)-underived; primary; basic

4)-*in biology, a)* primordial *b)* **designating species very little evolved from early ancestral types**

Two items that can be primitive:

A) a primitive person or thing

B) an artist or work of art that belongs or is suggestive of an earlier period

So we have several definitions of "primitive". Let us see whether we are more *evolved* than our ancestors were. *If you are like I am you pride yourself on being as modern (or up-to-date as anybody who ever lived on this planet.* That does not mean that you have the newest, furthest-out concepts of diet, wearing apparel, music, art, speech or behavior. *It is simply that your concepts of life are fully evolved and mature.*

Your great, great grandfather was not as evolved as you are. He was probably all wrapped up in religious phony-ness. It is amazing how long the same craziness can persist and people do not seem to have evolved at all from their primitive beliefs. Religions have changed only when people change and the people, most of them, are still quite primitive. It was once an idea of advanced people that "time" would lead to lead to more solutions of the problems of mankind. But that was only a dream. The natural disasters that have occurred over the ages have led to a paganism that is full of beliefs in all sorts of gods, Instead of higher ethical and moral development people have reverted to a more primitive form of religion.

Organized religions failed to answer the natural questions that arose in the face of such catastrophes that humankind has experienced. We, who are more evolved, had hoped for a more intellectualized form of religion. But that did not materialize. The guilt of the constant disasters of Nature that organized religion blamed us for, was too much for us to handle. That together with the guilt of killing of millions of Muslims who became much too roguish for the world to accept, were the causes of our reversal in morality.

I must confess that the dreadful experiences that the human race has gone through are much too much for the normal psyche to absorb. The usual belief is that there had to have been some outside malignant source for such anti-human behavior to exist. The great Mother Nature had, for eons, been so kindly and considerate that even the most evolved of persons had difficulty in realizing that this kindly Mother Nature was the source of Ice Ages and the floods that accompanied the melt-down of the same ice that was our oceans once upon a time. I can see the reasons why the most evolved of persons would lose their confidence in the human capacity to handle such an experience.

But that is when that confidence is so important! One simply cannot cast his lot with any old god and expect a beneficial result.

Only the human mind, stressed-out though it may be, is able to deal intelligently with the problems that Nature inflicts on us.

The human mind is limited in its capacity. The greatest aspect of humanity has been the discovery (in the year 8,007, of the capacity for Extra-Sensory-Perception, which has always been located in the pineal gland for eons of scientific neglect. So we must wait thousands of years, if that is long enough, for the human mind to evolve still further.

One of the problems is that some of the human beings kill off some the best minds and strongest bodies that ever existed. Estimates have it that 6,000,000,000 of the best minds have been killed off during the ages that preceded this article. During the "atomic age" over one and millions of Muslims have been eliminated without changing the basic beliefs of Mohammedanism! That shows you the implacable strength of ignorance and the effects of heredity on ways of life. Millions had been killed as "witches" by religious fanatics. Millions had been killed in various futile wars, and millions had been killed in artificially-incited acts of prejudice and bigotry. How much longer this blood-letting will go on with the human race still able to meet its commitments is questionable. If we lose more people where will the new humans come from?

It is amazing how in the year 9,556 the great majority of residents of this planet place their critical decision-making in the hands of make-believe creatures who has no vital connection with them at all. If you think that the preceding story is all made up, think again. It comes (indirectly) from the myths and history of real people. All that was changed was the names of the writers, the names of the people involved and the names of a few of the gods. **The details of the stories are true, as far as myths and history go. I would place limited trust in the philosophy of the author.**

Imagine, if you are able, no matter how primitive you get, that a goldfish can speak to you and tell you that a flood is coming! What in the world did those people use for minds! Imagine believing that reeds or a hollow tree-trunk are the way to escape from a flood! Imagine believing that drivel about deities hating infidels and wanting to drown them! Imagine believing that it is better to die by blowing yourself up than to live in this world! Imagine believing that Allah will kiss you to welcome you to heaven *and then will give you seventeen virgins!* (This comes from a society which treats women worse than dogs.) The whole world is primitive in the worst sort of way and probably deserves to be drowned if it does not become civilized soon!

Imagine if you can put yourself back to 1935 that people believed that the Germans history and created a war that killed *20,000,000 soldiers, plus* the six million Jews murdered in those concentration camps. And there are lunatics about who doubt that story all-together! They don't doubt it because it is not representative of reality *but because they still hate the Jews!*

Hatred is evil. It is madness. I wonder what we can do about it. It takes normal living and twists it. Wars may come and they may go. Millions of Muslims were slaughtered in the wars in the second millenium and the remnants still hate "infidels!" **This article is written in the year 9,556.** If mankind continues on his course of madness I don't blame any god for wanting peace at all costs.

The world, right now, is crazy.

Author's Note:
Did you see what I just did with this story? I have been looking at programs (on TV) on the melting of ice for years. But not one of those programs dealt with this very important problem of a human basis with the screamingly funny letters that people actually wrote. That's because I am a "writer" instead of a scientist. I did the same thing with history with "Manfredonia" and with "Cristoforo Colombo". Are you not proud of the way I tackled these subjects? First of all, what is the real truth of these stories?

You may wonder how I came to all this information. Most importantly, I read voraciously: anything about anything. Secondly I looked up on the internet for information about the Great Floods. I found an article by Jonathan Adams "Global land environments since the last interglacial." That was absorbing but not for this story. Then I found an article about Noah's Ark in the Wikipedia free encyclopedia. It was also not enough for this story. Then I found **"Flood stories from around the world".** *That was* **IT.** *Although it was labeled* **"Flood-Myths"** *it was just what I wanted. There are as many myths as there were survivors. It is impossible to tell what the 'authors' of these books 'made up' and what were the original myths. The maps are my contribution to mythology*

Then I read about the "Ice Age" in the **Wikipedia** *encyclopedia. It was very interesting and I used vital components to fill out and give the impression of scientific accuracy to this tale. But the "meat" of this story is the mythology of the Flood Victims found in both the* **Wikipedia** *and the "Talk origins of the flood myths from around the world." The basis of all writing is the education of the author and his imagination. This is so unreal it is difficult to believe that there is a great truth behind it all. Is there anything more unbelievable than the history of the Earth?*

The "floods" covered all the lowlands on the Earth to a minimum of 130 meters, which is roughly 400 feet. This means that the center of the North American continent for the recurrent floods was under seawater separating the Eastern mountains coast from the Rocky Mountains by over 1000 miles. This created the North American Sea! The lowlands include the Mississippi Valley and the Great Lakes and all the farmland in about thirty or forty States.

The Middle East is mostly lowlands .Thus it was natural for this area to be flooded almost entirely .The former Golan Heights and the area around King Solomon's Mines might be islands. All the rest of The Middle East would be inundated entirely. Parts of Egypt, of course, and Libya would be islands due to their height.

Some areas would be flooded due to the lengthy intense rains (hundreds of years!).

They have been flooded before, years and years ago. Such an area is on the "continent of Australia", where I created a long lake on apparently low areas.

The continent of Australia was the victim of severe volcanic activity adding very much land to the already largest island on the earth. The natives of the new Australia did not have to do much digging for artifacts because there were hundreds of artifacts of one of the World Wars, many remnants of warships that demonstrated the futility of warfare as a means of solving international problems. Terrible enemies became the best of friends after these wars. Didn't you say, "The world is crazy right now?" Oh, it must have been me! There are now islands called, Allah's Islands. They are part of the former Indonesia which were mostly Muslim and after the expansion of Australia, which must have cost millions of Muslim lives, I thought it was sensible to name them "Allah's Islands."

I noted an article I once read which stated that the South Pole was once in the tropical islands of the South Pacific. My choice for this freeze-out for the future was the Fiji group of islands. No reason: Fiji it is!

RE-CREATION

This is a wild one! I get my inspirations, often, from the History Channel on television and this is one of them. The program that I saw late on the night of the 9th of October in 2007, dealt with "Mega Disasters". It had no personalities involved and was simply something that "might occur". That is where *I* come in. If it *can* occur it *will* occur on my pages and it will have a personal context.

It all began when, for some reasons, methane gas has come out of the Earth. Methane gas is very explosive and dangerous to human beings and all other animals. It has a distinctive odor. There was a program recently, on the National Geographic Station on TV about methane gas from the organic detritus that lies under the ice and snow. That is likely to replace the oxygen in the air in case of a warming of the Earth and destroy all life!

On this program that I saw there were scenes that revealed methane gas coming out of the bottom of the ocean! I do not know which ocean was involved. Incidentally, you can drive your automobile on methane gas. There is a technique for keeping a load of chicken dung in the trunk of your car (if you are not particular) and the methane gas that the dung produces can work in your car. The trick is to ignore the aroma of the chicken-dung!

Apparently there is a real danger of an explosion of some sort wherever methane gas accumulates and it does accumulate under the ground in large amounts. That would account for the "mega catastrophe" that appeared on Television; a catastrophe full of explosions and flames.

But the program did not say "where" this might occur and "what" the consequences might be. I feel, as an author of short stories, that I am particularly well-qualified to decide the what, where and when of a story.

Apparently all through the Middle East there were vague threats of a colossal earthquake. From Israel to Turkmenistan, from Egypt through Pakistan including all of the well-known oil-producing nations well known formerly as "greater Araby" and Southern Russia there were vague rumblings of a distinctive but unknown nature.

What does a first-class nation like Israel do in such a case? Their first obligation is to see to it that as many people as possible get out of the country to relative safety because, in this day and age, one never knows the extent of an earthquake. There might be a tsunami and since Israel is essentially low-lying a flood would take a tremendous toll of the population. The earth beneath the Mediterranean Sea all the way to Italy and Greece was involved in this series of quake-threats.

Secondly, the safety of the world was involved. Israel has (it is rumored) over 100 atom bombs. During a flash-fire and explosion this could lead to a real catastrophe. Those atom bombs had to moved. "Where" and "how" I will leave to the Israeli Military, but I think that war-planes and naval vessels to get them out of the Mediterranean Area would be preferable.

The military and civilian organizations would have to prepare for some serious mega destruction and a great many injuries and deaths. Wherever the populace went it would have to be out of the Mediterranean area. Ships to take five million people? Implausible! Friendly nations? In this world? Even the United States has to be eliminated from consideration. The main consideration would be to save as many Jewish lives as possible. This is the opposite from the Muslim countries where the populace would probably be happy to die! Anyhow, I have to leave the Israeli nation to its problems and get on with this story.

I must tell you what steps every Muslim nation took to protect itself. They all took the usual steps for earthquakes. They organized medical care so that a minimum of suffering from injuries would take place. Death, they all assumed, was in the hands of Allah and there was nothing anybody wanted to do about that.

It never occurred to Pakistan to secure their atomic bombs. Pakistan, as you know, is entirely mountainous. It is not that they didn't care; they just never thought about the subject. The possibility of a tsunami was not germane. The wealthy oil magnates from all the Muslim countries, by the way, flew with their families to the safety of Switzerland.

Russia, Italy, France, Nigeria and Greece took as many preventative measures as they figured to be necessary. None of them even considered the possible occasion of a tsunami at all. Of course this was a fatal form of neglect. Turkey, however, took medical and military pre-cautions and carried many people from the low-lands and moved them temporarily to the hills. They also thinned-out the crowded cities and moved those people to the hills. This saved them many, many lives. It was an act of Grace from Mother Nature to give the time to save all those people.

The character of the rumblings underground was different from every other occasion. It lasted for months and created much inconvenience. The food and drinking- water problems alone was considerable. The economic problems were a form of catastrophe. There was no way that geologists, at this time, could figure out what was going on. Meteorologists claimed that everything was normal yet the air-pressure was subnormal. Science failed to estimate the explosive nature of the problem. Nobody thought about methane gas because there were no fires and no odor from the gas which was deep in the ground. But many trillions of cubic feet of that explosive gas was finding its way between the tectonic plates and the other interstices throughout the Earth of the Middle East. The stage was being set for a mega catastrophe.

The President of Israel offered to help with the medical aspects of the coming tragedy. His efforts did not even receive an answer from the twenty nations to which he addressed his remarks. Praying was the main activity of the multitude in every country. Imams in every Muslim country were certain that Allah would "take care" of the Jews for the problems that would come from earthquakes. He ultimately would "take care" of the guilty and the innocent but His punishment would have nothing to do with their guilt or innocence.

The prime minister of Iran at just about this time (it was close to two o'clock in the morning) decided that he was hungry. He pressed the button that rang a bell in the kitchen. The "help" were used to the Prime Minister's peccadillos. They knew that "the boss" worked under great tension all day long and he sometimes forgot to eat. So they knew that they had to ask him what he wanted, although it was always the same thing when he ate so late at night..

"What would you like to nibble on at this hour?

"I don't want to nibble. I want to eat. I'm starved! Please make me an egg-beater omelet with the whites of two eggs added and some non-fat cheese, some onions, some red sweet peppers and some celery and some mushrooms. And don't use any butter when you fry it. Use non-fat margarine. Bring that to me with a pot of coffee and some toast with some sugar-free jelly. And make it snappy!" (This was spoken in Arabic, which the author does not know. But he does know that the Prime Minister was on a diet that told him that he was either a candidate for a heart attack or a stroke. As a Type-A-Personality he could drop dead in a second, especially if he had a sudden severe fright!)

In less than ten minutes the food was ready. The chef brought it in himself. "Don't you get tired of that same old breakfast, Sir?"

"At this hour I have to have something I am used to. By the way, take a look at this report that was just faxed to me! It is scary!"

The chef reads out loud, "Emergency! Urgent! There is something just about to happen, *but we do not know what it is.* The symptoms are that we are about to have a tremendous earthquake but we are not certain. There is something peculiar going on with our tectonic plates. Make sure that people are out of their houses and as high up in the hills as possible!"

It was early that morning, about two o'clock, when an errant flow of lava touched off the fire and explosion that literally rocked the Earth. It was somewhere under Pakistan, which does not usually have volcanoes any more, that the fiery lava touched the quintillions of cubic feet of inflammable gas that had soaked throughout the Earth under all the oil-producing countries. *The explosion that ensued separated over twenty-five hundred miles of the Earth's crust to a depth of three thousand feet and lifted the whole mass convulsively at a speed that elevated the sextillions of tons of earth into the air and threw it all almost out of the Earth's gravitational field!* All of a sudden we had a new moon! It did not shine...yet...and was not perfectly round. But a new moon there was!

The Holy land was at last in the sky! All the human beings charred and still on fire were suddenly in the sky! If there was ever a twist to Fate this was **it!** There it was, with most of the world's supply of oil on fire and smoking in the sky! Pakistan's twenty atomic bombs exploded when the new "moon" was on fire on the way to its orbit but that was like nothing compared to the loss of the entire country. There was utter surprise when the total of "Araby" went flying through the sky. All of the Middle East from northern Egypt to Israel, Saudi Arabia, Lebanon, Syria, Abu Dhabi, Kuwait, Iran, Iraq, Pakistan, parts of India and parts of Russia (where oil was produced), Kazahkistan and their neighbors went into the sky creating a new space-body with all the characteristics of a new moon.

And what was left of the Earth? A vast series of waves from the Indian Ocean and the Mediterranean Sea came all at once in a tsunami against all the shores left in the Mediterranean area: in Turkey, Cyprus, Greece, Italy, France, Gibraltar, Nigeria, India, and North Africa as far South as Kenya. All the islands of the Mediterranean Sea were overwhelmed and there is no need to tell you of the loss of life and physical damage to every place those gigantic waves hit. The Black Sea joined waters with the Mediterranean Sea. Southern Russia was inundated. There was a new "ocean": an extension of the Indian Ocean.

The Israelis ultimately had to perform one of those Biblical miracles to get one of the northern African states, which had friendly relations with Israel, for four million of their people. But they still lost one and a half million people to the tragedy. The entire Muslim population and all the Christians were lost in all the states that were almost entirely Muslim Millions of people were also destroyed to the elements in the lands bordering on the Mediterranean Sea and in Russia and India. The whole world was shocked at the losses that it had sustained. Parts of India were also missing due to the undermining of a portion of that country abutting Pakistan. While a new moon was a novelty the cost would forever remain prohibitive.

The resultant tsunamis and earthquakes are beyond description.. Floods went beyond the lowlands in every Mediterranean shoreland. Fiery lava emanated from Italian volcanoes and places in Greece, Turkey, Southern Russia and Afghanistan and in the bed of the Mediterranean Sea. *The former "Araby" was now a part of the Indian Ocean* as well as the newest body of water. The former Mediterranean Sea extended beyond the Black Sea to create an Ocean of sorts. To say that a total of a billion people were lost or were displaced would be an understatement.

A new concern was the probable presence of methane gas in the oilfields of every country that produces oil. Scientists determined to study that problem immediately. *It is important to visualize the nature of this problem* : suppose these scientists determined that methane gas was deep in the ground in Texas, or California or Pennsylvania, where oilfields abound. We do not need any more new moons. And we certainly do not want any tsunamis or fires or earth-quakes. What can we do to ameliorate the situation?

How can we get rid of the excess of methane gas? It is being produced twenty-four hours a day. It is a naturally produced product from the Earth itself. Can we manage a way to suck it all up and cast it into the air? Can we find out why and where Nature makes this dangerous gas in the first place? If we cannot find a way to eliminate this gas we have to expect to repeat this story ad infinitum". Oh, I know. You are bothered by the idea of a new moon. That is just a possibility but the presence of the gas is real if you can believe the History Channel.

ROMEO AND JULIETTE

"**Y**ou are forbidden to see Jason ever again! Your father and I are definitely against a romance that is useless and can only lead to trouble!"

With her parents so set against her boyfriend, Roberta Canton had very few alternatives. She was only fifteen years old and Jason Banker was sixteen. They loved with a love that was deeper than any imitation romance–far deeper than they imagined. What were they to do?

In the pottery class, was a special course in the Crediko High School that a "special" teacher had planned to break the tension of the more serious courses: mathematics, science, economics, English composition and historical appreciation, that everyone who wanted to "get ahead" took. "Pottery Planned" was a chance for friends to be friends and kidding around was de rigeur while each student took his (or her) efforts at "creation" to the kiln and had to wait for half an hour while the colorful clay artifacts were permanently baked.

Maureen Andante was one of the students who took her work seriously but that didn't stop her from kidding Roberta about her Canadian accent. Apparently Robbie was only peripherally aware that she had a French accent when she spoke. She took the ribbing graciously but let Maureen know that her Bronx accent (Maureen's parents came from the Fordham Road section of New York City) was equally "obnoxious". Both girls got along very well.

"I'm having problems with my parents," said Robbie.

"Are they still serious about their opposition to Jason?"

"Absolutely, this morning my Mom told me that if I want to go to this school I would have to stop seeing Jason. We have to come up with some plan. I can't take too much of this stuff!"

"Well, what is the basis of their opposition?"

"They object to his having no money. I told them that we weren't getting married until he had a profession and had a bank account. They were concerned that we might have sex and that opened up a whole can of worms."

"Are you having sex?"

"No. Not yet. I would just have it as soon as possible. I get kinda antsy all the time but Jason wants to wait. He's more honorable than I am. But my folks are worried anyhow."

"Maybe your folks know you better than you think."

"They don't know how I feel. They're just afraid on general principles. They forgot how love feels; if they ever knew!"

"You sound like one of those heroines in the movies!"

"That's what my folks think. They accused me of being like the female in Romeo and Juliette."

"You know what happened to *them*?"

"Well, that's one possibility!"

The clock rang out telling them that the cups they were making were finished baking. The conversation ended and Maureen promptly forgot about it but Robbie was "in a mood" and had a problem that didn't want to go away.

Jason was a "man" of principles. He firmly believed in the policy of "taking the bull by the horns." So he phoned the Cantons and arranged to see them both when Robbie was out of the house.

"I'd much prefer if you would trust me more and allow me to see Robbie anytime we want to." he said.

"It's not a matter of trust," lied Mr. Canton. "It's just that we don't think you are the right sort for our little girl."

"That's *your* problem. You think of her as a little girl when she's a fully-developed young woman and should be treated with the same respect you owe to every adult."

"That's one of the reasons we don't like you," replied Mrs. Canton. "You are not very respectful to us."

"I guess you expect respect when you tell a young man that he's not good enough for you to have in your family. That attitude is for the birds! If you want to know what I think, you guys are very ordinary people, nothing special. You have delusions of grandeur. That's it--delusions! And some day you'll get what you deserve! I think our conversation is over. I wish I could say 'It's been a pleasure' "And he walked out of the house before they could say what was on the tip of their tongues.

It was then that there appeared on both their computers (Robbie's and Jason's) the suggestion that a joint suicide effort would be the best way for their getting to heaven together and the best way to punish the Cantons.

Robbie and Jason saw each other in school and in the afternoons, when Mr. and Mrs. Canton were at work. They agreed that whereas they wanted to be together the only way they could share a life was to end it. They began to figure out what was the simplest, most dramatic way to share the ending of this life. Robbie had already written a suicide note on her computer; under "letters to go." Jason had not written his letter yet: he was waiting. Robbie kept looking at her letter, editing it endlessly. To suggest that she was more interested in the ending of her life than she was in living it would be true. She was overly-playing the role of the "abused child" in a tragic manner. It had only one conclusion.

Jason was more sensible. He had gone to her parents, which was a total failure. Now he had to go to *his* mother. His father had died years ago. When he explained the problem to his Mom she was shocked that the Cantons had not accepted her son on any conditions. After all, he was only sixteen years old but he was used to being the 'man of his house' ever since his Dad had died. He and Roberta were the 'only' children in their families. Mrs. Banker told her son that he should see his sweetheart surreptitiously as much as possible and to have their attorney speak with the Cantons and see how he felt about threatening them a little bit. Her philosophy was, "The world hasn't ended yet." She had been a young widow with a small child and knew whereof she spoke. She had no idea that the two young people had been planning on suicide.

Mr. Irvin Maugham was a well-respected attorney-at-law. He did not think threatening people was a good idea. He went to see the Cantons on a Saturday afternoon, before the ball-games were on television. He was awfully hurt when those people didn't have a single kind word to say for his client. He felt he had to remind them that Jason was an only son, the head of his family for years, had top grades in school and planned on becoming an attorney with an extra degree in economics. He was as honest as the day is long and the only fault Mr. Maugham could find with him was that he had fallen in love with the wrong girl.

"Jason is really in love with Roberta," said Mr. Maugham," and wants to give her the whole wide world. Could the Cantons relent a little bit and make an arrangement to limit the frequency of the young people's 'dates'?"

The Canton's reply was as unyielding as possible. It was then that Mr. Maugham, Esquire, offered a suggestion that a judge might feel differently than the Cantons. The set of their jaws told Mr. Maugham just what he was afraid it would. He told the Bankers what he had said and what *they* had said.

Jason simply replied, "There's more than one way to skin a cat!" Whatever that might mean, certainly it didn't suggest suicide.

Jason and Roberta decided to kill themselves by being run over by a train. They had visions of being hit by a speeding express train which goes over a hundred miles an hour. They planned to simply walk in front of the train as it sped toward them. You know how small towns are. There is a passenger station with its exposed tracks. It's a cinch to step out in front of a speeding train

They kissed a fervent kiss, as Jason had presaged on his computer and timed their end perfectly. The only item that was wrong was that on *this* day Eastern Standard Time became Eastern Daylight Saving Time and the trains were an hour's time different. A CSX freight train, going about fifty miles per hour, hit two young persons in a tight embrace. Of course it killed them. They had timed their deaths perfectly.

Everybody in the town of Grapefruit Park was shocked. The Cantons were sure that Jason Banker had instigated the suicide. Mrs. Banker, Maureen Andante and Mr. Maugham knew better. Was there a way that Jason and Robbie could have gotten their romance on the road without suicide?

South Florida Sun-Sentinel March 22, 2003
TEENAGE LOVERS STEP IN FRONT OF TRAIN *Sweethearts who compared themselves to Romeo and Juliet die in an embrace-*
By Mike Schneider,The Associated Press

ORANGE PARK-As the CSX freight train drew closer, 15-year-old Brittany Chisolm and 16-year-old Sean Blanchette stepped onto the track and kissed each other in a tight embrace.

The conductor tried to stop the train but it was too late.

Chisolm's parents told her recently that she could no longer see Blanchette. Classmates said the two high-school sweethearts were inseparable. But no one knew they were contemplating jumping in front of a speeding freight train.

However, detectives investigating Thursday's incident found several copies of a suicide note in the teens' homes. "Brittany and I are desperate. I vowed that death couldn't keep us apart and it won't". Blanchette wrote in the note. "I hope us doing this will be a reminder of how love can still be in this age; that we are a true Romeo and Juliette."

Volusia county Sheriff investigators on Friday positively identified Chisolm's body. The teenage boy's body hasn't been identified yet.

Sandra Lumbery, 15, a 10th grader at Deland High School, said there was no sign that her classmates wanted to take their own lives. "she was full of life and made people smile" Lumbery said.

"They were perfect together and made a great couple". Several classmates pointed out that Blanchette was considered the class clown.

Chisolm always enjoyed good-natured ribbing about her Canadian accent. Her classmates described her as always upbeat. "She could be really funny" said Michelle Pescatore, 16, who had a pottery class with Blanchette and Chisolm earlier in the school year. "She's from Canada and we used to make fun of her accent". "They were always holding hands and hugging" she added. Blanchette and Chisolm were always seen kissing and hugging in the hallways of the Deland HS according to classmates.

The authorities and police investigators found several notes, computer messages and notebooks outlining plans to run away and possibly kill themselves, said Gary Davidson, a spokesman for the Volusia County Sheriff's Office The couple was last seen on Wednesday. They had abandoned Blanchette's car near the town railroad track. But a 22-year old man and two other teens found it with the keys to the ignition and drove off, according to the Sheriff's office. The three were charged with grand theft.

VICK

My job is to create the punishment for Michael Vick, who has been found guilty of a series of crimes that derived from his providing the funds for the gambling related to dog-fighting. I am a judge with all the powers to make my decisions "stick."

Who is Michael Vick? He is a highly competent football player in the NFL. Is Mr. Vick in the same category as Tiger Woods and Michael Jordan, in which by a brilliance of performance these men are the most exciting athletes and the most efficient sports technicians to watch? Nobody interested in sports would turn off his television set while watching a game in which Vick is participating. That should answer your question.

What are the actual crimes that Mr. Vick is accused of committing? There are several crimes. First of all he admitted that he funded the actual fights between the dogs. He, with his coterie of friends, procured the dogs, organized the fights, arranged for the medical treatment of the injured animals and arranged for the destruction and discarding of those animals that were moribund after these fights. He also admitted to funding the betting and seeing to it that everything went business-like for these contests.

What is the range of punishment for these crimes? Michael could be incarcerated in a prison for anywhere from one year to five years. He also could fined for the court costs and, depending upon my considerations, he could be fined for up to one million dollars.

I have already thought out this case and the severity of his crimes. First of all, we must take into account the nature of Michael Vick's work. He is in professional football: as bruising, rough, intimidating a job as there exists. I ask you to consider twenty-two men who are rarely under six feet two inches tall, who weight from 225 to 400 pounds each and are dressed with cleats on their shoes and wear a helmet that is a potent weapon. They are all in the pink of condition, can run as fast as a sprinter and are not afraid of using their considerable weight as a weapon as well. Tackling a ball-carrier can be as violent as possible, depending on how sensitive the referee is. All in all, I'd say it takes untold courage and considerable talent to simply play the game of football. *In a way, it is very much like putting a bunch of dogs in a ring and saying, "Let's you and him fight!"*

Who are the owners of these football teams? Mostly they are business people who have made hundreds of millions of dollars (or more) in various businesses. Are they particularly moral or considerate men? If you like the idea of buying and selling flesh as a living, that's your answer. Anyone who thinks that professional football is a place where you can say what you want to and have the freedom of expression and of action that our constitution guarantees is clearly mistaken. One of these bruisers can't even change his job if he's unhappy or can make a lot more money. There are "regulations" that make certain aspects of slavery a thing of the present instead of a thing of the past.

Who is the National Football League? It is the accumulation of all these business people and they have "laws" to see that no one makes a buck at their emporia without cutting in a sizable chunk for "the owner". The parking lots, the tickets, the hot dogs and other refreshments and the T-shirts, balloons and other doodads are a source of income for these moguls. Can you sell hat-dogs without cutting the owner in? If you want to risk life and limb, you'll do that.

This limited democracy is where Michael Vick works. And the laws are written by and for whatever the businessmen think is good for them.

So we have established that Michael works in a locale that is remarkably like the place his dogs work in. Does any owner care when his paid hands use their helmets as weapons? Does he care if a 380 pounder hits a 225-pound quarterback? Doesn't he want his tacklers to be as rough and "definitive" as possible? Doesn't he actually relish the colossal brutality of it all? *Isn't it all a lot like having dogs fight?*

How much does a top-notch football player earn? Rookies, I'd say, earn half a million dollars a year. Super-men like Michael Vick earn about $17,000,000 per year, plus what they earn in the ads for shoes, T-shorts and bric-a-brac of all sorts. When legal cases like this are postponed until the end of the season it costs Michael Vick close to $21,000,000.00. How much of a crime did he commit, if he already has to lose $21,000,000.00? Do you know any other crimes that would cost the perpetrator that much money? How much would the owners (the NFL) lose if Michael were to be set free today, with certain considerations? Wouldn't they, rather, make more money? Certainly the owner of the team Vick plays on would *double his earnings if he could get him to play.*

Don't talk to me about morality. If there is a more brutal and horrendous "sport" like dog-fighting I have yet to witness it. They call it a "sport" yet those innocent helpless dogs are treated like total criminals. If there was a more venal more abhorrent "game" than professional football I don't know what it is, with the exception of boxing and wrestling. They are just as bad, maybe even worse. More-over the "laws" that the industry makes for the benefit of the owners are sheer hypocrisy. But there is something exciting about all these "sports"!

So I have decided that Michael Vick should be set free at once, provided he goes to a psychotherapist for a minimum of two years and he apologizes formally on television for the embarrassment he caused to the NFL and the considerably sensitive members of the viewing audience and pays one million dollars for court costs and for the Federal Government's fine. It must be added that any further dog-fighting or any investment in betting will be punished to the fullest extent of the law. If I felt that my actions would modify the "sport" of football, but it is so unaccountably popular that I would be a spoil-sport of the first order. But dog-fighting is a different crime.

The other men in this case can have their freedom as well, if they pay a fine of $250,000.00 and apologize formally on television and if they understand that any further dog-fights or betting problems will be punished to the fullest extent of the law, which I will be adamant in pursuing.

Author's note: I took this story and brought it to the football team of the University of Miami, Florida to read it. They loved it! It was honest, sane, concerned about dogs, and said some things about the forms of modern capitalism that bring back the grubbier aspects of slavery.

CRISTOFORO

The winds were northeasterly and, although the sun was bright, the sails were filled with a warm breeze and all was well on the three sailing vessels that followed a due-West course. How else could you reach India from Palos, Spain, if you did not go due-West? (After his first trip to the Americas he modified his direction to West-Northwest to better reach Hispaniola). A brief stop was made at the Canary Islands where the plan was to add a few gallons of fresh water to the supply of that vital liquid.

The owner of the Pinta, who was forced by the Queen and King of Spain to take his ship on this cruise (he did not want to go!), had sabotaged the rudder of his ship to start off with. It took three weeks to be repaired, which must have been a strain on the Admiral who had waited for years for this opportunity. The Nina, also, received in the Canary Islands new square sails (square-riggered) to replace the triangular sails (latine sails) and was then the fastest of the three vessels. She was able now to speed at five miles an hour!

Cristoforo Colombo, who kept two sets of books (logs), did so with the utmost cleverness. He was afraid that this trip to who-knows-where would be so tedious in the long run, weeks upon weeks. The men were likely to become critically upset. Who knows what was in the minds of such men most of whom were experienced sailors who were used to traveling towards a definite target instead of a simple "Asia"? There was considerable information that the sailing community had to learn about geography. They also had a lot to learn about science, philosophy, history, religion, social studies and how to live in this complicated world History takes its own time.

So Cristoforo kept a double set of 'logs': one was the accurate log of his journey, the other was a duplication of the exciting events that transpired, with a few key weeks left out of the time that had elapsed between the Azores and whatever date he figured the men were likely to get restless. Very clever, I would say. So he could point to that log to show that it was not *that* long a voyage. The men did not have calendars or clocks or any means of communication with any other person who was able to keep track of the trip.

The crews of the three vessels, the Nina, Pinta and the Santa Maria, totaled eighty-seven men. (I have here the name of every man! Thank goodness for the internet!) It is amazing to me that all these men were willing to go on an exploratory voyage of unknown character. Only a few of these sailors were criminals who were offered their freedom from prison if they would take such a risky trip. It seems that prison has "known" risks, but this exploratory trip had risks that were "unknown".

To describe the daily experience of these crewmen, first of all, they were not spoiled rotten by the luxuries we accept as our daily due. The diet of these crews was beans, bread (mostly moldy, as time went by) very little fresh fruit (the limes and oranges that the British sailors took to prevent scurvy had not been known about until the discovery of America plus one-hundred years. They had mostly preserved meats which had insect life in it, no canned food, no coca colas or other soft drinks and no cookies or cake whatsoever. Grog or other alcoholic beverages were a luxury that never made the print of history books. Only in the movies did sailors have grog or rum or wine. They hung live animals on slings on the decks to have as much fresh meat as possible. Any fish they caught in transit and any birds that were foolish enough to get in the clutches of the crew were additional fresh food. That strangely, rarely occurred. Their diet was really boring, but did they know it?

The world (outside of the Orient) had not reached that level of affluence where sugar and spices were an everyday dietary occurrence. That is why Cristoforo took this trip in the first place: to find the countries that produced these spices and to establish trade routes with those nations. The utter lack of refrigeration for food-stuffs meant that food soon showed signs of spoiling and one way to hide the smell of rotting meat is by the use of a multitude of spices. Did you ever wonder why frankfurters and salami are so highly spiced? Need I tell you that such foods conceal a whole world of rottenness?

Silk was an extra lure to India and China (called Cathay). Silver and gold and other precious metals were added prizes for the paupers who sailed these ships. Only the Captains were not paupers. Cristoforo had his own source of income but he was never really wealthy until he had discovered the Americas.

What did the men do to pass the time of day? During the daylight hours all of them were busy on their jobs on the ships. No one was excess baggage. Nothing was mechanized; every aspect of life at sea had to be hand-wrought. The trimming the sails, the steering, the cleaning of the decks, the preparation of the food (and the cleaning up of the garbage), the care of the sails and the cleaning of the privies had to be done by hand. For a privy they hung seats off the handrails of the deck!

There was no "free time" available at all. When storms arose there was obviously a shortage of hands. The Captain was busy navigating and directing the steering of his vessel and had a multitude of responsibilities at all times. He would have no free time at all with his manifold responsibilities. Instead of cabins (which modern crewmen sleep in) the crew slept on the hard deck, or whatever rope lay about on deck. There was no relief from the intensity of the sun in those long, work-filled days.

All-in-all the life of sailing men was dreadful.

Cristoforo was not a Celestial navigator. He was, for many years, used to navigating by "dead-reckoning" He had come from Genoa in Italy, originally, and in the Mediterranean area one did not have to concern one's self with the problem of latitude. Anywhere in that area you had to travel by ship was in about the same latitude or within a few degrees. He had difficulty dealing with Celestial Navigation and the subject of longitude. He also had a Genoese idea of distance.

His "league" was based on the Roman Mile, which had 4,060 feet. Our mile has 5,280 feet. His "league" would be 4 nautical miles long whereas the Spanish and Portuguese navigators used "leagues" of 4.9 nautical miles. This is a difference of .9 nautical miles. He was more inclined to employ dead-reckoning which was a lot chancier. But Celestial Navigation was more modern. He tried, many times, to use Celestial Navigation (use of the stars at night to guide one), but always seemed to foul it up. He was plenty knowledgeable about astronomy but was unable to handle Celestial Navigation. Cristoforo was the Captain of his ship and the Admiral of the little fleet of ships under his command and had the "last say" on which method of navigation he would use. Of course the other ships in his convoy had professional navigators, but they had to follow the leader.

We have electric lights which enable us to stay up until all hours of the night reading or watching television. But candle-light was the technique of Cristoforo's nights. Did you ever try to read by candle-light? TV was four hundred fifty years away. And electricity was almost as far in the future! These men had a simpler way of living.

It is true that the basic needs of life depended upon the quality of one's hands, the degree of determination to get along in this world and the physical ability to create an interest where a world was waiting to be discovered. However, to put one's self in the place of a member of Columbo's crew is almost impossible. How does one eliminate the innominate items of social, historical, and political progress? How would one create an interest where a void existed: a pregnant void, but a void, nevertheless?

The claim was made in the Catholic History of Christopher Columbus that a mutiny never started on his first trip. I find that estimation to be specious. *He planned on such an eventuality and his duplicate logs attested to that fact!* Of course it occurred, but this was an item that was obvious from the beginning of his trip and it started "from the top!"

Let us retake this trip from the Canary Islands, which were a few miles off the coast of Spain. It is necessary to intellectualize the facts that history provides in order to get the true story.(Did you recognize his name as being originally Cristoforo Colombo? In Spanish his name was Cristobal Colon).

Rodrigo de Escobedo was the secretary of the fleet. As such, he had the full confidence of all the Captains of the Nina, the Pinta and the Santa Maria. He had a vast knowledge of sailing and he was really indispensable. He was the man who was going to make up the documents of agreement when the fleet reached "Asia". He was the man whom anybody who was anybody had to speak with when any economic issues arose. He had the full confidence of Cristoforo Columbo and the owners of all the ships.

It was in the Canary Islands, which had an unsettled population, that the Captain of the Pinto, Martin Alonso Pinzon, approached Rodrigo de Escobedo the secretary of the fleet. Rodrigo was quartered on the Santa Maria. Martin and Rodrigo were old friends, having sailed together on ever-so-many voyages. Martin had something to discuss with Rodrigo on behalf of the owners of the Pinta, Gomez Rascon and Christopher Quintero who disliked the voyage altogether.

Martin asked Rodrigo, "What do you think of Cristoforo as an Admiral?"

Rodrigo was careful in his reply, "I think he struggled for years just for the privilege of making this voyage. He deserves a lot of credit for that."

"Don't you think that his technique of navigating by "dead-reckoning" is out of date and that he should be using the more modern "Celestial Navigation?"

"What are you really trying to say? I should have as many pesos as there are Captains who use dead-reckoning. He is the Admiral of this fleet and their Royal Majesties would not have chosen him for this job if he was not competent."

"Well others, not I, haven't the same confidence in Cristoforo that we have."

"If you mean Gomez Rascon and Christopher Quintero they were forced to include the Pinta because otherwise they would have spent quite some time in jail, according to their Majesties. They never would have taken this voyage otherwise. They are not the adventurous type."

"Well, I see that you have your confidence in Colombo. If he never gets to the Indies what would you say then?"

"I'm not one to lead a mutiny. We all understood that this was an adventure; an attempt to reach unknown lands by ship instead of overland. Vasco Da Gama was successful at the overland method but that is too dangerous with all those lunatics anxious to protect their turf with all kinds of weapons. Even De Gama was jailed, in of all places, Genoa. I'm satisfied, so far."

"I hope you are satisfied when weeks or months go by and he can't seem to find land."

"If you had spoken with Senora Dona Inez Peraza, the mother of Guillen Peraza, who became first Count of Gomera you would have learned something valuable. He is a real explorer who saw land far to the west every year for years. You would feel better about our chances. Cristoforo said that in Portugal a man came to their Majesties in 1484 to get a vessel to find land which he claimed he saw every year that was just under six weeks away. He claimed they were the same size and shape as the Azores. I have no problems with Cristoforo and you are speaking for two guys who are real trouble-makers."

"We will leave things as they are, for now. I trust you not to mention this to Cristoforo."

"Of course."

From the port of Gomera, on Grand Canary Island, the fleet left on September 6, 1492 to find the lands of spices, silk and gold. Not one word concerning Colombo's navigational techniques was mentioned (as far as I know).

Every day (a day has 24 hours) the three vessels averaged 80 to 200 miles which was the mileage that most sailing vessels were able to sail. Time was not everything for those men. The Admiral had to reprimand the sailors who steered the Santa Maria at times because the course was due west and he noticed that they tended to steer the vessel in the direction of west northwest, which actually would have taken them to the continent of North America, probably in the neighborhood of Florida or Georgia! But that extension of this trip might have taken another few weeks and we do not have the confidence that the crew would have gone on for that length of time without the signs of land which could not be denied.

The crews and their leaders of these ships were motivated by a form of greed of which they were not fully aware. Greed takes many forms. It will be noted that all of the crewmen were palpable paupers. Anything made of precious metal was valuable to them. Any clothes made of silk and any artifacts made of baked clay were valuable to them. Spices of any sort were of value to them.

It would be interesting at this time to quote *from the actual log of Cristoforo Colombo* to see how the exciting threat to his powers as Admiral would be resolved. It should be a relatively painless experiment. Most logs are pitifully boring, but not this one. After all, it is the discovery of the Americas with all the glory that is coming to Columbus. *It has a certain tenseness!* (italics are the author's.)

Friday, August 3,1492: Set sail (*these are the actual words of Christopher Columbus!*) from the bar of Saltes at 8 0'clock and proceeded with a strong breeze till sunset, sixty miles or fifteen leagues south, afterwards southwest and south by west, which is the direction of the Canaries. *(There were a number of overcrowded ships that left the same port of Palos at dawn before the Colombo group left. They were loaded with Jews who were attempting to escape extermination at the hands of their Royal Majesties, Ferdinand and Isabella. It is essential, apparently, that glorious Spain should remain free of the contamination that a different religion can provide. It seems like only yesterday that the Moslems were defeated in a Holy War and driven out as were the Jews. Author)*

Monday, August 6, 1492: the rudder of the caravel Pinta became loose, being broken or unshipped.(?) It was believed that this happened at the contrivance of Gomer Rascon and Christopher Quintero, who were on board the caravel, because they disliked the voyage. The Admiral says he found them in an unfavorable disposition before setting out. He was in much anxiety at not being able to afford any assistance in this case but says that it somewhat quieted his apprehensions to know that Martin Alonzo Pinzon, Captain of the Pinta, was a man of courage and capacity. Made a progress, day and night, of twenty-nine leagues.

Thursday, August 9, 1492: The Admiral did not succeed in reaching the island of Gomera until Sunday night. Martin Alonzo and the Pinta remained at Grand Canary by command of the Admiral, he being unable to keep the other vessels company. The Admiral afterwards returned to Grand Canary and there with much labor repaired the Pinta being assisted by Martin Alonzo and the others. Finally they sailed to Gomera. They saw a great eruption of names *(?)* From the peak of Teneriffe a lofty mountain. *(Sorry about the poor English. This has been translated a couple of times. This is from the original. Author)* The Nina, which before had carried latine sails *(that)* they altered and made her a square-rigger. Returned to Gomera on Sunday, the 2 of September with the Nina *(and Pinta)* repaired.

Sunday September 9, 1492: Sailed this day nineteen leagues and determined to count less than the true number that the crew might not be dismayed if the voyage should prove long. In the night sailed one hundred and twenty miles at the rate of ten miles an hour, which makes thirty leagues. The sailors steered badly, causing the vessels to fall to the leeward toward the northeast, for which the Admiral reprimanded them repeatedly.

Monday, September 10, 1492: This day and night sailed sixty leagues, at the rate of ten miles an hour, which are two leagues and a half. Reckoned only forty-eight leagues, that the men might not be terrified if they should be long upon the voyage.

Tuesday, September 11, 1492: Steered the course west and sailed about twenty leagues. Saw a large fragment of a mast of a vessel, apparently of a hundred and twenty tons but could not pick it up. In the night sailed about twenty leagues and reckoned only sixteen, for the cause above.

Friday September 14, 1492 Steered this day and night west twenty leagues; reckoned somewhat less. The crew of the Nina stated that they had seen a grajao and a tropic bird, or water-wagtail, which birds never go farther than twenty-five leagues from the land.

Sunday, September 16, 1492: Sailed day and night, west thirty-nine leagues and reckoned only thirty-six. Some clouds arose and it drizzled. The Admiral says that from this time on they experienced vary pleasant weather and that the mornings were most delightful, wanting nothing more than the melodies of the nightingales. He compares the weather to that of Andalusia in April. Here they began to meet with large patches of weeds, very green, and which appeared to have been recently washed away from the land; on which account they all judged themselves to be near some island, though not a continent. According to the opinion of the Admiral, who says, "the continent we shall find further ahead."

Monday, September 17, 1492: Steered west and sailed above fifty leagues and reckoned only forty-seven: the current favored them. They saw a great deal of weed which proved to be rockweed. It came from the west and they met it very frequently. They were of the opinion that land was near. The pilots took the sun's amplitude and found that the needles varied a whole point to the northwest on the compass.

The seamen were terrified and dismayed without saying why. *(Possibly a subconscious anxiety about the whole trip.)* The Admiral discovered the cause and ordered them to take the amplitude again the next morning, when they found that the needles were true! The cause was that the star moved from its place *(Sic!)* while the needles remained stationary. At dawn they saw many more weeds, apparently river weeds and among them a live crab, which the Admiral kept. He says that these are sure signs of land, being never found eighty leagues out at sea. They found the seawater less salty since they left the Canaries and the air milder. They were all more cheerful and strove that their vessel should out-sail the others and be the first to discover land. They saw many tunnies and the crew of the Nina killed one. The Admiral here says that these signs are from the west, "where I hope that high God in whose hand is all victory will speedily direct us to land," This morning he saw a white bird called a water-wagtail, or tropic bird, which does not sleep at sea.

Wednesday, September 19, 1492: Continued on and sailed day and night another twenty leagues; experiencing a calm. This day, at ten o'clock in the morning, a pelican came on board and in the evening another. These birds are not accustomed to go twenty leagues from land. It drizzled without wind, which is a sure sign of land. The Admiral was unwilling to remain here beating about in search of land, but he held it for certain that there were islands to the north and south, *(which)* was in fact the case, and he was sailing in the midst of them.

Here *(due to the lack of wind)* the pilots and other people made their way to the Santa Maria *(in small boats)* , and compared logs. The reckoning of the Nina made the four hundred and forty leagues from the Canary Islands; that of the Pinta four hundred and twenty, that of the Admiral four hundred.

This is in the Log but modified) Suddenly, someone spoke up, in a voice that was brusque and not at all respectful to the Admiral. It was Christopher Quintero, the owner of the Pinta. He glared at Columbo and spoke accusatively to him, "I don't where you are going and I want to remove my ship from your fleet! You are an incompetent."

Columbo was surprised at the vigor of this attack but was in a good humor notwithstanding. He spoke as though he were speaking to a child, "You don't know where we are going. As a matter of fact their Majesties, Ferdinand and Isabella gave me a contract to explore the Ocean Sea just to find what appears to be some strange lands which we might find within a couple of weeks, if not sooner. If we land on some peripheral islands of the Indies, we will have reached the source of the spices, silk and gold that everyone wants. If we don't find the Indies we will find some other place, with a fine climate, possibly fertile land and fresh water so that Spain can move thousands of people here to establish ongoing towns with the possibility of great profit. There may be all kinds of metallic ore where we are going. Didn't you have that understanding in the first place?"

Quintero was not at all palliated, especially at the tone of delivery that Colombo used. "Don't speak to me in that tone of voice! You are known to be an incompetent. You are unable to master Celestial Navigation, which any damned fool can understand and use! Also we are all aware of the number of responsible people who have turned you down for a variety of reasons. The most common reason has been that you have no idea of the size of this Earth. They figure if you don't how big the earth is you would get lost in no time at all. And all those advisors to the royalty who turned you down: can all those experts be idiots?"

At that time Colombo chose to argue like a lawyer, regardless of the manner of speaking that Quintero used to him. After all, the man had come up with some arguments that appeared to be valid. "In terms of the advisors to the royalty, yes they are invalid. What kind of advisor, for instance was the confessor of Queen Isabella, who recommended that I lose my Captaincy. He was a cleric with delusions of grandeur. What is this man's experience at sea? What is his experience in the world? How does he dare participate in such a discussion! And the other "experts": how many of them have been to sea? Who knows what kind of background these meddlers have had? It takes a certain bravery and imagination to go on an exploratory voyage. These are qualities that *you* will never have. You are completely devoid of bravery and imagination. You are totally unknowing of the respect that you should have for an Admiral. I have in mind just the kind of punishment that you deserve."

*This is still in the Log but modified:*Quintero gasped as he realized that this Admiral had his life in his hands. "You are not going to punish me for speaking up honestly, the way I have done! I have just expressed what everyone here believes and just did not have the courage to say."

Colombo did not lose his "cool". He knew that it was a matter of a few days until they reached land; wherever it was. But Quintero had put him on the defensive, which is no way to treat an Admiral. Cristoforo then asked the assembled Captains and owners and their supporters, "What do you fellows say? Am I an incompetent? Am I an imaginary fool who does not know where he is going?"

Rodrigo de Escobedo, secretary of the fleet, spoke first, "There is a timidity among us that contradicts the excitement of an exploration. Who knows what sort of land we will find tomorrow or next week? Will it be the Indies or some other land? Are we not interested in the future? We are on an adventure, a profitable one I hope. We cannot look on this trip in any other way. I, for one, have the greatest confidence in Cristoforo Colombo; as an Admiral and as a Man."

Martin Alonzo Pinzon, Captain of the Pinta, spoke up next. "We signed on to do a job of exploration. We cannot be nit-picking about our Admiral just because of some personal problems we may have. I find nothing to complain about in the way Cristoforo has handled this exploration. He did not show his exasperation when Quintero and Rascon Gomez damaged the rudder of the Pinta. He did not show the anxiety that I knew he was having. He is a sailor par excellence. And he is a good friend."

Vincent Yanez Pinzon, the Captain of the Nina, spoke up next, "We recognize a professional sailor when we see one. Cristoforo Colombo is a professional sailor if I ever saw one. We signed on with him when we might have been sailing around to all the ports we have seen a dozen times. He is my leader and I am pleased to follow him wherever he goes!"

That told Colombo exactly what he wanted to hear. He had to deal with Quintero as firmly as possible. It is fortunate that this form of "mutiny" was blood-less. But a threat to the Admiral's power and his basic philosophy had to be dealt with in a firm manner.

This is in the Log but modified: Colombo then spoke, "This is early in the day. After they have had a good lunch I would like to see that Cristobal Quintero and Gomez Rascon take one the dories that Quintero owns on the Pinta and stock it with an adequate supply of water and food and by three o'clock this afternoon those two men and anyone else who wants to go with them will leave for Spain. We will see how well they can navigate, how much time it will take them, and how safely they can get there. You may have one of the extra compasses and my gear for Celestial Navigation and an extra sail. You may reach Spain in four to six weeks.

"Give my regards to their royal Majesties. Tell them that you couldn't wait to see the Indies." (*Quintero and Rascon never made it to Spain.......Author*)

The over-riding question is, "Did Colombo contrive that 'mutiny' just to get rid of a couple of trouble-makers and plan it a few days before the crew really got bothered by the incessant delays? If you looked at the rest of his log he wrote, on Wednesday, October 10, *(from his genuine log)* "Steered west-southwest and sailed at times ten miles an hour, at others twelve, and at others seven; day and night made fifty-nine leagues; reckoned to the crew but forty-four. Here the men lost all patience and complained of the length of the voyage, but the Admiral encouraged them in the best manner he could, representing the profits they were about to acquire, and adding that it was to no purpose to complain, having come so far, they had nothing to do but continue on to the Indies, till with the help of our Lord, they should arrive there."(*These were the very words that Colombo used!*)

You understand, don't you that this author was brought up by a very manipulative father. There is something about Cristoforo that reminds me of my Dad. It wasn't until a crisis arose that he had planned out in detail that you realized it was all his responsibility and it was too late to act except the way he had planned it! This includes using the name of "our Lord."

This story has most of its material taken from the internet. I used AOL to get the story of Christopher Columbus from the Catholic Encyclopedia, from The Journal of Christopher Columbus, from an article in the Wikipedia, the free Encyclopedia. I also sourced-out a few articles that were very descriptive of the ships, the crews, the diet, the navigation, the logs of Cristoforo Columbo (one of his many names), the wages of the crews and the general history of western Europe in the fifteenth century. I also looked into the John Patrick Sarsfield replica of Columbus' ship the Nina through the courtesy of the Peace Corps. Also, the Mariners' Museum had articles on the Age of Exploration, also a long article named The First Voyage by Keith A. Pickering, research done apparently from 1997-2006. The quotes from Columbus' Logs are from the Wickipedia Free Encyclopedia.

Sources that attempt to prove that Columbus was a Sephardic Jew are not in any way convincing. His religiosity in the Catholic religion is typical of its day in the fifteenth Century. The number of researchers into Columbus' life is daunting. This author tried to examine Columbus' motives as well as his personality, with moderate success. This was not a psychiatric study, of course, although that might have been a good idea.

This is my preface to this book. It is also the inspiration for this story.

EPIGRAPH

"At every crossway on the road that leads to the future, each progressive spirit is opposed by a thousand men appointed to guard the past. Let us have no fear lest the fair towers of yesteryear be sufficiently defended. The least that the most timid among us can do is not to add to the immense dead weight which nature drags along. Let us not say that the best truth always lies in moderation, in the decent average.

Let us think of the great invisible ship that carries our human destinies upon eternity. Like the vessels of our confined oceans she has her sails and her ballast. The fear that she may pitch and roll on leaving the roadstead is no reason for increasing the weight of the ballast by stowing the fair white sails in the depths of the hold. They were not woven to molder side by side. Let us ride with the cobblestones in the dark. Ballast exists everywhere; all the pebbles of the harbor, all the sand on the beach will serve for that. But sails are rare and precious things; their place is not in the murk of the well, but amid the light of the tall masts, where they will collect the winds of space."

Maeterlinck "Our Social Duty"

THE CARETAKER
An Almost True Story

Alzheimer's disease is a dreadful condition that usually strikes the elderly. Rich or poor, famous or infamous, whatever your status, Nature is not impressed. Former President Reagan, and Charlton Heston (who played the roles of Moses and Jesus and the hero in Planet of the Apes) now both have to deal with an awful change of identity: actual dementia! The symptoms, from which my beautiful, youthful wife also suffers, include gradual loss of memory, gradual dissolution of the ego and sense of self, incontinence and, ultimately, total loss of reason. Such individuals become entirely defenseless, growing physically weaker. They are unable to get up from a chair or a bed and even forget how to swallow! *(Did you know that swallowing is a learned procedure?)*

How does one care for such a person? How long can one last if he tries to assume the entire burden of mother, father, servant, cook, shopper, medical aide and emotional support for someone who looks at you across the breakfast table and says, "Who are *you*?" Does she remember it if you reply, "I'm your husband Ed. We've been married nearly sixty years!"

Statistics show that seventy percent of the caretakers who are members of the immediate family pre-decease the person they are caring for! There is untold tension involved if you are a spouse of the patient. Upon the advice of numerous sources we tried a day-care center as well as trained women caretakers who came into our home for about eight hours a day to help old Dad help his wife.

After losing about thirty pounds I could see the "handwriting on the wall." There will be in our future, ultimately, a full-time nursing-home or a full-time caretaker who will live in our home taking most of the burden from my shoulders. Do you know how much this can cost? In the Northeast of the USA a nursing home can run as high as seventy-five to a hundred thousand dollars per year! The caretaker you hire has to have a day off each week and this can cost over two hundred dollars a day for her replacement. And how about a two-week vacation each year for your caretaker with pay at her regular salary *plus* in excess of two hundred dollars a day for her replacement for two weeks! Before you realize it we are talking about real money!

If you get your help through an agency half the salary goes to the agency. At over two hundred dollars a day the caretaker only gets one half of that. The agency gets the other half. If your caretaker is not a citizen or doesn't have a green card or a work permit she will work for a hundred-fifty dollars a day or more. But you will not be able to take any of that off taxes. Also you would have to be pretty grubby not to help provide medical or dental care for this person and she will not have the benefits of social security or the unemployment laws.

The following story, as it unfolds, will prove to be a tense drama. Because I have been in the vortex of the endless swirling waves that have engulfed me I felt it important to describe in detail the basic problems involved in getting a caretaker. The nature of the people we employ is an unknown quality. You bring some stranger into your home not truly aware of the complications that have engulfed them as they have tried to compete for existence in this complex world. *Let me tell you right now* that the drama about to unfold slowly in these pages was entirely unexpected. All I wanted to do was hire a caretaker for Janice.

It was in December that I found an ad in the Sun-Sentinel, the local newspaper for Boca Raton that advertised simply, "Help for the ill and the elderly." That ad was just what I needed. After a phone call to the secretary an appointment was made for the woman who owns the agency to visit our home in order for her better to evaluate what our needs were and what kind of people we were. Jan was at the day-care center when the woman came to visit me. I was not about to disturb Jan's sense of security any more than necessary so we met while Jan was away.

Actually, two people were at the door when I went to reply to their ring. There was the head of the agency and her husband. Both were very handsome people; neat, clean and bright, with all the savvy one would need to run such an agency. This does not mean that they exhibited any sense of humanity or guilt over taking half the salary of each person they would send me. It just meant that they were very shrewd business people who knew what the market required and were willing to meet that demand.

Mrs. Caldwell answered as many questions about their "product" as I could ask. Were the employees certified by any schools for caretakers? Were they able to cook? How much "cleaning" should I require of the woman? Where were these women coming from? I didn't want a semi-savage from the wilderness somewhere in the tropical islands or South America. I told Mrs. Caldwell that I really preferred a helper from Eastern Europe, like Austria or Slovakia or Poland. Such women clean a home like crazy, they can cook the kind of food that we know we can eat and they usually can speak to me and my wife intelligently since they have quite some education. That was my prejudice and I was showing her how little I knew of the world.

She informed me that she didn't have anybody from Europe. Almost all her women came from the islands of the Caribbean and Central or South America. But they could cook and clean and were all certified in varying degrees. It was then that I made my usual error. As I often do, when the conversation gets boring, the temptation to make some kind of a joke becomes too great to resist. "Well, I was hoping that, perhaps, you might be able to find a disinherited young and beautiful princess from some Eastern European municipality who desperately wanted to care for an educated, comfortable elderly couple."

The attractive blonde agent did not smile indulgently. Her husband didn't smile at all. He had never said one word except

"Hello." and "Goodbye." Instead, the agent said, "Well, I don't have a princess from Eastern Europe but I do have a surprise for you. I actually have a young woman, practically a child, whose family, she says, was royalty in the jungles of Central America. She says any prospective employer has to meet her parents who would come by and evaluate you and your place and have to give their approval for their daughter to work for you. *That's even wilder than your suggestion!*"

"Are they head-hunters?" I asked facetiously; but actually I was serious (and came very close to the truth!).

"I have no idea. If you want to meet the young woman I can bring her here at your convenience."

"There's nothing for me to lose," I replied. "Can you bring her here tomorrow? Jan is at the day-care center from 11:00 to 5:00.

"We can make it at about 2:00 P.M. How's that? Meanwhile we can extend our search and try to find someone in the normal range of caretakers, in case this doesn't work out."

"Fine. See you tomorrow at 2:00. Shall I prepare lunch for you?"

"That won't be necessary, thanks. I can afford to pay all kinds of insurance but not for gratuitous food-poisoning or gastroenteritis!"

"You're mean! Attractive and intelligent, but mean! (Her husband nodded his head, quietly.) See you tomorrow."

Tomorrow actually arrived on time and so did that employment agent and her job applicant. As the "job applicant" stood at the door I was particularly impressed by the youth and beauty of the young girl who wanted to take care of my beautiful but ill wife. "Where's your husband?" I asked the agent, thinking he was still parking the car.

"I keep him as far as possible from youngsters like this one. He's a "second" husband and I remember the problems I had with the first one."

"Well come on in. Let's not have this interview on one foot." And so they entered our lovely little apartment. The young lady was immediately impressed with the beauty and the sparkling cleanliness of our place. She walked all around the few rooms and visited the patio with its close-up view of the tenth hole of the golf course. I had made up my mind in advance not to allow my natural proclivity for pretty young women to affect my judgment *this time.* But that was yesterday."

They sat on the large leather couch in the "second bedroom" which we used as a den and TV room. Although I had set out a couple of colorful dishes with nuts, chips and dried fruits, neither woman wanted any of that stuff. They were "all business" and weren't about to be distracted.

My first question to the applicant was, "How old are you?"

"Just nineteen."

"What experience have you had for this kind of a job."

"Practically none, but I am willing to give it my best effort."

"Of all the jobs available why did you choose this field for your employment?"

"I was hoping to be able to go to college. Working for any agency doesn't pay much more than the minimum wage but they know where the jobs are. I figure that I'll get my experience working for someone like Mrs. Caldwell here. Then, when I learn to be really efficient I'll go out on my own and maybe earn as much as twenty or twenty-five dollars an hour. That would help me go to college. I simply must get an education and that's that!"

The kid was adorable. She had confidence and had planned her answers very well. Although she was mistaken about getting $25 an hour this was no time for such a discussion. I had to struggle with my male hormones to keep my mind on the situation at hand. I sincerely doubted that she had anything like the same problem.

"You realize that there is nothing intellectual about this job. It is menial work: cooking, cleaning taking care of a lovely lady who is often incontinent. She is still a very attractive lady but the lights are gradually going out in her eyes. She used to be a beauty and was the most popular professor at her university. It would be a tour-de-force if you could engage her in conversation and not just sit around feeling sorry for her. You could help her take walks to get some exercise, help her bathe, help her with eating and dressing and provide enough pleasant company to keep her from getting depressed. What do you know about any of that?"

"Practically nothing. But I am a human being with much compassion and endless patience. One of the reasons I chose this field was to impress any college board and any of my potential future constituents that I am a thorough-going humanitarian. I want my people to know that I am not afraid of hard work, even menial labor and to show my people that I can empathize with the poorest of them."

"You do seem to have a regal bearing about you. Do I infer from your remarks that you are thinking of going into politics?"

"In a way, yes. My family has been the rulers of a relatively small tribe in Central America for over a thousand years. I am in direct line to become the next ruler of our tribe. It will be necessary for me to find a way for the few thousand members of our tribe who have been driven out of our land to return and re-assume our position of power."

This kid was serious! She meant business and already had the attitude of a potentate. Despite my reservations about whether she could handle the job I was offering her I had to be deeply impressed by her reasoning and ambition. Was she going to be good for Janice? Could she bring some of her good cheer and positiveness to bear on my sweet, lonely wife? Would this female phenomenon impress even that victim of Alzheimer's and possibly create a powerful stimulus to counter-act the chemical erosion of her mentality? As a youngster would she soon become bored with her job? Was I day-dreaming? Was I asking the impossible, as usual? Probably.

"You can take all the time you need to evaluate me." the youngster said. She must have been reading my mind. "I am not going to take just *any* job. I'll be selecting a home for myself just as you are selecting someone—some stranger—to live in your home."

"First of all, you are to be admired for your mature approach to this problem," I said. "I have no doubt that you will ultimately achieve your goals. But whether or not to employ you is not a decision that is for me alone. Although everything you do to help my wife removes burdens from my body and mind that will benefit me as well, the decision is not mine alone. I am not sure whether Janice is past having the ability to decide something as important as this. We will see. You must allow me some time to evaluate this situation. You and Jan will have to meet so that she can evaluate you. I am sure she will take kindly to you, but will you have the range of qualifications to aid my wife? I don't know yet. Tentatively, I am in favor of accepting you for this job. If it is possible, you might come by with Mrs. Caldwell around 7:00 some evening soon. We can probably make a decision at that time."

The young princess, for that is what she was, looked directly at me, knowing in her brain and in her heart that I really couldn't find a sensible reason to reject her, despite the fact that she was not officially certified as a medical caretaker. I am equally sure that she had already decided that this was the job and the location that she wanted.

"That's a great idea. Any evening soon would be fine. Besides I know you would like to meet my parents. My father is the recently deposed King Amoku of the Eastern Mayan tribe of the kingdom of Belize. My mother is the former Princess Anana, from a Mayan tribe in Chile. My parents would not permit me to live anywhere that did not meet with their approval. I think that once they meet you both and see your lovely home with all those books and the computers and that electronic piano and your well-cared for garden they will be quite favorably impressed. I see a book up there that has your name on the jacket. Are you really an author?"

"Yes. I have done considerable writing since I retired ten years ago but only this book, so far, has been published."

"Oh! I could help you do typing and all that sort of thing!" She seemed genuinely excited.

"Great! Let's invite your folks for this Wednesday evening at 7:00 o'clock. I wish I could invite them to dinner but you have to know that one of the many talents I do *not* have is cooking."

"Oh, we'll forgive you and come long before our dinner hour."

And so it went. Did you notice that not one memorable word had been spoken by the employment lady after they had been seated in the den? Not one! Do you think she noticed that we (Naina and I) had been so bound up with each other that it was as though we had been entirely alone?

I had met a genuine young princess. My blood-pressure must have risen a few degrees and I felt forty years younger. It remained for her to impress Jan that she could add some positive qualities to our lives and not just bluff her way at our expense, which would be considerable.

When Wednesday evening came around and our guests entered our brightly-lit little apartment I had a chance to observe four magnificently attired natives from Central America in their tribal costumes. They wore multicolored gowns and sandals that seemed to be woven from a fabric like tapa-cloth, which I had seen in other primitive areas of the Pacific. The employment agent, Mrs. Caldwell, was not present, She had called to inform me that we could "handle things" from this point on. Attractive as she was, she was not missed. I do not wish to appear guilty of overstatement as to our guests' appearance. They were, in a word, *spectacular!*

I write this as a man who has seen much of the world and its creativity. But not on Fiji, Hawaii, the Solomon Islands, New Caledonia, New Guinea, the Philippines, Mexico, Europe, North Africa, Israel, Japan and the islands of the Caribbean did I ever see more outstandingly beautiful costumes than these four people were wearing. But who were the four people? Well, there was Naina, the princess who was applying for the job with us. There were her parents, the deposed rulers of a tribe from Central America and there was Naina's younger sister, Talura, a raving beauty of sixteen, who rivaled her sister in attractiveness and regal appearance.

All four of these people walked and even sat with an erect posture that made them seem taller than they actually were. Talura did not possess the softness of demeanor that characterized Naina. Her eyes were black and piercing. I had the sensation that she was looking right through me and she possessed a natural capability that could instill fear—groveling fear—in the hearts of lesser folk. She also had a physical appeal that, it seemed to me, would not be satisfied with anyone less than a god—a minor god, perhaps—but someone with legendary powers. This young lady had an aura about her. She had an intriguing, mysterious persona.

When they all met Jan, who was sitting, partially dozing on the recline-able leather chair in the den, they were more impressed than anyone might have expected. I guess that being so close to someone whose existence has been a daily part of my responsibility for many years allowed me to cast into a sort of limbo the reasons we got married in the first place. Her beauty and intelligence which made her so popular as a professor at the university were even secondary to her soft and gentle approach to all the vagaries of her life. All this was apparent to these Mayans who probably had never met anyone personally who had taught English literature and existentialism, social studies and history at a university. This treasure that I was protecting was the victim of a mind-depleting disease and their hearts went out to her.

Naina, especially, but even Talura, went at once to Janice and tried to bring her into our conversation—and they succeeded! I knew right away that Naina would do a world of good for Jan. It was simply a matter, now, of reassuring her parents that no harm, only considerate treatment would come to their daughter.

Everyone then went into the living-room to which I had brought some trays with things to nibble on: nuts, dried fruits, cheese and crackers, potato chips and salsa, tiny gefilte-fish (balls made of ground whitefish) with red horse-radish and a separate platter with strips of roasted red peppers and small strips of mozzarella cheese. As a tour de force I included the only foods that I know how to make very well; a bowl of chicken salad a la Edgardo and a bowl of egg salad Valedor. It was food for a king—a Jewish king—but Amoku and his family ate as though I had prepared some rare delicacies.

By the time we got to the subject of Naina's being allowed to work for us the subject was practically moot. King Amoku broached the subject in this way: "When Naina works for you how will she ever be able to leave your warm household to go to college?"

I had thought about that beforehand. "The same problem has occurred to me" I said, "It is the eternal question that arises when you have a young person in your home who must inevitably leave to establish his or her own life with college love affairs, jobs and marriage on the calendar. While the youngster is in your home your family life is expanded. It is fulfilled. You and she have all the benefits of the kind of attention and selflessness that only a loving family can bestow. Frankly, we have missed that since our young men left home for good. This is the kind of love we are prepared to offer her. Her future is *her* future, and we have to accept that graciously." I had told her parents just what they wanted to hear.

Her father replied, "This is even more than we have a right to ask of you. She will have to work hard and be sufficiently loving to deserve what you have described" Naina nodded her head in affirmation of her father's opinion. We all seemed very happy that the discussion had taken such a positive turn. But after an awkward pause I felt that Amoku had something further—something controversial—that needed to be said. I knew exactly what he would bring up but apparently he and his wife had discussed this with Naina beforehand. So it was his wife, the queen of their tribe, who said," Naina has admitted to us, when we brought up the subject, that she feels attracted to you, despite your age, and thinks that you are of a like disposition. What are your ideas on this subject?"

I had never expected such a frank discussion, especially brought up by a girl's mother. It was of the utmost importance to all concerned that I answer the question with honesty, delicacy and grace. "If I were twenty years younger I would have great difficulty answering this question honestly. But I am nearly 87 years of age—even though I may not appear that old—with a sick wife whom I love and respect. I know that young women are frequently attracted to older men, but if Naina were still attracted to me after six months it would be more like committing incest with a member of your immediate family. This also happens, on occasion, but we must try to put it into perspective. Although my male urges are at least as strong as they have ever been I must confess that I am an older man of limited strength. I have had a serious operation that has had an unfortunate result on my ability to perform the way I used to do. This ability, while it has not been entirely destroyed, has unfortunately done something to the man I used to be. I think that Naina and I will do what is proper and sensible. That is all I can say on that subject."

The queen then looked at her husband and they both nodded. He spoke up, quite embarrassed, "That sounds very fair and reasonable. We simply had to judge for ourselves the sort of home Naina was going to be dealing with."

Talura then surprised us all by speaking up in what seemed to be a serious tone of voice. "Where does that leave *me?* What about *my* physical desires*?*" None of us had anticipated such an overt sense of humor from that normally serious young girl. Her folks were non-plussed and it remained for me to answer humor with humor. "The fact that you express that desire as a question is evidence that you have not met the man of your dreams. I hope that you don't dream of an ancient man. I have to deal with one problem at a time. If I told you *my* dreams you'd be shocked!"

Within a few minutes they had all left, but I noticed that Naina as well as Talura had stopped to hug Janice and pat her hands. Jan was completely at ease with this young Naina. She even reached out to hug Naina and kiss her cheek.

Janice surprised us all by saying, "What a beautiful family!"

On the following Monday Naina moved into our apartment, and into our lives. Two men, apparently members of her tribe who lived in Fort Lauderdale had brought Naina and all her belongings in a small van. I think it was a Toyota Sienna. All she had was three small valises and a twelve by twelve inch cardboard box. I had prepared ample closet space for ten times as much stuff and had prepared some linens for her. She would reside in our den and any time I had to use the computer she had to accommodate to my requirements. Naturally, I would be considerate.

Of course everything worked out very well with Naina. She was clean and orderly and exceptionally attentive to Jan, who immediately loved "the little Princess", as we called her. There was plenty of time for Naina and Jan to take walks to give Jan the fresh air and exercise she needed. Naina's cooking was simple and not really good enough. I bought her a couple of cook-books for simple cooking and asked her to practice. I would buy all kinds of food and was the guinea-pig who did all the food-tasting. After a couple of months (during which time nobody got sick---- or gained any weight) we began to have decent meals: not gourmet, but tasty and nutritious. What was most remarkable was that even Jan ate foods that were not prepared in our customary manner---even foods she didn't like—-in order to encourage Naina.

One little matter has to be mentioned. It really has to be mentioned, whether you will believe it or not, despite some provocative behavior by our "little Princess." When Jan had to take her daily shower she usually needed some help, especially in getting into or out of the shower-stall or even turning on the water to the correct temperature. Alzheimer's had taken the last of her pride and of her ability to fend for herself. Jan had never allowed any of the other "aides" to help her bathe. That was left for me and I hoped Naina would help her. Naina agreed and so did Jan.

That evening I saw Jan being led gently towards the bathroom. She was wearing her green dressing-gown. *But what was Naina wearing?* One of our white towels *around her waist—and nothing else!* When I saw this sight I said, in mock fury, "I'm absolutely speechless! I'm shocked! I'm stunned and incoherent with rage and....and I don't know what else!

Naina calmly replied, "I know what else. For someone incoherent with rage you thought of four great adjectives and didn't cover your eyes at all."

"Of course not! I'm not that old or that infirm or that stupid!

"Well, in Belize children used to run around naked until the age of eleven or twelve. We didn't get excited by nakedness. It's natural. As a princess I was expected to be covered all the time but I used to strip off my clothing and run around naked like the other kids. I didn't want to be different, until a certain age."

See what I mean? I had to suffer this way, and in other ways, for several months. Meanwhile there were other surprises that Naina had to offer us. Instead of sitting around like couch potatoes watching vapid programs on television, we had long discussions and Janice participated in a limited fashion as well.

It all started when Naina expressed surprise at all the history and social-study books we had in our small library down here in Florida. "You have quite a library but you don't have any books that deal specifically with Latin America. How come?"

"Frankly, we have had only a limited interest in that area. The classes Jan taught were in English literature and a branch of philosophy known as Existentialism as well as the historical impact of North American history upon the society we live in. And I taught the historical and economic aspects of the Franklin Roosevelt years including the causes of the great economic depression that we suffered through in the nineteen twenties and thirties. One simply cannot be a specialist in everything. However, I realize now that we could have broadened our range of interests with great advantage. We'll have to change that as soon as possible. Perhaps you could give us a thorough history of your native land together with an overview of the history of Latin America as it relates to your tribe and its history."

I figured she would know what any South American high school graduate would know plus some political events that applied particularly to the nation of Belize. But I was totally wrong. She started a discourse more well-informed and more accurate than an encyclopedia about her part of the world. More than that, she ultimately recited as many folk-tales and as much of the "folk-history" as she could recall, which was indeed extensive.

One afternoon, while we three were sitting on the patio overlooking the Boca Teeca golf-course I asked Naina a simple question about her people." Your parents and you seem to have a modern, up-to-date morality. Is your religion Christianity or does your tribe have its own religion?"

"Of course we have our own religion. Our tribe is older than Christianity and our people have lived in the Americas for at least ten thousand years. But several hundred years ago some invaders with all kinds of weapons forced our people to accept–on the surface only–many of the precepts of Christianity. Some so-called holy men visited my ancestors whom they considered to be savages and gave them an ultimatum: either convert to Catholicism or be slaughtered! Nowadays, there is a group called "The Mob" that gives you such an offer that you can't refuse. These were Holy Men? Didn't they recognize that *they* were the savages, not us? Their religion may have spoken about good will towards men but not one of the invaders lived up to that credo.

Men from strange countries would steal and kill to get someone else's land. They took whatever woman they wanted and had no regard for her purity or affections. They disregarded our religion and our family customs. Their priests were also savages. They preached those Ten Commandments but because they themselves were not allowed to marry they had no regard for normal sexual conduct and they took young boys as bed-mates–which is disgusting—or they took our women, claiming to be privileged as Holy Men. Never did we learn of a Spanish or Portuguese or English white man who did not steal or kill for gold or for personal power. And worst of all, they had a macho belief that denigrated all things feminine, as though women were beneath men in the eyes of the divinity. That's terrible!"

Janice then spoke up, which was a surprise to me. "I saw a show on television recently which showed that the Mayan tribes were all very brutal and killed people for religious purposes. Is that still true or is that just a part of your ancient history?"

Naina was delighted to have gotten Jan so interested in her people that she forgot to be sick! "I'm so glad you are really interested in my people! We actually have our own form of morality. The Mayans who were our ancestors, thousands of years ago, really were very brutal and, outside of survival, life itself was not a primary consideration. Our ancestors had to think about survival of the tribes against the brutality of the climate and of nature itself and then they had to defend themselves against other tribes. For these reasons they became quite paranoid, like the Zuni tribe of American Indians, which lived within itself and any stranger was looked upon with murderous suspicion. But one small portion of the great Mayan people became my particular tribe. We are an offshoot of the Mayan people who did *not* believe in the killing and did *not* have brutality at the core of our religion. We learned to defend ourselves without shedding blood!

"You see, we believe that blood contains the heritage of a people. All of your ancestors are in your blood--like ghosts. So since all people are victims of superstition, our particular superstitions led us to believe that when you commit bloodshed you let loose an unknown quantity of spirits. When blood is shed by accident the "preachers" have to clean it up with red sand to eliminate the existence of someone's spirits. They mix dark red iron ore with white sand. It is a very serious experience when blood is shed. That is why we do not use swords or spears or guns in wars, in fights or in games.

"The past is revered by us as the source of life, of strength and of culture. We must not lose any of that through bloodshed. Otherwise my people do not believe in ghosts or spirits. We only believe in one God and that is Mother Nature. We believe that God is a feminine entity. She is not a ghost or a spirit but a force. And She cannot be prayed-to. We believe that a fragment of the Eternal personality exists in every living being. That fragment is called a "*solu*"...the same as the soul. This *solu* can be prayed to for strength and solace. There is no other power to appeal to. Each *solu* is your own most essential element—your own personal essence. You must not kill or abuse anyone because you might commit damage to his *solu*.

"No one knows what happens to the *solu* when you die. Most people believe it returns to the "source", but no one dares take a chance with that piece of the Eternal Personality."

"But," Janice asked, "You mentioned that a whole army of Spanish troops was destroyed by using poisons. Isn't that killing?"

"Of course it is. But ours is a religion of Nature. Nature has her own ways and her own reasons for the killing of animals and plants all over the universe. Killing is a natural phenomenon and mankind has to protect itself from whatever agencies threaten to destroy him. The idea is not to shed blood and thus release those spirits of the past. But when strangers come into your own land and your home with ulterior motives you have every natural right to defend yourself. Only a misguided fool would accept destruction without lifting his hand in self-defense.

"With that purpose in mind our tribe developed, over many years, various poisons that kill painlessly and immediately, without the shedding of blood. Those who are responsible for the production of poisons never, but never, have been known to use them for personal reasons. Those poisons are meant to defend the tribe, only."

"What types of poisons have been developed, and how do they work?" I asked Naina.

"I know a lot about them because I am in line to assume leadership of this tribe when my father passes to the Great Beyond. We have certain people trained to produce these poisons, which are of many varieties. In fact just a few families are privy to the ingredients and manufacture of these poisons. Most of the poisons have the ability to cause the blood to coagulate in one's blood-vessels within a couple of seconds, as though you had been given the wrong type of blood in a transfusion. Most of the poisons are odorless, colorless and tasteless. Thus, when a few hundred Spanish invaders came to our shores and killed several of our people they all died in about four minutes after drinking water from a poisoned well. The rest perished when incense was burned by a priest at an open-air meeting of the soldiers. The priest did not die because he was wearing a mask that concealed a bladder of fresh air under his hood.

"Some of our citizens are very adept at blowing darts with a blowgun. We all learn to become adept at that pastime. But when an enemy invades our country he may suddenly become aware of a barrage of poisoned darts coming at him from behind every tree and shrub. As a result of our methods of defense we are actually feared by nations who have great armies. and much superior forces. They prefer to leave us alone for fear that our "technicians" will come into their own lands and destroy them. In this way we have been able to defend ourselves until just recently."

"You mention that you were able to destroy large groups of invaders. How did you do that if you couldn't shed blood?" I asked.

"Well," said Naina, who was just warming up to her tribe's history. "What you may not know about Belize is that there is a very long chain of barrier islands that protect us from tidal waves and the full force of hurricanes. Those islands must be at least one hundred miles long. They lie about a mile or so off the coast of the mainland and make it very difficult for sailing vessels to approach our coast. Strangers have to come into the coastal waters many miles from our homes and they thus give us plenty of warning that they are coming into our area. When the Spanish (or English) figured out how to come into our waters we allowed them to land.

If they were peaceful we invited them to great meals of native foods and drink. It simply never happened that they were respectful of our culture. They always gave us some ultimatum that demanded that we surrender our sovereignty to them and provide all the gems and gold that we had.

What my ancestors did, when they saw the nature of the invaders, was bury their gold and gems deep in the ground where it came from originally or threw it into the deepest waters. Because we could not or-- would not–shed blood we poisoned their food or traded poisoned goods or poisoned the chickens that were given to the invading forces. They lost thousands of men over the years. Most of our neighbors also became fearful of our jungles because even the air around them was poisoned by our chemical specialists. They never suspected what was going on.

When the Spanish and English came to our shores in immense sailing vessels we set them on fire by surrounding them with rafts filled with hay–which they thought carried traders or "friendly natives"—we then set our hay-filled rafts on fire. Those rafts caused their wooden vessels to burn to the water's edge. Our men escaped from the burning rafts by leaping into canoes which they had on board hidden under the hay. Many large ships were destroyed this way. Those soldiers who had landed on our shores were poisoned before they could harm a single one of our people. Even a suit of armor could not keep out the poisons. It wasn't until foreigners came to our shores in metal ships that they made any real threats to our people"

"That's very exciting. You couldn't deal with them by force of arms so you used poison and fire to fight back. That's amazing!"

My next question was obvious. "What happened recently that your family was thrown out of power and had to leave the country?"

"Oh. That's a very unfortunate story. Our people have long been what modern politicians would call "liberal." That means that we have long believed in human rights, in the rights of women to be equals in every activity in our society. We were liberal in all aspects of education and allowed the deprived and the victims of abuse in other lands to come to our shores to try to live the good life that we are so proud of. And so when certain African nations continued their depravities against various natives of their own country, we welcomed with open arms any of them who applied for admission to our country. Foolishly, we had the idea that the whole "emergency" would be a temporary thing: that when the ruffians who had assumed power in their countries had ultimately been replaced by rational people these refugees would naturally want to return to their native lands.

But the ruffians never seemed to leave and these people have stayed with us for about seven years. While these immigrants were told that they must adhere to the rational, humane laws and customs of our nation, not all of them behaved as we wanted them to. They abused the democratic election mechanisms of our nation and violated our strictures against killing. Before we were able to deal properly with these scoundrels they had seized power by force of arms and sent any objectors out of the land of their birth to be refugees all over the world. My parents and the leading members of their establishment were allowed to immigrate to the United States. Actually, they are all here in Florida."

Janice had been listening very seriously to the young woman's tale of woe. Surprisingly she spoke up, "If ever I heard a more concise exposition of any subject from any of my students I cannot remember it. Not only do you have a mastery of your subject matter, you have a natural teaching ability to explain it lucidly and interestingly. I'm very proud of you!"

So it was with enhanced respect for our "little Princess" that we grew to live with more and more dependence upon her. I knew how much stress and physical labor had been involved in the personal care I had lavished on my wife plus the normal range of chores and duties that come with living in this modern civilization. Naina had taken over almost all of the chores that had to do with Janice as well as many of the household duties. Even though we hired some 'cleaning-ladies' to do the heavy cleaning every two weeks I began to wonder when she would start to show evidences of the stress that had been transferred to her. But she seemed to thrive on it.

Those who think they know me might be surprised that I took so long to bring up the subjects of sex and marriage. They may consider me as frequently rash and precipitous in thinking and behavior. But those who know me best know that I rarely make important moves without due analysis of all sides of a question. Rarely would I make a decision that might endanger the emotional or physical status of my family. And so it was, one evening long after dinnertime had passed, while Jan's eyes were closed as she semi-dozed, that I asked Naina the question that had been uppermost in my psyche for a couple of months. "How seriously does your tribe take their marriage vows?" This was calculated to open up the entire subject of the male-female relationship that my endless supply of testosterone impelled me to investigate. I was not going to rush into anything.

"Very seriously, "she replied. Had she fallen into my trap? Had I been falling into *her* trap all this time? "We do not have divorce or extra-marital adventures. Ours is a small tribe and everyone would soon know about it if a man wanted someone else's wife. Of course there are rare exceptions in the event that a man cannot perform his marital duties or one of the parties is very ill for a very long time. Like I know about such things because an uncle of mine had been severely injured and his mate had the moral right to seek a lover. It was called a moral right although it was entirely physical. Divorce, under any usual circumstances, is impossible.. Here in America it is just the opposite. At the first sign of incompatibility many people don't even try to correct the situation. Some judge simply gives them a divorce. I read that some movie stars have been married five or six times. That is immoral to us: to me especially.

"You know, Doctor Ed (a name she decided to call me) when a couple in our tribe decides to marry the initials of each mate are tattooed discreetly on their foreheads. This lets everyone know that they have a lifetime partner. Look somewhere else! That is totally civilized. It forces everyone to try every alternative to correct interpersonal problems without giving it all up. You learn to mature and to use your will-power to correct some faults you may have that bother your partner. You learn to give as well as to take."

Notice that by being so serious about the subject she had bypassed what I really wanted her to discuss. I learned from that girl more than anyone could have imagined. One day, after Naina had been in our household almost two months, I asked Naina about the Mayan people: where did they come from and how have they changed over the centuries. Is it true that the Mayans still believe in human sacrifices and the blood-letting that were once part of their religion? What happened to all the warriors who must have existed to conquer all of the smaller tribes?

"Big surprise coming for you, Dr.Ed" she answered gleefully. She was about to destroy all my preconceived notions, as well as all the misinformation that I had told her was in the Encyclopedia Brittanica (that I told her I had consulted before I asked my questions!).

"As you know, Doctor Ed, the original humans who first emigrated to this continent and to South America, came from Asia. There is only a 30-mile strait of water between the furthest stretch of Alaska and the Easternmost tip of Asia. Currently the people who occupy that part of Asia are called the Chinese. But we do not know who lived there 20,000 or more years ago. The two features they did have were slightly slanted eyes and a pigmented skin. It could have been yellowish or slightly tan.

"It is probable that in a very severe winter the thirty miles of water between the two continents can freeze over—sometimes for many years---maybe for many centuries, as during an ice-age. An ice-age lasts for a long time.

"The men who came to North America over that ice-bridge explored a great part of the West coast possibly as far down as Mexico—or further south. When they returned to Asia they told everyone what they had seen: ice over several miles deep in the North and immense forests with giant trees. The fishing was great all over with orange colored fish and in the far South the sun seemed to shine all year 'round. Most people did not believe any of those stories. Orange-colored fish, indeed!

Some of the families who heard these stories were very adventurous. They took their wives and children with them for the next trip and several whole villages decided to settle in the new, sunny, fertile valleys that they had heard existed well over two thousand miles South of the iced-in areas. They must have first settled in Southern California or Mexico, because the seeds they brought along with them from Asia would grow very well in a warm climate. It did not take much urging for these families to leave Asia, which was undergoing its own ice-age. It must have been a trial to walk all the way to Mexico!

"They had dog-sleds, you know, and larger animals that we call the Yak, which supplied them with transportation and even milk. Of course, by staying near the coast they always caught plenty of fish."

"They must have been very sturdy people," I observed. "I wonder if they had fire or any metal-work, like hooks or spears."

"My ancestors did not mention metal, except for gold and silver. But if they knew how to look for one metallic ore they must have had a clue about the others. For many purposes they used animal bones for clubs and for spear-heads to catch fish. But they did have fire. You cannot live through an ice-age without fire, so my ancestors often mentioned fire in their oral histories. You know how primitive people are with their stories and songs. They would sing from one generation to another the interesting stories of their past experiences. If there was a flood or a particularly cold stretch of time they would mention that in their songs. And they also had songs that recited the names of people who lived long before our parents. You know, so-and-so begat such-a-man and he begat so-and-so.

"But they did have fire. My ancestors often sang about fire, which they used to cook food and to warm their clay huts and tepees. They would keep the controlled fires alive by feeding it small branches and straw in a large clay pit. They must have smoked some kind of pipes or cigars because they were growing tobacco for well over a thousand years! And they had many drugs...medicines as well as psychedelic drugs...which they could find growing wild in the woods.

"After many centuries, perhaps thousands of years, other immigrants came to the coasts of Central America. By that time our people had occupied most of North and South and Central America. Some of us were called Indians, others were called Mayans. In thousands of years all kinds of changes can happen to people. It has been estimated that in North America alone there were over ten million American Indians before the Spanish and British came to the Islands and the mainland. Some new immigrants had come to Central America by huge reed rafts that they "sailed" and navigated using the ocean's natural currents. I think they must have come from Egypt, because they started building huge triangular stone memorials to their great kings in Egypt. These were pyramids and only in Egypt and Central America are they found.

"They were very clever, being adept at surgery on human beings as well as being able to read and write in their native language. They even had books, or folios, that some of their intelligentsia had written. But mostly the earliest men carved their writings into flat stones. They got along very well with our people and when we showed them some of our gold artwork they outdid us by far with their artistry. These newcomers just didn't seem primitive to our ancestors. Our people knew real talent when they saw it.

"There might also have been some Melanesians or Polynesians who arrived on the West coast of Central America, following the Humboldt Current the way the Egyptians followed the Atlantic currents. Our people mated with these newcomers from the East and the West. We found them to be creative and very strong and interesting, since they, too, had a long culture behind them. They had a different religion from ours, sort of Paganism, but it fit well with our religion which also thought of the primary deity as being Mother Nature. We both thought of the one real God as being Nature and then we had a bunch of subsidiary gods to handle things like crops and storms and good luck and rainfall and so on. There's nothing to argue about there. So what if we might have been mistaken about some of those things?

"Whom could we hurt by simply believing? Nowadays religions are so touchy, so paranoid, so much under the control of their priests that a simple thing like believing in your own deity seems to threaten them somehow. That's part of what my ancestors would call, "the madness that drowns out all reason." In fact, these so-called religions denigrate reason—and women. They want everybody to believe unproven dogmas from invisible powers and for unnecessary purposes."

Most probably it was not apparent to that little Princess, but I had fallen hopelessly in love with her. Hopelessly it was because what could I offer her that such a young person of such a different culture could expect of me? Besides, I really wanted her to get the handsomest, young, virile Prince that her history demanded for her. If I judged her correctly–and I did–she would not yield herself cheaply or gratuitously to anyone whose culture and standards were as foreign to her as ours were.

I had gradually become aware of how gross and self-centered our culture is. Sure, we think we practice the Judeo and the Christian morality. But we don't. We have none of the simplicity of her people or even of our own ancestors. We are too involved with the material aspects of life—too much rich food and a concentration on the acquisition of wealth; of jewelry and expensive cars, lavish homes and investments that are supposed to multiply our wealth and provide a care-free life-style and an old-age of sunshine and endless pleasure. We never seem to have learned how to be *unreservedly* social people. I will let my readers decide for themselves where we went off the deep end.

It occurred to me that Jan and I had only recently become aware of a particularly sane and sophisticated people in the Mayan tribe from Belize that had produced Naina and her parents. They really practiced a philosophy of "survival of the fittest." What *we* do, by contrast, is to save the weakest with our antibiotics, heart and other organ transplants, blood-transfusions, pills and ointments for an endless collection of discomforts and itches. Physicians of all varieties are making fortunes by preserving the viability of people who are not truly alive any more. It is as though we are injecting an anti-embalming solution into all the old folks in our know-it-all, obsequious way.

Physicians generally, in their arrogance and self-adulation, really consider themselves the anointed of God. It is only when one of them gets seriously ill himself that his mortality becomes apparent to him, as he goes through the mill from doctor to doctor, specialist to specialist, MRI to MRA, blood-tests and the seemingly endless expensive experiences of doctors and nurses and more and more tests until the truth finally dawns upon them about their mortality and morbidity.

Our Princess comes from a culture that does not curry the weak. If one is indeed the victim of a dread disease they provide food---sustenance. Your hunting days are gone because they have practically no modern medicines. Malaria, cancer and diabetes are killers. They kill the Mayans fairly promptly. We drag out the sentence so that everyone can make a great living out of our miseries. (Janice's pills cost $62 per day for a hopeless disease. The doctor's get $78 for a five-minute examination. Day-care centers get $78 for half a day. Care-takers get $70,000 for a year of service).

Naina's tribe doesn't believe in embalming the dead. After you die you're *supposed* to rot. We postpone the situation until we have festivals over the dead sometimes we carry the corpses by jet planes for thousands of miles while we get all dressed up in goin'-to-meetin'-clothes to shed our communal tears. Many thousands of dollars later we plant the victims into the ground and many folks erect monoliths to prove how important they are. There are many people who make a living off the dead: preachers, embalmers, livery drivers, cemetery owners, stone-carvers, party-givers, camp-chair manufacturers, coffin-makers, even obituary departments of newspapers charge big money for their services. It is a wonder we can afford to die!

One afternoon, while Jan was sort-of dozing, I left my computer to ask Naina another—actually, it was the same old question. Naina had really gotten to me. I was finally impelled to ask her, openly, about sex. After all, as old as I am, I'm still sort-of a man. "What about sex in your culture?"

Naina squinted at me as though I was a bug under a microscope. "I've been waiting for a stripped-down version of that question since the first minute Mrs. Caldwell brought me to your home." (So have my readers been waiting for this.) "Well, without sex there would be no people," she said. "Apparently they enjoy it in every way very much. We, as children, didn't have to be taught much since we always had access to all those explicit stone and wood carvings that have made the Mayans so popular. But sex itself is not a primary concern to us the way it is to the Europeans. North Americans are as prurient as a covey of baboons, if you have any knowledge of anthropoids. Baboons, higher apes and American men and women share a primary interest in sex. We Mayans are descended from the Orientals and other ancient people who came to the Americas on those reed barges. We have slightly slanted eyes like the Orientals, slightly dark skin like the North Africans, especially the Egyptians, and a tendency towards flab in middle-age like the Melanesians and the Polynesians. The Orientals, because of their vast numbers, would seem to be most interested in sex, although you'd never suspect it to look at them." (And here she giggled like a school-girl, covering her face with her hands.)

I waited for her to continue, perhaps to express some personal note, but she is much smarter than I am. I was well aware that when I mentioned sex she became verbose and pedantic. She left it for me to ask more personal questions. I don't know if it was wise or not, but I declined the gambit and let the subject drop right there. Talking about it would simply not lead to sex with this girl. That was the last time I ever had a formal discussion of that topic with her.

"We have a serious problem here, with the Professor," was the reply to my silence. Apparently we were having difficulty starting up another conversation. But Naina did reach out to hold my hand. It was a warm, positive gesture. We sat there for a while just holding hands. After a while I arose intending to walk back to my computer I couldn't resist the opportunity to kiss her on the cheek. Naina surprised me by pulling my head down so that our lips met in a long, deep, delicious kiss. In this way we had sealed our understanding; without words.

Janice, who we thought had been dozing, suddenly spoke up, "At last! I was so bored with all your sparring about!" and went back to pretending to be asleep. That was the beginning of a real, soul-satisfying affair!

Days later Naina said that she was quite impressed that Jan had gone back to college after having two children and even had a third son while studying for her Doctorate. She had taken to calling Janice "The Professor" and was really was convinced that women could lead and govern. Jan was sitting back, as usual. We were never certain whether she was fully awake or could listen to our conversations whenever we had them. In fact, Jan did the unexpected when she opened a full-fledged discussion with the Princess. "You seem to be entirely aware of your tribe's history. Have there been any women leaders of that tribe?"

The Princess was quite pleased by Jan's interest in her tribe. "Why, yes! About three hundred years ago there was a series of three women who led the tribe after a plague of some kind had hit all the eligible male leaders. In fact, I am named after the first one, Queen Naina Oomalah. They say I even look like her, but all we have left is a couple of statues. I think the sculptor must have been in love with her. He made her look so beautiful. He poured his soul into that statue and made her appear so attractive."

"Well," said Jan," I think you should go to the best university to study international relations and whatever courses you would need to lead a nation. You are a genuine princess and have a long history to live up to. I think you can do it! We'll help you, won't we, Ed?"

"Of course," I said. "She'd have to study history, science, anthropology and probably some psychology. Also, you *must* learn about communication technology. We'll help you look at the syllabi from every college and University that teaches all those subjects. You'd have to study advanced courses in economics and civics. Civics is important in order to know how a government is organized. You should also be educated in languages and the literature of the whole world. The world has grown much smaller since the development of all our forms of communication and even China is now just around the corner.. The past is important, of course, but the future is where you will have to live. The present is simply here only for a moment. Tomorrow is forever and that's where you will have to live. When you study psychology you will learn about the influence of the media on people's thinking. You have a lot to learn, but you have a good head start. We are amazed at how much knowledge and maturity you have already.

"We are not a wealthy family but we care for you and will help you as much as we can, as though you were actually one of our children. I have in mind encouraging you to apply to a fine university that would be so impressed by your appearance and qualifications that they would be pleased--and honored--to have you matriculate in their school. But we would be pleased to help you with some of the expenses that such a prestigious school will engender." I sat for a moment in silence, wondering whether we were not offering her more than we could afford.

The Princess was overwhelmed by our interest in her future. She was well aware of the nature of the government that now controlled her tribal area. Although the Mayan population far outnumbered the African-Americans who now ran the place they were repressed and prevented from voting. Our Princess had a long, tough road ahead of her, with sudden death if it seemed that she posed a threat to any indurated clique.

One afternoon I had an inspiration. "How much schooling have you actually had?" I asked..

"I graduated from high school in Ft. Lauderdale in June and took a few courses at a local community college this fall."

"You don't seem too inspired by any of that, do you?"

"Well, *you've* inspired me more than anybody. It's going to be a long struggle and I just didn't know how to begin. But you've lit the spark that had almost died out. I'm really excited!"

"Why did you actually take a job like this, helping a tired, sick old lady? It pays less than seven dollars an hour and is a dead-end job."

"Oh, I went to this agency and told them I'd like employment helping people who couldn't help themselves—and here I am!"

"Doesn't your family share any ambitions with you? Your parents are charming—genuine royalty. And they're not old at all! I'll bet that they are no older than our sons."

"My Dad is fifty-eight and Mother is about forty-seven. You remember that they did not leave Belize voluntarily. They were told by the military that they could leave or be assassinated. They have never been employed by anyone before. My folks are the leaders of our tribe. All expenses have been paid by the community. They have no real money of their own. My parents were tremendously popular and as such presented a threat to the ruling clique who now control Belize.. My folks are supported, even here, by the tribe, many of whom are here in Boca Raton, in Ft. Lauderdale and in

Miami. We can consider ourselves lucky to have been able to leave, five years ago, and that we were not shot in the streets. It really hasn't been easy for them."

"Or for you!" said Jan. "You are in line to become the queen if you can return. We have to do something to help make that possible!"

"Yes. In fact, my Dad, who never got discouraged in his life before, told me that I could be the ruler of our people—and even our country—as soon as I get ready. I think his diabetes is beginning to take its toll. He has been training me for that position but the world has become more complicated than he knows. I'll really need the college training that you mentioned: and more! "

"You will need a great deal more than just college training. You will need political and military allies who can exert pressure on your behalf. Perhaps a former President of the United States, like Bill Clinton, and the American military could advise you as to the proper procedures to use, with an implicit threat to the Africans who have taken over your nation that their control of Belize is displeasing to us and that you are ready to replace them. All you have to do is to show everyone that you are serious and qualified and we will do our part by trying to get some political and military help for you. Do it! And soon!"

We have never seen anyone "light up" the way that kid lit up. She was practically incandescent! We just admired that girl! How brilliant she was! And how educated, even without college! Of course it would have been more convenient for Jan and me if she were more knowledgeable about cooking and home-making. But you can't be everything, can you? This kid was a Princess; genuine royalty. She knew just what attitude was most impressive to her people and was never "play-acting". She was not "assuming a role" or "acting" the way Ronald Reagan did when he became President. This youngster was brought up with solid values which she was not about to sell cheaply for power or influence, nor was she beholden to any group except for the best interests of her tribe and her nation. She was determined to see that her tribe recovered their lands, recovered their independence, maintained their ethnicity and thrived in whatever forms of endeavor could preserve their people-hood.

And so, one rainy afternoon when we didn't dare leave the house because of the wild windy rain, the thunder and the lightening, Naina, Jan and I decided to work out the plans for applying to a university. It was now in early January and we figured she had plenty of time left to apply to a top-notch school and also to study whatever courses they might still require for admission.

"Which schools do you think I should apply to?" was Naina's first question.

"It may seem a deep gamble, but I think, considering the qualifications you have and the regal aura you project when they meet you in person, that you should aim for the top and let them know that you are only applying to just one school, their school, because you have every confidence that they will accept you. You must not cower before their stature because they are only human at best. They are not gods nor are they infallible. You have to ask them for every possible benefit and bonus that they can offer to a student who has your qualifications and your lack of financial resources. Let them know in a modest way that you will both be the losers if they reject you".

"Oh, how could I say, 'You will be the losers if you don't accept me!'?

"Well, it does seem immodest but it's true! Don't you think their public relations men will capitalize on having the future ruler of a nation among their students?"

Finally Jan and Naina gave me positive signs, so that I was able to say, with assurance, "Okay! I have spoken! The school is Princeton University! It's an hour from our home in New Jersey and a wonderful place for your education."

"Great! I will immediately go into my room and type up a draft of the letter for admission to Princeton University----if the Professor doesn't need me at this time."

"Go ahead, please, Princess. It will give me a chance to catch up on some sleep I forgot to get last night." replied Janice

I accompanied Naina to her room and offered her some suggestions as to what the college needs to know, what credentials she would be enclosing, what she should mention of her personal and family history and the reasons for selecting only Princeton for her education. The following is the letter that she took less than an hour to write (and print out on the laptop I had bought for her):

Admissions Department,
Princeton University,
Princeton, New Jersey.
Sirs,

My first thought when the idea of college arises, is "Princeton". This is the only application I am sending out and I feel certain that you will accept me.

I am a native of the nation of Belize, a tiny country on the East coast of Central America. For over a thousand years my family had been the ruling aristocracy of our tribe and of this nation. When, in the nineteenth century, we were conquered by Great Britain, my family was still permitted an abbreviated enclave of rule within the borders of this nation. We are an off-shoot of Mayan (Meso-Indian) origin and have struggled to maintain our ethnic purity all these years. By the way, despite what you may read in the Brittanica, our tribe is not composed of bloodthirsty cannibals.

My father, King Amoku, is a youthful man who was recently deposed as ruler of the nation of Belize by a junta of black immigrants from Africa whom we had welcomed as refugees from the violence and irrationality of their native lands. They do not seem to want to understand democracy. While our leaders have encouraged African immigration these people do not reciprocate our generosity. They have threatened my family and many of our tribal members with assassination if they did not leave promptly for any country that will take us. Five years ago the United States accepted over a thousand of us, with the proviso that we behave ourselves and don't get into trouble. That was the easiest part.

King Amoku is not well and I am next in line to succeed to the rule of my people, who number about 750,000 souls. While we are living in Florida, pro tem, I have every intention of getting an extensive education at Princeton in order to rule my people properly in a broad-based, humane and democratic manner. When the time is appropriate we shall return to our homeland where I shall exert every effort to re-establish our hegemony over our traditional grounds, despite the threats of violence that have flown about us.

When re-established in Belize I shall run for President of that country which was an English-speaking democracy and strive to expand opportunities for all to be able to work in peace and harmony. In order to enhance my efforts I plan to bring in American economists, psychologists and social-workers to aid me. We shall seek economic investors and outside help to raise our living standards to the maximum of our capacity. We want to increase our reputation as a place of refuge for all honorable people, despite our unfortunate experience with certain immigrants.

For all these purposes I deem Princeton a primary source of education. After a Bachelor's degree in Government and International Relations, I intend to pursue an MBA degree at Princeton to best avail myself of the necessary aid in maximizing our nation's economic potential.

Currently I am employed full-time by a family who are very supportive and encouraging to me in my ambitions. My employers are a former Full Professor of English at Fairleigh Dickinson University, who currently suffers from Alzheimer's disease, and a retired Dentist who is a published author and former teacher and lecturer. I am a full-time "care-taker" for Professor Janice and perform many services to make the life for her and Dr. Ed as comfortable as possible. I will require a full subsidy from Princeton which I assure you will be quite painless. If you so require me I shall reimburse you in full in due time. The more I learn at Princeton the easier it will be for me to repay you!

Enclosed are a transcript of my records of education, my documents of immigration, the results of my SAT tests and a few articles published in the National Geographic about my tribe and my country. Also enclosed are photographs of me and of my family and a letter from the current President of Belize, stating that he wishes us well in the United States because we know what our fate would be if we were to dare return. This is in writing.

I look forward to your reply. Of course it is possible for me to appear at a personal interview. If you have someone authoritative in this area we might have that interview down here because right now I am sorely needed to care for Professor Jan. Cordially,

(Crown) Princess Naina.

A reply came back in ten days:

Princeton University Admissions Office

Dear Princess Naina,

Please go for an interview at the office of the President at Florida Atlantic University, in Boca Raton. The current President is a graduate of Princeton who has served on our admissions committee in the past.

You may call his office at 561-988-6000 and arrange a convenient time.

Yours truly,

The next day Naina called that number and arranged for an interview. Four weeks after that interview, which took place on April 2nd, Naina received this form-letter from Princeton University:

Dear Princess Naina,

Congratulations! You have been selected to start your studies at Princeton on September 12, 2003.

We have agreed to subsidize your entire educational program and your living expenses on the proviso that you perform adequately as a student and as a citizen. This means that you must achieve no less than a "B" average for all the years you attend classes at Princeton and that you absolutely never give us cause for disciplinary attention for any moral or social infraction. There will be no requirement to reimburse Princeton for your tuition and the support funds.

An accompanying pamphlet describes our policies in full.

Please fill out the forms enclosed for course selections, dormitory choices and food preferences. Also please make a choice for type of room-mate.

Again, congratulations! For any questions or advice you may write, phone or E-mail any of the numbers listed below.

Cordially,

This was indeed a whirlwind accomplishment. Jan and I wondered about getting another care-taker but we felt very proud of the way we had guided Naina on the road to education, power and achievement. Of course, all we did was to offer her good advice. The young princess has all the instincts and capabilities to achieve her goals. What she needs now is a little more good luck and a satisfactory fall of the dice when she chooses to return "home" in about six or seven years.

Naina's parents were extremely proud of their Number One daughter and when we invited their whole family to a dinner (that Naina had mostly prepared) they arrived at precisely five P.M. on a gorgeous May day.

"Welcome, your highnesses! Until you get to taste the fabulous cooking of your daughter you may have your choice of appetizers and refreshments that Naina and Doctor Ed have prepared for you." (Some of the foodstuffs and drinks were prepared by Doctor Ed, except for the three dishes of Mayan delicacies and the brisket that I had no hand in at all.)

While we were sitting on the lanai, enjoying each other's company, I asked a question that I was certain had an embarrassing answer, but I simply had to ask it. "I am sure that the reason Talura has not come with you is that she has a date with a magnificent demi-god of a man and prefers, as all young people do, to spend an evening with someone closer to her age and interests."

"I wish that were true," said her mother. "But Talura has a peculiar interest in a different kind of chemistry. She spends much of her time learning about the chemicals, the poisons as well as the beneficial medicines that our medicine-man, who came to the States with us, produces in great secrecy. I know that Naina has informed you that we do, occasionally, have to defend ourselves and for this we have our own chemists."

I was about to say, "That's really strange." but there was so much that was unusual about these people and about the subject of poisons that the royal couple had mentioned that it seemed wiser for me to drop that subject right there.

"Well, Talura is always welcome in our home and I hope she knows it."

"Certainly," replied King Amoku. He really looked distressed. "We are not going to pursue this topic any further today, but I will only add that we are concerned about our child. Anything might happen....."

Naina had heard all this. Our apartment does not lend itself to very much privacy. However, she did seem to have sustained a shock of some sort from something one of her parents must have mentioned to her. The color of her face seemed to have paled. Were those the beginnings of tears in her eyes?

Incidentally, both she and her parents, when they looked at each other had some strange extra-sensory exchange that seemed to fly through the super-charged air. This left me in no doubt that something "ultra" was going on. But what was it?

Naina tried to break up the sense of foreboding that had overpowered us all. "Here's the greatest meal you've ever had!" she exclaimed. Her pride in the brisket of beef that she had made was real. (Jan had surprised us by remembering the 'formula' for that dish and by supervising its preparation.) Together with the three Mayan dishes we had a sumptuous repast. What did they want to drink? Everyone settled for Lipton's iced tea!

By the time the "evening" was over, everyone seemed (on the surface) to have phased-out the troublesome problem that had been exposed earlier. But does anyone reading this story have even the suggestion of an idea that the members of our little party could truly shake off the pall that had crept into our souls? Even Janice, whose feel for interpersonal relations seemed to have mostly vanished, admitted to me, after the older couple had left, that "something had given her the creeps" about these people. I said that I felt the same way.

Naina resumed her job with us without any comments about her family's problems. She was a mighty busy young lady, having the ever-increasing level of care in our home and having to renew, big-time, her studies so that she would not fall behind when she got to Princeton. She even matriculated at the University of Pennsylvania for the summer months to take a number of courses that would better prepare her for the studies at Princeton. Guess who paid for her tuition and who lent her one his cars to attend those courses.

We all know that many high-school and college students are dedicated "eager-beavers". Naina would have to compete with all those bright-eyed but almost heartless youngsters from the best schools in the world. From New York to Los Angeles, from London and the Sorbonne, from public and private schools, such as the best of the Catholic schools and the Yeshivas the brightest students came to Princeton. Going to school at this level was not simply learning college-level material and regurgitating it in exactly the way that the instructor expects of you. Going to school at this level is much like running for national office. You have to show by your face and your bearing that you are up to any challenge, that you are just as eager a smart-ass as any kid from the best schools anywhere.

We planned to leave Florida sometime early in the month of June. Usually we left for the North in early April in order to be able to spend Passover with our family. But this year was different because of the youth of our caretaker and the need for Naina to see much more of her parents, whom she might not see for six months. She needed to do lots of shopping for clothing, which she could do best with her mother and to get some things for her room. She already had a laptop computer and printer-scanner-fax-copier combination. Guess who paid for all that stuff. We sent twelve parcels up North by UPS and loaded the car to the hilt.

We prepared the defenses of our treasured little apartment against the possibility that some cataclysmic storm might hit our area. I have always overdone my security measures where-ever we have lived. Sometimes my preparations were justified, as in last Fall when a humongous bolt of lightning struck a large palm tree outside our lanai, severely damaging the hurricane shutters we had installed. Our apartment was not damaged at all, fortunately. Naina helped me caulk the lower rims of the doors and patio doors against the 20-inch rainfalls that occasionally besiege the Boca area. Was this a very costly apartment that I was protecting? Not really. But, if all it takes to protect your property is a few hurricane-shutters and some caulking, the question is moot. Actually, I love that little apartment!

Naina was all excited that we were going to drive all the way up to New Jersey, stopping for two nights at motels in Florence, South Carolina and Fredericksburg, Virginia. We had planned on leaving on Saturday morning and this was already Friday morning. Naina called her parents to bid them goodbye. She had met with them at a local restaurant a couple of days before. If anything unusual had transpired she would not have been able to conceal it from us. Her father and mother were far superior actors, having spent a lifetime dealing with all sorts of unusual occurrences.

So when Naina called her folks on this Friday morning, her mother wished her a fine trip and was forced by an emotional reaction of some sort to hand the phone to King Amoku. As she listened to her father Naina turned as pale as anyone could turn without fainting. She listened very respectfully and then was barely able to whisper to her father, "Of course. This afternoon at six o'clock. Here is Doctor Ed." She handed me the phone.

I was absolutely stunned by the news that King Amoku presented to me. It seems that Talura had died suddenly. Her father did not wish to discuss it over the phone. "Would we wish to join them at a function in honor of Talura at six o'clock?" Of course we accepted his invitation.

We would not allow Naina to perform any more of her duties for the rest of that week. I called the agency and hired a lovely Jamaican woman to take care of Janice for about twelve hours a day. Naina trembled like someone with Parkinson's disease. Nothing in her life had prepared her for what had occurred. Loss of a sibling is a dreadful experience, especially to a young person who has so far been shielded from such traumata.

We took care of Naina as though she was one of our own children. Princess or not, she had sustained a serious psychic shock and reacted the way any normal, serious girl would. Outwardly she soon recovered her poise and spent nearly two hours preparing her "image" for the notable people whom she would soon be meeting. Jan and I knew nothing about these people and were basically interested in accompanying Naina and protecting her from any more "psychic shocks." Actually, we had no real place at the evening's function and should, more sensibly, not have been invited. But apparently King Amoku and the Queen cared very deeply about us and loved us for the way we felt about their daughter. They almost considered us "family."

At six o'clock promptly we arrived at the residence of the King and Queen. Jan and I were dressed in dark clothing, befitting our traditional conceptions of a funeral. Naina and their family and friends were dressed in their multi-colored native costumes, with black armbands on their left arms, above the elbow. Naina's beauty had never been more outstanding despite her sorrow and her loss. She knew and we suspected that her intent was political: to leave no opportunity unmet to impress the ruling class of her tribe about her fitness for any role that they might demand of her. Gone were the tremors of her hands and of her lips. Gone was the girlish fright and shock. She was a Royal personage at a time of national disaster: calm, cool, under control and totally aware.

As she entered the acre or so of ground that extended beyond her parents' home she paused to greet and listen to the condolences of her fellow tribesmen. She neglected no one. Her kiss on the cheek of the Mayor's wife was classic. Her handshake with the Secretary of State of Florida was pure talent at international relations. I wondered what she still had to learn!

And when she came to us at the tail end of a long line of well-wishers she ostentatiously enveloped Janice with a heartfelt hug and a kiss. And for me she reserved a lingering touch of her lips to my cheek. It was then that she revealed her pain, for she had difficulty repressing a deep sigh that I might prefer to describe as a sob. She held me until she recovered control of herself. Would you believe it if I state that I actually felt honored that this young Princess cared so deeply about us and chose us for support?

At about ten o'clock the last of the well-wishers and notables had left. It was then that King Amoku and his Queen and Janice and Naina and I sat down for a late dinner. It may seem ridiculous to state that I have searched and researched my mind but I am simply unable to remember what we ate. My emotions got the better of me. I knew that, sooner or later, the real mystery of Talura's demise was going to be revealed. For Jan and me to be involved in the intrigue of an entirely different culture was not only exciting: it might prove to be dangerous.

We ate sparingly but whatever drink they served was potent. It was subtle in its ability to relax our tense muscles, a by-product of the cares of the day, without being a soporific. I began to suspect that we were being used. Perhaps we were like butterflies being prepared to be pinned to a board in someone's laboratory.

The justification for my restless psyche was ultimately to be pronounced by King Amoku himself.

"Dr. Ed, I must say that your expression is that of a champion chess-player considering and reconsidering the subtle moves of his opponent. The first move I must make is to assure you that you are not our opponents. In fact, of all the millions of people in America, you and Jan alone have been understanding and generous to our family. For that reason we feel that you must be told the entire truth about our beloved Talura and her tragic ending." (By the way, where was Talura's body? No one said a word about it.)

At that moment King Amoku unleashed a deep, prolonged sigh, the product of only the kind of pain that can accompany the death of one's child. His wife could not conceal the trembling of her hands and of the muscles of her neck. She and Amoku were in the deepest pain possible.

Taking a deep draft of that potent drink, King Amoku started the unraveling of the mystery of Princess Talura's death. "I mentioned to you just recently the unusual interest that Talura had in the chemical procedures that are the basis of our system of national defense. As Naina has told you, our ancestors had devised undetectable poisons to place in the water, in the food and even in the very air that our enemies might breathe so that they would never suspect that we were capable of so dealing with soldiers and even statesmen who threatened our existence.. Needless to say the identities of the chemists who created these poisons was a closely guarded secret. The talent and the training for these chemicals has been kept in a couple of families for over a thousand years.

"Tolura had an uncanny form of intelligence. She would have been a dangerous leader of the secret police. She would have thrived as chairman of the CIA. And as brilliant as she was, that cold was her nature. She rarely could kiss or hug anyone with true affection. Janice was one of the few people to have gotten her affection. She only gave gifts if there was a reciprocity with someone of considerable influence. She never said to anyone, "I love you."As far as we could tell she was simply incapable of love.

"Tolura was also incapable of empathy for the poor or the elderly or the disadvantaged. Strangely, the only persons she ever said that she liked were you and Jan. As a Princess second in line to lead our tribe she was totally unable to express care for our people or to understand their needs. The only interest she had was in chemicals----in poisons! She also, on only a few occasions, expressed the attitude that she would adopt if by some chance she would become a leader of our tribe. "That's not the way I would behave if I had control over these people!" she would occasionally say. "They are too soft; too forgiving. They are too generous for their own good. Those people should be eliminated!" she would say about some of our elected leaders. We knew what she meant by 'eliminated'.

"Somehow she made friends with the chief chemist of our tribe. He called me a few months ago to advise me about her serious interest in those poisons. But I mean *serious!* I warned him that she should never actually learn how those chemicals are made. Also, that she should never get her hands on any of them. And I warned him to remember whom she shows any antipathy towards and whom she, slyly, cultivates as her friends. We had to find out if she seriously wanted to 'eliminate' anybody.

"He replied that he was concerned that she had shown a sudden interest in his eldest son, who, besides being very handsome and personable, was also involved in the manufacture of the tribe's poisons.

"A week ago the chemist called me. He said Talura had disclosed that some day she might be the leader of our tribe if anything happened to me and Naina. He seemed genuinely upset over her ice-cold expression, as though she had been thinking about that a great deal. Then he said, "I guess I should have told you last year that she had said, "After a certain age we don't need our families."

She just blurted it out as though she had been talking to herself. You have a serious problem with that beautiful young woman."

"Yesterday, the chemist told his son, his chief assistant, to phone me and tell me that about 15 cc. (About a quarter of a cup) of the purified poison was missing since about ten o'clock in the morning. Talura had been there for about an hour and later phoned that she was going to be back at their lab at about 4:00 P.M. to pick up her sweater which she had forgotten to take." Then the young man asked us, "Is there anything else you wanted us to do?"

King Amoku then continued," I asked to speak with his father, immediately. His father, our faithful old friend, confirmed that about 15 cc. of a most potent poison was missing and that only Talura could have taken it. He advised me and my wife not to drink or eat anything in our home if Talura had been in the house since 10:00 AM. He also advised us to phone Naina at once to give the same precautions to her. This was just yesterday, Tuesday. I told him to take the usual precautions and that we would call him back within the hour. Talura came home from the chemists for lunch and then went out to the library for something for school. Upon the advice of the chemist we gave some of the milk from the fridge to the dog. Nothing happened. We gave him some coca-cola. Nothing happened. We got him to sip some of my wife's pea soup and the dog went into an immediate coma and died. Talura never liked pea soup and wasn't likely to drink it. But my wife and I certainly would have perished because we had planned on having some of that soup for dinner.

"After consulting with my wife I immediately called my chemist and told him what had happened. I ordered him to take the following steps: when Talura comes back for her sweater he was to offer her a coca cola. She can never resist a coke and she trusted that chemist implicitly. That would be the last drink she would ever have.

"When Talura returned for her sweater she seemed a little excited and her face was flushed. The chemist asked her what was so exciting. She replied, "Oh, I got some great grades in school today and I feel very encouraged!" She accepted his offer of a coca-cola and at the first sip she went into an immediate coma and died. Her blood had coagulated, irreversibly, in every tissue of her body."

Naina then spoke, in somber tones. This was the first time she had spoken in what seemed like hours. "Talura was going to drop by our place at about five o'clock. She said she wanted to have some of my delicious cooking." she said to her father. "I think she might have been after me, too. If her ambitions were to assume the leadership of our tribe the only way she could do that was if you and I were dead."

I did not mention it but it had occurred to me that if she killed Amoku and the Queen via the poisoned pea soup, since Naina had also planned on heating some of her mother's pea soup for us that day, Jan and I might have fallen victim as well as Naina.

This internecine skullduggery was entirely strange in our lives. For the royal family to be raising the equivalent of a viper in their home for sixteen years only to discover unequivical proof that her parents and sister were targets for assassination was more disturbing than an Agatha Christie novel. To forestall such a dastardly plot and to give the villain a dose of her own "medicine" is equally as diabolical.

Why were my hosts not crying? Why was Naina not in tears? After all, villain or not, Talura was the only other member of their immediate family. I had to ask the only pertinent question, "Could you not have called the police who would have discreetly put Talura in a mental institution where she could get carefully-supervised psychiatric therapy?"

Amoku had tears in his eyes when he replied. "If what she suffered from was a form of paranoia or schizophrenia we might have taken a chance on the bad publicity and the probably incompetent medical services. But one has to know in his bones what he is dealing with. If a person is in fact a "bad seed", an individual with a built-in diabolical madness that is part of her basic nature, not a psychiatric problem but a genetic pre-disposition to hatred and murder, then what therapy could a court-appointed psychiatrist achieve? Talura had the true Mayan blood-thirst that our branch of the Mayans was lucky to have been lacking." He paused, barely able to continue.

"Talura was a beauty; a dark treasure. She was a pleasure to observe. She was brilliant and very competent, but evil. We have lost our evil treasure...I loved her."

And so, the King and Queen who had just lost their youngest daughter now kissed "au revoir" their eldest daughter, who, in the natural course of events was to lead their tribe back to Belize. They would all return to their traditional home, back to the semi-primitive life that combined intelligence of a high order with the ability to live off the land and a culture that accepted nothing but loyalty and communal love from its fellow-tribesmen.

Janice and I ultimately lost our new-found treasure, whom we loved and admired, to "a greater cause". And I, personally, lost an interest at an age when such a loss is irrecoverable and not to be believed..

THE DEATH WISH*
A MURDEROUS MYSTERY

Those who read and enjoy history should not be greatly surprised at the twists and turns of human stories. But even a history buff such as I am had to be shocked--even startled--by the unexpected shift in the nature of the characters in this tale.

I thought that the characters were relatively normal who had presented themselves to me in the preceding story. That story seemed to have a decent enough ending with a relatively satisfactory conclusion to the problems of Naina and her family. But I must confess that events as they began to unfold after Naina had been accepted by Princeton University were a stunning surprise for me. Even my own character, as I participated in the developments, took a sharp turn towards the savage who inhabits even the best of us. Sorry about that.

As you may recall, the exiled King Amoku learned that his beautiful younger daughter, Tolura (AKA Talura), had poisoned the food that she expected her parents to eat one night. Later the same afternoon she was supposed, also, to visit her sister, Crown Princess Naina, who was employed as a care-giver for my wife Janice. The only persons who stood between Tolura and the Crown of the Mayan tribe of Belize were King Amoku and Crown Princess Naina.

*This is a sequel to the narrative, "The Caretaker."

The King, upon confirming the actuality of Tolura's plans learned, also, that she was going to pick up her sweater which she had left at the home of Omooru, the master chemist of the tribe. She had left her sweater there when she had stolen some of Omooru's poison. Amoku ordered his old friend Omooru to see to it that Tolura would become a victim of a poisoned drink herself. Amoku felt that his daughter was a dangerous psychopath who had apparently inherited the blood-thirst of the Mayans which had not been present in her family or most of the members of her tribe for many generations. Thus we are privy to the exciting and almost unbelievable continuation of this story.

It is now about two months after Naina had left Florida with us and had traveled with Jan and me to our home in New Jersey, near Philadelphia. We had evidence that Tolura had died from having imbibed some Coca Cola which had been laced with a tasteless, undetectable poison. A funeral had been performed for the dead princess, although her body was not brought to the funeral and none of the other tribes-people had been informed about the circumstances of her death. Jan and I had assumed that a funeral without the "corpus delictus" was one of the customs of that particular Mayan tribe. Nobody asked about it. It was not until a while later that we learned the truth about her poisoning.

After we had come back to New Jersey we had to employ another caretaker for Janice because it would have been impossible for Naina to have maintained such a taxing job and attend a college such as Princeton at the same time. Jan and I decided on how much we could afford to donate to her education and set that money aside in a special checking account for her to draw upon as needed. She proved to be unusually frugal and only drew out what she could not avoid drawing of those funds. For the summer months she registered for some courses at the University of Pennsylvania, close by. Naina's ambition was to study whatever was mandatory to prepare her to take the throne of her country as an educated and properly-trained executive.

It was on August fifth that I received a phone call from King Amoku in Florida. He said that he, without the Queen, would be at the Philadelphia airport, which is nearby and would be staying at the Hampden Hotel in our town for a couple of days at the most. The purpose of this visit was not social. It was for him to discuss with Naina some critical matters that had arisen. Also, Amoku was bringing along the son (Mikala) of his friend Omooru, the chemist who was so important to the history of their tribe. Amoku specifically invited Jan and me to participate in their discussions.

Needless to say, we were quite surprised. Of course Naina and I met the King and his guest to bring them to their hotel. Jan was left behind, under the care of Sylvia, the new caretaker. When Amoku and Mikala got into our car he immediately said that as soon as they checked into their hotel they would spend the rest of the day discussing the important matters that were so demanding. Before anyone could say anything else, after Amoku had spoken, I just had to break into their thoughts with an observation.

"There are two tough-looking men who were on your plane and are in the taxicab that is following us real close. Shall I try to shake them off our trail?"

Amoku smiled as he replied, "Those are my bodyguards. They follow us everywhere we go. They will have the two rooms on each side of us. One man will be in the hall all night with a cell phone. They were allowed to carry weapons on the plane: blowguns with poison darts!

Naina laughed and informed me, "I always called them Woolu and Boolu. They're crazy about me!"

When we arrived at the hotel we were hurried into the suite of rooms they had reserved and I was pleased that Amoku called room service and ordered drinks and sandwiches for everybody in his party. He asked the guard who was not stationed in the hall to search all the rooms, including the bathrooms and the closets, for any hidden microphones or tape-recorders. Both guards were informed that they would be official "food-tasters" for all the food and drinks that we would have, but they were used to that job for years. I am very grateful to "Woolu" and "Boolu" for being so devoted and caring to that royal family and of course I am appreciative that the food and drinks were both safe and delicious.

As soon as the phones were cleared I called Sylvia, the new caretaker for Janice, to find out how my wife was faring in my absence. Sylvia has the medical training that Naina doesn't have and years of experience that really are required to provide the best care for a sick older lady like Jan. Sylvia reported that everything was okay at home and not to worry about anything. I didn't mention where we were but in case of emergency she could reach me on my cell phone.

Finally, King Amoku spoke. His guards were no longer in the room and could not hear what we were discussing. "You are correct if you think that what I have to say is of importance. For at least the past year there have been serious discussions between my advisors in the tribe and me concerning a suggestion I had made in May of last year. As you know, we have now been out of our country for nearly six years. I asked them all, 'When do we ever expect to return to Belize, or do we surrender our homeland to those savages who have killed so many of our people and seized control of our government? They have made life miserable for everybody who remained in the country.' I had gathered all my advisors around me to figure out a way for us to return and retake control of our government. It is now time to enhance our plans and finalize them. I wish to return to Belize in a matter of months!

"Among my advisors are Omooru and his son Mikala, whom I have had the pleasure of knowing since his birth nearly twenty-three years ago. They, too, are royalty and must have a say in our future. It was my conception that we might land in neighboring countries and move surreptitiously across the borders into Belize to stir up a revolt by our people. Since we do not shed blood what other means do we have to seize control and drive out our enemies? Whom could we get to do the attacking of our enemies? How would we use the only weapons at our disposal on a relatively modern enemy who has all those automatic weapons and even a certain amount of poison gas?

"We have not as yet formulated any definitive plans and that is why we are here today. We need your imput. I want my darling Naina ultimately to assume her rightful role as ruler of our tribe and leader of the country of Belize. Do you have any ideas on the subject, Naina?"

Amoku, at this point, looked very thin and tense. I thought that he was under some unmentioned pressure and that his health was giving way. Naina also looked at him very long and hard and, as though she had read my mind, she then spoke." I can see, father, that you share our obsession to return to our home before the spirits carry you away from us. We are all here to make your decisions less onerous and to lead in all the physical aspects of retaking Belize. "There are many phases of this problem that must be considered. First of all there is the overall plan. Then there is the all-important question of who is savage enough among our gentle people to do all that killing by poison. And then there is the question of how do we lead our people whom we have left nearly six years ago. We have been in a pleasant never-never-land while they have been suffering at the hands of those brutes from Africa all this time. Do we still have their affection and respect? Can we count on their support? Can we lead this revolt from Florida or shouldn't we be on the soil of Belize, risking our own lives as they risk theirs? Can we answer any of these questions right now?"

Amoku was delighted with Naina's grasp of the situation. He then looked at me, a gaunt, sunken-eyed look such as a lost man might direst towards a divinity. "What ideas do you have, Doctor Ed?"

Whereas I would usually jump right into a discussion and spew a multitude of ideas that might (or might not) be half-baked, this was not the occasion for an impulsive stranger, who really was ignorant of the basic statistics of the problem, to shoot his mouth off and exacerbate the situation. So I decided to ask as many pertinent questions as I could think of to clear the air—and *then* offer some suggestions.

"First of all," I asked, "how many of the enemy do we have to deal with? How many grown males and older teenagers and how many women and children are there? What is their educational level and how much power do they actually have? What sort of weapons do they have and are they located all over the country?"

It was Mikala who had all the answers to my questions. "They are really a fifth-rate power as nations are rated. There are only about five thousand males of all ages and about one thousand teenagers of both sexes beyond the age of fifteen. They only have the cast-off weapons they could buy cheaply on the open market. Their leadership is clever but crude. No real talent there. None of them have ever gone to college, they don't know anything about technology and none of them have very much education. The dozen or so men who created all these problems for us are dirty and tricky but they have no idea about military strategy or tactics.

'What they are is crooks; thieves and rough and tough. They were driven out of the Ivory Coast of Africa for very good reasons and I would like nothing better than to ship them all back to get the punishment they deserve. In all there are about twelve thousand of them, including women and little children. By the way, these people are very ignorant and superstitious. If they were to experience an "impossible" catastrophe they would fall apart."

This account was unexpectedly brilliant and thorough. We all looked at this young man (aged less than twenty-three) with a new-found respect. I had to ask some further questions and get some more answers before I could even dare to make any suggestions. "Could you tell me how modern or advanced Belize is? For instance, are there paved roads everywhere, especially leading to the neighboring countries? Are there military stations to guard these roads, like near the borders? What sort of airports and shipping does Belize have? Can helicopters land near paved roads anywhere? Does anybody in Belize have computers? Do you have any railway lines? What sort of banking and mail systems do you have? Do most of the homes have electricity? How prevalent is air-conditioning: like in private homes, in office-buildings, in the houses of congress or parliament? Are your enemies really sophisticated enough to be able to bug your phones or your hotel rooms or to attack you on airplanes?"

Amoku answered me this time. "Of course we have paved roads, except up in the mountains, and there have always been guard posts at the borders with Mexico, Nicaragua and Costa Rica. We have three airports; one large one on the outskirts of the main city and two smaller ones. You could land a helicopter anywhere except in the mountains, which are pretty rugged. But there are large clearings even there. Our big airport can take big planes like

747's. Our port can take the largest ships there are, but most long passenger vessels, like the Carnival, don't come to us because we have a barrier reef about a mile or two from our shores and they are afraid to hit some coral reefs in turning around. Our port is really a deep-water facility–thirty to fifty feet deep, for the most part.

"Our banks and postal system are quite modern and sophisticated. So is our telephone system. Everything is automated, much like the USA and every public building is air-conditioned and computerized. Most of the homes for the middle class and above are also air-conditioned and have computers. Every grade school teaches computerization and almost all employees and students have cell phones and computers. You've seen my daughters and Mikala. Could they get along in this modern age without computers and cell phones?

"Our enemies are not at all sophisticated. They have to hire "hit men" to go after us and bug our phones. Our phones here in the States have been bugged for over five years. When I called you from Florida I used a cell phone."

Amoku, as gaunt and exhausted as he seemed to be, was able to answer all the questions I had asked. He also appeared to be recovering his strength as he spoke. But I had one key question to ask. "Okay. That's all very important, but who amongst this tribe is savage enough to lead in all the poisoning that will have to be done? I can't see anyone like that in this room, although Mikala could well lead the people and so could Naina. But I cannot see them doing the actual poisoning of water, air and food, which will have to be done. I have in mind someone who might have been perfect for the job, but that person is no longer with us."

King Amoku shifted uneasily in his chair. When he looked directly at me he had tears in his eyes. I thought he might be on the verge of a breakdown, but he spoke in a soft voice and stunned us all by what he had to say. Only Amoku was not surprised by my question.

"You are very perceptive, Doctor Ed. I am so pleased that we chose to include you at this time. I have some news that might answer your last question. You may remember that when Tolura had placed poison in our food and would probably have poisoned all of us in order to get the power of tribal leadership, I asked my dear friend Omooru, Mikala's father, to give Tolura a fatal dose of the same undetectable poison that she had placed in our food. I had felt that Tolura was an untreatable psychopath and exceptionally dangerous.

"Omooru, who never argues with me and does whatever I ask of him, gave Tolura, instead, a poison that does not kill and does no permanent damage to any of the body's tissues. It throws the victim into an instantaneous coma for a few days and the victim comes out of this coma very slowly. In this way we can control an enemy without killing him—or her. Omooru's explanation, when he told me what he had done, was that we had all thought of Tolura as being the perfect selection of the savage but brave and intelligent person to lead the assault against our enemies.

"We had been trying for months to figure out who that Dark Angel would be and Omooru took definitive steps not to destroy our own Dark Angel. Why kill her? Why not chastise her by letting her know that we are at least as clever as she is and caught her in the violent act of trying to poison her own family? We could then try to use her "talents" in the revolt against our enemies. She is perfect for that job and might even be repentant for what she had tried to do.

"But Omooru had a problem. Maybe he had given Tolura too strong a dose of the 'medicine'. She stayed in the coma for nearly a month and as she was slowly coming out of it he called me and told me what he had done. When I went to see her, my darling, beautiful child, I cried and cried. But as I approached the couch she was sitting on I noticed a great change in my Tolura. She had lost quite a few pounds and her skin seemed to have darkened. She was the embodiment of the dangerous Mayans we have differed from in our fortunate history. She didn't say one word but looked through me as though I had been made of glass. What had we done? Her attitude also prevented me from speaking. We simply stared at each other. There were no words to express how she and I felt.

"I had thought that she was dead until Omooru's call a month later. We never have a corpse at a funeral. We, in our tribe, prefer to let our imaginations revolve about the recently departed and not allow a coffin or a burial sack to interfere with our remembrances of the serious loss we have incurred. So we had held a funeral for Tolura. I had instructed Omooru as to the burial.

"We have a principle in our tribe: the family she comes from do not talk to the dead and they of course cannot speak to us. Tolura, to us, was now dead. The Priests had said the prayers for the dead for her. What could we now do about that?

"I decided to let Omooru or Mikala say to her whatever we had to say. They are not members of our immediate family. Tolura had no idea that she had been in a coma for a full month. She was physically very weak. Nobody could bring up the proposition at this time for her to lead a revolt. I am not sure that I was glad she was alive. She didn't smile or speak at all." Amoku paused to wipe the tears from his eyes. He suddenly seemed so shriveled and so ancient. "This was our last little girl who had grown up so strangely!"

Naina went to her father and hugged him and kissed him on the cheek. How could anyone not love this dear, troubled man? I too hugged him out of sheer affection and I noted that Mikala hugged and kissed Amoku as though he had been his own father. Naina then said to us all, "I'm going to go back to Florida to take care of my parents and forget about college for now."

At this Amoku straightened up and said very firmly, "No way, my love! You were honored by being accepted by Princeton University and that's that! Only one thing would keep you from finishing your education there." We all knew what he meant by that remark.

Mikala then spoke up but we were not sure to whom he was directing his words. It was very much like a soliloquy. "You read about family turmoil in Shakespeare and never expect to see it right before your own eyes. You read in history books about the troubles of the Hebrews and the Armenians and the Kurds and never think that your own tribe would have similar problems. History never stops repeating itself! People must be stupid!"

I could see that Naina had, almost suddenly, developed a new respect and affection for that young man. And why not? He was perfect for her: intelligent and sensitive and a fellow tribesman.

My place in her life was immediately a thing of the past: a fond memory, but old news.

Amoku must have seen the qualities of this young man and subtly brought him to the attention of Naina: successfully. It was like someone finding a gem that was lying at her feet all along.

"Well, what is the next stage of our discussion, father?" was Naina's way of covering up the intensity of her gaze while Mikala was speaking.

Amoku was quick to reply, "We have to develop our plans more highly; the plans that we barely discussed until now. Doctor Ed asked a lot of questions but that was to learn more about the nature of our land and its captors. Now let's hear if Dr. Ed can come up with some practical suggestions."

It really was not my province to take a leading role in their discussion. Certainly they knew their problems better than I did and they would benefit only marginally by what I might have to say. And so I really surprised myself by the savagery of my thinking. As an American, Jewish liberal I was not supposed to think this way. Perhaps it was their Mayan background that encouraged me to say the primitive things I said. Perhaps the fact that I had just finished reading the stories of Flavius Josephus and was inflamed by the actions of so many tyrants against the people I love. I don't know what impelled me to recommend murder and violence: but I did!

"Since you do not believe in guns and bloodshed it is more difficult--trickier--to deal with your enemies. And they *are* your enemies! You must know that these individuals from the west coast of Africa are but a very few generations from out-and-out savagery and primitivism. They are not at all as educated, as generous and as civilized as your people are. All they can understand at their stage of development is, as the Bible says, 'An eye for an eye, a tooth for a tooth'. Your whole tribe and your nation must reciprocate in the same degree of inhumanity and ungodly behavior that *they* used in Belize, or you can never be rid of them!

"So you have to do all of the following suggestions and more:

1) You have to send a delegation of highly-trained and highly-motivated young people to Belize—surreptitiously.

2) This cadre of young men and women will train perhaps two thousand youngsters from your tribe in the art of using the blow-gun with poison-tipped darts.

3) Also they must be trained in the art of silently stalking people in the cities and in the fields and forests. They must learn how to insert your poisons in the intake portions of air-conditioners so that you can wipe out a whole houseful or an office full of people in a very few minutes. Since your poisons are undetectable *you* should be undetectable as well, so that you can make a quick, lethal strike anyplace in your country without giving yourself away.

4) You must aim primarily at the male leaders of your opposition. You understand that you don't have to kill their families if that can be avoided. For families you could employ the drug used to immobilize Tolura. You could use the same drug, if possible, when you immobilize an office full of people. You don't have to *kill* everyone: just the military, the police, the leadership and those who have been bleeding your treasury.

5) You must have someone train you so that you can train your young people how to place poisons into an air-conditioning system to immobilize the maximum number of policemen, soldiers and other people in their barracks, homes and offices.

7) You must immobilize the leadership in your House of Representatives, or Parliament in two minutes' time by poisoning the air they breathe. If you station a group of youngsters with poison darts at every entrance and exit of a building they can nail those who try to run away from the poisons inside.

8) You must train your people to kill as many policemen and soldiers as possible the very first day of your revolt—you can't give them a chance to use their automatic weapons, their bombs and artillery shells. And they may also have poison gas, somebody said. They could wipe out your whole tribe in less than a week. You have to pre-empt them!

9) A certain large cadre of your young people will sneak up to each residence that your enemies have and poison their air-conditioners. If they don't have such a device you have to prepare a device that spreads poison quickly through the air of a house— possible a battery-operated electric fan! This all has to be done

before anyone can phone for help or use a weapon. You will not be using any firearms so your advantage is good training and surprise: and total dedication to the job at hand *without human sensitivity*. This is war ----a defensive war!

10) You must plan, in advance, that no airplanes, ships, boats or vehicles of any kind will leave your shores or your land if it carries one of your enemies. You must plan to disable every vehicle and boat and airplane without an explosion. A half pound of granulated sugar in the gas-tank will prevent almost any engine from starting! You must have a sufficient number of blow-guns at the shores and airports to discourage escapees.

11) Your leadership has to take the airlines, the passenger-liners and the cargo ships into their confidence and let them know that not one individual can leave Belize until you give the all-clear signal—probably within 24-48 hours.

12) You must see to it that all military and police guard stations on all the highways and everywhere else are immobilized quietly with one poison or another. You must not give even one guard an opportunity to use his cell-phone to call for help or support. Death must be instantaneous for all such men.

13) You must not allow any man, woman or child to leave your shores or get to a neighboring country. Those men who may have valises full of gold or gems or securities must be apprehended and immobilized permanently.

You have a critical need for quickness, efficiency, insensitivity and organization. It is all a matter of planning."

The silence that followed my remarks was as palpable as a brick wall. Amoku was the first to speak up, as well he should be. "I see that you caught some of that Mayan blood-lust from Tolura! I must say, as you sit there with that tentative smile on your face, that you really out-savage the rest of us. But that is exactly the way we must behave. And knowing this is why my advisors have been undecided in their advice to me. Everyone's afraid he will be called "a savage", but that's what war really is and if we are to retake our country from those 'bad guys' we have to defeat them overwhelmingly. The way you suggest is the only way we can beat them."

But Naina spoke up in a very humanistic manner. You couldn't help loving someone who speaks as she did. "But father, we must be careful not to encourage our young people to think of surreptitious violence and the use of poisons as a way of life. That is the way of Tolura and must not be encouraged!"

"Well, Naina," said Mikala, "You know how proud we are of our history of non-violence despite the fact that we used poisons for many years to keep from being over-run by alien marauders. We really are a wonderful people to have fought that way for several centuries and still we have become such a model society for all to admire."

Amoku added, "I agree with both Naina and Mikala. We have to do what we have to do but we cannot have a model society if our behavior is always based on a threat of violence."

"I'll agree to that wholeheartedly," said Naina. "But I have another point to bring up. We have heard from our friends in Belize that the many millions of dollars in our national treasury have dwindled to so little that we are unable to pay for the education of our youngsters. The present leaders have not been spending that much money for the public good so we have to assume that it must have been stolen. What can we do to prevent that?"

"I'm glad you mentioned that, Naina," I replied. "That's one of the main reasons to block off all exit routes from Belize suddenly and totally, to prevent anyone from carrying anything valuable out of the country."

"Also," said Naina, thoughtfully, "It is very probable that they could have sent millions into Swiss bank accounts or other off-shore accounts by mail or E-mail or direct deposits. We have to check all their phone and electronic records and get our hands on all the private papers of those men who could have had access to our treasury. It can't be many people, but I am not sure if we can recover all that cash."

Mikala continued where Naina had left off, "I'll bet that once we get our hands on their private papers we can learn their account numbers, where-ever they are deposited. We can then put pressure on the banks to return our money."

"Yes," said Naina, mischievously, "And if they refuse to repay the stolen money we can send Tolura on a trip to Switzerland as a convincer."

"You could do worse," added Amoku seriously. "They are all a bunch of crooks, the savages who stole our money and the Swiss banks. They are all unholy!" I was surprised at the vigor and intensity of our dear friend Amoku.

"We have to organize all these great ideas," Naina continued, "and appoint people whose responsibility it will be to effectuate them. It is only proper to widen the base of our activities so that it will not appear to be simply a family matter. Since my Dad is well into the planning for this exploit can we hear how far he and his advisors have gotten already?" Naina has that practical turn of mind that is more interested in the brass tacks of solid accomplishment than in dreams of the future.

Amoku immediately responded to his daughter's implications. "Of course we have considered most of the suggestions that you all have come up with, but you have actually gone even further than we have accomplished. My advisors and I have come up with two people who will lead the revolt in Belize. Mikala will be the overall leader. The leader of all the attack forces with all that poisoning you mentioned, st of which we had already worked out before I came to visit you, will be Tolura. Of course, everyone knows she is dead, so she will have to change her identity.

We thought she might even wear a mask part of the time, but she really has changed physically so much that most people would not recognize her. She has a hard, intense look on her face. She never smiles and even her posture has been altered, since she acquired an aspect of muscular tenseness which has changed her back and shoulder muscles. I must inform you that that child has been converted into almost a caricature of the most inhuman Mayan terror who ever existed. I am not certain how long such a person, even at her age, can live with such a twisted personality.

"Omooru and I discussed with her, finally, the fact that we had been considering her for the task of leading the assault forces on our enemies. She looked at us as though we were criminals and said, surprisingly." Of course. I did a cruel, primitive act against my parents. I must have a criminally insane mind, according to your estimation. Therefore only someone like that could lead the poison attacks on our enemies. If that is the case, I accept. I will be pleased to make up for my actions against my family to free our tribe totally from the aliens who have taken over our land. You can count on me to train the teenagers to use all the vicious techniques that I have been dreaming about since we were driven away. You can count on me. Because I am legally dead I must have a new name and a new identity. I will be the "Dark Priestess" of our tribe and will dress appropriately. Give me my orders. Give me the young people. Give me whatever supplies and support I will need and I will be the perfect Dark Princess."

Omoku then spoke. "That was my beloved child acting out so intensely the role of the "bad seed" that she really and truly believes it herself. It is more than sad, but she will do a superb job for us and may, actually receive some therapeutic values from her realization that doing something important for your people is the way to live a normal life. Mikala will be her boss. He will help her and support her and we will provide all the help she will need." Amoku looked exceedingly tense.

Mikala spoke up,. "I *hope* to be able to control her. She gives me the impression of someone on the verge of going beyond control. What can be done to restrain her from going beyond the feasible and rational in her behavior? After all, the way to succeed in life and especially in a war is not to take the emotional path but the rational path. The time for play-acting is past. It was part of her childhood and has no place when the success of our revolt—and our lives—are at stake."

"That is entirely up to you." said Amoku, "She has rejected *this* father figure but requires another. It is now for you to speak to her in exactly the terms with which you just spoke to us. Tell her about play-acting. Tell her about the importance of unemotional judgment as contrasted with getting angry or excited and making an obvious, predictable response that our enemies are expecting of a young person. There will be no mass killings except for those with armaments and positions of authority and those who attempt to interfere with your plans. They must be destroyed. You must inform Tolura that the same drug that was used on her should be used on women and children and elderly people. We will not tolerate mass killings, for any reason at all."

But I had a question that required an answer. "How about your legislature now composed almost entirely of aliens who have voted for all those terrible impositions on your people? Should they be punished as well and to what degree?"

Naina replied, "That's a good point. Were they acting on their own or because they were fearful themselves of the military and the leaders?"

Amoku had a quick rejoinder, "They were given orders to plunder our nation, to destroy our businesses and our educational facilities. They stood to gain by taking over our shops and factories and our land. I insist that they are all supremely guilty and should be punished. I leave it to the people on the ground in Belize about what to do with them; whether they should be killed or simply immobilized. When you return home, Mikala, you will ask around about these people. Do as your countrymen request, but make sure it is a rational decision, not an emotional one. Either way these people have to be rendered powerless and if kept alive, they must be placed on ships and sent back to the Ivory Coast where they came from less than six years ago."

Mikala took up the side of the story that I had hoped he would. "Regardless of the reasons "why" they voted as they did, each vote was a criminal act under the laws of our nation. They violated our laws against bloodshed. They cast aside our religious observances. They gutted the curriculum of our schools. They deprived almost all the Mayans of the means for a livelihood. They stole untold sums from our treasury and altered the gentle, liberal, educated nature of our country to a harsh, ignorant police state. And they drove so many of us out of our own beloved country. I am not like Tolura, as a rule, but I would let Tolura loose against those legislators. Immobilization is not enough of a punishment for them!"

"Well spoken, Mikki," said Naina. "I'm almost afraid of you myself!"

"Well, I'm sorry you're frightened. That was not my intention at all. I was aiming at our enemies. You *are* a friend, I assume?"

It suddenly occurred to me that Naina was teasing Mikala the way she had teased me for almost two months. Of course she had to agree with everything "Mikala" had said or else our entire meeting was undermined and she could not have wanted that at all.

Amoku sensed that aspect and looked at Naina in a questioning, intense mode. Naina looked back at him and pretended to hide a smile behind her hands. In the midst of all this seriousness Amoku and I detected the love-play beginning between the two that Mikala hadn't quite picked up yet. As "Doctor Ed" I had picked it up the second day that Naina had stayed with us but was helpless before it for a long time.

"Where does this leave us now?" I asked "Is there a role for Naina in all this?"

"Of course," said Amoku. "She is a vital part of the planning and executive committees. She is at the top of the hierarchy, with me. As soon as the police and military aliens have been "neutralized" we will all return en masse. We will take up exactly where we left off. The same people if they are alive who ran the government will take their old positions. People will retake their old businesses, regain their old lands and homes, the old curricula will resume at the schools and Naina will be right in the forefront of our activity. She will be directing people in the schools, in our parliament and in our government to return to the democratic ways of our recent past.

'She may have to postpone her education for a few months to help in the revolt and the transition, but then she can return to Princeton to complete her education. We need her common sense and her humanity, we need her liberal approach to our problems and we need someone to help eradicate the effects on our teenagers who will have been trained in the use—and the philosophy—of violence. They have to re-learn the teaching that violence begets violence, and Naina, without having to go back to college even for one day, is capable of re-teaching all those kids, who will be poisoning five thousand or more enemies, that there is a better way to live in peace."

I was impelled to speak up at this point because my heart was so full of admiration for these Mayans. "I must say to everyone here that I am not aware of any nation in the world whose leaders are so reluctant to employ violence and whose genuine beliefs are as moral and honorable as this group right here and right now. I am very impressed. This is "Dr. Ed speaking from his heart."

Amoku had some final words for the occasion. "I think we have done all we can do for this stage of our planning. We will return to Florida and start recruiting as many young men and women as we can, with the constraints of secrecy being uppermost in our minds. We shall gather the elders in our group of advisors and inform them of our plans. In fact, Mikala will work with us and we shall include a large percentage of younger members of our tribe for our executive council. We need them in every way. We will formulate a list of those who will be the first to return surreptitiously to Belize and start our training methods with the young people we will need. We will not spread the word around too much but a revolution is not supposed to be a secret. It just should not get to the enemy.

"I will need to consult with Naina and Dr. Ed again in Florida. Maybe you can bring Janice down with you and spend a few weeks– or as long as it takes–refining our plans and thinking of details that we haven't even begun to mention yet. I would like to see the first cadre of revolutionists leave for Belize in less than three or four months, if possible. Much depends on the health of Tolura. If she still seems frail in a month or so we can delay our preliminaries for that length of time. Meanwhile Mikala will be on the look-out for someone else to take Tolura's place. We cannot simply depend on one little girl for our revolt. We already have several young men in mind, but right now there is only one Tolura."

Amoku wanted us to stay for dinner but I had to get back to Janice. Naina stayed on for more discussions and for dinner. I came by at ten o'clock and brought her home with us again.

Early the next morning Amoku and his party left for Florida. That evening Amoku and the queen went to visit Tolura, who was still living with Omooru and his family, a couple of blocks from Amoku. She would never again stay at her parents' home. Since she was legally dead and the prayers for the dead had already been said for her, the tribal laws dictated that she could never again resume normal family life. But her mother, who had not seen Tolura for almost a month, simply had to see her and reach out to her "little girl", regardless of the laws.

According to Mikala, who was present when the King and Queen came into his home to visit with Tolura, it was a most unusual scene. Amoku was overly tired, having flown from Philadelphia that very day and not having rested at all. His health was a matter of conjecture. Such tension in a person with diabetes is not recommended. Certainly the impending revolt against the enemies of Belize had to put a great weight on his constitution. And now he was visiting his beautiful but strange young daughter who was not living at her own home but in the residence of a friend. And it was this friend, Omooru, who was the chief chemist responsible for manufacturing and storing the most dangerous poisons known to man. It is no wonder, then, that Amoku's hands trembled and his blood-pressure was highly elevated.

As for Tolura, let it not be supposed that she took any pleasure from seeing her parents in such a state of tension and stress. She saw her father as a changed man, and the changes disturbed her. She had never seen her parents so aggravated. Her heart went out to them. The only problem was that she was unable to express her feelings of love and sympathy. Some psychological wall existed between her deep feelings and the manner with which she was able to demonstrate her sensibilities. All that she was able to do, to show her feelings, was to say to them, "I think you are both over-tired. The best thing you could do right now is to go home right now and take a nap!"

Of all things for a daughter to say! Not, "I've missed you!" or, "I dearly love you both. Please don't be so upset." or, "Is there any way that you can forgive me for what I've done to you?" Nothing like that escaped from her lips although it was in her heart and ready to be expressed. All she could say was, "I think you are both over-tired. The best thing you could do right now is to *go home right now and take a nap!*"

Amoku and the Queen took it the wrong way. Talk about putting salt in a wound! They smiled a strange smile to cover their pain and soon said good-bye to their hosts and their daughter.

No sooner had they left than Mikala exploded in a dramatic tirade against Tolura. "How could you treat your parents like that!? Instead of apologizing or saying something nice to them to soothe them, you dismiss them with, 'The best thing you could do right now is to go home right now and take a nap!' What a creep you are! What a heartless little savage! Didn't you see how ill your father is? Didn't you see how your mother has developed a nervous twitch that she can't control? Do you think they get a decent night's sleep? Ever? What do you suppose brought this on? Do you think it is possibly due to their darling, beautiful daughter poisoning their food? You poison everyone's life around you, you savage!" He almost burst into tears but turned aside because he didn't want Tolura to see him cry.

Suddenly, Tolura herself burst into tears! The dam had broken. She cried uncontrollably for over five minutes. Mikala watched her coldly all that time to determine if she was play-acting or if she was truly sincere. When convinced of her sincerity he made a bold move. He telephoned Amoku whose residence was three city blocks away from his home.

Amoku had just walked into the house and answered the phone. Mikala said, in a firm voice, "Your highness, we have a little girl here who wants to speak to her Daddy!" And he handed the phone to Tolura, who eagerly grasped it and spoke through her tears to her father. "Oh Daddy! I'm so sorry! I'm so sorry for all the mistakes I've made! I do love you and Mommie so much that"---She stopped speaking and stopped crying at once. She had heard a "thud", as of someone falling to the floor at her home. She immediately told Mikala what she had heard. He immediately called 911, asking for an ambulance to be sent Amoku's residence.

By the time Mikala and Tolura had run the few blocks to Amoku's home the ambulance had arrived. There was nothing they could do for Amoku. He had sustained a massive cerebral hemorrhage and was dead before he hit the floor. His wife saw at once that he had succumbed and simply held his face in her hands and kissed it.

"I was on the extension line in the kitchen when you called," she said, and heard what you said to your father. 'I'm so sorry! I'm so sorry for all the mistakes I have made! I do love you and Mommie so much.' Your Daddy loved you too, Tolura, and so do I. It was very thoughtful of you to call. I am certain that Amoku died with his mind at peace. And I am at peace as well." And her hands had lost the trembling that had plagued her for months.

Of course, we in New Jersey had no idea that all this was going on. Amoku had just left this very morning. Here it was about nine-thirty at night and we had just learned about it as a result of Mikala's phone call. We asked him to delay the funeral until at least two days had elapsed because Jan and I and our new caretaker were coming down to Florida. Naina was going to take an early morning flight to Ft. Lauderdale airport and we would be flying down later that day to the West Palm Beach airport, which is a little closer to our apartment in Boca Raton. We intended to rent a car for a week or two.

I immediately ordered four tickets from U.S. Airways over the phone. I did not buy a return ticket for Naina, however. She would not be coming back to New Jersey in the foreseeable future. By seven o'clock the next evening we had all been transported to Florida. We opened up our lovely apartment again and, after Jan and the new caretaker, Sylvia, had gotten comfortable, I drove to the neighborhood Publix to purchase some food and drinks and then I had to drive for about forty minutes down to Ft. Lauderdale to visit with Naina and her mother. Hey! Here I am, nearly eighty-seven years old, and running around doing all kinds of errands as though I were a kid of thirty-five again!

Naina had already been sworn in as Queen of her tribe but the elders had planned on a more expansive ceremony at a later date. They had decided not to let anyone beyond the immediate family in on Amoku's death at this time, for fear it might have a deleterious effect on the revolt that was planned.

Of course I paid my respects to the former Queen, Naina's mother, and had a long talk with Mikala. I made sure to impress on that capable young man the full confidence I had in his approach to all the matters he had become involved in for all the past few months. But the critical matters of the revolt and Naina's ascension to the throne of her tribe were not matters that needed any expansion on my part. I was just preparing to leave for Boca Raton when Naina approached me and said, "The elders and I have something to discuss with you, Dr. Ed." and she led me to a sun-room where seven elders were waiting for Naina and me. Among those "elders" was Mikala, which told me that he ranked very highly in his tribe, and rightly so.

A wizened old man spoke first. "With the permission of our new Queen, I have something of importance to say."

Naina promptly agreed, "Elder Boku, you may speak."

"Is there a possibility, Doctor Ed, that you could procure for us a whole staff of advisors tor our new Queen? She will not be able to attend Princeton at present and we urgently require some of the brainy people you had mentioned to her who could advise her majesty and us on matters of politics, economics, psychology and history. We wish to make our little country as efficient and as strong economically as possible. We also have to enhance our sense of historic relevancy in order to fit into the modern world." No one had told me that Elder Boku had been the president of the university in Belize.

Naina added to Elder Boku's speech. "You had mentioned to me, several times, that some of America's best public citizens might agree to help us. Can you flesh that idea out a little bit, Doctor Ed?"

As she said that "Doctor Ed" she looked at me in such a manner that I really wanted to rush over to her and donate a hug and a kiss to 'her majesty'. I hoped that my restraint was not visible to anyone present.

What was requested of me was not something in my exact powers. All I could do was to promise to make a series of urgent phone calls to those whom I respected in public life. "Well, thanks for your confidence. All I can promise to do is to call those whom I feel can help you and you can take it from there. Frankly I have always had the highest respect for Former President Clinton and his staff when he was in office. If I were doing this for my own country I would suggest a more leftist or socialistic approach.

I really feel that items like the ownership of a nation's natural resources should rest in the hands of the government, so that the public—and the government–.would not have to pay excessively for minerals, for oil and for forest products. That would also keep millionaires and billionaires from running your government. Also I would recommend governmental management of a complete health system and such projects as social security and unemployment insurance, care for the elderly and laws for the vast array of manufacturing that establish your deep concern for the ecology. Your goods have to be competitive in price: affordable to your own people as well as to those overseas. You must encourage the manufacturing and retail abilities of your country.

"President Clinton is a centrist. He correctly judged the mood of his country when he was running for office and adopted a centrist mode in his policies, which annoyed many Liberals, including me. In your country, which is nowhere near as prodigious in size and capabilities as the United States, a more left-leaning program would meet your needs and still get to the same relative degree of efficiency. I will ask Former President Bill Clinton to gather together his idea of a satisfactory group of economists, business-managers, social-services specialists and even election specialists and have them all meet with Queen Naina and you at your convenience. This has to be done practically at once, at the same time that other individuals are preparing for your revolt. You must have an organized plan and appoint your leaders of each department before you move back into Belize. You simply cannot land on that holy ground and not know what to do. You cannot afford to make key mistakes and alienate the very people whose support and welfare you wish to preserve. I do not know how long it will take for me to organize your economic and social aides but I will know better in a few weeks."

Then it became time for me to return to my wife in Boca Raton. Naina would stay at her mother's home until she moved on to Belize, where the community would build her a new palace for her own use. The funeral for Amoku took place two days later, in relative secrecy. Since no one besides Omooru and his family knew that Tolura was still alive she could not officially attend her father's funeral. However, several people did notice a black-clad, heavily-veiled young woman sitting at the rear of the hall, who kept dabbing at her eyes with a handkerchief. This young woman left the hall before the others and disappeared from sight, permanently. Amoku's body was not at his funeral, just as Tolura's was not at *her* funeral. But Amoku was really dead, alright

The next morning a meeting was held by Naina with all her elders and advisors as well as Mikala. Somehow, perhaps from some previously hidden source of talent, Naina conducted her first meeting with a charm and an efficiency that more experienced politicians might envy. She had all the acumen and confidence— and some of the 'trickiness'–of an old 'pro'. She informed her group about Amoku's trip North, just a few days ago, and what had been discussed. She summarized what each person at the meeting in New Jersey had said. As though she had taken notes she gave as accurate a 'precis' as it was possible to give. Naina really had a photographic memory. She showed the intellect and the instincts of a professional manager and politician. She appointed Mikala as the leader on the ground in the revolt for Belize. She mentioned that they had come up with a person of superior leadership ability and bravery to be in charge of the military–the poisoning–campaign.

This person, for obvious reasons, could not be named at this time—if ever. Because there would be so much killing of the aliens in such a gruesome manner, it would be totally inappropriate to name the people involved. After all, this person has to come back into the tribe and try to lead a normal life.

"I find that proposal reasonable and am prepared to accept it." said Queen Naina. Everyone agreed, but except for Mikala and Omooru not a soul even suspected that the "military general" was Naina's sixteen-year-old "dead" sister, Tolura. By the way, Alexander the Great began his career, in much more primitive times, when he was only sixteen years of age. He, too, had spent all the years of his childhood "dreaming" about military action against Greece's enemies.

Naina then outlined the broad plans for the invasion and revolt against their enemies. She then suggested that every day at eleven A.M. there would be a meeting at her house of all the people who were currently in attendance. "Oh, by the way," she said, almost casually, "Do we have any members of our tribe who are certified air-conditioning experts? Let me know, please."

The meeting ended and, I said my good-byes to everyone there. Most of them had never met me before. Naina came over to me and expressed her love for Janice. "I'm going to have some friends come to your house in New Jersey to bring some of my stuff down here to me. I don't think I left any of my belongings in Boca. Most probably my chances of going to Princeton—after all you did to help me get into that school--- are in vain. I'll have to write to them in a day or two. Princeton was just a great dream, but so is the present reality. Perhaps I might be able to take some courses by mail. We will see.

"Do you think you could hang around a few more days to give us some more imput in our project?" Of course I said, "Yes!" We were alone at the time in the foyer of her home. I made a move to kiss her on the cheek, sort of a 'social kiss.' She kissed me, instead, squarely on the lips with a kiss that was anything but "goodbye". But it *was* a goodbye kiss nevertheless. She was now no longer a teen-ager, a student and a care-taker for my wife. She was now Queen Naina of her tribe and would some day, hopefully, be President of her country. *And*, she now had a prince who was eager to marry her. He just didn't know it at that time!

All the plans initiated by Amoku and his advisors, including Doctor Ed, were eventually put into effect. The planning and training took about six months. In exactly two days, as Amoku wanted, Belize was free of its invaders. The alien police and military, as well as the hundred-and-eighty-man legislature, were destroyed the first day by a well-rehearsed series of poison-attacks led by Mikala and Tolura and the youngsters from Belize. Those aliens who were not executed were immobilized and placed on passenger ships; destination the Ivory Coast of West Africa.

The plans to have a semi-socialist government in Belize, was immediately put into effect. Former President Clinton was able (and willing) to create the kind of Government that would provide a Liberal Democracy for that Central American Republic. There remained just a matter of cleaning up the few economic issues that were in need of care. The Swiss banks which had deposits of one hundred and eighty-three million dollars that had been stolen from the treasury of Belize were reluctant to send back any of the funds. But they reconsidered and gladly sent all the money back with eight percent interest after a series of unfortunate accidents happened at the main offices and two of the branch banks and one luxurious resident hotel in Zurich. It seems that some dreadful poison had somehow gotten into the air-conditioning system of those beautiful buildings and over a thousand people were in a coma for about two weeks. Most of those affected were the executives and employees of the very banks that held the stolen money.

What a dreadful experience that was for the Swiss! So many of the "victims" promised to be more God-fearing souls in the future, especially after the amazing coincidence that sixty-two executives thought they were having tension headaches and then they thought they were experiencing heart-attacks. What a coincidence! Nobody knew exactly what had occurred, although one Swiss clergyman was sure it was the work of the Jews! When Tolura and Mikala returned from their trip to Europe they were pleased to learn that all those millions of dollars were now back in the National Bank of Belize. It has also been reputably reported that King Amoku, now on a golden throne in heaven, was seen smiling broadly for days. A day in heaven is our equivalent of a hundred million years.

THE LIVE SEA SCROLLS

Dr. Benno Amita
Hebrew University, College of Antiquities
Jerusalem, Israel 12/12/00

12\12\00

Dear Benno,

Unquestionably this letter is disturbing you at some deep, dark mystery involving one of those endless "digs" on Israeli soil. What I am writing to you about is another of those wild-goose chases that I have been running on for decades. But please listen carefully while I describe my latest adventure. It may be important.

Two days ago I went with several friends, most of them known to you (Drs. Artur Harshai, Werner Uebermann and Rafel Ben Aryeh), to re-visit the Qumran Caves. Of course we did not make any new discoveries. We merely went there to visit yet one more time the scene where the so-called Zealots hid those marvelous scrolls of Holy data.

Our guide was a man with apparently grand delusions and it took all our will-power not to stuff his mouth with good Israeli mud. (It had just rained heavily!) His claims to being a direct descendant of David were matched by his assumption that we were ignorant tourists. I was the only scientist who lent a sympathetic ear and also "pumped" him for any possible data that could lead us to some revelations that we simply know lie unrevealed in those hallowed hills.

About two hours after my return to my hotel that same young guide made an unexpected appearance at the door to my hotel room. He practically pushed his way into my room, quietly closing the door and locking it behind him.

"Doctor," he whispered hoarsely, "Please do not speak. Just give me the honor of your attention and take very, very seriously what I have to reveal."

"Go ahead....." I started to say, but he spoke with such a tone of urgency that I was compelled to listen and, and perhaps, to believe what he then told me.

"My name is Karnon. I am a direct descendant of King David. My family has shared a secret for two thousand years, waiting for the appropriate time and the appropriate man to whom to reveal this secret. From what we have been able to determine, you, too, are a....."

"Direct descendant of King David," I interrupted. "That has been a belief in our family since time immemorial. How could you know?"

"We know. We are so few in this world that keeping track of blood relatives is a genuine possibility."

"I now have confidence in you, Karnon. Please speak on. I shall try not to distract you, although that may be difficult."

"Sir, we know your reputation as a student of antiquities and we feel that this is the time and that you are the man to give this exceedingly valuable artifact." He then drew from under his long jacket a fairly large cylindrically- shaped packet.

He paused, almost stifled with anxiety. "Take this, please. And may *Hashem* (God) have mercy on your soul!"

Stunned as I was I had the presence of mind to ask one important question, "Where did you find it?"

"You know what it is?"

"I can guess...This is a small clay jar from the caves where you make your living. showing off your expertise to tourists. Be aware, Karnon, you will perform a serious disservice to the Hebrew nation and your ancestors if you are involved in a fraud of any kind."

"Oh! Oh! May the Almighty torture me for an eternity if I have perpetrated anything but an honest serious opportunity for you and for Mankind!" He dropped to his knees and wept. "And now I shall never go to those caves again!"

As I thanked Karnon he turned pale, as though by his having discharged this trusted mission his reason for existence was all but gone. His appearance became like one of those fanatics who were willing to take on the world for the cause they believed in. Was he, then, a descendant of the Zealots, as well?

He left as abruptly as he had come to me and, I must confess, it was with unsteady hands that I unwrapped the packet. I placed it on the bed so that, in my anxiety, I should not create damage to my gift.

When unwrapped, all there was to be seen was a most unprepossessing baked clay jar in "Israeli brown"—a reddish-brown, smooth exterior. It was certainly not a thing of beauty. The orifice to the jar was sealed. I was careful not to shake the jar so that a possibly very dry manuscript would not be damaged.

This jar, which was about twenty inches long and about ten inches in diameter, was delicate and light. The clay itself, while rough, seemed to have been baked in an unusual way, so that it possessed a glass-like quality, which could have rendered it waterproof. Even the cap of the vessel was baked the same way and it was apparently sealed with a low-fusing porcelain or glass which required a degree of heat that would not damage the materials secreted within the jar. This vessel, with its contents, was created to last a long, long time.

I write to you, my dear Benno because I need you to help in opening this vessel and then quickly preserving whatever is inside. No man in all the world can do this better than you can. You may reach me at the Reboah Hotel, here in Jerusalem. Needless to say, absolute discretion and silence on this matter are essential. I have sent this letter to you by special messenger provided by the Israeli Army. I must add that I have not dared to leave this room for the past twenty-four hours! Regards to Ziporah, Sincerely, *Ariel*

It must have been less than an hour after Benno had received his letter that Ariel received a phone call from him. Ariel answered it in his usually flippant manner. "Good-morning! Say something important!"

"Ariel you rascal, how are you? Haven't you left that room yet?" Of course it was Benno: jovial at all times but deadly serious in his work.

"Don't laugh, Benno. Someone who notices everything will start to wonder why I have my food sent in. I'm beginning to get "the creeps". What if my phone is tapped? This might become a dangerous situation."

"Alright Ariel, I will send my two sons, Moshe and Amram, to escort you and whatever you have to my laboratory at the University. They are big bruisers, wearing Army uniforms; special services branch. They should be at your place within half an hour. Ask who it is before you open the door. When you ask, "Who is it," they will reply with my wife's name. Okay? Meanwhile, relax....on second thought, don't relax!"

And so, Moshe and Amram escorted Ariel and his "gift" to the laboratory of Dr. Benno Amitai where they arrived at about 11:00 A.M.

An hour later Benno, mopping his brow, agreed that the jar had every aspect of legitimacy. "One thing, Benno, makes me feel that there may be something phony here," said Ariel.

"What's that?"

"None of the other clay jars found in the Qumran caves were baked like this. None had this glass-like impermeable surface. Who could have baked this jar so differently? Oh, and there is something else. This jar is so small compared with most of the other jars they found. If someone went to all this trouble to create this situation and then hide it so it might not be found for millennia, his ideas must be of great importance, yet he only used a relatively small jar to contain all the important data he wished us to have.

"It is possible that this was baked a generation or so later than the others. The Romans had, by then, developed a knack for baking porcelain onto clay in a finer way than the Greeks had used. Also some Orientals had developed that knack to a fine art. It is possible that some Hebrew porcelain specialist was trained in the Roman or Chinese method of baking porcelain. This also makes me feel that this jar is more recent by perhaps half a century than the other jars, which were done during the Roman occupation about 2000 years ago. Also, the fact that this jar is baked differently than the other jars might mean that the previous artisans may not have survived the stressful times they lived through. They may have perished with the others on the Masada."

Ariel replied, "That all makes a lot of sense. Meanwhile how do you propose to open this sealed jar without damaging its contents? They may be so light because they may have deteriorated to the point of becoming almost a powder."

Benno might have seemed as though he was bragging. "Here in the lab we have hermetically sealed cabinets and work-tables upon which we can set this jar when we work on it. Thus we will let no outside air or moisture into the work area. We will use– don't laugh–a high-speed dental drill with diamond-tipped bits to remove the cap of the jar by drilling away the sealant. A gentle suction device will continually whisk away the grindings."

And this was exactly the procedure Benno and his assistants used. It was completed in a surprisingly short time. When the sealant was removed the cap was also removed. This was done by using a "gentle" blowtorch and turning the cap while the sealant was softened, but that also provided a surprise. The cap had been screwed onto the neck of the jar! This had never been done for the other jars that had been found and should have been an additional aid in preventing moisture and air from entering the jar.

The jar was then tilted almost upside down and a fiber optic light was placed so that the contents could be seen and then removed. The jar was held in a firm, yet cushioned clamp while Benno and his aides were prepared to use specialized mechanical means to remove the contents. However, yet another surprise awaited the scientists! The scroll that lay within the jar was not crisp and dry like all the previous scrolls. By having been placed in a water-proof and airless chamber for at least 2000 years the contents were still about as pliable and manageable as when they were inserted! The scroll, made of parchment, was enclosed, for a cushioning effect, within rolls of a tissue-paper-thin fabric likewise composed of some animal tissue. Not one of the previous scrolls had provided such an opportunity for examination and study without the hazards of severe aridity and difficulty in flattening the manuscripts without multiple fractures and even loss of valuable portions of the texts that were to be studied.

When the scientists had discovered that they could almost easily unwrap the insulating tissue and the scroll itself, everyone was simply "dying" to have a look at the scroll itself. It was surprisingly clear and readable, although the "print" was much smaller than that found in the other scrolls, accounting for the larger amount of data held within what seemed like a smaller scroll. Benno understood everyone's desires to read further, but he called a halt to the reading after just a few minutes. He then made a sensible statement, "Now that we have revealed the nature of these contents, we will re-roll and re-wrap the scroll and place it back into the jar. It will be kept in a vacuum chamber until we can bring in the other scientists who will photograph it, take a small portion of it for carbon-dating, we will even take a sample of the ink to find out its nature. Meanwhile, our scholars will read the Hebrew (and Aramaic) and record it, on film as well as in writing. Then another group will translate the contents into Modern Hebrew, English, French, Italian and Arabic. This will all take a few months, if we are lucky." While answering questions Benno proceeded to re-wrap the contents and replace them into the jar.

"Dad, what struck you most about the document?" asked Amram.

"That's a good question. I only had, as you noticed, a very brief time to examine the document. Actually, I didn't examine it at all—I just barely got a glimpse at it. I was afraid to handle it too much. But one thing is certain; there is much less Aramaic here than in the previous scrolls found. This has to be at least 50 years more recent than the others. And I can't tell you how surprised I am that the scroll has remained so pliable."

Ariel seemed troubled, despite the great progress made. "Benno, this must not be revealed until we study its religious and political aspects. Heaven only knows what's in this document. It could be explosive!"

"My sons and I will sleep here. You, too, can have a cot sent in. But there is one thing I simply have to say: I have never been so excited in my whole life! The excitement and anxiety about this whole enterprise stimulated all of the participants to work as quickly and as efficiently as they could. In less than two weeks the technical aspects, such as determining the age of the document and the nature of the ink it was written with were established. (The age of the document was the year 122 Anno Domini) also, the entire manuscript, which was rolled up like a Torah was laid out on a ten-foot long table and the photographers then took pictures of every kind including color, black and white, video, regular movies and still shots and put their results on paper on tapes and discs, on video tapes and motion-picture reels. This entire series of operations was facilitated by the fact that the scroll was in such marvelous condition. There were no problems with finding missing pieces of a dried out, fractured document, or trying to unwrap a metal scroll which had suffered a molecular redisposition of its particles and thereby produced a loss of much data.

As I stated, all these wonders were accomplished in about two weeks. And then two specialists were brought in to translate the entire document. What could be so difficult if the men actually knew their Hebrew, right? Aha, the problems were manifold. First of all, the document was much longer than we had assumed by the deceptively small jar it was in. The print, which was done by hand with a very fine brush, was less than half the size of the print used in all the other scrolls we had seen. What the document lacked in height it made up for in its length. Someone very wordy and conscious of his importance to his community as well as sure of his ideas as a philosopher made certain that he got all his pertinent ideas down in writing.

And so it took over four months for these two specialists to translate the archaic Hebrew and Aramaic, as well as the occasional Greek and Roman expressions interspersed in the document. The Jews have always added many words and idiomatic expressions to their Hebrew, depending on how long they had been under the occupation of some alien power, or even how long they had been the actual occupiers of alien territory, where their soldiers and political personnel began using the native language of the area they were occupying. All these factors were involved in the long time it took to translate this particular document.

But finally these men brilliant and talented, printed out on their computers the translations into modern Hebrew and into the Americanized form of English that most of the world is using today. I think I should mention their names, to give them some degree of honor when all the credits will be given out. David Mamelov and Chaim Kluger were the two translators. Other men would later be brought in to use their translations to re-translate the document into Italian, French, and Arabic.

In the week or two that it took Benno and Ariel to bring to a printed fruition their many weeks of labor, they found that, instead of experiencing a let-down of sorts, their work was only magnified in ways they had not anticipated. They had produced a small book with the history of this particular Dead Sea Scroll that they had all been working on. Ariel was particularly effective in descrbing their efforts because, instead of being a specialist in only one field, he was multi-disciplinary in his training. And so his "book" was from the point of view of a person trained in the antiquities, in art and general literature, in religion and in history and political science. He could be called a "generalized maven."

What was apparent in all the aspects of this document is the fact that this scroll was the actual philosophy of the author, not, as many of the scrolls were, portions of the Hebrew religion or of the Bible. As such, it is not surprising that this scroll received "special attention." It was immediately apparent that this author was an important personage in his own right.

When Chaim Kluger and David Mamelov wrote out the Hebrew and English versions of the scroll it was not a religious critique of the work but simply the literal translations into modern Hebrew and into English with David and his friend, Chaim Kluger, getting the credit for the translations and Benno getting the credit for the scientific aspects of the accomplishment. Everything looked like a success so far.

It was about a week afterward that the series of translations and Ariel's book were sent to the specified authorities. Those unfamiliar with the speed of computers might be surprised at the rapidity with which all these things had been accomplished. They had been copyrighted, of course, and had been sent to the Prime Minister, the Minister for Security, the Chairmen of several major religious Jewish organizations in Israel and the Chairman of the commission that had been set up to deal with all matters pertaining to the Dead Sea Scrolls. A copy had been sent to the President of the University in Jerusalem.

It was while waiting for an uproar to arise and an endless barrage of criticism and vitriolic vituperation from all the self-proclaimed authorities to wash over them that a totally unexpected tragedy shocked the entire group that was involved with this scroll.

A body was recovered from the Dead Sea that was proven to be that of Karnon, the guide who had led Ariel and his party through the Dead Sea Caves and who had singled out Ariel to be the recipient of the latest unknown scroll. Israeli authorities confirmed that Karnon had been tortured beyond belief and that his body–dead or alive–had been thrown into the Dead Sea within the past two or three days. Why? Who would want to kill a tour guide? Why torture him? What could he have to reveal? If he gave information to his torturers what was the information? Who else would now be vulnerable to some vicious secret plot in revenge for the information that Karnon might have given under duress?

Practically no one could have had a chance to read the translations since they had only just been sent out by hand-delivery. Some of the intended recipients were not at home or at their offices and their copies were not given to any other recipient. They were brought back to Benno and Ariel. Copies had not yet been given to the Vatican or the Archbishop of Eastern Christianity, nor had they been given to the Ayatollas or the representatives of any other country except Israel. So was it an Israeli who was responsible? What did he have to gain and what did he think he had lost by Karnon's actions?

Ariel and Benno and their team knew they were in treacherous waters when they embarked upon the newest scroll project. They now feared the long hand of some secret cabal that they had not as yet learned about.

But the Israeli police and the Mossad (the Israeli Secret Police) were not as baffled as were the scientific team of Ariel and Benno. The next day the Mossad picked up four men and a woman in Rome, Istanbul, Paris and Jordan. By investigating all the passenger lists for every mode of transportation leaving Israel in the past forty-eight hours they had put together a scenario that rivals "The Day the Eagle Landed". Since they had already known the list of people who had come into Israel in the past several months they had to compare incoming with outgoing travelers and voila! They found their suspects!

Who were these people? They were part of a cabal that is under the tight direction of the Vatican, the French Secret Service and the Iranian Secret Police. They had originally been attracted to Karnon because of his abnormal braggadocio. Why did a tourist guide have to tell everyone his actually glorious family history? Who was he, really? Did he actually have some secret connections after all, or was he simply a braggart—or a liar?

So they followed him everywhere. They found that he no longer went to the caves as a tourist guide after he had made one single visit to the apartment of Dr. Ariel Schiffman in Jerusalem. His behavior was so nondescript and his credentials so negative that there simply had to be something unusual going on for him to make a visit to a noted Professor of Antiquities at a classy hotel when he had never even gone to a college before in his life and actually had quite a lowly job.

So they took him into custody and drove him to an area near the Dead Sea, which was quite deserted at night, and proceeded to interrogate him. Acting as though he had a blithe nature, he said that he couldn't believe that they were interested in his duties as a tour guide. And what else did he do that could interest a vicious cabal? They couldn't figure it out and he didn't volunteer anything. His cigarette gave the cabal an inspiration. They jammed the lit cigarette—and others, also, into his skin in various sensitive areas. After three hours of burns, cuts and beatings he finally revealed that he was indeed a descendant of King David that he had never lied about that, and that if being proud was a crime the whole Israeli Army was guilty as well.

"What business did you have at the apartment of Dr. Ariel Schiffman?"

"First of all, I think you should know that Dr. Schiffman is also a direct descendant of King David, which is an honor. I knew he was interested in antiquities because he and some friends, whose names I never heard, had visited the Caves and I was lucky enough to be their guide. I thought that he should know that I didn't think there were any more Dead Sea Scrolls because I had been surreptitiously searching the area for ten years and couldn't find a trace. That would put his mind at rest and let him devote his time and his energy to more practical enterprises." But it was after six more hours of torture, at which time the rosy glow of dawn was rising in the East, that he finally said three words, "Another small scroll..."and died. His body was unceremoniously tossed into the Dead Sea, where it continued to float because of the high concentration of salt in the water. Karnon's pride had been his undoing.

While the police and the secret service did not reveal Karnon's death the incident was "leaked" to Benno by a friend on the police force. Benno's work was of such importance that he had to have access to all sorts of information so that he and his work could be protected. The Government knew about his "connections" but allowed them to exist. Needless to say, a quiet form of terror now was in effect among the few participants in the newest Dead Sea Scroll affair, and Karnon's family (especially his sons) were also quietly retrenching and preparing to leave for unknown parts.

When the transcripts of the newest scroll were finally all distributed to the selected Israeli officials, they read the material, several times, with unbelieving eyes. They all agreed to be present at a meeting at the University which Ariel and Benno would chair and speak on the subject. Ariel would spend a half hour, or so, reading the transcript, and then the important leaders of the clergy and the government would discuss their opinions of it all. First, of course, each individual had to read that material several times to make up his (her) own mind about it, so that everyone would be thoroughly informed of its contents before they discussed and debated whatever was controversial.

The date set for this discussion, news of which was withheld from the public, was March 4, 1990. The entire area was under police protection, but every man in the protective entourage was personally investigated by the Mossad, so that this collection of the nation's leaders would be secure. Apparently the Mossad had learned from the four individuals who had murdered Karnon that they were instructed to destroy anyone and everything pertaining to this last Dead Sea Scroll. Was there any doubt that other such teams were on the job in Israel?

The answer to that question came on March 3, the day before the conclave. Chaim Kluger, who was one of the two original translators, was in his office at the University when he received a phone-call from someone he knew quite well. "Chaim," the woman said, "'I have some unusual information for you that I think you should know about at once! May I come to your office right away?"

"Certainly," said Chaim.

Within twenty minutes, this woman, Rosalie Lubovich, the wife of the professor of Arabic Literature at the University, was at Chaim's office door, with another person who was strikingly handsome and apparently of Arabic descent.

"Come in," said, Chaim. "Oh, I see you have Hassanein El Barani with you. What's going on?"

"Oh, I didn't know you two knew each other. That makes it easier to discuss this."

"Why don't we sit here, near the table and I'll mix a few drinks."

Hassanein spoke up, "We do not have the luxury of time. May we discuss why we are here?"

"Of course."

Hassanein apparently had been planning what he was going to say with great care because he raised his hand, as though asking for the floor then he paused a few moments to order his thoughts. "We have learned from various sources about what has happened to a man named Karnon. He was a gentle man and did not deserve to die the way he did. We also know about the newest scroll. However, you may be stunned to learn that there is yet another scroll, somewhat larger than the one Karnon brought to you that holds great promise. It was found sort-of plastered into the wall of the fourth cave that was supposedly cleaned out thirty-five years ago. This is an early scroll, of course, and should be looked into promptly. I have it at my apartment here in Jerusalem. If you wish I can bring it to you in a large valise and no one will know anything about it since you have rights of passage here and we are your friends. "

"Well, we are so busy here, these days, I don't see how we could get through the security they have set up. That scroll has waited two thousand years. Can it wait another week?"

"We have the opportunity to bring it to the French team, which, I'll admit, has not distinguished itself with any degree of fairness and integrity. But we need the money it will bring and we know you want and deserve the chance to study yet one more treasure of antiquity."

"Let me make a quick phone call and I'll speak to you in a few minutes."

"Fine."

Chaim went into the bedroom, closed the door and dialed the number for Benno's lab. He knew that every call he would make was being recorded by the Mossad. Benno was not at his lab. He dialed Benno's residence. He wasn't there. He dialed Ariel's office. He wasn't there. He dialed Ariel's residence at the hotel. Ariel's wife answered and got Ariel to pick up the phone. "Ariel, two secure friends of mine, Rosalie Lubovich and Hassanein El Barani claim they have another Dead Sea Scroll, somewhat larger than our latest one, and they offer to sell it to us. When I tried to stall them they hinted at a possible French offer but, why I don't know, they prefer selling it to us. What should I do—I'm at my office at the University."

"Could be a phony, but what would they get out of it? We have Benno and Zipora here in the living room, let me get Benno to discuss it with you. If I had my way I'd stall them a week or so. Here's Benno." Chaim went on to explain the situation to Benno, who took almost forever to reply. "It sounds phony. Let's figure out what chances are we're taking: if the thing is a fraud they won't get paid. If it's wonderful we'll pay them more than anyone else. If he needs the money today he's out of luck: we have to see the merchandise first and he can watch us while we open it up and check it out. Let him bring the thing to my lab. I'll call whoever's there, I think it's Amram., and he'll accept the package. No one gets into the lab but you and Amram. You can bring them into the foyer. If they don't accept these conditions let them sell it to the French."

"Got it, fine."

Chaim explained the circumstances to his two friends and they agreed. The price was left open, but they knew the reliability of those with whom they were dealing. It was agreed that Hassanein and Rosalie would deliver a fairly large valise with a Dead Sea Scroll in its container within an hour and forty-five minutes. They left abruptly, forgetting the niceties of departing from the office of a friend.

Chaim left his office and walked across the campus of the University to the office in building Lvov where Professor Benno Amitai had his office. He waited, with only Amram as company for nearly two hours. At that time Rosalie Lubovich and Hassanein El Barani made their appearance. The two men let the friends of Chaim come into the foyer of the 'Laboratories for Research into the Antiquities.' Amram didn't want to talk with the two strangers. He knew Rosalie as one of the most regressive individuals in all of Israel. He knew Hassanein as one of the few Arabs acceptable to the University, but he also knew that he was a rough and tough homosexual. He suspected that Chaim was a "female" participant in a ring of homosexuals who had their activities at discreet places in the capital. He "smelled a rat" but since his father had allowed these people to bring their scroll and Chaim's loyalty was indisputable he allowed them only as far as the foyer.

Chaim asked if he might open the valise to, at least, take a look at the scroll in its clay container. Rosalie asked Hassanein if he wouldn't prefer that he open the valise so that there would be no chance of anyone dropping the scroll before Benno had a chance to see it. Chaim agreed. Hassanein said, at that moment, "You know, this great moment would have been the perfect occasion for those drinks you offered us." And he smiled his most beguiling smile at Chaim, who was duly embarrassed.

Hassanein proceeded to lift the valise onto the couch in the foyer, explaining that he didn't want the scroll possibly to fall onto the floor. He opened the two hinged snaps in front of the valise, took a key out of his hip pocket and tried to turn the key in the lock. It was the wrong key. Rosalie, impulsively, said, "I have another key in the car. I'll be right back." And she left immediately. Hassanein reached into a different pocket and found another key. He tried that key in the lock. At that moment a tremendous explosion occurred, completely destroying about seventy-five or more feet of the laboratory and the waiting room, killing Hassanein, Amram, Chaim and Rosalie, who was in the hall just outside the door. Smoke poured into the air-conditioning ducts and spread throughout the building. The intense fire completely gutted Benno's laboratory. But the blast did not affect the scroll that was under study because that had been secreted in a vault elsewhere. Two fanatics, part of a world-wide web of fanatics, had made a statement.

The conclave of leaders on the subject of the newest Dead Sea Scroll was postponed for two weeks to allow the police and Moshav to make an investigation and to allow the mourners to get themselves together.

It was on the eighteenth of March that the conclave was held, in a state of aggravation and mourning that has had few parallels in Israeli history. As previously arranged, Benno and Ariel were the leaders of the discussion and planned to answer any questions that may come from the floor. The plan was to have pre-written questions submitted and replied to first, then there would be more questions and even debates from the floor.

After the usual introductory remarks and introductions, Dr. Ariel Schiffman was asked to read the entire document from the Dead Sea Scroll in a loud and clear voice so that the recitation of that revolutionary thesis could have its full impact. Ariel rose to speak when called to the rostrum. He spoke in modern Hebrew. Simultaneous translations into English were provided.

Ariel's reading of The Document

"The following document translated into modern Hebrew and simultaneously into English is a remarkable story that might indeed shake the world. We give this scroll no name or title. We only can swear to its authenticity. We take no stand on what it says but do vouch for its honest position in the hierarchy of important documents in the history of Mankind. Read it as a student of history, as a student of religion, as perhaps a man of *Hashem* (God) or as a man of science. This may be the last Dead Sea Scroll, but it is certainly the most revolutionary and most exciting we have read so far. The following words are directly from the document that was brought to us by the late Karnon, *alav a sholem,* (May peace be with his soul) who paid with his life for his desire to bring to the world an artifact of human creation that he knew, somehow, had earth-shaking potential. Please bear with me in this trying time for the effort it will take to read, in an even tone, this long and significant document."

THE DOCUMENT

"My name is Ephraim, son of Marya and Yosef. My ancestors spent years in bondage to the Egyptians before Moses led them across the bed of a branch of the Red Sea to freedom. They spent many years wandering in the desert before they reached the place known as *Eretz Yisroel* (The land of Israel). As a result of that personal history no power can remove from my soul the consciousness of being a loyal Hebrew.

My life and that of many of my ancestors have been dignified by a continual effort towards growth and progress in the use of reason in our beliefs and behavior. We have often been at odds with the ruling classes because we have never been tied to the past. We have always been identified as those who looked to the future for our own people's development. We have always looked askance at the use of myth and unreliable "historical" data that were supposed to guide us in the right direction.

Although the current weakness in the character of our people has lasted well over 200 years, with our nation divided into

269

many sects, including the Zealots, (who are almost fanatic about observance of the Law. They are militants who are unafraid of the Romans and their satellites, King Herod and his entourage); the *Osim* (Doers of the Law); the *Pharisees* (who are devout, but beholden to Herod and his pro-Roman minions); the *Sadducees* (Tzadikim) and the *Nozrim* (Nozarenes).

We all know that all of these sects are Hebrews whose life would be meaningless without the Judaic Laws and the belief in Jehovah, our one and only God. However, any student of our history can agree that our people share one particular trait, which explains a great deal about the turmoil we currently face here in *Eretz Yisroel* (Israel.) That trait is almost ludicrous, wherein every other Jew thinks he is a leader and there are currently more leaders than followers. However the world may interpret this trait, it does not mean that we are necessarily so divided as to be sinking to our doom. It means that our religion and our history encourage individual thinking and a certain personal relationship to our God, who is the only entity that truly understands the Hebrew people.

As to the Romans, history shows that all despotisms ultimately come to a bloody end, especially when the common man recovers his sense of self-interest and the courage to lead his own life in his own way comes to the fore. During this period, which the Romans would call "pro tem", we personally may not survive. But the Hebrew people must survive. Hopefully our internal divisions will have healed by then. It is with this hope that I write these prescriptions for proper belief and behavior. It is with these prescriptions that our Hebrew people may better survive, and, as Isaiah said it, "be as a light unto the world."

Thus, I have placed my "philosophy", as the Greeks would call it, in a sealed jar to be hidden from the world until some loyal descendants of King David deem it appropriate to reveal these words to the world. You who finally receive these thoughts whether you have been handed this clay jar in two or three millenia from now as the Romans would say it will know that the personal and communal ignorance and destructiveness of Mankind will have been characterized by virtually constant wars and depredations. Your history will demonstrate a return to atavistic behavior by high and low alike and what may be described as an insane, imaginary conception of Man's place in the Universe and of the true nature of his God.

You, who now read these words, know that my estimations have been accurate. What I cannot be sure of, at this time, is that the intellect and soul of Mankind will be ready, even two or three millenia from now, to re-think its existence and live in the less primitive status that their forefathers dreamed about. I hope so. Man's existence on this earth is not guaranteed. The destructive potentialities that will be developed over the years will bear the possibility that mankind might well destroy not only himself, but the Earth as well.

It would serve no useful purpose for us to castigate the Romans for being barbarous. History itself will put them in their place. Likewise, it would serve no useful purpose to castigate those among us Hebrews who have aided the Roman conquerors expecting some exalted position or great recompense for their perfidy. Ordinarily, it would not be appropriate, either, to name those who, taking advantage of the weakness and disorganization of the Hebrew people at this time, have started new sects that are hypercritical of our religion and are so divisive among us that many simple folk do not comprehend their treachery to our people and its historical importance. And yet, since this document is part history and part philosophy, the truth must be told about our times, spoken with the honesty of a moral and righteous man with the true facts of our current situation explained to whoever is interested in our legacy. History must be served.

The reader of this document is entitled to know who has written it, where he comes from, his political and religious affiliations, his achievements and rank in his society. And so I repeat that my name is Ephraim, a Hebrew whose bloodlines run to the earliest days of our nation's existence. One of my ancestors was our fabled King David, a most illustrious and talented man. My immediate family and many of my ancestors have lived in the area around Nazareth for many centuries. My parents were Joseph and Marya, poor farm-people who nevertheless had abiding faith in the goodness of Mankind.

My elder brother was Emmanuel, a simple-appearing man who attracted large crowds of adherents wherever he went as an itinerant religious speaker. He made his living as a carpenter, but he had no home of his own. Somehow he remained celibate, possibly due to the influence of the Osim, which we considered strange for a Hebrew man in the best of health. Emmanuel and I were similar in that we seemed to have a calling for dissemination of the Judaic Law and the inculcation of the desire to be righteous. Hence, my brother was known as Emmanuel of Nazareth and I was known as the Teacher of Righteousness.

Both Emmanuel and I belonged to several of the sects that made their appearance in our time. We found that the Osim are a particularly gentle and giving group, eager to be friends with everyone, even the minions of the untrustworthy Herod. From the Osim we acquired an ability to listen and to try to understand the problems that people had with their religion and their relationship with God. The Osim are also known to have the ability to promote the healing of illnesses and each devotee who trains with them for a period of three years acquires their learning of the healing arts. Emmanuel and I both trained with the Osim for three years.

The Tzadikim and the Pharisees appear to us to have become undermined in their loyalty to the Law and to Hebrew ethnicity. They seem to be subverted by the Romans and their loyalty to us is suspect. This I can say even though one of my Mother's uncles was a Tzadik. Normally this would be an educated and knowledgeable man, but this uncle was also suspect, since he never took steps to protect either Emmanuel or me from the violence that was fomented against true Hebrew leaders by the minions of Herod.

Emmanuel met a dreadful death at the hands of the Romans, most probably because he (and I) had also been members of a very zealous group who were religious to the point of inciting violence among their adherents. Emmanuel suffered greatly as he died, mostly, I think, because his ambition to correct the fallacies in human nature were thus brutally abbreviated and he wept that all Mankind should obey the Judaic Laws of God and he cried out that God should not desert Man the way He was deserting him. Emmanuel's body was removed by our friends and carried to Nazareth quickly. Nobody else has ever seen the grave they prepared for him.

Some years later there was in Jerusalem a man known as the Wicked Priest, Ananas by name. Ananas had a most vicious streak of inhumanity that he employed to secure his own power and maintain that power for a long time. Since I was known as the Teacher of Righteousness I came into conflict with Ananas and his henchmen many times. Ultimately, at his behest, a group of strong, misguided Hebrews were impelled to try to kill me. They almost succeeded. They beat and slashed me they broke my bones and threw me over a parapet of Herod's Temple. They threw tiles and bricks down upon what they thought was my corpse and would have indeed killed me if my friends hadn't come and covered me (the way one covers a corpse) and carried me away. Seeing that I was still alive, my friends secretly, at night, carried me in a small wagon to the city of Jericho, where I lived in seclusion until I had recovered.

However, that fall from the parapet and the bricks that hit my head, made it impossible for me to walk, and my left side was —and still is—almost useless to me. Only the love and charity of these fellow-Zealots ---those who were known to be zealous for the Judaic Law ---preserved my mind and my body for all these years. When I was well enough to travel I was carried by mule up to the top of the cliff community about twenty miles south of Jericho where I continued my teaching of Righteousness and supervised the writing of numerous scrolls in which our truly religious folk deemed it important to preserve forever, if necessary, the Law and the history and the myths of our people, which are so vital to a civilized society.

This Zealous community was an arm of the same community that existed in Masada and all over our land, especially in Jerusalem. We even had members who were in the Tzadikim and the Pharisees. It was they who surreptitiously sent the treasure of the Temple to be secreted all over Israel so that the Romans and even the perfidious Priests could not get their hands on it. Ananas and his group were sure that I was dead, especially since word spread that I had died and there was much mourning in the land. Also, unbeknownst to me at the time, some of my fellow-Zealots cornered Ananas and did to him what he nearly succeeded in doing to me.

As I reached my eighty-second year I learned that the Roman legions were planning to annihilate the spirit of our people by destroying all of our strong-points, in Masada (the cliff community beyond Jericho, which we code-named Damascus to confuse the Romans), Jericho itself and other places.

Since I would have been no use as a fighter against the Romans—I was a liability, in fact, since I was personally so dependent upon my friends for mobility---I prevailed upon them to see that I was given a mule and two attendants to carry me to another very small village about twenty miles south of Masada, beyond the end of the Dead Sea, where I had once seen a series of caves and an almost invisible path up a cliff where I chose to live. Since my wife had died years before, my two sons were selected to accompany me into the wilderness, where I planned to write these words and have the scroll hidden for posterity. I was most fortunate to have left the cliff community several months before the Romans launched their attack.

This history will not be complete unless I tell the story of The Liar, the man who, more than any other, has succeeded, so far, in creating a new religion from certain aspects of Hebraism and from Pagan rites and beliefs that seem to be attractive to those who do not have the feel for Hebraism or the inclination to undergo the strictures of our principles and the limitations on personal behavior that our religion prescribes.

The traitor named The Liar by almost all who knew him, was originally a Persian Jew named Saul of Tarsus. Because of his small, compact build he is called The Small One by the Romans. Paulus, in Latin, means 'The Small One.' Almost everyone in our country knows about the tainted background of this Paulus. But it is possible that you reading this document 2000 years from now may not be aware of the violent, dishonest nature of this brilliant man. He knows that the Hebrew nation has been beset by numerous troubles, such as an occupying army of brutes that has been here for over 200 years, as well as the divisive tactics by the nation's priesthood who are in the pay of the Romans and who are actually traitorous to their own people. Accordingly, these are not the best of times for us, making it difficult for us to survive intact.

Paulus has been in the employ of the corrupt Priesthood who gave him writs to annihilate any and all who pose any kind of threat to the rule of the Priests and the Romans. He actually admitted these facts in his commentaries that were distributed widely several years ago.. He was on his way to the cliff community near Jericho when he had a seizure and actually fell from his horse. Whether it was a seizure like he had had many times before in his life or whether it was due to the brain-confusing powers of certain mushrooms that he was known to have purchased in Jerusalem or whether it was the true voice of God speaking to him we do not know. But suddenly he claimed he had an epiphany that my dead brother Emmanuel, whom he had never met, had spoken to him and asked Paulus to stop persecuting him. Anyone with all his senses knows a madman when he sees one. This Paulus had a strange vision—he says—and from that moment on he has been intent on subverting the Hebraic religion and creating a new religion based on Hebraism and Paganism.

This man, brilliant in his efficiency, has been expounding the accomplishments of the late, beloved Emmanuel (a Zealot, as I am) who gave his life as a loyal Hebrew. Emmanuel is the focal point for this new sect. Paulus has created a movement based on the belief that Emmanuel was a Messiah who came back from the Dead (which no one else has confirmed) and promulgated a new religion based on our religion but which includes many aspects of Paganism. Since there are many more ignorant Pagans than Hebrews, this is a clever ploy to expand the possibilities of this new "creed." The adherents to this new creed are not expected to exert the self-discipline that characterizes our religion. Meanwhile, this effort is dividing our Hebrews in our time of troubles and confusing many simple folk who think the new creed is a form of Judaism, which it is not.

The critical point of failure in Paulus' preaching is the opinion that Emmanuel is a son of God and is a Messiah. Not since Isaiah created the concept of a Messiah has anyone promoted this idea of one person being a Messiah as vigorously as this man. Emmanuel himself, who opposed such an idea, also opposed the employment of pagan concepts in our daily lives to stimulate greater interest among our people. He was a gentle but firm leader who was, as I am, a Teacher of Righteousness within the Hebraic Laws. Emmanuel encouraged us to carry swords and to await the time to break free of the Roman chains. While Emmanuel admired the philosophical ideals of the Osim, he found them to be too pacifistic for the requirements of our time.

It is beyond the concepts of a reasonable man to understand how people can trust the so-called visions of a known traitor and murderer (Paulus admitted that he had instigated the murder of Stephen) and instead of promulgating the benefits of Hebraism as he has been asked to do several times, we have discovered that he has been exhorting the innocent crowds that he attracts to join his new religion. We find that to be traitorous. He has admitted several times to opposing the Hebraic Laws, yet he claims to be a loyal Hebrew and some people still trust him.

Many people simply have the need to believe in something, almost anything, that can be a combination father-figure and giver of rules. It does not matter to them that what they believe in violates the bounds of reason or that myths, visions and impossible miraculous acts are supposedly performed by this imaginary leader. This need just to believe in and also pray to an imaginary God is nothing new. Usually new creeds are created by clever, unscrupulous men posing as visionaries at just the time when human beings in their area are going through their time of troubles.

Just as takes place in the human body when its resistance is at its lowest point then some disease takes hold and overcomes the bodily defenses, so are we now subjected to the development of a threatening new creed that bids fair to divide and confuse our populace while we are at our lowest ebb due to over a hundred years of brutal occupation following another period of brutal occupation by military forces. We haven't had a chance to be ourselves for so long that it is a tribute to our faith that we have survived this long as a distinctive entity. And we will survive even longer, regardless of what sort of substitute religions make their appearance at our expense.

One can wonder why some people have to believe so urgently that they do not exercise their native-born power of reason to figure out that the very basis of the new religion is admittedly false and based on violence. When a large structure is built it cannot last if it is erected over mud or sand. Some sort of solid, impermeable natural object must lie below the foundation or the structure itself will not be trustworthy. One must wonder why those who must believe in something, or anything, do not take this into consideration.

It is true, though, that Hebraism itself has among its basic documents considerable myth and many references to miracles and patently impossible events that even the faithful cannot accept, in all honesty. But we all know that the origins of these stories took place in much more primitive times than we have today and are much like the myths of other primitive peoples. Also, many of our Biblical stories were concocted as teaching methods to inculcate certain deeper concepts that had a moral or social value.

And so there is a difference between history and myth. History is supposed to be an accurate record of what actually transpired in the past. Myth is often the creation of shamans, priests and seers who create these stories to "teach a lesson" in proper behavior to the people in their purvue. There have been many mythological figures in our "history" and each one represents a focal point around which is built a social statement that we need to believe. Adam and Eve are mythological. They are in our sacred documents to let us know that there are certain aspects to being Godly that it is safer for Man not to know about. Knowing "The Truth" about every aspect of the Lord may incite us to abuse that knowledge and perhaps even destroy ourselves.

There is a legitimate place for the mystical in our lives. Most individuals conceive of some mystical influence when there are so many areas that defy our state of knowledge and the logic that we might employ to explain the forces of nature that we can all observe. There are sensations of some supernatural forces about us whenever we think about death or eternity, or infinity or even when we observe the restless power of the sea, the implausibility of chance, the vast blackness of the universe at night and the vast blueness that seems to go on forever by day. It is not wrong for people to attribute some spiritual presence to these mysteries of our universe.

After all, we are relatively tiny beings in a seemingly endless mechanical world where our loudest shouts are like those of a child when we try to get the attention of that mysterious being who has created everything. When alone at night one can get the feeling of his one-ness with the universe at the same time that his skin seems to crawl with the un-named fear of utter helplessness. It is no wonder that we feel the urge to pray to that un-named being that we imagine lives out there somewhere and whom we simply must communicate with for our needs. This is a normal, but a primitive sensation, which should dissipate when our range of knowledge ultimately removes most of the mystery of our universe. It is useless to pray to this universe but it is not useless to pray to one's own sense of godliness, which will help us considerably.

We must beware of a primeval cast to the mind which can carry mysticism to abysmal depths with reversions to primitive chauvinism. They close the gates to freedom of thought and freedom of expression with certain segments of the population being treated as vassals with an unjustified sense of superiority being applied to males and a denigration of females, as well as a chauvinistic pride of one tribe over the well-being of its neighbors. This often leads to violence as a way of life, which is not at all a humane way to live.

Life and its values do not end with the religiosity of the zealous few. The world will keep expanding, its problems and its opportunities growing into the void created by the obliteration of useless ideas of the past. The future may be frightening but it will be unbelievably productive and creative. We must not be so mired in the teachings of the past that we cannot welcome the future whole-heartedly.

The past is holy for what it has accomplished but the future of mankind is equally as holy and must be embraced without losing our love of the Law and our ethnicity. Details involved in expressing a belief are never important enough to cast your neighbor aside as unclean. We have survived Greek skepticism, the brutality of the Persians and the Romans and the domination of the Babylonians.

We must now survive those elements of our society that present flaws which would be fatal in any people who hope to leave their mark on history. We have always been able to stretch the fibers that bind us to our God because the God we are bound to lies within us, not within some mysterious stranger in the skies or within some priesthood. We must apply the reasoning methods of the Greeks to the natural inclination towards mysticism.. There is, in all of us, a native fear of the unknown, but we must not revert to the idolatry of the cavemen. This is said despite a feeling that some answers about Nature may be forever unknowable.

Those who have allowed themselves to think deeply about the human condition, or who have not been constrained to fear questioning our habits of living, must be aware that Man created the concept of God. Man created God and God (Nature) created Man. Mankind needs God to solidify his grip on morality and ethics. God does not need Man any more than he needs birds or tigers. God is the force behind the Universe. Who is to say what He (or It) requires?

But Man, who understands pitifully little of the causes and effects within the Universe, had to create the concept of a deity with human qualities, with a sense of propriety, with a temper and with the senses that Man endowed to Him. God had to be like a very powerful Man, and Man, unbeknownst to himself, has in reality arrogated the powers of a mini-god to his own being, so that he can have someone who can hear and see him and understand his needs. How else can one converse with the infinite?

And yet, despite this Man-created deity, He is not entirely imaginary. Life is so brief and the path is so treacherous that some form of superstition is almost necessary to cover over the painful areas that are burned into our psyches. Living as we do, on the edge of an abyss where an infinitely cold, deep blackness lies before us, waiting for us to make a serious misstep, it is no wonder that Man has sought for a powerful friend to guide him. Mystery looms in every direction and so Man had to create a God with the morality and ethics that he needs to live by to keep from falling into that abyss. Thus, the God who lives in Man's mind can be spoken to, man-to-man. He can be appealed to and praised, in moderation. He enjoys the songs and dances that are performed in His honor. The ambivalence that exists is truly not a weakness. It is a tacit recognition of the fact that Man wants to be controlled by the God that he has created.

In terms of the reforms prescribed by Emmanuel and me, we have to open the doors to those who question and doubt, who want to believe but cannot, who are Hebrews to the core but are not devout. There are none, except fools and pagans, who will doubt the wisdom of the seers and the Laws of the sages and who will not respect the history of our very special people.

To reiterate an idea hinted at earlier in this scroll, there is a great difference between history and myth, especially if one is going to base his theories of life upon the facts that are presented to him. As an example, Job was not a real person. He is a mythological figure created to teach us not to lose our faith regardless of how much we may suffer. Job is, in reality, the Hebrew people. We are often led to think that perhaps God himself believes in suffering as a means of weeding out the weak and maintaining the strong.

It is not Job but we who suffer interminably for our sins, for our ambitions, but mostly for our beliefs, which usually conflict with the Pagans who surround us. We have always suffered and probably always will suffer in every generation until Israel herself has become purified and can truly live as a "light unto the world." The world itself, at that same moment in time, will tire of its aimless cruelty and fear the consequences of its venality and its self-destructive ways. They will someday realize that Man may be threatening the security of our Earth itself and then at a conclave of world leaders, seeking a way to rescue Man and his Earth, we will come to use Reason and Humanity as levers to perform that chore.

So here is the crux of this scroll of ideas: it lies in the concepts of Reason and Humanity. Man must not be indicted for his failures if he has made serious efforts to civilize himself. Perhaps that aforementioned conclave of world leaders should include military, theological, political, philosophical, scientific, educational and other influential leaders to discuss the problems of Man's failures.

Without such an open discussion of well-intentioned men the human race is doomed to an escalating vortex of violence and debasement, carrying all those whose lives even border on that vortex down to their ultimate destruction. There will be wars and wars within wars, cults and sub-cults, theories and concepts and plans of all sorts but all will come to naught as the whirlpool of barbarism carries to the bowels of the Universe the good and the bad and the unconcerned.

What we think of as God does not indict Man with taunting satire, vituperation or denigration. He has given Man only a limited capacity to govern himself. At this stage of Man's development he still needs a parent, a father-figure, perhaps: perhaps, also, a threat of punishment, to help control his atavistic impulses. Without such a figure, it has been thought, even if it is only imaginary, man will strike out wildly in all directions, sacrificing the good with the evil, all on the altars of some misguided perceptions. Perhaps this is the secret conception behind Paulus' use of Emmanuel as a god-like figure that tempts the imagination and has no human qualities that one can dislike. After all, he is now dead, killed by the Romans to whom he was a threat. Paulus claims that he heard the dead Emmanuel's voice. What Paulus unquestionably heard was the fearful voice of a guilty conscience, the cry of terror that only he himself could have created.

In ancient, primitive societies men had very little understanding of the forces of nature, whether it was forces such as wind or rain, great heat or snow, the coming of spring or the dying of leaves on the trees in autumn. And early man had no knowledge of the forces that lived in his own nature, the conflicts of jealousy, the pain of thwarted ambition or the loss of good fortune, the temper that accompanies greed or the love that greets a dear friend or a spouse. Man in his earlier days was a relatively highly-developed animal who was beset by almost every conceivable misfortune and who spent his brief lifetime afraid of the dark, afraid of what he thought were spirits in trees and bushes, in rocks and running water, in the sun and the moon, in the stars and the clouds and above all, in the endless blackness of the sky and the lack of understanding of our origins or our termination.

This constant fear and lack of answers to even the simplest questions ultimately had to be addressed by the wise men of each tribe. And so the concept of gods was created as an explanation for every phenomenon in nature. In order for Man, primitive Man that is, to deal on a respectable level with these gods they were given names and one soon learned to make demands on these gods if one wanted to grow a crop or to receive relief from a prolonged dry spell. One demanded or begged the gods for their help. Then there developed the idea of prayer which was actually an abject declaration of helpless dependence upon these many gods for a chance at a decent life.

All sorts of sacrifices and dances and gifts were prepared for these gods and it was not long before some clever rascals called themselves shamans or priests or intermediaries of some sort between the gods and Mankind. As such, the intermediaries soon developed considerable power because everyone wanted something from the gods and they were willing to surrender much booty and power to these intermediaries to receive the blessings of the gods.

As I write this it occurs to me that perhaps the present times are not much different from primitive days. Does not that recitation sound very familiar to you? You are reading this perhaps two or three thousand years from now and I am willing to wager that even in the year two thousand (or three thousand) from now there are priests and other so-called intermediaries who capitalize on your fears and insecurities. Do you see the problem that Man faces when he cannot solve the complex problems of nature especially his own nature and he has to depend upon crass, clever men like Paulus to receive your prayers. Of course he cannot deliver even the faintest proof that any one of the gods will give you what you desire.

Emmanuel and I had this all figured out while we were still youths. We came to the conclusion that there is nothing wrong with the Hebraic theology that a little reform could not correct. In this reform movement that we started we made every effort to stay within the Hebraic Laws, because they were created by very intelligent and trustworthy men and we respect them and their memories. However, Emmanuel and I also had an epiphany, just as

Paulus did only we did not eat of the sacred mushrooms or depend upon false visions to create our concept of the nature of God. And it is exactly that concept that we spent all our waking hours teaching to the Hebrew public, whether it was on the Hebrean Hills or the banks of the Jordan or even along the shores of the great sea.

Our concept was to use reason instead of fear of the unknown. What we could not understand about the universe we cast into a basket entitled the Future. Questions about the origins of the universe, eternity and infinity were placed into that "Future" basket, knowing that at this stage of Man's knowledge and experience we will not even try to solve those puzzles. Perhaps you, the men of the future, have already solved many of these problems. Similarly, we found that there are problems that men have that arise from their own natures, from within their own brains. We have not solved the problems yet of what the Greeks call the psyche. We are not ashamed to place those problems into The Future Basket. We do not know yet what causes the winds and the floods, the scorching sun or the freezing cold on the mountaintops. These too are placed in The Future basket.

But notice that we do not attribute each poorly understood phenomenon of nature to a separate god. That would make no sense at all. It is more reasonable to state that there is one incomparable God of all the universe comprising all of nature. It would not be reasonable to pray to such a cold and distant deity. How can one pray for rain to the creator of the universe, the spirit that runs the motions of the stars, the force of the oceans, the birth and death of millions of animals and plants the world over? How can one expect a personal appeal to such an alienated force to be productive? It cannot. It simply is unreasonable.

So why do we always pray to God and offer our promises to Him and beg His forgiveness when we commit a sin? How can we ask God for strength in battle or recovery from illness or to produce a growth of a fine crop of wheat? Why does Man allow himself to be controlled by a God who does not care whether Man lives or dies, suffers or succeeds, grows old or dies young? How can you pray to an impersonal deity?

The answers to those questions are what Emmanuel and I taught to our Hebrew brethren and would gladly teach to the whole world. The answers completely exclude the need for a priesthood or an organized clergy, because man does not require an intermediary between his own personal deity and himself. Clergymen should be considered teachers of righteousness and their temples should be called schools. No clergyman or priest ever had the ear of a god or any influence with Him. That entire concept has been fraudulent from its inception perhaps forty or fifty thousand years ago.

The God you pray to is yourself! No one wants you to be as healthy, wealthy and wise as you yourself want to be. No one cares whether you succeed or fail any more than you do. No one knows how much you suffer when you are ill any more than you do. No one loves you any more than you do. It is just that self-respect and self love that has to be encouraged the way you would think some extraneous God can do it. If you think that you are so ill that some impersonal God whom you grovel before and make all sorts of promises to can help you recover you have not been using your mind. You have been under the influence of thousands of years of misinformation by shamans and priests and medicine men who want you to depend on them to act as intermediaries....for a price. The price you pay is your self-respect and control over your own life, and in some cases actual gold.

There is only one God, of course. That is the God of Nature of the entire Universe and all that is in it. This Nature is a mechanical God, a cold, impersonal, chemical deity who has no qualities that imitate human emotions nor can it hear or see or feel the way humans can. This God is creative beyond anyone's conceptions; timeless, with no beginning and no end, with no senses to tell whether it is light or dark, wet or dry, human or animal, plant or mineral, yesterday or tomorrow. This is the way God should be, the greatest power and the most creative and the most invincible force in the Universe.

But He doesn't have a mind or a personality, nor does He or She care about you as a miniature since caring means to have an emotional relationship, which God does not have. The fact that his entire Planet is limited in its life and can have its own time of troubles we can leave to the future. Mankind will only live and thrive on a Planet that is as youthful as ours.

However, the greatest creation that this awesome power ever constructed is precisely that puny little Man, with his marvelous brain, his intellect, his ability to see, feel, smell, touch, sense, hear and taste the way we always conceived that a God can do. This Man who, primitive though he is, can actually build his own home, can farm his land and tame lesser animals to serve him. This modestly-sized creature can bake bread and make boats that can ride on the waters, he can organize into families and nations, he can fight enemies and reward friends, he can love and be loved and he can hate. Man, in his own small way, has a touch of God in him, powers that he doesn't even suspect exist. It is this Godly power that actually lies in Man that he must depend upon for his survival.

Do you actually believe that some being up there in the sky can care about you and do something for you? Really? Do you actually believe that a priest is a man of God, with powers that you do not have: that he has the power to act as an intermediary between you and the awesome power of Nature? Really?

However, if we develop a philosophy of ethics based on reason only, rather than on the Torah and a morality based on learning and natural creativity instead of what has been considered God's commandments it can ultimately be rejected as being man-made rather than God-inspired. That is, unless we consider Man's mind and creative powers as being part of the God-given spirit that sets us apart from every other species in the universe. That is the ultimate answer to the spiritual element in religion. The spirit found in Man is a heavenly creation!

This thesis of the God-like nature of Man could sweep the world as a replacement for all other religions that have a form of ethics and morality at their core. This form of Hebraism could become a Universal religion, applicable as a Universal Governance of Man. Therefore, since Nature another word for God is universal so the spirit of each man is an individual deity to be treated humanely and revered and respected worldwide. National and ethnic entities are all equal in value and deserve equal respect. When the time comes that all men are regarded as elements of the one God, Israel will be the Messiah proclaimed by Isaiah. And why not? This spirit of enlightenment should reign! Can any other form of universal governance be superior for Mankind?

A man can have a dialogue with the God who lies within him. He can argue, challenge, beg, pray to and listen to the answers he receives. Specialists in self-understanding can study Man and aid him in strengthening his bonds to this God. They can aid him to develop his "psyche" as a sturdier entity. Self-understanding and increased psychic strength are the secrets of Man's future development into a truly deified species.

Some very clever person once said that God helps those who help themselves. Nothing more true has ever been said. If you are in battle and you need almost superhuman strength to withstand an enemy's charge you are likely to pray to God for that sudden burst of strength. If you succeed or if you fail it is YOU who have produced the strength to succeed, or were just not able to produce the strength you needed, so you failed. When you sought outside help to make you stronger you were, in effect, trying to urge yourself on to greater effort.

The man in the sky or the man in the moon cannot help you any more than you can help yourself. *You are* all the God you need! (*Italics are by the author*) You have a modest amount of that Godly spirit and strength, creativity and common sense that is responsible for Man's having lived so long on this earth. There is only one God, Nature, and He has placed in your mind and body a large amount of His own power, so that when you pray to God you are actually praying to that part of Him that exists in your own brain. You are praying to the only personal deity who can help you survive yourself.

The Priesthood in Jerusalem looked with horror upon the teaching of Emmanuel and myself. We had left them out in the cold and they looked on dispassionately as the Romans killed Emmanuel and they themselves came close to destroying me. What *we* have been teaching is respect for the moral laws of Hebraism, the use of reason rather than myth and superstition in your relationship to your deity, and above all, the employment of every form of humane behavior towards your fellow man, regardless of what creed or ethnic background he comes from.

I am aware that Man has accused God at times for Man's failure to control his passions, to deal with the elements, to extract from this truly bountiful earth the wherewithal for a satisfactory existence. These are not God's failures; they are Man's. Man has sufficient intelligence and inner strength to live well and with mercy to all. But mankind is taking too long to move from the primitive to the civilized. He allows every sort of liar and cheat and despot to deprive him of his independent thought and freedom of development: like ants led by blind ants, like goats led by other goats who cannot see much further than their horns, Man has become the tool of nefarious leaders. This does not have to be so: with ants, yes, with goats and sheep, yes. But Man!—Ah, Man! He has a God-like capacity to think, to measure, to plan, to calculate, to remember, to dream, to hope and to love. There God gave us his own powers. Do we dare to use them?

What our people really need to do to begin recovering from this latest overwhelming by an alien power is to change our leadership away from the toadying, hypocritical, egotistical priests and politicians who have set themselves above the level of the common man whom they claim to represent. All people who find that they are controlled by such a leadership should rise up and challenge their leaders. Meanwhile, this has been painful and destructive to our morale.

What our people need is to create a body of instructions so that Man can better understand this God who lives within himself, to learn not to abuse Him, not to make demands that are unnecessary and unreasonable and not to use his enormous power for trifles. A method must be devised to address this Godliness without the groveling, without the bending of the knee or the bowing of the head. This God within us is our personal representative, our friend, our strength and our redeemer. He knows how to forgive and how to forget, just as He knows that you have strength of mind and strength of body that you have never tried consciously to use. Each person who believes in himself can get the most out of his mind and his body, if the correct methods are employed.

Unfortunately, this is something we may have to leave for the Future. The violence of these times has affected the normal composure of our people's minds. We have to have appropriate leadership to instruct people how to make the most of their inestimable assets. We have been unable, under these conditions, to effectuate this plan. Hence this scroll is put away for a few thousand years. What we must not confuse is mental strength versus physical strength. No one person has a stronger God or a better God than another man. People will soon discover that a sensible, reasonable approach to their potentialities will lead to a more productive society a more humane society and a more understanding society; with a better balance of the components of their psyches.

Constant fear or depressed attitudes will vanish as one knows that he is getting the most out of his potential and one must ever strive to get more and higher results from his mind and his psyche. Increased respect for human life, with its component of Godliness, will be an immediate result of these efforts. The use of Godlike powers within the Hebraic morality and respect for this newly discovered sense of humanity will terminate interpersonal and international conflicts. When one realizes that his relatives, his neighbors and his associates all have a portion of this true God in them one will desist from instigating any serious conflicts.

Ethnic pride will be increased as one's joy at his tribe's successes become more apparent. This normal competition between peoples is healthy and part of the God-given design of nature. But competition to the point of violence is where mankind has the potential to differ from lower animals. Self control, self-understanding and love---genuine heart-felt regard—for your fellow-man are all primary characteristics of a mature, Godlike human being. This is not like the system of Greek gods, who were in reality examples of humans who wished they had godlike powers but were generally undone by their by their all-too-human faults and weaknesses. The Greek system of gods-acting-like-human beings makes for interesting reading and displays better than anything the fallacy of indiscriminately giving godlike attributes to unbalanced personalities.

Part of our teaching has been to de-emphasize the primitive belief in an afterlife. There never has been any evidence that there is either a heaven or a hell to await the good and the bad. These conceptions are the products of very clever imaginations of seers and shamans who needed some lever to bend primitive minds to their way of thinking. Such unreasonable, un-proven theories have no place in a reasonable society. We have ample reasons for behaving properly without having some childish ogres like the devil or primitive dreams like a heaven to lead us on.

The system that Emmanuel and I envisioned and taught has been essentially a self-respecting and humanity-respecting belief that can exist without a clergy or any intermediary device that denigrates Man's innate greatness. Each man can feel a newly-discovered sense of that greatness that will not be encumbered by chauvinism or selfishness. Self-love is not selfishness. A balanced personality is not a sterile or impotent force.

Details for teaching this approach to the nature of *(Hashem)* God and the nature of Man can be propounded by Teachers of Righteousness of any generation that has an understanding of the dreadful self-destructiveness of Mankind. Once a decision has been reached to accept these principles and the techniques created to effectuate that decision Mankind will rise as though a great weight has been lifted from his mind and from his psyche. The Godliness of Man will come into its own.

This has been completed in the ninety-first year of my life. This jar has been baked in the newest Greek manner to provide maximum imperviousness to moisture of any kind known to Man."

Ariel finally concluded reading The Document. It had taken nearly two hours. He was surprised that during that entire time everyone had listened respectfully. Apparently this was such an important event that the usual picayune needling and arguing was not apropos. There were occasional gasps of surprise from those who had not read the document thoroughly beforehand. There was no applause at any time nor were there audible comments made.

Ariel dabbed his brow with a handkerchief and to the stunned, silent conclave of perhaps fifty noted clerics, leading politicians and specialists in the antiquities who were sitting there in deep thought and even astonishment, he quietly announced that, "I will now ask Moshe Amitai to read aloud the questions that you have submitted in writing and either Dr. Benno Amitai or I will reply, if we can. Answers from the floor will be honored." Still, there was an unnatural silence.

Ariel felt constrained to speak again before Moshe could start reading the questions. "I know how you all feel. If you applaud whom do you honor? The old man wrote this in the desert nearly two thousand years ago. If you disagree violently with what he says because it seems to undermine thousands of years of belief by our revered ancestors how can you hate him? After all, this Zealot, who had been on Qumran before it was razed, who had lived when the Hebrew community was torn---as when isn't it torn---with dissension, the kind of dissension that can cost you your life.

"And lastly, who has the *chutspah* to disagree with his historical facts? These questions that Moshe will read show a particular interest in the definition of *Hashem (God)* and especially with his agreeing that there can be more than one God for the human race: there may be five billion Gods!. That is no surprise to the historians, the paleontologists and philosophers who tacitly accept that the trillions of people who have populated this planet for over a billion years *had* to have more than one concept of a divinity. So what's the problem? You can't go to shul (synagogue) this Sabbath and believe in the power you've always prayed to? Is that the problem?

"Moshe please read these questions and then we will find out why everyone is so silent. I've never seen a collection of such brilliant and important people Jewish people to be so silent!" There was no good-natured laughter at Ariel's attempt at levity. This event did not lend itself to levity. Ephraim had made a painful impact on his twenty-first century listeners. The questions that Moshe read were, for the most part, academic in their content such as, "Does not Ephraim differ from all his contemporaries? What evidence have we ever seen that anyone in that area at that time agreed with him?" Another questioner asked, "Actually, our own religion has fostered an independence of Mankind. What Jew isn't an independent individual? The fact that they pray for luck, for victory in a contest, for good weather or good health is merely the plea of normal human beings wanting something that they haven't the physical or mental strength to effectuate. Basically, we actually do cater to Ephraim's idea that, "God helps those who help themselves."

Another questioner asked, "Isn't this man, Ephraim, an odd-ball, a crank who had a chance to tell every idea he ever had, wrote it all down and expected to change the world? Who was he, anyhow? We never heard of him before." And someone else protested, "If Ephraim undermines the Christian Church, the Muslim Church and even has basic differences with our own religion why are we giving him so much attention?"

A very tall, intense man with a wry sense of humor rose to reply to that last questioner. "Anyone who can think clearly and offer rational alternatives deserves to be heard. Ephraim was listened to and admired by several generations of Jews in his own time and he has been revered as Saint James by the Christian Church for over two thousand years, although he would have turned over in his grave if he knew he had been "sainted" by them. Apparently he and Emmanuel were the first 'Reform Jews' and look at what they got in return!"

Most of those questions received the anticipated replies from Ariel and Benno. Some of the questions were also replied to by David Mamelov, the last surviving translator of the scroll. He, more than anyone, was warmly treated by the audience. People who were: educated highly-trained individuals in the audience volunteered many of the answers. The anticipated uproar and arguments had not arisen.

That is, until one man raised his hand to ask a question. When recognized, he was asked, as every questioner from the floor was asked, to give his full name and his field of expertise. Of course, everyone present knew this man because he was an ardent left-wing, irreligious man whose arrogance and what some people would call his ignorance were legion. As he rose to speak, two people started to leave the room. Ariel asked them to stay a while.

His question, which wasn't really a question, was, "My name is Mordecai Gur. I am chairman of the People's Party of Israel. I know for a fact that the team that put together this entire fraud is part of a fascist plot! It is part of a cabal to undermine our beloved Jewish religion and cause us to be laughing-stocks before the whole world. I think the entire team should be investigated and indicted for treason!"

Benno rose to reply to his accuser. He stood tall and dignified but there was a tell-tale twinkle in his eyes. He made certain that there wasn't a sound—not a cough or a crinkle of paper before he would speak. "Everyone who knows Mordecai Gur knows that when he speaks most of his audience leaves either for the bathroom or for another cup of coffee. He is a a very stimulating fellow. He stimulates both ends at the same time. He also has an agenda. Every idea or plan that he has must be cleared by Moscow or the Comintern before he is allowed to make it public. His love for the Jewish religion, which is something new for him, must be what he remembers from the years before he was Bar Mitzvah. For the past fifty years, or so, his love for Jewry is a reflection of the same love for the Jews that the Bolsheviks have always shown. Is there one synagogue in the world that can brag that, "Mordecai Gur is one of *our* members?" Not really. Has anyone ever seen him in any *shul*, (synagogue) even on a Sabbath or a Holy Day? Not really. It doesn't happen.

"But, surprisingly, Mr Gur has something in common with the ideal Jewish man that Ephraim was describing. He is a rugged individualist. He doesn't ask anyone or any power to provide for him what he is unable to provide for himself. I disagree with almost everything that he believes in but he does have that spark of godliness that Ephraim described. He *is* for the common man and the underprivileged. He *does* want to lead a moral life and help free the oppressed. He *is* a thorough-going Jew, albeit irreligious, but his entire political spectrum and that of the group who pay for his living is mistaken. For this mistake and the trouble he has caused us we should hate him. *But he is so Jewish in his behavior that we love him and cannot take him seriously.*

"To Mordecai and everyone else I must emphatically state that we are not frauds. We have documented every aspect of our work. We have been the object of a vicious cabal that has killed Karnon, the tourist guide who brought us this scroll. They have killed Chaim Kluger, that brilliant little genius who helped translate this scroll. Two suicide bombers, Rosalie Lubovich and Hassanein El Barani also took the life of one of my sons, Amram. In the face of such a vicious and dangerous cabal we have stood our ground. Can anyone in his right mind dare to call us fraudulent?"

Mordecai Gur rose to rebut the accusations made by Benno. He looked at the distraught face of the man who had just lost his son and had worked so diligently to produce the entire panoply of documents about this one scroll. Mordecai looked at Benno and Ariel, the greatest intellects he could ever want to see. Suddenly he burst into tears; real sad, uncontrolled tears. Between sobs he apologized to Benno and Ariel and the whole team of workers on this project. He addressed the entire assemblage, as his voice recovered its timbre, "Everything Benno has said is unfortunately the truth. I came here under orders to denigrate these wonderful people and the brilliant work they have done. But I apologize. I was terribly in error and the people I work for are equally in error. There comes a time when you have to be a *real Mensch* (Man). This is that time for me." And he burst again into tears as he sat down.

The assembly then discussed how the religious groups should meet to figure out how to deal with Ephraim's religious statements. After all, he was a deeply religious Hebrew who had seen Mankind at what had seemed its worst. Those people in the assembly who had also lived through the Holocaust years had also seen Mankind at its very worst. There was a consensus among them that unquestionably Ephraim had a surprisingly modern and youthful outlook on mankind's problems. He actually was, as he described himself, a man who was not tied to the past. Why should these modern theologians and socially-minded thinkers not open their minds to Ephraim's well-thought-out ideas? They decided to do so, as soon as possible.

They also, most importantly, resolved the question of whether to forward copies of the translated scroll to the Vatican, to the Archbishop of the Eastern Orthodox Church, to the French Department of Antiquities. The Prime Minister of Israel sided with the faction that supported such a generous offer, "You cannot keep secret from the world such an important document. Besides, it wouldn't be long before they would get "bootleg copies". It seems that Israel has everything to gain by being magnanimous in this matter."

The President of Hebrew University expressed reservations in that matter "Remember when De Vaux, that scurrilous Catholic priest, withheld the first hundreds of scrolls from Jewish view and wouldn't allow any Jews to work on the scrolls in any capacity for thirty-five years. Such an anti-Semite was not working alone. He was under orders from higher-ups in the Church. I think it would not be in our interest to be so yielding. They would not appreciate it and we would be in for scurrilous attacks. I'd wait a year or two."

The Chief Rabbi of Israel settled that debate by clearing his throat noisily, which was always a signal that he felt an almost God-given right to speak at that particular moment. "Generosity on our part is the only proper way to behave. Besides, it will put the others on the alert that we are no longer the weaklings that they used to deal with. We are the strongest power in the Middle East. We also have a secret service that can tell the world a great many ugly secrets about the governments and institutions that might try to denigrate our people. They have something to fear and we do not. I say, let them see the scroll. They may be on the defensive for years to come once it is revealed!"

That settled it. Ariel and Benno were instructed by their academic "superiors" to prepare suitable copies for the foreigners and to forward them their copies as soon as practical. It would be beneficial if the whole affair could have been concluded with good nature on both sides.

Suddenly, a raucous voice penetrated the persistent hum of voices speaking in a restrained and dignified manner. It was

Avrum Lubovich, the widower of the suicide bomber, Rosalie,* who had killed and been killed in order to destroy the scroll that might change forever the nature of modern religion. Avrum was a fanatically religious man of honorable intent but his devotion to a literal reading of the Holy Scriptures and its controlling applications to everyday life were in conflict with most practicing Hebrews. They did not believe as he did and occasionally deep, bitter gorges appeared between the two philosophies. Can one consider a fanatical belief a philosophy, when the definition of 'fanatic' is "a frenzied, excessively enthusiastic, uncritical (unreasoned) devotion," whereas the definition of philosophy is, "a pursuit of wisdom a search for general understanding (a reasoning) of values and reality...."

This hypercritical man, Avrum, was like the rest of his sect, so impossibly certain of his beliefs that he felt it to be a sin even to question, to evaluate, to reconsider or to investigate the source of those beliefs. Was he dangerous? Only when some agency or group makes a determined effort to do all those aforementioned intellectual efforts which might cause Avrum and his co-believers to feel threatened.

The Jewish people have not survived all these years without a critical analysis of their religion: Maimonides and Rabbis Akiba and Rashi were devoted to their religion but that did not require them to be uncritical and unreasoning. The Jews have been like chameleons, forced to scurry between the cracks of historical forces, yet their religion never required them to reject the present for the unpleasant past or to create subterfuges instead of using the word "God."

*Rosalie, in effect, had been a 'suicide' bomber since she knew the power of the bomb in the suitcase and by running out of the room into the hall and standing right outside the door she was aware that she would be killed. Religious Jews are not supposed to commit suicide, but Rosalie tried to have it both ways.

Being uncritical and unreasoning is not the way to go in a modern world that needs, more than anything else, a sense of camaraderie, a feeling of 'belonging' to one another. It appears that those members of Avrums sect are the weak who require a stern, unforgiving, primitive father-figure who forbids even the mention of His name.

Yet Avrum spoke up, "It is not in the interest of *Hashem* to bring back from the dead the words of people whose beliefs and intentions are suspect. We are satisfied with our religion as it is. "It is written!" There is no need to disturb our confidence in *Hashem* and His Word. My own inclination is to destroy that scroll and let its ashes be thrown away. Jewish people do not dig up the dead. We are not grave-robbers. Let the ghosts of the past vanish into the air!"

An agitated, graying, stern gentleman then rose to rebut Avrum. "I am Yuri Olvenu, Chairman of the Scientific Institute of Israel. The differences between Avrum Lubovich and me are like a bottomless abyss. Doesn't Avrum realize that the past will always be with us, but that we were given an intellect to learn to move on from the past to a newer and better future? While it is true that every new child born today carries in his genes a replication of the human genetic history that extends back for thousands, perhaps millions, of years. This new child was given a modern brain to *use the lessons of the past* and create a healthier, safer life for his future.

"Of what use is that highly developed brain if one dare not deviate from some of the customs of the past? Doesn't one who possesses a healthy brain have a right to re-evaluate the past and do what he thinks is better for him than some old ways that were just about good enough for the *shtetl* (small town) and the tents in the desert? Must we be so deathly afraid of God that we dare not even use His name? Must religion be a condition of continual fear of some invisible power? Is that conducive to a healthy mentality? Must we be in a state of constant cowardice? Is that supposed to be what Judaism is all about?

"Must we all be in the bondage of a fanatical belief that refuses to think, to reason, to find out how and why we are here? By destroying this scroll, which was the intention of Yuri's wife and her friend, we would be destroying the thoughts and observations of a man who actually saw and knew one of the last great Hebrew prophets! Must our religion become the stultified remnants of a great belief that it became in the stifling atmosphere of Eastern Europe under the Czars?

"Our race is known as *'Homo Sapiens,'* "Man with the power of Intellect." If anyone wishes to live by sacrificing the main aspects of his intellect: the questioning, the investigating, the creativeness, the free thinking about the past, present and the future, well--that is *his* prerogative. *We do not burn books. Hitler did!"*

Avrum didn't treat those remarks to an answer. The assembled intellects then engaged in some further, desultory debating on the topic of the arrogance of intellectual cripples and then concluded with its original decisions. Avrum left, flushed as though he had been slapped in the face a hundred times and humiliated beyond belief.

Within a month the Israeli government had made discreet contacts with the Holy See, at the Vatican, the Office of the Archbishop in Constantinople, the Office of the Ayatolla in Cum, Iran, and the State Department of France, asking whom it was proper to speak with concerning the latest Dead Sea Scroll. Of course, they knew exactly whom to contact, but in matters of State it is necessary to "go through channels."

It took about three months before the Israeli State Department received answers from the various State entities. No one seemed to be in a hurry. The replies were all virtually identical: "We are not interested in your translations, which are herewith returned to you. Send us the Scroll and we will do our own translating and interpreting. This Scroll is legally the property of The Vatican (The Eastern Orthodox Church, The Ayatolla of Islam, the Department of Antiquities of The Republic of France, etc.) and as such you cannot expect that Scroll to be returned to Israel, which is not regarded as a legitimate State." By the way, the correct address to have sent that scroll, when sending it to the Vatican, would have been to "The Offices of The Inquisition, care of the Vatican." When Cardinal Ratzinger (who has since become Pope!) was in charge of that office for many years this scroll would have been sent to the equivalent of the Grand Inquisitor and we Jews know a little about that sort of thing.*(Cardinal Ratzinger **was** the "Cardinal of The Inquisition!")*

Israel was then no longer interested in dealing with any authorities who felt that way. The translations in all applicable languages had already been copyrighted worldwide. They were then published in each language and distributed worldwide. Each translation gave due credit to those who had found, translated, cared for and preserved the document. A brief history of this particular scroll was included, as well as several articles describing the key arguments made by Ephraim. Also, a summary of historical points made by Ephraim were added, because it is those historical data that were most likely to create the uproar that was expected.

Needless to say, many of those serious, honorable individuals and groups who felt that a portion of their religious beliefs were undermined by something written by Ephraim, expressed their astonishment—even dismay. However, in a respectful, civilized manner they met to discuss procedures to deal with changes that might have to be undertaken in their religious observances.

Some individuals and groups expressed a more critical tone, holding "The Jews" responsible for a world-wide cabal aimed at upsetting Christianity and Islam, as well as The Jewish religion itself! Reactions were frequently violent, with synagogues and even cemeteries being vandalized, necessitating the creation of Jewish self-defense forces all over the world. Many governments refused to supply protective personnel.

Frequently, individuals and groups took action against their own churches, synagogues and mosques, castigating their own clergymen as frauds, hypocrites and even robbers (Sic!) "for taking so much money for a phony religion."

Iran prepared its armed forces for a Holy Jihad against Israel, with the enthusiastic support of every Moslem state. The Vatican preferred to work 'underground', sending out agents to sabotage as many Israeli installations as possible and having its media unleash a barrage of anti-Semitic abuse. The French government, who are masters of deception especially against their own people, had supported for over forty years the anti-Semitic clergyman, Father Roland De Vaux, Chairman of the Rockefeller Museum in

Jerusalem, who misrepresented nearly every aspect of the Dead Sea Scrolls for almost half a century and refused to allow any Jew to even see the scrolls, no less read and interpret them.

(These are true stories. There is nothing false about them. The author.)

The French sent out agents with the explicit mission of locating and destroying the scroll that Karnon had found. If they were successful and after there would no longer be a scroll to contradict them, they would then accuse Israel of having perpetrated a massive fraud against Christianity!

In America the religious right wing, who rate among the world's leading fanatics and hypocrites, had a "field-day" in its anti-Semitic explosions. "How dare those God-benighted Jews take Jesus from us!" exclaimed the Reverend Jerry Falwell. This is the man who wrote, published and distributed many thousands of copies of a book accusing former President, Bill Clinton, of murdering his best friend and ally. He had no proof, of course, and Clinton, at a function a few years later, greeted Falwell with decorum and even put his arm around the "Reverend". "It's only politics!" someone thought he heard Clinton say. *(You thought Clinton was smart?)*

But *this* "religious" explosion was more than just "politics." It was sheer hatred born of fear and cowardice. "Whut we gonna do without Jesus?" cried out one Senator from Alabama. Can you imagine a Senator from Alabama without Jesus?

Neither the FBI nor the CIA made any effort to stem the tide of violations of Jewish civil rights. The President of the United States, an ardent, born-again Baptist, washed his hands of the whole affair. "Some foreigners' civil rights are not my concern. Them Jews have to take care of theirselves!" American Jews are foreigners?

However, the Israeli Foreign Minister had an 'epiphany'. Speaking to the American Secretary of State on the phone, he sought to defuse the whole issue. "Suppose we send that scroll to the United States on an El Al airplane. Suppose we donate it to the Smithsonian Institution where it can be displayed in its hermetically-sealed case for all the world to see protected by Americans like the Declaration Of Independence? Would you accept this gift from us? After all, *we* didn't write this thing. *Our* religion is taking a beating as well as yours is. What do you think?"

"That is very magnanimous of your government, sir. But I shall have to consult with the necessary authorities and get back to you soon." And so, for a period of three tumultuous months, Israel waited while the American Executive, Legislative and Judicial branches consulted, discussed, threatened and *were* threatened, studied and finally decided about this momentous offering by the Israeli Government. It would not be productive to repeat the slurs, accusations, criticisms and expressions of pure hatred that were bandied about during those "intellectual" adjudications. But humanity finally won out and the answer was, "Yes, thank you. The American people appreciate your generosity."

From then on, Israel made all sorts of preparations to forward the scroll in its hermetically sealed case, with several copies of all the translations made in six languages, in an El Al airplane. There would be a limited number of Israeli commandos on board, who would be screened by the Mossad, to accompany and protect the scroll. Dr. Benno Amitai, the brilliant scientist who had opened Karnon's clay jar and had organized a team to study every aspect of that two-thousand-year-old document and then translate and describe it, would be assigned to go to Washington in charge of that prestigious mission. Israel's Chief Rabbi, Foreign Minister and the President of the Hebrew University in Jerusalem would precede the shipping of the scroll by a day or two, while every detail was set in motion. Israeli fighter planes would accompany the El Al passenger plane for four hundred miles over the Atlantic Ocean.

Everything was set. The scroll, the plane, the VIP's, the fighter jets, the personnel who were finally ready to go on the plane with the scroll: everyone checked out for loyalty and efficiency by the Mossad. Ariel spoke up as he accompanied Benno to his seat in the plane, "You said, the minute you opened up the jar that contained the scroll that 'This is the most exciting moment of my life!'. This new mission is going to be the most prestigious event of your life. I want you to know that you have everyone's love and best wishes on this mission."

Ariel and all the others who were not to go on the flight soon had to leave the plane. Their hearts pounded as they watched it take off; each one wishing that he was on that flight also. The fighter planes had already been in the air going through all kinds of defensive moves.

The El Al plane crossed the Mediterranean Sea in a due westerly direction, staying clear of the territorial waters of every bordering nation. As the plane reached the area of Malta, a new group of Israeli fighter planes took off from a Maltese airfield to relieve the first group who were almost out of fuel. They would protect the El Al vessel until it was four hundred miles over the Atlantic. On this very black night, it was 4:30 AM on March 18, 2002, exactly one year after the Conclave at the Hebrew University in Jerusalem when Ariel and Benno had made their first presentations of the scroll's contents to a prestigious assembly of notables.

That was the last time anyone ever saw or heard that plane or its contents or its passengers. That airplane simply vanished. No ship or other aircraft claimed that they had seen it. It was flying at 40,000 feet. The plane, LS 194, was incommunicado so that no friend—or enemy—could trace a call and locate the vehicle. No one had been told which course the pilot would take to Washington: the Southern route, towards Central and South America, the Northern Route, along the Arctic Circle, or a median route, perhaps at the 30th parallel. That plane simply vanished. This has never happened to an El Al plane.

There had been no SOS or "Mayday" messages from a distressed pilot, no bright flashes indicative of an explosion in the sky. Engine failure? Explosion on board? No artifacts were found floating on the water. Total silence. Hit by a rocket? High-jacked to South America or Africa, in broad daylight? Possibly, but after two more weeks of silence no one had made any claims about that plane.

Washington, frankly, was not sure how to react. If such a thing could happen to an El Al plane with their impeccable safety record then no one would be safe in the air: not even Air Force One. Scary. Disturbing. But some people were relieved. "The Scroll" was lost probably destroyed. This meant that those cries of "fraud!" and "cabal!" could be revived. It was not a good day for Jewry. It was a great day for bigots and Ecclesiastical fanatics.

But Benno and Ariel had figured this all out in advance. Benno gave up his life so that Ariel might surreptitiously ship the *real* scroll by Israeli submarine. And that depended on how the world reacted to the loss of what it supposed was the real scroll. The drama of sending it by plane, and the publicity that surrounded it, was superb. Even the bitterest enemies of Israel had to admit that it was a tour-de-force that gave Israel a new lease on life. Ariel was hoping that world reaction would be sympathetic, generous and humane. But no. Such was not the case. Whatever media contacts were controlled by Islam, by the Catholic Church, by the religious "right" everywhere in the world, by the knee-jerk-anti-Semites who need no urging to belittle the Jews—all their media and the "sermons" of every religion denigrated the value of Ephraim's words. Suggestions were heard, "It's a good thing that damned scroll was blown up, if there ever *was* such a scroll!" Efforts were made almost everywhere to locate and destroy every copy of the scroll and its translations.

Taking this all in, Ariel came to a conclusion that nearly cost him his sanity. As Ephraim had said," What I cannot be certain of at this time is that the intellect and soul of Mankind will be ready, even in two or three millenia from now, to re-think its existence and live in the less primitive status that their forefathers dreamed about." Patently, the world is not ready. Intelligent people would ask, 'What should be done with this ancient scroll?'

After mourning the loss of his dear friend, Benno, and after mourning his deepest disappointment at the state of the world, Ariel came to his conclusion about what should be done with the scroll. He went to Benno's lab, which was now under the control of Moshe Amitai, Benno's talented son. He asked Moshe to bring the original scroll from the hermetically-sealed vault it was in and to rewind the scroll as tightly as it had originally been, and to re-wrap the thin tissues that had encased the scroll originally. Then, together with a letter that Ariel gave to Moshe, the scroll was to be re-inserted into the original jar and the original cap from the jar should be replaced and sealed with a low-fusing porcelain similar to the kind that was used on the 2000 year-old jar. There is a low-fusing porcelain, like glass, that can be melted with a small blowtorch that can be applied without damage to the contents of the jar. When completed, the jar would look exactly as it had appeared when Karnon first brought it to Ariel.

With a military escort of chosen and trusted men, Ariel took the reconstituted jar to a rocket base in the desert, where Israel kept rockets of all types. Having already cleared this project with the Israeli authorities, Ariel then had several technicians wrap the jar in some material that would insulate the jar and its contents from the extremes of temperature and moisture and violent attrition that it might experience. The encased jar was then placed securely in the interior of an exceedingly small satellite, even smaller than the satellite that carried the first living being—a monkey—into space many years ago. This satellite was carried by one of Israel's eighty-four intercontinental missiles. (It was an atomic-powered missile.) It was lifted off and sent into outer space at 1:53 AM, Israeli time on April 2, 2002.

Whereas most satellites that circle the Earth do so at about 250 miles from ground zero, this satellite, driven by an atomic propulsion system that does not produce the wild fiery glow of the usual liquid-oxygen propellants, was sent a distance of several million miles into *really* outer space to the surface of one the moons of the planet Jupitor which is very inhospitable. This moon is known to have sulphuric acid as the basic content of its air and as such was not considered as a possibility as one of the "planets" that might sustain life. The chances of locating and recovering this satellite by any means now in use is about one in six septillion tries—about the same odds that accompanied the finding of the original scrolls under the earth in a cave in a desert in the Middle East. That took 2000 years. It might take almost as long to find again the wisdom and history of Ephraim.

The rocket quickly disappeared over the horizon. The blackness of the night and anti-detection devices installed on board insured that, except for the few men working at the base that evening, no other power could have detected the flight of that rocket and its precious cargo. The computer that captained this intercontinental rocket had been given instructions to come back to Earth in the waters south of the tip of Africa after it had discharged its satellite. Those waters, especially at night, especially in the cold violence of a winter night, are so forbidding, that one would have to be out of his mind to try to recover that rocket, even though it had been propelled by an atomic reactor.

At 8:00 o'clock that same morning Ariel got into his jeep in front of his hotel. Heavy-hearted at the world's failure—heavy-hearted at the loss of his friends and the failure of their project, he went to his office, cleared out his desks and files, went home to his wife and children..

"What are all those papers? And why in the world are you home so early?" his wife asked.

"These are all my records. Tomorrow morning I'll tell them at the University that I have quit. I am no longer interested in antiquities and I am no longer interested in the future of Man. We are going to move to a kibbutz where we can live out our lives on the land, with God in his heaven and nature in her usual mood. We will live on the bounties of the earth." Then he burst into tears which took over three hours to be quelled. His wife and his sons, who were so proud of their "Man" were sure that he would recover his usual cheerful and vibrant self. Only you and I know that he will remain depressed for the rest of his life.

To Posterity,   April 2002,

The enclosed scroll, written on parchment and wrapped in very thin animal tissue, was written by a Hebrew prophet in approximately the year 90 in the Common Era. The translations enclosed, in Hebrew and English, tell you that this prophet had serious reservations about the religions of the world and he offered historical data that undermined the basis of most of the world's leading religions. He knew that in the year 90 Mankind was not a mature enough species to appreciate what he assumed were revelations of the truth about their dependence upon philosophically untenable spirits and beings and artificial creations of some ecclesiastic minds. As he says in this scroll, "What I cannot be sure of, at this time, is that the intellect and soul of Mankind will be ready, even two or three millenia from now, to re-think its existence and live in the less primitive society that their forefathers dreamed about."

He was correct. Although his writings came to light and were revealed two thousand years after having been written, the world rose up as one angry, frustrated, vicious man and rebelled against his revelations and his "prescriptions". They even struck out against the Hebrew people who had translated his works, as though they, and not mankind's own primitive nature, were responsible for the problems that have beset this world.

Efforts were made by several highly-regarded religious entities to destroy this scroll. In reality, what they tried to do was destroy the truth that might have destroyed their ecclesiastical leadership and, at the same time destroy the imaginary basis that has been the source of solace for billions of people, as well as a primary source of friction and violence and misunderstanding for thousands of years. The consequent violence was understandable: to some it was kill or be killed. And they actually did kill, with the cold sureness of executioners performing a social service by executing an enemy of the public. This has been the nature and level of und erstanding of the human species until now, in the year 2002 of our age.

Whoever finds this scroll is not lucky. If mankind has not improved in its respect for integrity and human life, then your life is really in danger. We tried to disseminate the rational words enclosed in this scroll to the intelligent people of our time. But the violent upheaval that swept over our "civilization" forced us to send this scroll into outer space in the year 2002 hoping that by 4002 or possibly even 7002 it will be reclaimed and land on fertile soil to take root. We have sent this Space Machine to the actual dark surface of one of the inhospitable moons of the Planet Jupitor. It will be a long time before anybody can find this scroll.

You may wish to know something of the history of this scroll and the nature of our society at this time. A man named Karnon, a true descendant of King David, found this scroll in a cave in the Dead Sea area of Israel. Karnon gave this scroll to me to study, translate and disseminate throughout the civilized world. My name is Doctor Ariel Schiffman. I am a Professor of Antiquities at the

Hebrew University in Jerusalem, and I, too, am a direct descendant of King David. Karnon was tortured and killed by ecclesiastical fanatics. Dr. Benno Amitai's son, Amram, was killed with one of our translators, Dr. Chaim Kluger, by two suicide bombers, one a Jewish woman and one a Muslim man.

Dr. Benno Amitai, a true genius with rare antiquities, was the head of the team that investigated, translated, studied and preserved this scroll faultlessly. He was killed, with a whole crew on an Israeli plane, when they publicized their effort to donate the original scroll to the United States of America. Their airplane vanished somewhere over the Atlantic Ocean. What their killers do not know, is that we did not send the original scroll by air but were surreptitiously planning to send it by Israeli submarine to the Americans for safe-keeping. When the world expressed, in the most vicious terms, their joy that the scroll was lost and blamed the Hebrew people for all their problems, we decided to conceal this scroll again, this time in a satellite far from the turmoil of the earth. In a separate jar, also sealed to protect its contents from moisture, are the translations we made into Hebrew, English, French and Arabic.

My age is 46. I have a wife, Yelena, and two sons, Adam and Abel. I am six feet tall, weigh 186 pounds and wear a full beard. My wife is beautiful, aged 41 and weighs 134 pounds. We eat well and live well, and try to maintain a balanced, healthful life for our sons. They go to school daily, are well-built, have girl-friends and are interested in world affairs. Each person in our family has his own computer and a "cell" phone, which we currently consider the ultimate in "belonging" to the world of information. We have a family library of six thousand books, all sorts of musical instruments, a valuable collection of paintings and statuary. As you can recognize, we have many of the ingredients of a wonderful life style.

We are relatively well-informed but not pleased with the world we live in. Bigotry and violence are rampant. A large portion of the world is populated by people whose religion stifles any competition and which seems to encourage violence and xenophobia. This is a dreadful situation, especially in the light of what Ephraim, the Hebrew Prophet, who wrote the enclosed scroll, had predicted.

Most economies in the world today are run by monopolies, which control the policies of their governments. International monopolies will ultimately become the order of the day. Frankly, we are concerned about what each day's news broadcasts will reveal.

If your world is the same as ours is, or worse, at your stage of civilization, please do not even open up this scroll or the translations. Put them back into much further from the earth or possibly on a further planet than Jupitor and hope that by another seven millenia we will have a more presentable society. It is entirely possible that the corrections of our societies may take a few million years. Who knows what the future will bring? Mankind, by then, might be more inclined to accept the prescriptions that have been written in this scroll. This is sent to you with every hope that our ultimate confidence in the powers of reason and the principles of humanity will prevail.

Sent with our love for humanity and our respect for you,
Ariel Schiffman

*Ariel's note to "posterity", enclosed with Ephraim's scroll in the satellite, on one of the moons of the planet Jupitor.

References

Baigent, Michael, Leigh, Richard, *The Dead Sea Scrolls Deception* .Simon & Schuster, New York, NY.1993

Barrow, R.H. *The Romans*. Pelican Books, Baltimore, MD. 1949.

Berlin, Isaiah. *Against the Current, Viking Books,NY,1959*

Braun, Lev. *Witness Of Decline:Camus*, Fairlegh Dickinson Press, Teaneck, NJ, 1974

Campbell, Joseph *Myths To Live By*. Bantam Books, New York, NY. 1972

Dawidowicz, Lucy. *What Is The Use Of Jewish History*, Shocken Books, NY,1992

de Vaux, R.oland, *Ancient Israel, Social Institutions*. McGraw-Hill, New York, NY. 1965

Dimont, Max I. *Jews, God and History*. Signet Books, New York, NY. 1962

Eliade, Mircea, *The Myth Of The Eternal Return*. Harper Torchbooks, New York, NY.1954.

Frazer,James G., *The Golden Bough*. Doubleday-Anchor, Garden City, NY.1961.

Freud, Sigmund., *Psychopathology In Everyday Life*, Mentor Books, New York, NY. 1951

Freud, Sigmund, *Civilization and Its Discontents*: W. W. Norton, New York, NY. 1961

Friedman, Maurice. *To Deny Our Nothingness*, Delta Books,1967

Glueck, Nelson, *Rivers In The Desert,*Grove Press, NY, 1959

Greenstone, J.H. *The Messiah Idea In Jewish History*:Jewish Public.Society,Phila, PA. 1906

Golb, Norman, *Who Wrote The Dead Sea Scrolls*. Scribner, New York, NY. 1995

Heidel, Alexander, *The Babylonian Genesis,* Univ. of Chicago Press,1942

Hertz, J.H. Editor,"*The Chumash"(The Pentateuch and The Haftorahs)* Soncino, London. 1992.

Heschel, Abraham. *Between God And Man,* The Free Press, NY, 1959

Kaplan, Rabbi Mordecai.*The Purpose and Meaning Of Jewish Existence,*Jew. Public. Soc, Phila, 1964

Kertzer, Morris. *What Is A Jew,* World Publishers, NY, 1953

Kushner, Harold. *To Life,*Little, Brown Co.,Canada, 1993

Kushner, Harold. *Who Needs God,* Summit Books, NY, 1989

Matt, Daniel. *God And The Big Bang,* Jewish Lights Public., Woodstock, VT.1996

Miller, Rabbi Allan, *personal communication,* 1970

Moscati, Sabatino *The Face Of The Ancient Orient.* Doubleday-Anchor,Valentine, Mitchell, Ltd., NY. 1960

Russell, Bertrand, *Why I Am Not A Christian,* Simon & Schuster, New York, NY. 1957.

Schulweis, Harold M., *For Those Who Can't Believe,* Harper-Collins, New York, NY. 1994

Shanks, Hershel, et al, *The Dead Sea Scrolls After 40 years.* Biblic. Archeology Society, Washington, DC.1991-2.

Shanks, Hershel, Editor *The Biblical Archeology Review,* Biblic. Archeol. Soc., Washington, DC. 1995-2001.

Smith, Homer. *Man And His Gods.* Little, Brown & Co., Boston, MA. 1952

The New Testament, King James Version., Edited by Roland M. Frye, Houghton Mifflin, Boston, MA, 1965

Toynbee, Arnold, *Christianity Among The Religions Of The World,* Scribner, New York, NY. 1957

Vermes, *Geza, The Dead Sea Scrolls, In English.* Penguin Books, London, England. 1962

Yadin, Yigal & Sukenik, Eleazer, *The Dead Sea Scrolls,* Lychenheim & Sons, Ltd., Jerusalem, Israel

MANFREDONIA

There are certain people who are unusually creative very original and have an inordinately impressive impact on their society. Such a family is the Manfredonians. We do not have much ancient history concerning this family but we do have enough to formulate an exciting tale. This story is as true as the history books, which are as false as they can be.

Let me tell you something about "history" and you can make up your own mind what you are willing to believe. Did you ever have an incident that you were involved in: perhaps it was a police action or an accident? How was it reported in the newspapers? Accurately? They left some crucial details out? They fouled up the whole story? That is history, darling. This is the situation as it is. The public has to believe it or not. There are all kinds of "vested interests" and the usual inefficiency involved in history or your own story. When it comes to religions there is the subject of *belief*, which does something to the real truth of the matter. So "history" is what you are asked to believe, regardless of the truth.

It says in the encyclopedia (I looked up the whole topic of Manfredonians on the internet) that the Manfredonians were "conquered" by the Greeks. This must have been about eighteen hundred years or so ago. Because there was much intermarriage between the Greeks and the Manfredonians they were an exceedingly handsome Jewish 'family': both males and females.

This "conquering" must have occurred in the north of Greece, in Macedonia, close to Albania, because the entire 'family' became, over the years, tall, blond and blue-eyed. The area of northern Greece that they lived in was the area that produced Alexander The Great.

As history hints at it this 'family' must have had something tragic happen to it and the entire 'family' was forced to move to Italy, in the area of Foggia. King Manfred had built it in 1256 after the whole town was destroyed in the earthquake of 1233. There had once been a flourishing Greek colony in Sipontum, (Sipontum was an area that had natural disasters and historical disasters) which had fallen into the hands of the Samnites but was recaptured by King Alexander of Epirus in 335 B.C. He was an uncle of Alexander the Great. King Manfred had produced enough power to leave an estate and his name on the township was Manfredonia.

Nobody seems to have any idea what the name of the Jewish family was who had lived for fifteen hundred years or so in Greece. It might have been Cohen or Levy or something else. After the destruction of the Second Temple and the formulation of Christianity the Hebrews were displaced and wandered all over the Mediterranean countries.This family landed in Northern Greece. They came from the mountainous area of Israel and they felt at home in that exhilarating, fresh mountain air in northern Greece as contrasted with the city folk, which included most of the Hebrew people at that time.

Nobody has recorded the contributions to Greek or Italian society of this Jewish family, as contrasted with the French and German and English societies to which the "Manfredonians" subsequently moved. This remark does not infer that such an original and talented family did not make any contributions to the society in which they lived. It is simply that history did not attribute much to that family. What families of "strangers" contributed anything substantial which the history-books would acknowledge?

The first incident that we can relate took place in Prussia, the largest and most powerful "duchy" of the Germanic States. In the late 1860's, Otto Bismarck, the creative leader in those States, developed the idea that if he could weld together the various "duchies" into a master-state, like the United States of America, he could create a Germany that would be able to organize the Germanic states into one powerful entity. This "new" Germany would be competitive with France and England. He got his ideas from a man named Manfredonia, who was a very wealthy resident of Prussia. This Manfredonian was not a state senator or representative of any kind. He was simply an impressive personality who had the idea that in unity there would be strength. He was tall, blond and blue-eyed, just like the Aryan ideal of the Germans.

Germany had considerable talent and creativity and a military that was based on the armies of Prussia, the largest and most powerful of the Germanic States. The Germans were also tired of the French who were always showing off their military prowess and were anxious to conquer the world. They never succeeded in that ambition.

The role of government was especially active in the industrializing policy of Germany due to the theories of Manfredonia. The State played a pervasive role in the initiation of economic development as well as in education. This man was a "bug" on literacy, saying that, "an industrial revolution is useless if only the business people are educated." He also invested heavily in agriculture, intimating that an industrial State that is reliant on someone else to supply its food has a fatal flaw in its economic system.

The fact that Manfredonia was Jewish had nothing to do with his ideas. He was just a private person (citizenship was not to be granted to Jews for many, many years) who loved Germany and had these ideas which he told personally to Bismarck. In 1870 the new Deutschland (Germany) was created by a vote of the representatives of all the business interests. The first country that got a taste of the "new German military power" in Europe was France. She was beaten at the same old game and this set the stage for World War I. The British and the French were primarily responsible for World War II. You have to read and understand the true history of Europe to know about that.

Among the first victims of the new Deutschland was this man, Manfredonia. He was executed as an enemy of the State, as a Jew who didn't know his place. He had kept after Bismarck to see that everything was just done right and some people did not like such behavior from a Jew. The name Manfredonia may not appear often in the history of France and Germany but that is not unexpected. Which wealthy men want their names publicized as "the power behind the throne"? The fun of the game is to have your ideas put into effect and all the "right" people know who's responsible. It has always been thus and it still is that way.

One of the Manfredonians was a clever artist whose specialty was vehicular design. He "borrowed" the concept of the vehicle that used 'tracks' (as in the caterpillars) to go through the mud and irregular soil that was invented by a man named Richard Edgeworth in 1770 for the Crimean War. This was "modernized" in 1885 by Gottleib Daimler.(also Jewish?) Manfredonia's artistic drawings of the first "military tank" was a total surprise to the military establishment of Prussia. It was so artistic! It was instantly manufactured by the infant automotive industry in Germany. This was in about 1911, before World War I began.

Of course, knowing what we do know about the Krupp Company and the Military Industry, notably Vickers, in Great Britain, (they are all branches of the same company!) it wasn't long before the British had the same tanks, designed by Manfredonia. This vehicle was further refined by Colonel Ernest Swinton who managed to convince Winston Churchill to use these tanks in World War I. (Did you know that the British did not bomb the Krupp factories in World Wars I and II? The Americans bombed the dickens out of the Krupp company because they were the main manufacturers for the Nazi Army and there were no American military companies that were partners with the Germans.

When this Manfredonian was executed as an enemy of the State (he was accused of giving the design to the British!) they found drawings of much more highly developed tanks, more like we saw in World War II. He had extrapolated the more highly developed engines which were not invented yet and figured how much weight those engines could carry. Don't think those drawings were not used in World War II! Did I just hear you say, "It isn't fair?" In this world there is no such thing as justice.

Another of the Manfredonians was a top-notch chemist. He worked at the German chemical company, I. G. Farben that produced Bayer Aspirin and Aniline dye, among a host of other chemicals. Nobody at the chemical company knew that Manfredonia was Jewish. He was tall, blond and blue-eyed. He was a perfect Germanic type! He also was a brilliant chemist. He thought up the idea of having a gas that could be fired by ordinary artillery shells that would paralyze enemy troops temporarily. He had thought of but did not recommend poison gas. That was left to the Germans who used mustard gas for the first time against the Allies after Manfredonia was executed as an enemy of the State (He was an enemy of the State because he was Jewish!) If there was any device that was inhumane it was Chlorine gas and Mustard gas. We must never under-estimate the chemical know-how of the Germans. Did I hear you mention Zyklon? I.G. Farben was very versatile and had an American branch that manufactured, among other items, Bayer aspirin. We did not bomb the I.G. Farben plants in Germany.

There was another Manfredonian named Emil, who was exceptionally proficient at aeronautics. He was exceedingly concerned after seeing that the newest model of transportation after WWI was used by the Germans, the French, the British and the Americans in military conflicts. He re-designed the MIG brand of aircraft while working at Messerschmidt in WWII, with two other men. It was the French in 1915 who really were 'way ahead of the Germans in aeronautical design and designed the original MIG-type aircraft but they lost interest in military matters for some reasons: political reasons. They got what they deserved.

The "M" in MIG is for Manfredonia. He was very artistic and his drawings of the potent MIG aircraft were a delight to behold. He was also a victim of the Concentration Camp, Bergen-Belsen, when it was discovered that this man, who would otherwise have been a hero, was Jewish. Emil was put in a "shower" where Zyklon (a powerful poison gas) was substituted for water. I could swear I just heard you mutter, "It wasn't fair"? As though the world is supposed to be equitable!

There was another Manfredonian, an officer in the German army. He was tall, blond and blue eyed . He was exceedingly conservative, as most wealthy people are and originally admired the policies of Hitler. He was a cousin of Hitler's. A (true) tale is told of Hitler's mother being a Jewess, a Manfredonian, who was related somehow to that officer. She worked as a domestic in the family named Schickelgruber where the old man of the family took advantage of her and she had an illegitimate son named Adolph. She also had several daughters who were mentally deficient. For publicity's sake Hitler was more concerned that his sisters were mentally deficient than that he was part Jewish. One of his sisters committed suicide. (These are historical facts!)

History tells that this woman would not confess who the man was who had these affairs with her. Anyhow, Hitler always liked this "cousin" especially since this cousin had admired Hitler's book, "Mein Kampf" and was an enthusiastic supporter of Hitler's campaign to become the Prime Minister of Germany. This officer was certain that Hitler's attitude towards the Jews was a ploy that was guaranteed to help him get into power. It never occurred to this Manfredonian that the anti-Semitism that Hitler exhibited would wind up as the source of the holocaust. He had thought, as many people did, that Hitler would say anything to get into power. They figured that there was a lot of truth in what Hitler had to say and if they got tired of him they could simply vote him out of office. It did not work out that way.

This Manfredonian was heroic on the North African front where he lost an eye, his right hand and two fingers of his left hand in combat against the Arabs. When he learned that all those Jews, including many of his relatives, were sent to concentration camps he made the usual excuses on behalf of the Nazis. He just could not believe it. First of all, he was like the average German who might not have supported such an extreme policy against that unpopular minority (the Jews. When you think about it the natural impulse was to take over the Jews' successful businesses and their bank accounts and portfolios and to ask no questions. He had thought, originally, that those concentration camps were like "boot camps."

When Hitler found out that his relative had been such a hero he invited him into his office and offered to change his name to Claus Schenk Graf von Stauffenberg which was originally the name of a member of the aristocracy of southwest Germany. So Claus became a Nazi. Claus von Stauffenberg had easy access to Hitler's presence.

Ultimately Claus found out that Hitler had carried out the anti-Semitism in a way that von Stauffenberg could not accept. Hitler also had made too many desperate gaffs in military matters. The entire Russian attack was a mistake, similar to the errors that Napoleon had made. Hitler did not learn by history. *Der Fuhrer* had also failed to figure out just where the Allies were going to land on D-Day and he failed to send those Panzers, gigantic tanks, which he had and which were ready to be used effectively against the invasion forces. *(These are facts gleaned from an encyclopedia. Of course, they have been interpreted "my way".)*

Many Germans became disaffected by Hitler's tactics and his strategy, especially when it became apparent that Germany was losing the war and they had to have somebody to blame. Hitler had allowed Rommel, who was his master tank commander, to commit suicide. Hitler gave Rommel an opportunity to escape the mock trials which were prevalent when he (Hitler) discovered that many of his top officers were involved in plots against his life. Instead of finding out what he had done wrong in the eyes of these officers he carried out many executions. He actually had written a book on how to lead his country down the bloody path to the everlasting bonfire. "Mein Kampf" was a plan to lead Germany to that eternal series of flames. *(Have you ever had a chance to see the pictures of Germany after WWII?)*

Von Stauffenberg would never have been comfortable inquiring about Hitler's mistakes until others on the staff of Hitler expressed, discreetly, their dissatisfaction to him. They figured that Claus had an "in" with the Boss and he might say something to Hitler to change his course. But von Stauffenberg knew that Hitler was beyond being "corrected". Those who spent much time in Hitler's presence knew that madness was amok.

Among the leaders of the conspiracies of the day (*these facts came from an encyclopedia; they were also on the internet)*, were General Hans Oster, head of the Abwehr Military Office; a former Army Chief of Staff, General Ludwig Beck; Field Marshall Erwin von Witzleben; General Friendrich Olbricht and Colonel Henning von Tresckow who commanded Army Group Center in Operation Barbarossa. The top man in the conspiracy was Admiral Wilhelm Canaris. Thus did a cabal arise, with the ultimate decision being to assassinate Hitler as soon as possible.

The story of von Stauffenberg bringing a briefcase that was loaded with a tremendously powerful bomb is well-known and has been variously told by all the media. There have been at least 16 films made of this assassination attempt, including the latest one with Tom Cruise, named Valkyrie (Walkure). This is all in the history books. There were heroics in the whole story of the making of that bomb and the setting of the briefcase that contained the bomb beneath the table where Hitler and his whole staff of Generals were planning the next moves against the Allies. This is certain. But why didn't von Stauffenberg stay to see that everything went as planned? He left the briefcase under the table and departed from the meeting! Someone else kicked that briefcase behind an enormous leg of the cluster of tables, far enough away from the figure of *der Fuhrer* to assure his survival.

It would have been much more effective if von Stauffenberg had committed a suicide bombing (as many Arabs do today) and then no one would have kicked the briefcase aside. Von Stauffenberg could have seen to it that the bomb would have gone off sooner, also. (There is a footnote in the Encylopedia which infers that perhaps von Stauffenberg thought that he might have a chance at taking Hitler's place, which he could not do if he was dead. This piece of venality led to a failure of the assassination attempt.) Maybe Von Stauffenberg felt that blood was thicker than water!

Hitler survived, although he lost most of the use of his left hand and arm. He was desperately shocked. He (Hitler) probably attributed his survival to "God" whom he figured probably wanted him to stay alive! As long as he lived Hitler had a pronounced tremor in that left arm.

The cabal was completely broken up as only the Nazis could break something up. Von Stauffenberg was executed and Hitler had no compunction in the hanging of the rest of the cabal. Most of the cabal was hung with piano wire, instead of rope. Talk about savagery!

I do not know what happened to the rest of the Manfredonia family but if you knew Adolph like I knew Adolph he would clean out the people named Manfredonia completely. Fortunately they did go under several different names and we never know who is a Manfredonian and who is not. (Schickelgruber?!)

Note:*This is not an entirely true story. It just seems like it. It has a lot of truth in it, particularly about Hitler's sisters and the way the cabal were hanged and about the way the way the bomb was left by von Stauffenberg. Also, a Jewish man did invent poison gas, as described.*

Sun-Sentinel

Phone: (954) 356-4600
Fax: (954) 356-4609

Earl Maucker
Senior Vice President & Editor

October 4, 2007

Dr. Edgar J. Goldenthal
173 Concordia Circle
Monroe Township, NJ 08831

Dear Dr. Goldenthal:

I received your letter requesting permission to reprint some articles originally published in the South Florida Sun-Sentinel to go along with some of your own personal writings and essays about those articles.

I saw nothing in your request that would give me pause, so if you want to include copies of those articles as they were originally published along with your short stories, it's fine by me.

I was impressed with your perspectives. Congratulations on finding a publisher for your short stories and poetry.

Sincerely,

Earl Maucker

Sun-Sentinel · 200 East Las Olas Boulevard · Fort Lauderdale, Florida 33301-2293 · (954) 356-4000